HELEN BARBOUR was born and brought up in Lichfield, Staffordshire, and now lives in North London.

She began her working life as a journalist on the *Express & Star* evening newspaper in Wolverhampton, and has written for the lifestyle magazine, *Complete Wellbeing*, and for the mental health charities Mind and OCD Action. She blogs as The Reluctant Perfectionist about living with obsessive-compulsive disorder, perfectionism and anxiety.

Helen enjoys red wine, live stand-up comedy and adventurous travel and experiences, which have included trips to the Arctic, ballooning and a tandem skydive. Her life's ambition is to figure out what 'good enough' means.

The A to Z of Normal is Helen's first novel.

Find out more at www.helenbarbour.blogspot.com or follow Helen on Twitter @HelenTheWriter.

G000143908

Praise for *The A to Z of Normal*

Clare loves her boyfriend, Tom. So why is she panic-stricken when he asks her to marry him? Because marriage means living together. And that means he will find out what she's really like…

In *The A to Z of Normal*, Clare inhabits a world in which extreme order and ritual rule. She arranges her belongings with military precision. The simplest of acts have to be done in a particular manner with dizzying attention to detail. It's no wonder that keeping her compulsive behaviour secret from those closest to her proves exhausting. She wants to change. She tries to change. As she searches for a 'cure', however, her life becomes ever more complicated and, at times, she appears bent on throwing away her happiness. The way she is going it seems less and less likely she will ever make things work with Tom.

Helen Barbour understands the nature of obsessive behaviour and writes about it brilliantly. She explores a tricky subject with sharpness and humour. I found myself willing Clare on, wishing she could free herself from the stranglehold of her destructive compulsions. *The A to Z of Normal* is a funny and poignant story. If ever anyone deserves their happy ending, it's Clare.

– MARIA MALONE, Author and Ghostwriter (Cheryl Cole, Tony Hadley, Eamonn Holmes, Mica Paris)

The A to Z of Normal

HELEN BARBOUR

To Jane,
   with warmer wishes,
      Helen Barbour

SilverWood

Published in 2015 by SilverWood Books

SilverWood Books Ltd
14 Small Street, Bristol, BS1 1DE
www.silverwoodbooks.co.uk

ISBN 978-1-78132-381-6 (paperback)
ISBN 978-1-78132-382-3 (ebook)

British Library Cataloguing in Publication Data
A CIP catalogue record for this book is available from
the British Library

Set in Bembo by SilverWood Books
Printed on responsibly sourced paper

For my parents, Joan and George Barbour

Acknowledgements

Thank you to Greenacre Writers for their friendship, encouragement and editorial input: Aditya Ashok, Lindsay Bamfield, Gema Belamonte, Rosie Canning, Linda Louise Dell, Christine Freeman, Liz Goés, Lianne Kolirin, Meral Mehmet, Raj Persaud, Carol Sampson and Bettina von Cossel.

Thank you to the Romantic Novelists' Association for supplying a critique under their New Writers' Scheme – in spite of the fact that my novel isn't a traditional romance – and giving feedback that reassured me I wasn't wasting my time as a writer.

I'm also grateful to the following.

For answers to research questions: Catherine Allen, Susan Beck and Heather Ferguson.

For reading, proofing and commenting on various drafts of my manuscript: my mother, Joan Barbour, Tina Cadwallader, Janet Collier, Maria Lugangira and Maria Malone.

For passing on second-hand electrical items to replace those that had failed me, including IT equipment essential to my writing: my sister, Alison Barbour, my partner, Pete Gettins, Nicola and John Lawson, Rob Smith and Mark Stewart. These donations were invaluable when I reduced my working hours (and salary) to write this novel.

Thank you to my mother for her financial backing of my publishing journey, and to Pete and the rest of my family and friends for all their moral and practical support.

Finally, this book is in memory of my friends, Penny Montgomery and Nicki Price – inspirational women who always believed in my writing. I wish you were here to see this.

Prologue

We arrive home before our guests. I stop on the doormat inside and bend down to take off my shiny, black shoes.

'Leave them on, please,' says Fiona.

I twist to look up at her standing on the step outside. 'But Mummy didn't—'

'Please, Clare. You can hardly wear your slippers. Not today.'

Mummy didn't let us wear shoes in the house; we always wore slippers. She said it was so that we didn't tramp dirt in.

I stand up straight and look at my feet. I don't want to tread on the carpet.

'Clare, hurry up. They'll be here any minute.' She gives me a little push and I jump sideways off the mat, out of her way. 'Go and help Daddy in the kitchen, while I open the windows. It's roasting.' My sister is even bossier, now that Mummy isn't here.

She closes the front door and disappears into the living room, her long, red hair flying out behind her, like Mummy's did when she was angry or in a hurry.

I'm standing on the floor between the mat and the wall, which is almost the same as being on the mat, so I don't mind too much. Fiona will be cross if I stay here, though, so I tiptoe over to the kitchen door.

Daddy is leaning against the sink, looking out of the window. I don't think he needs help; he doesn't seem to be doing anything.

Still on tiptoe, I hang onto the doorframe. 'Daddy?' I whisper.

He doesn't move.

The doorbell rings. Daddy turns around. 'Clare! I didn't know you were there.'

'Fiona said I had to help. I—'

'Good girl.' Daddy pats me on the head as he walks past into the hall.

I undo my shoes and take them off. Daddy opens the front door and Fiona comes out of the living room to stand next to him.

Holding my shoes tightly by the straps, I climb halfway up the stairs behind them to watch.

As the people in black clothes squash in, the house gets darker and darker. Even without Mummy, it was bright and sunny – as if she hadn't really gone. Now they're spoiling everything. I want to make them go away, all the people, their noise and their darkness.

There's only one thing I can do to put things right.

Before everyone is inside, I run upstairs and into my bedroom. I push the door shut and lay my shoes down next to it, on their sides, with the soles touching. Mummy would be pleased with me for doing that.

I go over to the dressing table. The nail varnish bottles are lined up exactly as I left them. There's a tall, skinny one in the middle, with fatter, squarer ones either side. Then the round bottles, then, at the very ends, little sample bottles. The same number of every shape and size on each side.

I sit down on the stool in front of the table. The seat is velvet and my fingers push backward and forward over its softness. I stare at the bottles. There are seventeen, filled with swirly varnish that sparkles in the sun, from a purple one on the left, to a bright red one on the right. I have more, but they don't fit the pattern; they're hidden in the drawer underneath.

Mummy gave me most of them, but only to play with. She said I wasn't to use nail varnish until I was eleven. The rest are from Fiona. She only lets me have one if she gets bored with the colour. There's a light blue, a green with glitter, and a squidgy brown. I like the brown best: it's like melted chocolate.

I push the stool back, so that I can see them all in one go. So that I can stare and stare until I feel better. Until the muddle in my head goes away. I push my fingers faster and faster over the velvet seat. Rub, rub, rub.

It isn't working; I still don't feel right. Something is wrong with the bottles.

I close my eyes, wait a few seconds, look again. Of course! They're not exactly in the middle of the table. What a silly mistake. I have to move them all a bit to the left.

I pick up the purple one. A clump of hair slips out of the band around my head and falls across my eyes. I stick out my bottom lip and blow upwards. The hair floats up and back down again. I put the purple bottle in the right place, half an inch along, and pick up the next, a cherry red.

10

'Clare? Clare, are you upstairs?' Fiona's voice startles me. The bottle I'm holding bumps the one beside it. I hold my breath as it wobbles.

'Clare, will you please come down!'

I can't leave the line all broken up, so I carry on arranging the bottles, but more quickly now.

Someone is stomping up the stairs. Across the landing. Towards my room.

I organise the bottles faster and faster. My heart is thumping so hard I can hear it in my ears.

Fiona throws open the door and it crashes against the wall. The dressing table shakes, the bottles rattle. A funny noise comes out of my mouth; it sounds like a puppy whimpering.

'What on earth are you doing? You're supposed to be downstairs.' She reaches out her hand. 'Come on, Clare, please.'

The bottles pull me the other way. My fingers are shaking, as I move another one.

'Clare, will you stop messing about and come with me.' Fiona drags me to my feet. My legs knock against the dressing table and most of the bottles fall over. The line is ruined. My head droops, my eyes fill with tears.

'Clare, I'm sorry. Did you hurt yourself?' Her voice is gentle. She squats down in front of me.

'No, it's not that.'

'Oh, sweetie.' Fiona sighs. 'It's all right to cry, you know? I miss her too.' She strokes my cheek.

'I know.' I'm not crying for Mummy, though.

'You've been very brave. You just have to be brave for a bit longer.' She glances down at my feet. 'Where are your shoes?'

I point towards the door, still sniffing.

'I told you to leave them on.' She stretches to pick them up and then kneels in front of me and plonks them flat on the carpet. I pull a face, but she doesn't see.

She lifts my feet, one at a time, and pushes my shoes back on, yanking at the straps as she does them up. There's a dusty mark on the shoulder of her black dress; I wonder if I should tell her.

'There you are, all smart again,' says Fiona. 'Don't your shoes look lovely with your white ankle socks?'

She stands up and takes my hand, and I let her lead me out of the room. I walk on tiptoe, until she notices.

'Clare, why are you walking like that? You're not a baby. Walk properly or you'll fall down the stairs.'

I don't want to make her more angry, so I do as she says, though Mummy would be cross.

In the living room, people turn to look at us. I only know a few of them. I try to hide behind Fiona, to become invisible. They lean down to hug me and whisper in my ear, but I can't hear what they're saying. All I can hear is my heart pounding. All I can see are the fallen bottles.

Fiona leaves me after a while. She has to walk around with the food: trays of sausage rolls and cheese on sticks and two kinds of quiche. Like Mummy did for Christmas parties. Fiona looks just like Mummy, except that Fiona's smile is sad.

Daddy is wandering around the room as well. He looks sleepy, confused. He comes to talk to a lady who is fussing over me. Although he looks down, he doesn't seem to realise I'm there.

I creep away to sit on the arm of the sofa, near the door. From here, I can see the stairs.

Everything feels so wrong. I have to sort out my bottles to make it right again. Only that will stop the itch in my head. I know it will start again, though. It always does. Maybe a hundred bottles would stop it, or a thousand, or a million?

There's no time to take off my shoes or to tiptoe; I run for the door. I have to get back upstairs. Back to my bottles. Back to normal.

1

Champagne froths into my glass. As the bubbles subside, so does my euphoria, displaced by rising panic. The waiter tops up the flute. I wish he'd stop. He should divert the flow of celebration to someone more deserving.

He serves Tom, bowing his head and offering a Mona Lisa smile. 'Congratulations, sir, madam.'

Tom beams. 'Thanks.'

The consequences of accepting Tom's proposal are suddenly obvious. The realisation of what I've done overwhelms me. Adrenaline floods my body; my heart races.

The waiter turns away. I wish I could go with him. His stiff, black-jacketed back disappears through the kitchen doors. I don't want to be alone with Tom; I don't know what to do. What should I do? Oh-my-God-what-should-I-do? The desperate mantra ticker-tapes around my head.

'Clare?' Tom's hand touches mine. 'Hey, beautiful. You're miles away.'

I force a smile.

He lifts his glass. 'To us,' he says. 'I love you so much, Clare.'

'I love you, too,' I say. If I didn't, this would never have happened. My unthinking *yes* was a product of that love. A love that overruled logic at the instant Tom proposed.

We clink glasses.

As he talks of our future, I think *I can't marry you; I can never marry anyone.* Why not is something I'm ashamed to admit.

I should have seen this coming. Tom asking me to dress up and refusing to explain why. The exclusive restaurant, instead of the usual Saturday night takeaway. The way he picked at his food.

He's wearing an ill-fitting suit; the sleeves are too short, like a child's hand-me-down blazer. As he talks, he tugs at the cuffs that won't cover his wrists. Between tugs, he jiggles the knot in his tie, lifting his chin and stretching his neck, as if he's being strangled. He's more used to tee shirts. I feel sorry for him, struggling to contain his bulky frame in the unfamiliar clothes. He's handsome in a suit, though.

'What d'you reckon, Clare?' he says.

I have no idea what he's talking about. 'Whatever you think is best.'

'You're happy to move into my place, till we get somewhere of our own? You've mentioned selling up and getting out of the city.'

I shiver. The air conditioning is set too cold for the end of March. 'Of course.'

'It'll be great living together, not just seeing each other at weekends.'

I shiver again. 'Yes, great.'

I grasp the stem of my flute and turn it, around and around. I have to say something; I have to explain. Words whirl in my head, but won't settle in the right order.

'You don't mind about the ring?' Tom reaches across the table and takes my left hand in his. 'Not getting one, I mean. I thought you'd prefer to choose?' The skin around his blue eyes crinkles with worry. 'Would you rather have had one?'

'No, you're right. It's nicer to choose.'

He smiles. 'Better than being stuck with something you don't like?'

'Absolutely.' I can't work out what to say with him in front of me. 'Excuse me, I have to go to the bathroom.'

Pulling my hand free of his, I stand up. I retrieve my handbag from the back of my chair and peer around the restaurant. The lighting is more murky than romantic. The waiter catches my eye and tilts his head at a door behind him.

It opens onto a long corridor; the Ladies is at the end. Inside the cubicle, I lean against the wall. Think. *Think*. I shut my eyes and try to focus. The cistern drips. Think, think, think.

I open my eyes. It's no good, I can't backtrack with a lie: tell Tom he's not the one, or it's too soon, or I don't feel the same. I can't hurt him – or myself – that way. Nor can I tell him the truth, not here: in the restaurant hush there is nowhere to hide awkward words.

For tonight, I will have to continue my deception by omission; a deception I've maintained since we met. A different kind of untruth, which I'd convinced myself would do no harm. Yet I'd always known it would catch up with me if we stayed together. And

I do want us to be together; I do want to marry Tom. I just don't know how to.

I abandon the cubicle and go to the mirror to put on fresh lipstick. The red is stark against my pale skin. I take a tissue from the box next to the basin, to dab at my lips. Beside the tissues is an orchid in a pot: nine flowers on a couple of long stems. Their creamy petals bleed pink. The plant looks artificial, although there's soil at its base. I finger one of the petals.

My mobile jangles with the arrival of a text. The sound makes me jump and my hand catches the plant and tips it over, spilling soil across the marble surface.

I stand the plant up, brush the scattered soil into my hand and lean over to drop it into the bin. Straightening up, I notice that some of the plant's petals are now bent. I lift the edge of one of them, concealing the split, but the wound reopens as soon as I take my finger away. I turn the damaged flowers to the wall. Tears sting my eyes.

I pull out my phone and, through blurred vision, read a message from Tom, *U OK in there?* He hardly ever texts; he must be worried.

Out in a min, I reply.

Message sent, I put the phone and my small make-up bag back in their usual places in my handbag. I glance inside to ensure everything is where it should be and close the zip. The glance wasn't enough. I unzip the bag and touch each item as I mentally check it off. The moment the bag is closed, I want to check again. I clench my fists. Once more won't do any harm. I open, check, close. But can't let go of the zip. Maybe just once more.

The door swings open. I lift my hand from the zip and lean towards the mirror to pat down an imaginary stray hair. A woman walks in behind me and stands to my right, smiling as our eyes meet in the glass. I can't continue with an audience. I don't want to leave, but I have to.

Tom looks up and smiles as I reach the table. 'I thought you'd run out on me!'

I return his smile and sit down. 'Sorry, there was a queue.'

'So, what do you think about dates?'

'Dates?'

'For the wedding. How about autumn?'

'This autumn?' I take a sip of champagne. Red lipstick tarnishes the rim of the glass. 'There's no hurry.'

'Is that too soon?'

'No...' I fiddle with my glass. 'I mean, there's no hurry to decide tonight.'

'Sorry, I'm getting carried away.' He laughs. 'Funny to think we met at a wedding and suddenly here we are, planning our own!'

In the taxi home, he puts his hand on my thigh, as he so often does when we sit together. Wherever we are, the gesture makes me feel loved, secure. I wonder now whether I deserve that love. Whether, if he really knew me, Tom would love me at all.

2

At Tom's cottage, his old golden retriever, Charlie, struggles out of his basket and hobbles up to us on arthritic joints. Tom pulls a balled-up tissue out of his trouser pocket, unwraps it and picks out a couple of cubes of steak. Charlie wolfs them straight from his hand.

'Good boy.' Tom pats the dog's blond head, which matches his own.

'I didn't see you sneak those off your plate.'

He winks. 'Years of practice. Got to look after my boy, haven't I?' He tugs gently at Charlie's ear.

Charlie shambles over to me, claws clicking on the flags, and sniffs around the hem of my dress. 'Sorry, Charlie. Nothing from me.'

He limps back to his basket.

The cottage is freezing: there's no central heating, only portable heaters. In spite of that, Tom has already flung off his jacket. He works as a gardener and appears immune to the cold. I don't share that immunity. I hug my coat to me, reluctant to give up its warmth. The stone floor's chill seems to seep through my shoes and up my body.

He goes into the kitchen. 'Do you want coffee?'

'Please. Can I put the heater on?'

'No need to ask. This'll be your home soon.'

That thought only makes me colder.

I flick the switch on the heater and follow him. 'Won't your sister mind if I move in? I mean, it's her home as well.' Tom bought the cottage with Liz, the middle of his three younger sisters, who lives and works in Hong Kong.

'No, it's never been a home to her.' He turns on the kettle. 'She only ever viewed it as an investment. Now she's with Paul, and they have Hannah and Joseph, she doesn't plan to come back here. We can buy her out when we're ready to move on.'

I can't even imagine moving in, let alone moving on.

In bed later, Tom slides his hand underneath my fleecy nightshirt. 'Sexy outfit!'

'It's cold.'

He gently pinches my left nipple. 'So I see.' He circles his palm over it.

A twinge of desire stirs in my groin. My heart isn't really in it, but I move closer and mechanically mirror his caresses.

I baulk at faking an orgasm, though.

Tom's fingers falter. He lifts his hand to cup my cheek. 'You okay, beautiful?'

'Yes.' I stroke his face, trying to erase the look of concern. 'Come here.' I pull him towards me.

As I wrap myself around him, he moves inside me. He comes quickly, watching me, watching him.

Still panting, he says, 'Are you sure you're okay? Would you like me to—'

'No, no…thanks. I'm fine. Just tired.'

He hesitates. 'So long as there's nothing wrong?'

'Of course not.'

'Okay, then.' He lies down and drapes his arm over me, already drifting off.

As soon as he's asleep, I ease his arm off me and slide out of bed. I put his dressing gown on and tiptoe downstairs, floorboards creaking underfoot. Charlie looks up hopefully and whines as I pass. Never mind Tom, a dog is an even more inconceivable housemate.

I go into the kitchen to make a cup of tea. Maybe in the peace and quiet, I can figure out what to do.

While I wait for the kettle to boil, I look around. Clothes hang askew on an airer at the other end of the room. A pair of muddy wellies lies next to the back door. The remnants of a DIY project litter the worktop: a hammer, a piece of wood, sandpaper and nails. I wonder if I could impose, and maintain, order if I lived here? Make Tom's home my own. Perhaps the solution to an apparently insurmountable problem is that simple?

Bending down, I stand the wellies up and position them so that the toes are level. A lump of mud on the end of one undermines the symmetry. I pick it off and throw it into the bin – which draws my attention to the fact that the bin isn't straight. I nudge it with my foot until it's parallel to the edge of the flag it sits on. Except, that must be wonky, because the bin is now at an angle to the wall. Floor or wall? I can't have both. The wall, a more obvious mismatch, wins. The recalcitrant flag still grates.

The tools and materials on the counter prove a challenge. I arrange the hammer, wood and sandpaper in descending order of size, from left to right, and then the problems begin. Tiny flaws in the work surface tip the heads of the nails this way and that, as I try to line them up next to the sandpaper, making it impossible to keep them parallel. I have to devise a different pattern, alternating head up and head down and pressing the nails against each other, to prohibit movement.

The kettle has long since boiled. I pour the water and leave the tea to brew. My feet are freezing, so I grab a pair of socks from the airer. Its crooked display of clothes is a blight, but too big a project to tackle.

I turn my attention, instead, to one of the wall cupboards. Inside I discover a motley collection of tins, labels facing every direction but front. One by one, I turn them around and sort them, first by content, then size: savoury separated from sweet, large tins on the left and small ones on the right. Finally, I vertically align the labels in each stack. The effort of creating order out of chaos absorbs me.

'Clare, what on earth are you doing?'

I drop the tin I'm holding. It bounces off the counter onto the floor, denting the rim. Tom is in the doorway, in his boxer shorts. His eyes are bleary, his hair tousled.

'I couldn't sleep. I'm just making some tea,' I say.

Tom bends to pick up the tin. 'With ravioli?' He reaches past me to put it back on the shelf – next to the rice pudding. I wince.

'Er, I was…looking for biscuits.'

His eyebrows arch. 'Still hungry?' He opens the adjoining cupboard and takes out some Jammie Dodgers. 'Here you are.' He puts the packet down on top of the hammer and wood, knocking them out of position.

I wince again. 'Thanks. I'll be up soon.'

'Okay, beautiful, but I know your secret now.'

'My secret?' My heart beats a little faster.

'Yeah. Midnight feasts!' Tom grins and walks out of the kitchen.

I look down at the counter, at the muddle of DIY materials. I look at the ravioli next to the rice pudding. And I realise that I will never make this place my own. This is how it would be if I lived here: a constant battle between my order and Tom's mess.

The battle would have to remain a secret one, though. I could never share with Tom the unwritten rules that govern my life. Rules that make no sense, yet are the only way to subdue my constant anxiety. I've never told any of my family or friends: they wouldn't understand.

Until now, it has been easy to hide those rules from Tom, too. We met six months ago at the wedding of a former colleague of mine and a not-very-close friend of his. Stranded next to each other on a table of disparate guests, we discovered a shared taste in films. Clinging to that, and each other, we navigated through an afternoon and evening amongst strangers. We went our separate, and distant, ways armed with phone numbers and promises to call. Hours of conversation and a couple of dates later, we were an item, albeit a long-distance one.

Our homes are far enough apart that we only see each other at weekends. Tom suggested alternating visits between the cottage and my flat. I insisted, as he works Saturdays, that I make the hour or so's drive north from London. A selfless and selfish offer he was happy to accept. So he has no clue what I'm like, because staying with someone else isn't an issue. My unbending, irrational need for order is confined to my home, my car, my desk. But one day this will be my home and the reality is, I can't wage a lifelong, private war against someone else's mess. If I don't fix myself, we can't get married.

Whatever it takes to do that, Tom can never find out how I am.

3

At two, I creep back upstairs. Before I do, I jumble up the newly segregated tins and put the wellies and bin back as they were. Wipe away any trace of my failed experiment.

Tom doesn't stir, as I slide back under the covers. I doze restlessly until morning, envying him his peace of mind.

I wake to the smell of flowers and the sound of Tom on the phone downstairs. Sunlight filtering through the curtains illuminates a bunch of golden narcissi on his pillow. On a piece of paper next to them is scrawled 'I love you' in his little-boy writing. The string-tied bouquet and sunshine fill me with a sudden hope that dissolves my night's fears. I kiss the note and hold it against my chest.

Snatches of conversation drift up the stairs. 'Have you told anyone else?...it'll be okay...lend you the money...Vicky, don't cry...'

Vicky. I might have guessed. Who else would phone Tom at – I lift my head and squint at the clock – eight-thirty on a Sunday? His youngest sister always has crises when the rest of the world is asleep. And she has more than most, the majority self-inflicted.

'Got to go...Clare's here...breakfast.'

I sit up, put the note and flowers on the bedside table, and hoick the pillow behind my back. Running my hands over my hair, I feel the spikes that plague my mornings. My hair defies control, in spite of a short cut, and a restless night is its greatest ally. I tuck what I can behind my ears. It's the best I can do until I get my hands on a brush and hairspray.

My need for order and symmetry extends to my appearance. I spend hours filing my nails into the same shape and plucking my eyebrows into identical arches. My hair, though, only ever fleetingly surrenders to my efforts.

The bedroom door opens and Charlie appears. He stares at me for a moment and then looks behind him.

'Come on, out the way, boy,' Tom says. Charlie trots in and

struggles up onto the bed. I shudder. Dog hairs and duvets do not go together.

Tom elbows his way into the room, carrying a large, wooden tray. He's already dressed: back in tee shirt and jeans. 'Morning, beautiful.'

He obviously hasn't noticed my hair.

'Morning. Thanks for the flowers.'

'It's a pleasure.' He leans down to kiss me, balancing the tray on the edge of the bed. Two glasses of orange juice, two mugs of tea, a teaspoon and a packet of sugar surround a dinner plate piled high with buttered toast. He puts one of the mugs on the bedside table next to me.

'Why do you taste of chocolate?' I say.

He blushes, as he places the tray on the floor and sits down, cross-legged, next to it. 'There was a bit of one of my Easter eggs left in the fridge. I couldn't help myself...'

'That's a nice, balanced breakfast!' The previous Sunday I'd hidden chocolate eggs all over the garden for him; I'd expected them to last him weeks.

Tom pulls two side plates out from under the dinner plate, loads them with toast and passes one to me. Charlie lifts his head and looks at me with his big, brown eyes, threads of saliva already glistening at the corners of his mouth.

'No, Charlie, you're not allowed bread.' I hold the stack away from him.

He lowers his head in defeat, dripping drool onto the previously pristine cotton, as he settles down again. I cringe and nudge him with my knee, through the quilt. He ignores the hint to vacate the bed, instead burrowing deeper into the covers. At least I'm not sleeping here tonight.

Tom stirs two sugars into his tea. 'This is great, isn't it? I love Sundays. Nothing to do except eat, drink and chill out. Every Sunday for the rest of our lives should be like this.' He bites into his toast, leans back against the chest of drawers and sighs.

'Was that Vicky on the phone?'

He nods, his mouth full.

'What was she after?'

Tom chews, swallows. Eventually says, 'Nothing. Just a chat.'

'At this time of day?'

'You know Vicky.' He pokes at the crumbs speckling his plate.

I don't, but I've heard enough about her to feel as if I do. 'She sounded upset.'

'What do you mean?'

'It didn't sound like a chat. Is she in trouble again?'

'It's not her fault, Clare. Things happen to her.'

Tom's older brother protectiveness sometimes blinkers him.

'What's happened this time?'

'Problems with Sam. As usual.'

'And?' I raise my eyebrows. 'I hear an and.'

He sighs a different kind of sigh. 'And she thinks she's pregnant.'

'Has she done a test?'

'I'm not sure. She said she's...' Tom shifts uneasily. 'A bit late.'

A bit late and, from the sound of it, already tapping him for money to have an abortion.

'She's probably stressed over Sam. That does weird things to your body. She'll be fine. She's old enough to look after herself.'

'I guess. I'll call her later, see how she's getting on.' He picks up one of the glasses. 'Juice?'

'Thanks.'

'I should have done Buck's Fizz, to celebrate.' Tom takes a gulp of the orange. 'You know, I'd have felt a right lemon if you'd said no.'

'Did you think I might?'

'Maybe. You might have thought it was too soon. And with me being divorced... I don't know. But things have been going so well. Touch wood.' He raps his fingers against the rim of the tray. 'Haven't they?'

'They have.' I reach over and touch his cheek. 'They really have. And everyone's allowed a second chance, aren't they?'

Tom turns his head to kiss my palm. I lift my hand away from his face and curl my fingers around the kiss.

'Mind you,' I say, 'some people might call it cradle-snatching.'

'Don't kid yourself! You're thirty-one, not twenty-one. I don't think a four-year age difference counts as cradle-snatching. A twenty-something girlfriend would be nice, though.'

I lift a pillow to launch at Tom's head. Charlie sits up and barks.

'Watch my juice!' Tom holds up his drink to ward me off.

I drop the pillow. 'You're reprieved for now, but I owe you a clump!'

In the light of day, marriage appears feasible. With every hour together, I become more optimistic. We take Charlie for a walk, stuff ourselves on a roast lunch at a pub in the neighbouring village and settle there for the afternoon with the Sunday papers. Tom's focus is the sports' pages, mine the general knowledge crossword.

'This is impossible,' I say. 'I'm going to look some of these up.' I pull out my mobile phone.

'Isn't that cheating?' says Tom. 'I thought the point was to test your general knowledge, not how accurate Wikipedia is?'

'I'm using my research skills,' I say.

'Cheating.'

'All right, clever clogs. You have a go.' I flip the crossword into his lap, covering the sports' section.

'If I get one, you're banned from using your mobile to finish it. Agreed?'

I hesitate. He only uses his phone for calls and the odd text. It's so old he can't even take photos with it and he has to resort to an ancient PC for his rare forays onto Facebook and Twitter. I'm somewhat more dependent on mine.

Tom raises his eyebrows. 'Do you want my help or not?'

'All right, then. Thanks.' It's a safe bet; the last half a dozen clues are tougher than usual.

He scans the blanks in the grid, while I flick through the lifestyle magazine.

'Shagbark hickory!' he says.

'Sorry?'

'Nine across, "Deciduous tree, a member of the walnut family". Two words, eight and seven letters. Shagbark hickory.'

'How on earth did you know that? The only member of the walnut family I know is the walnut.'

'It's the kind of thing you remember when you're a teenage boy studying horticulture.' Tom passes me the crossword. 'My work here is done. No more cheating!' He buries his head in the football results and I put my phone away.

We are so comfortable together – so normal that anything seems possible.

Driving home, I'm happy, hopeful. I can do this, I can. I will get better. We will get married. This is how our life together is going to be.

I'm happy until I step into my living room; then reality comes crashing in on me. It's as if I'm seeing everything for the first time. The room empty of clutter. The furniture positioned at set angles.

The magazines piled with corners lined up. Every object with, and in, its place. Unlike Tom's front room, where books and paperwork spill off shelves and out of drawers. Where tools and gadgets litter the surfaces. Where cables from electronic equipment make a Spaghetti Junction of the floor.

Every area of my flat is the same as the living room. Everything has its designated position, and everything is centred, or precisely angled, or symmetrical in pattern – whether tins, toiletries or flower arrangements. The rules extend to the contents of drawers and cupboards, to places no one can see. My home is a giant puzzle, with a rule for every piece. A puzzle no one else could ever solve.

Suddenly seeing it like this, I remember how hard my previous attempt at treatment was. I won't be able to change quickly or easily.

I pour a glass of wine and unpack my overnight bag. As usual, it takes ages. The problem isn't the unpacking, it's the military precision required in the putting away. I line up toiletries, fold clothes fit for a shop display, hang up my jacket with the arms tucked in just so. And just so takes longer when I'm already anxious. If something doesn't look right, I have to do it again. And again, and again. It's not just a look, though; it's a feeling. It has to feel right, too.

And then there are the interruptions. If something distracts me, I have to start the job again, to be sure I've done it properly. Something as small as a sneeze can throw me.

Tom's narcissi add to the challenge. The stems are too short for any of my vases, so I use a juice glass, but there aren't enough flowers to fill it. They loll against the rim, with an unfillable void in the middle. The only way to salvage the display is to space the stems evenly around the edge of the glass. That takes ten minutes – and then I realise that it isn't centred on the top of the bookcase. As I adjust the glass, the flowers shift and it takes another ten minutes to fix the spacing.

By the time I'm done, I've started my second glass of wine. In the living room, I pick up the phone to let Tom know I'm back and see the message light flashing. I hit *Play*: 'Clare, it's Fiona.' My sister. The last person I want to talk to. 'Clare? Are you there? Pick up if you're there. Clare? Oh, never mind. Call me as soon as you get this.'

She left a message during the week, but speaking to Fiona is never a priority. Our relationship is tainted by the fact that she brought me up after our mother died. I was only ten, Fiona seventeen. She's never let me forget that she put her life on hold for me. Our conversations are charged with resentment on her side, guilt on mine. If it weren't for her children, Sophie and Harry, I doubt we would speak at all. They make the sniping encounters with my sister worthwhile. Not that I let them come here. I fend off visits by claiming my flat isn't child-safe. Fiona seems happy to capitalise on that to avoid seeing me.

It has been just as easy to keep away friends, by meeting on neutral ground, and previous boyfriends, by inventing unfriendly flatmates. Although, on occasion, I've had to resort to more drastic measures, such as imaginary infestations of mice. Over the years, I've become ever more cunning and inventive – like an alcoholic.

Some people I can't keep out, such as plumbers, boiler engineers and delivery men. I suffer domestic problems as long as possible before giving in to the inevitable. At least those visitors don't touch anything outside their area of work and I can watch them, to see what I have to fix when they've gone. Unless they need to use the bathroom.

I scribble 'Call Fi' on a sticky note and tag it to the bottom edge of the phone's base unit, pressing the paper into place only when I'm sure it's straight.

Sipping my wine, I sit down to make my call to Tom, who picks up straightaway. 'Hey, beautiful. Are you okay? It took you a long time to get back.'

'I've been unpacking.'

'Unpacking! You only had an overnight bag. What are you like on holiday? You'll have to set out a week before me.'

'I had to put washing on. I should have called before I got sidetracked. Sorry.'

'Not to worry,' he says. 'Listen, I've had an idea. I know it's old-fashioned, and I've done it back to front, but I'd like to ask your father for your hand in marriage. What do you think?'

What I think is, *Damn, I forgot about Dad.* About telling anyone else our news. Once I do, it will be official, creating an added incentive – or pressure – for me to get better.

'Clare?'

'Yes, of course. That's a nice thought.'

'If I come to your flat on Saturday, we could look at rings in the afternoon and see your dad on Sunday, if he's free?'

My flat? He wants to stay at my flat? 'On Saturday? What about work?'

'The lads can handle it.'

26

'Are you sure?' Tom has been training Barry and Steve for months and still doesn't trust them unsupervised.

'We haven't got anything difficult booked, just a bit of clearing and tidying. I'm sure they can handle it.'

'What about Charlie?'

'He'll be okay for a night. I'll ask Vicky to stay and look after him. Sounds as if she could do with a break from Sam.'

'Doesn't Charlie get agitated when you're not around?' Desperation drives me to emotional blackmail.

'You're more important.'

After that, there is nothing I can say that won't sound churlish.

'I'm looking forward to seeing where you live,' says Tom. 'I'm beginning to think your flat doesn't exist!'

Right now, I wish it didn't.

4

So, I have less than a week until Tom's visit. Six days is nothing like enough time for a cure – especially one I have to effect on my own. I can't afford private treatment again and a referral will take too long. Besides, a therapist won't tell me anything I haven't heard before.

I only had treatment previously to save my job as an office manager. The role brought the perk of my own office, until building works elsewhere on the premises forced me into sharing with a colleague.

Up until then, all I'd had to worry about were the cleaners: the downside of a tidy desk is that it's the only one they bother to dust, and dusters snag things and knock them out of position. I had already developed a morning ritual of restoring order before I started work. Just as at home, everything has its given place. Phone at a forty-five degree angle in the top left-hand corner of the desk. Pen pot at the same angle in the top right-hand corner, with stapler, ruler and hole punch lined up next to it. Mug perched on the bottom right-hand corner and keyboard centred to monitor.

With the arrival of my colleague, I had to devise an evening ritual, too. Every night I stayed late to tidy, to preserve our office as an oasis in a building cluttered with paperwork, product samples and personal belongings. My tidying culminated in daily rows; her chief complaint was that she couldn't find anything.

It wasn't as if *she* didn't have quirks, including her insistence on always drinking her tea from the same oversized mug: a one-off promotional tool decorated with the company's logo. God help anyone else who used it. Arguments had broken out over this ugly piece of crockery. She'd even poured offending colleagues' drinks down the sink to liberate it for her own use. The office joke was that it should feature in the company handbook, so that newcomers were forewarned.

Eventually, though, she threatened to take out a grievance against me. Only my promise to change dissuaded her. No sooner did

I start therapy, than the building works were over and she moved out. To eliminate the risk of new intruders, I filled the space in my room with filing cabinets. Territory reclaimed, I relapsed into my old habits.

Those habits have hampered my career as well as my love life. It's difficult to progress when you spend more time ordering paperwork than dealing with it. I get by only because I've been doing the job for so long that it's become easy. Providing I avoid anything more demanding, I have sufficient capacity to accommodate my rituals. The situation is unrewarding, not least financially, but I've had no real incentive to change it.

Now I do. Now I have to find a way to beat those habits for good. All I need is a refresher course, a quick booster. I only wish it were as easy as a jab in the arm. I resolve to trawl the Internet for guidance after work tomorrow.

Plodding home through the rain the next day, though, the lights of the local library draw me across the road. They must have something more concise on the subject than the numerous sources available online – and a book will save the cost and effort of printing.

Inside a warm fug envelops me. The smell of damp coats and old books is comforting: it reminds me of library visits with Mum. I treasured being alone with her. Fiona, a cool teenager, derided spending her leisure time on books, but Mum helped me to find stories I would enjoy. Every week she picked one as a surprise. I saved those until last to read; they were always the best.

The visits stopped in the weeks before she died. She was too tired to stand for long. I wish I'd known the last visit was to be the last; I wish I could remember the final story she'd chosen.

Times have changed: computers have long since replaced the card catalogue. I would prefer the secrecy afforded by the cards. Shuffling through the index, nose close to the drawer, no one would know what I was looking for. Instead, I have to perch on a swivel chair in front of a monitor in the middle of the room.

A skinny, teenage boy sits next to me, at one of the public access computers. His right leg jiggles, as he scowls at the screen. In the Google search box at the top are the words 'How to pass GCSE maths'. He looks up, catches my eye. 'Yeah?' he says. 'Whaddya want?' The soft heel of his trainer bumps the floor as his leg jogs up and down.

'Er, nothing.'

His scowl deepens. 'Whaddya lookin' at then?'

'Nothing, I just wondered...' I gesture at my screen. 'Do you know how this works?' Acting dumb to deflect his aggression.

'Course,' he says, aggression replaced by contempt. He reaches across me to the mouse. Half a dozen clicks and an impatient nod later, he growls, 'Put in whatever.'

The cursor flashes in the empty search box.

'Thanks, thanks very much.' I make no move to type.

The boy stares.

A library assistant comes over. 'Do you need any help?' He doesn't look much older than the boy. He points at the blank box. 'Key in what you're looking for there.'

'I just told 'er that.' The boy sneers at me, before resuming his maths' quest.

I nod. 'Thanks. I'm trying to decide the best search words.'

The assistant hovers. 'What's the subject area? It's best to keep it general at first.'

'The subject area? Er...pensions.'

'Just try that and you should be able to narrow it down from the titles.'

'That's great, thanks. I'm all right now. Bye.' I lift my fingers to the keyboard, slowly spell out 'p-e-n'.

The assistant returns to replacing books on shelves.

I glance to my left; the boy is engrossed. I delete 'pen', type 'obsessive-compulsive disorder' and hit *Return*.

Disorder? The very thing I hate. I laughed when my therapist gave his diagnosis. Naming the problem didn't solve it, though. I completed the therapy, read the books, gave up my rules. Then threw myself off the wagon at the first opportunity. There was no one to stop me and, with my colleague's departure from my office, no longer any reason to stop. And I'm not that bad. Not like those who have no life beyond cleaning, or checking, or counting. I have a relationship, a job, friends. Everything was fine, until Tom's proposal. With those few words, my world unravelled.

The screen fills with titles. I read them as fast as I can, leaning forward to block the monitor. The boy gets up and I relax. Memorising the reference for a self-help book, I head for the relevant section.

Halfway there, I remember I didn't clear the screen. By the time I get back, someone else is hunting through the catalogue. I linger for a second, uncertain what to do. There is nothing I can do. And, after all, nothing to connect me to that search. My face still burns as I turn away.

I grab the book from the shelf, not looking inside it, and head for the self-service machines close to the entrance – only to find they're out of order. I'll have to use the counter. As I walk over to it, I turn the cover to my chest.

At the desk, I hand my library card to a different assistant.

'This is out of date.' She waves it at me. 'I'll do you a new one. It'll only take a sec.'

She fiddles about on a machine next to the main computer and waits. A line starts to form behind me. The assistant idly picks up my book, looks at the cover, and flips it over to read the back.

'There was something about this on telly the other week,' she says. 'This woman, she washed her hands, like, forty-seven times a day. She wouldn't let anyone touch her. It was really sad. She didn't go out or anything. It's a shame when people get like that, isn't it?'

'Yes,' I say. My mouth is so dry I can hardly speak.

Someone behind me sighs. I glance over my shoulder. Everyone in the queue can see the book.

I swallow hard. 'I'm doing research for my degree. I'm studying psychology.'

'Oh, yeah? Which uni are you at?'

'Er...Middlesex.' I'm suddenly sweltering in my light raincoat.

The machine spits out the new card.

'There we are,' the assistant says. She scans and date-stamps the book and hands it to me, along with the card. 'Good luck.'

'Sorry?'

'With your course.'

'My course? Yes, my course. Thanks.'

I scuttle out of the building, as if evading customs with a suitcase of drugs. The rain is a relief on my hot cheeks. On the library steps, I stop and breathe in the cool air.

The experience has stressed me. I need to tidy something to calm down. As usual when I'm in public, away from my own environment, I turn to my handbag.

I sit down on the wall outside the library. The rain drips down my neck and splatters my legs. It's hard to focus amid the noise of the street. I wait until a couple of chattering pedestrians have passed. Until a yappy dog stops barking. Then it's just the swish of tyres on wet ground: a white noise I can ignore.

31

Opening the main section of the bag, I peer inside. In the diffused glow of the streetlights, I check everything is where it should be, touching each item as I mentally tick it off.

Umbrella next to purse? Check.

Car radio and make-up bag behind them? Check.

Mobile phone in mobile phone pocket? Check.

Zip up the bag and open the outside, right-hand pocket. Quick, quick, before something interrupts me. The thought itself almost breaks my momentum.

Flat and car keys, spare keys to Dad's house? Check.

Zip up the pocket and open the outside, left-hand pocket.

Travel card, Tube map, lip salve, tissues? Check.

Zip up the pocket, then a final once-over to make sure everything is shut.

It rains all the way home, but I don't put my umbrella up. I don't want to risk breaking the magic by disrupting the bag's perfection. For the ritual, small as it was, has worked. The adrenaline rush of stress has subsided to a gentle throb of anxiety. A persistent throb that beats in my mind as my heart beats in my chest. Sometimes loud, sometimes quiet, yet so much a part of me that I can't imagine life without it. For good or bad, it makes me, me.

5

Back at the flat, I call Dad to arrange our visit. It will take him the rest of the week to psyche himself up for it.

The conversation limps along, as usual.

'Hi Dad, it's Clare.'

'Clare? Ah yes, Clare. Hello.'

'How are you?'

'Very well. Yes, very well indeed.'

'Good. Dad, I've got something to ask you.'

'Ah. I'm going out.'

'On a Monday? What are you up to?'

'I have, er, an engagement.'

'What kind of engagement?'

'Er, the photography group. Yes, that's it. The photography group.'

'Doing what? It's dark.' They usually meet at weekends for outdoor shoots.

'Portraits. Indoors.' Dad never uses twenty words if two will do, but he's acting cagey even by his standards. Maybe the portraits are nudes.

'Branching out, eh? That'll be interesting. Have fun.'

'Yes, I will. Goodbye.'

'Dad! That's not what I called about.' I roll my eyes at an imaginary audience.

'No? No, of course not.'

'Tom and I would like to come over on Sunday. Are you around?'

'Tom? Who's Tom?'

'My boyfriend, Dad. I have told you about him.' In one of our infrequent conversations, at least. 'Are you free?'

'I believe so.'

'I'll take that as a yes. Is three o'clock all right?'

'Yes, indeed. Very nice.'

'See you then, Dad. Love you.'

'Splendid, splendid.' Dad's voice fades, as though he has walked away without hanging up.

He's not good on the phone. He's not good in any conversation. After Mum died, he withdrew into himself: for two years he hardly spoke to me or Fiona. Years later, I realised he had had depression. Since then, he has never got the hang of talking to us. There's so much we've never said to each other – so much he doesn't know about either of us.

One challenge down, I tackle the next: the self-help book. My new bible, though I'm not yet born-again.

Armed with a glass of wine, I sit with the book on my lap. I feel like a smoker before their last cigarette: on the verge of giving something up, I'm unsure how I'll cope. There's no equivalent of a nicotine patch to get me through this.

I turn to the first page.

Two hours later, I'm filling in a questionnaire designed to show if I'm obsessive-compulsive. In my case the question is not if, but to what extent. It's hard to know how far I have strayed from normal behaviour.

The trouble is, it's like a multiple-choice magazine quiz. The sort that might tell you how well suited you and your partner are. After a couple of questions, you see a pattern. If you answer all As, you'll live happily ever after. All Ds, and you're such an ill-matched pair, it's a wonder you got past the first date. You might then choose to fake it, tick A, A, A and celebrate your fabulous love life. Or, at least, fudge some responses, to regain the middle ground between wedded bliss and acrimonious separation.

No point in my cheating on this one, though; it isn't for fun.

I have to award a mark between zero and four to a list of statements. I log a lot of fours. Three statements in, I realise the pattern: fours are not a good thing. All it takes to win the prize of 'probably' suffering from the disorder is twenty-one points. I have fifty-six. There's no 'probably' about it.

My reading is interrupted by a call from Tom. He launches straight into wedding talk. 'Barry and Steve want to be ushers. I'm not sure. I've not known them long and I've three friends I'd like to ask. I suppose I can have as many as I want. What d'you think?'

I don't think anything; I haven't considered the wedding at all. My time and energy have been devoted to tackling the practicalities of marriage as a state, not a ceremony.

'We need one of those wedding guides,' I stall.

'Good idea. Might as well do it properly, eh? Did you set things up with your dad?'

'Yes, we're going there at three on Sunday.'

'Okay. I thought I'd get down to London about midday on Saturday. Maybe we can grab a sandwich at yours before we hit the jewellers?'

I tot it up; we'll be together for about thirty hours, the majority in my flat. I'd rather run a marathon in flip-flops. Unfit as I am, I'm better prepared for any physical challenge than the mental one ahead of me. 'Fine,' I say.

It takes me the rest of the week to read the book. Until I've finished, I don't want to put its advice into practice. Like a student cramming, I read up until the night before Tom's visit.

With only a few hours to go, I begin my cure. It boils down to a simple tactic I knew even without opening the book: mess things up. A mess for me means as little, and as much, as moving something half an inch out of place.

I hide the book under the bed and look for something easy to start with; the cushions on the sofa catch my eye. They're lined up, tilted at an angle and overlapping. I bundle them up and launch them back at the sofa. Two fall off, one flops flat on the seat and the fourth lands in the corner at an attractive angle. I leave that one in place and try again with the three offending cushions. Throwing them all at once was a bad idea. Instead, I lob them one at a time, from several feet away. Like playing hoopla – and with about as much success. They plop down, topsy-turvy and scattered along the length of the sofa. Scattered, that's the key word. They are, after all, scatter cushions. Mine have never been scattered in their lives. They're the most regimented cushions in the history of home furnishings.

I tilt my head this way and that; I can't make them look right. I know what right is and this is not it. The solution is not to look at them at all; I turn my back on the sofa. I can still sense the cushions' higgledy-piggledy presence. The sensation is almost physical, as if something is off kilter in my body. But it's not in my body, it's in my mind; it's the mental discomfort of disorder that is now making me uncomfortable in my own skin.

Unsettled, I move on to messing up something else.

On the floor are magazines, piled in order of size, from the biggest up, and with the bottom left-hand corners aligned. I stretch out my right foot and push the pile. Now it just looks like a tidy one someone has bumped into. I prod it harder. The action makes me wobble and my raised foot comes down on top of the magazines. Their glossy covers skid away from under me. Falling, I land heavily on my left knee. I right myself and stand up. The magazines are all over the place. Perfect.

And so I carry on through the flat. Turning storage jars so that the labels face in different directions, unfolding and loosely refolding clothes, ruffling towels, nudging everything out of position.

Rebelling against my rules gradually brings a guilty pleasure. Like eating chocolate on a diet or sneaking an illicit cigarette. As with chocolate and cigarettes, there is a price to pay.

Usually, before I leave a room, I scan it from the door, to check everything is in its place. This time, I save that scan until the end – and become more nauseated with every room I review: my flat looks as if it has been burgled.

Tom will be here within the hour. It has to stay like this until he leaves tomorrow. Tomorrow? I don't know how I'll make it through the next ten minutes.

6

The station is only a few miles away, so I have half an hour to kill before going to collect Tom. I can't spend that time here; I might be tempted to start putting things back in their rightful place. Instead, I get changed and go straight out, moving quickly through the flat, so that my eyes don't focus on anything: reducing the mess to a blur allows me to pretend everything is as it should be.

The waiting room is freezing and, as I step out onto the platform to greet the train, the rain starts.

Tom gets off, carrying a rucksack and a bunch of red, pink and yellow tulips. 'Hey, beautiful.' He seizes me in a one-armed hug and kisses me. His lips are warm and soft against my cold face. 'I hope you like tulips?'

'They're lovely, thanks.' I take them with a smile, while my heart sinks at the prospect of arranging them. I only buy bunches of flowers of one colour; symmetry is easier to achieve, when the component parts are the same.

'I thought we could go out for lunch,' I say, 'rather than eating at mine.' I can't keep him away from my flat indefinitely, but every minute outside its walls is time off the thirty-hour sentence of his visit.

'Okay. Could we stop by your place first, though, to ditch my rucksack?'

'You can leave it in the boot for now. It'll be safe enough there.'

'What about those?' He nods at the tulips. 'They ought to go in water.'

'They'll be fine for another hour or so.'

Tom gives me a funny look. 'Can't we just drop into your flat?'

'All right, if you really want to. I'd just planned to eat first, before everywhere gets busy.' I don't want to arouse suspicion by labouring the point.

When we reach the car, I open the boot. He swings his rucksack inside and I lay the tulips next to it.

His arms now free, Tom grabs me in a bear hug. 'That's more

like it. It's good to see you, Clare.'

'You, too. Come on, let's go. I'm soaked.' I ease away from him and close the boot.

'You okay? You seem kind of grumpy.' He runs his hand through his hair.

'I'm not grumpy. I'm cold, wet and starving. I'll be all right once we're indoors and I've got some food inside me.'

Tom's mobile rings as soon as we get into the car. It's Vicky. In charge of Charlie and the cottage, she's already hit a problem: the front door won't shut.

'Slam it really hard,' says Tom. 'It sticks when it's damp. No, harder than that.' The crash reverberates down the phone. He grimaces. 'Is it okay now? Give me a shout if you need anything else. Say hi to Charlie. Bye.'

'How's Vicky?' I suppose I should ask.

'A lot better. She's not pregnant.'

'There's a surprise.'

'You were right – false alarm. She still wants a break from Sam this weekend, to think things over.'

'They'll make it up. They usually do.' I can't engage with her problems right now.

Tom slides the phone into the top pocket of his flannel shirt. It goes off again almost immediately. He sighs, as he flips it open.

'Really? Okay.' He sounds irritated. 'No problem. See you Monday.' He hangs up. 'Jeez, the first time I leave them alone!'

'Barry and Steve?'

'Yes. They've run out of work and want to go home. What the hell do I pay them for? If I'd known they were going to skive, I'd have taken the van instead of sitting on that blinking train.'

Tom's van is his only means of private transport.

'Maybe they started early?'

He grunts and puts the phone back in his pocket.

In the hallway of the flats, we bump into my downstairs' neighbour, Janet.

Tom introduces himself, before I can. 'Hi, I'm Tom, Clare's fiancé. You must be one of Clare's neighbours?'

'Yes, I'm Janet. I live downstairs. It's nice to meet you,' she says. 'I had no idea Clare was engaged, but she's certainly done well for herself. Handsome and romantic.' Janet nods at the tulips I'm clutching and winks at Tom.

'Janet!' Our acquaintance is a purely practical one. We've swapped spare keys and emergency phone numbers, but not confidences.

'Maybe we could all get together for a drink to celebrate?' says Tom.

Great.

'That'd be lovely,' says Janet. 'Ooh, must dash. I've left the bath running. Only came out to check the post.'

As we walk up the stairs, I grumble at Tom, 'What did you have to say that for?'

'Why not? She seems friendly.'

'She is friendly. She's just not a friend.'

Janet's not my type; she's too flaky. Always losing her mobile, running out of petrol, getting her utilities cut off. If I'd known anyone else in the block, I'd have given them my spare key. Instead, I labelled it with my name and decorated it with an orange ribbon bow, so that Janet couldn't forget whose it was or mislay it.

'Sorry,' he says. 'I didn't realise.' On the landing, he looks around. 'Nice building.'

'I thought you didn't like modern?'

'I don't usually.' He peers out of the window at the rear communal lawn. 'Pretty garden, too.'

'It's a bit of grass.' I unlock the door. 'Here we are, home sweet home.'

I'm suddenly light-headed with anxiety that this moment has arrived. For so many months I've avoided it, stalling even up to the last minute.

'Thanks.' Tom steps onto the doormat and puts his damp rucksack down on the carpet next to it. The bag tips towards the wall, hitting it with a metallic clunk, before sliding to the floor.

He takes another step forward.

'No!' Keys still in my hand, I claw at his arm.

'Ouch!' He jumps. 'What's the matter?'

'Sorry. Can you take your shoes off? Please.' Slipping the keys back into my handbag, I remove my own boots. I move inside and open the hall cupboard to reveal a rack with evenly spaced footwear on every level. Damn, I forgot to mess that up. My fingers tremble, as I crouch down and push a few pairs of shoes along, closing up the gaps between them to make more room.

Tom yanks off his trainers and drops them into the space. The wet, muddy ends of the laces trail over my best work shoes. I flick the laces off, put my boots next to the trainers and straighten them all as best I can without him noticing. Flustered, I stand up and shut the cupboard door.

'My mum had a thing about not wearing shoes in the house,' I say, 'and in this weather—'

'Mine, too,' says Tom. 'She still tells me off about it. Which way's the bathroom? I could do with a wash and brush-up.'

'Down there, on the left.' I don't want to let him out of my sight, but I don't have any choice.

He pads off in his socks, his heels visible through the threadbare weave.

Hoisting the rucksack up, I follow him. 'I'll put this in the bedroom for you.'

He turns back and reaches for it. 'Here, let me.'

'It's all right, I've got it.' A clasp has already scratched the hall paintwork; goodness knows where he'd plonk the bag next.

'Okay, thanks.' He disappears into the bathroom.

In the bedroom opposite, I prop the rucksack against the chest of drawers and go over to the dressing table to brush my damp hair back into shape, trying not to dwell on what Tom is up to.

Seconds later, he appears in the doorway. 'Just need to get my washbag.' He comes in, squats down and ferrets in the main compartment. 'Here we go.'

As he heads back to the bathroom, the rucksack slowly topples over, narrowly missing the bedroom wall. I wedge it upright again, wondering whether Tom has any proper luggage – with a flat bottom.

In the kitchen next door, I face my nemesis: the tulips. I don't know where to start in arranging them. There are different numbers of each colour, so a symmetrical pattern will be impossible. And tulips are wilful: their stems will twist overnight, destroying any pattern I do achieve. I admit defeat and slide the flowers into a vase in their existing state of disarray. The only thing I can control is the position of the vase: centred on top of the bookcase at the end of the living room. Imposing order in one corner does little to ease my frayed nerves, though.

Tom is still in the bathroom. I perch on the edge of the sofa to wait for him, avoiding looking at the flowers or the muddle around me. Staring at my feet, I try to work out, from the noises, what he's doing and what he might be moving. The bathroom door opens and closes. I pick up a magazine from the heap on the floor, but can't concentrate with someone else in the flat. The sounds now emanating from the bedroom distract me.

'Are you all right in there?' I call. No reply. 'Tom, are you all right?' He seems to be taking an inordinate amount of time; after all, it's not as if he's just stepped off a long-haul flight.

He comes into the living room. The smell of soap and toothpaste wafts in with him. His blond hair is dishevelled, with wet strands sticking to his forehead. I don't think he owns a comb.

'Fine, all done.' He looks around the room. 'This is a really great flat. A woman's touch makes all the difference.' He grins at me. 'And not having a hulking bloke or dog galumphing around! You must think the cottage is a shambles?'

'Of course not.' I throw the magazine back on the pile, turning away so that I don't see how it lands. 'I'll pop to the bathroom and then I'll be ready.' I have to inspect the damage.

My stomach flips at the sight. It's as bad as I expected from the sound effects: the towels hang at strange angles, the mirror and toothpaste have been moved, the toilet seat is up. I couldn't cope with the mess I made; this is so much worse. My hands shake as I put everything back in its normal position. I can't bring myself to tweak it to restore the post-obsessive, pre-Tom look I spent all morning on. I need to feel that I've regained some control in this nightmarish situation.

In the bedroom, the rucksack is still standing and the room appears unscathed. Then I spot Tom's washbag on the edge of the dressing table. To create space for it, he has pushed my toiletries to one side. Any semblance of a line, even the wobbly one I created earlier, has gone. The toiletries now also hide the photo I keep in the middle of the table: a black and white portrait of Mum reflected in the mirror of her own dressing table. She is brushing her long hair, her head tilted by the tug of the brush and a pensive look on her face – captured in a rare moment of almost stillness. It's the loveliest photo Dad ever took of her.

'Clare, are you nearly done? I'm famished.'

'On my way.' I'm desperate to sort out the dressing table, too, but daren't hang about any longer for fear of Tom catching me; I wonder how long I can avoid it.

We leave the flat and, while he makes his way downstairs, I turn and re-turn the front door key in the lock. Checking is the lesser of my obsessive evils. In spite of that, it always takes me several attempts to be sure the door is secure. The only thing that enables me to move away is to tag the action mentally, with a memorable word. If later I doubt locking the door, the word of the day reassures me.

The only word in my head now is help. Help, help, help.

7

At the third jeweller's we try, we have to wait for someone to answer the front door bell. A man in a dark suit materialises from a back room and reaches under the counter. The entry system buzzes and Tom ushers me in.

'How can I help you?' The assistant clasps his hands in front of him.

'We're looking for an engagement ring.' Tom beams.

'Congratulations, sir, madam. We have a large selection.' He indicates the display cases in front of him. 'Do let me know if I can be of assistance.' Stepping back, he positions himself a few feet away.

I peer at the cases. The artificially bright lights glint off the glass. Most of the rings cost more than I earn in a month.

'Tom, these are a bit pricey compared with the other shops,' I whisper.

The assistant clears his throat.

Tom glances at the price tags. 'They're within my budget.'

'Really? That's an awful lot.' I feel underdressed in jeans and an old fleece jacket. As if I have no right to aspire to such expensive jewellery. Perhaps I don't; a successful marriage is still unimaginable.

'Clare, it's your engagement ring. If I can't splash out on that—'

'Don't you need the money for something else? The business?'

'This is my money, not the business's. I want to spend it on you.'

'You could spend it on the honeymoon. That's for me, too.'

'A honeymoon doesn't last.' He touches my arm. 'Please, Clare.'

'If you're sure?'

'I'm sure. How about that one?' He points to a monstrosity of a ring, marked with a five-figure sum, and winks at me.

'Very nice, very large. If you insist—'

Tom holds his hands up. 'Okay, okay, it's a four-figure budget… up to any number starting with a two. Otherwise, I'll have to sell the cottage, the van and maybe even Charlie.'

'Poor Charlie! We can't trade him in for some over-priced bling,' I say.

The assistant coughs.

Tom glances at me, whispers, 'Clare, shh!'

I try to suppress the snort building at the back of my nose. Tom, lips pressed together, is also struggling not to laugh; his eyes water with the effort.

'Sir, madam, has anything caught your attention?'

I swallow hard, shape my face into more serious lines, and point at the nearest ring. 'Could I have a look at that one, please.'

It turns out to be three times Tom's limit. When we've spent sufficient time feigning interest, we move on to the real contenders. I'm trying on a white gold ring, set with one large diamond and a smaller one either side, when Tom's mobile rings.

'Hi, Vicks,' he says. 'What's the problem?'

I twirl the ring on my finger. It feels strange; I don't wear rings and I wonder how long it will take me to get used to it. I hold up my hand to show Tom. He nods.

'In the wardrobe in the spare room,' he says to Vicky. 'Got them? Okay, see you tomorrow.' He hangs up.

'What was that about?'

He takes my hand and looks at the ring close up.

'Tom?'

'I like this. Do you?' he says.

'Tom! What's up with Vicky?'

'Nothing. Sam's coming around tonight.'

'I thought she wanted time on her own?'

He shrugs. 'He called, wanted to see her. Looks like playing hard to get paid off.'

'Is that what she calls playing hard to get?'

'Clare, let's not worry about Vicky and Sam. Do you like this ring?'

'What's in the wardrobe in the spare room?'

We're the only ones in the shop and the assistant is listening, yet I can't let it drop.

'Clare, it doesn't matter.'

'It does matter. Why's she fishing about in the wardrobe?'

Tom sighs. 'Jeez, Clare, you're like a terrier. Vicky needed to change the bed in my room, that's all. She and Sam can't manage in the single guest bed.'

Which means they're going to sleep in ours. Charming.

He squeezes my hand. 'So, what about this ring? Is this the one?'

The cool metal still feels odd. No denying its beauty, though. 'Yes, this is the one,' I say. 'It's gorgeous, thank you.' Genuine excitement about our engagement fizzes through me. I stretch up to kiss Tom on the cheek; I'm so lucky to be with this romantic, generous man.

'Great.' He smiles and catches the assistant's eye. 'We'll take this one, please.'

'Tom, we can't, it's the wrong size,' I say.

'Oh, that's a shame. I wanted you to have it today.'

I lift my hand and shake it. The ring twirls like a Hula Hoop. 'See. They'll have to resize it. We'll pick it up another day.'

'Next weekend?' Tom looks hopefully at the assistant.

'Of course, sir.' He jangles his set of measuring rings.

Size sorted, we head home.

On the way, anxiety replaces my burgeoning excitement. Tom has spent less than fifteen minutes in my flat so far and that was hard to handle. Ahead are hours more. I break it down, trying to make it more manageable. It adds up to just one evening, one night, one morning and part of an afternoon. Not even a whole afternoon. Not even a whole day to get through. And Tom will be asleep and immobile for several hours of that. It still seems a giant leap from here to the sanctuary of Sunday evening. The very prospect makes me weary.

At the flat, Tom dumps his trainers on the shoe rack. A promising start.

'Fancy a beer?' I say.

'Thanks. Okay if I put the telly on? I'd like to catch the football results.'

'Sure.' I prefer him to be stationary, in one place, so that I can monitor what he's doing. 'I'll get the remote controls for you.' I move towards the living room.

'That's okay, I'll find them.' Tom cuts in front of me.

I hesitate in the hall and then turn into the kitchen. As I pour the beer, I listen. Silence. I open a bottle of Merlot.

'Clare, where did you say the remotes were?'

I knew he wouldn't track them down. 'In the coffee table drawer.' Lined up next to each other.

The drawer rattles open and shut. The television goes on a moment later.

When I take the drinks into the living room, Tom is leaning forward on the edge of the sofa, a remote in each hand. He has pushed one end of the coffee table out, to accommodate his legs. I put the drinks on the floor and pull at the other end of the table until it's straight.

'Sorry,' he says, still staring at the television. 'I didn't have enough room.'

'I know. It's just that it looks...' I lift the drinks onto the table. 'I don't want you to trip over it.'

I sit down next to him. A game show blares behind the match results.

'It's a bit loud,' I say.

Tom adjusts the volume and scrolls to the next page of results.

'When you're finished, can you leave the remotes on the table? I usually keep them there while I'm watching television.'

'Right you are.' He peers at the screen. 'Damn, two, nil.'

'Saves them getting lost.'

'Okay.' Tom closes the sports' pages and drops both of the remotes onto the sofa.

'Tom!' I retrieve them and lay them side by side on the coffee table, between our drinks.

He turns towards me and strokes my arm. 'Hey, beautiful, don't stress.'

He might as well tell me to stop breathing.

'All right if I leave you to it while I have a shower?' I say.

'Go ahead. I'll try not to get up to any mischief.'

After my shower, I shut the bedroom door and begin tidying up the toiletries on the dressing table. With the addition of Tom's washbag, there isn't enough room to line them up as usual. If I take the bag off, he'll only put it back. Better to move everything, so that it can perch on its own out of harm's way. It takes a long time to close up the spaces and create an alternative pattern; I'm too used to the old one. At least the temporary, new layout ensures Mum's photo is visible again.

Tom puts his head around the door. 'Can I come in?'

'Of course. I only shut the door to keep the draught out.' I reach for a pot of moisturiser to justify being at the dressing table.

'Thought I'd grab a shower as well.' He comes over and picks up his washbag, knocking over a can of deodorant in the process, which has the domino effect of taking down a tube of hand cream and a perfume bottle. 'Sorry,' he says, standing them up, all at sixes and sevens.

'No problem.' I cringe inside.

Tom disappears into the bathroom and I recreate my new pattern, now far too stressed to nudge it into something between obsessive and normal. It's not as if he'll notice the difference, the way he's barging around.

And so it goes on. Everything I see Tom undo, I try to fix. I simply can't leave things be; it unsettles me, grates on my nerves. All evening – through dinner, a film and getting ready for bed – I note what I have to put right, but can only do so when I'm alone; and I can't do much with him always close by.

Come bedtime, I'm exhausted. I feel like Sisyphus, repeatedly rolling his boulder uphill. I'm not sure how long I can keep pushing.

8

In the morning, I suggest a walk in the nearby park. It's cold, and has been raining again, but I have to get away from the flat. I drive the half mile there, so that we don't have to return before heading to Dad's.

I've escaped home, but not Vicky. She phones Tom five minutes into our stroll. He plonks himself down on a damp bench to take the call. I sit next to him, waiting until he's finished. He puts his hand on my thigh, giving it an occasional, affectionate squeeze as he talks. His monosyllabic answers are less than illuminating.

'What's up now?' I say, when he's off the phone.

'Sam's going home and she wants to go with him.'

'You didn't let her?'

'No. Charlie'll need feeding again before I get back. She didn't like it, though.' He runs his hand through his hair, scratches his head. 'I wonder if I should ring her back? Say I'll get an earlier train.'

'Tom, no! She has to learn. She can't always have her way.' The second the words are out, I realise I'm talking him out of an early exit from my flat. Damn.

'She's young, Clare, give her a break.'

'She's twenty-four, not a child.' I take Tom's hand, stroke the fine hairs on the backs of his fingers. 'She depends on you too much.'

'Who else has she got? Everyone's given up on her. Even Mum and Dad.'

'You should encourage her to help herself.'

'It's not that easy. You don't understand. You don't have all her hang-ups,' says Tom.

'I've got my fair share.'

'Like what?'

'You know...' I shrug as nonchalantly as I can. 'Doesn't everyone? Don't you?' My palms sweat, although I'm chilled from sitting still. I let go of his hand.

'I suppose.' Tom nudges me with his elbow and winks. 'So, you don't have any dark secrets I should know about? Before it's too late?'

'No. And if I did, and I told you, I'd have to kill you!' I get up. 'Come on, let's have a go on the swings.'

The dreary weather has emptied the playground, leaving us free to regress to childhood. I wipe one of the swings dry with a handful of tissues and sit down. As I push off, I dig my toes deep into the bark chippings coating the ground.

Tom hesitates in front of the next seat. 'Are you sure these'll take our weight?'

Swinging gently next to him, I say, 'I've seen children fatter than me using them.'

'Were any of them six foot three and thirteen stone?' He tugs at the chains and looks up at the framework. 'If I break my neck, it'll be you that has to feed me and push me around in a wheelchair.'

'You're just scared you can't go as high as me!' I kick at the chippings as I swing backward and forward.

'Oh, yeah?' Tom clambers onto the seat. 'A tenner says I can.'

'You're on.' I push harder, as he drives his swing into motion.

Five minutes later, dizzy and dishevelled, I have to admit defeat. 'You had a weight advantage,' I grumble.

'You can't say you didn't know,' he says. 'Let's try the seesaw.'

I fall for it. As soon as his end touches the ground, Tom stops, trapping me up in the air.

Legs flailing, I shriek in mock fear. 'Let me down! I bet you didn't do this kind of thing to your sisters.'

'Oh, I did a lot worse, believe me. It's in a brother's job description.' He leans back and gazes casually around the park.

'For younger brothers, not older brothers. Older brothers are supposed to look after their sisters.'

'Aren't you enjoying the view?'

'What view?' I scan the shabby terraces that border the park and the urban detritus at its entrance. 'Do you mean the shopping trolley or the mattress?'

'There's some nice artwork over there.' Tom tilts his head at a brick wall scarred by spray-painted hieroglyphics. 'It might be a Banksy.'

'Oh, ha, ha, you're so funny.'

'I know. That's why you went out with me in the first place.'

'Yes, you were hilarious at the wedding. Not so much now. Let me down, you cultural heathen!'

'Not until you've told me the other reasons.'

'Okay!' It's a well-rehearsed game we play. 'I went out with you because you're handsome.'

'And?'

'And you pulled out my chair and helped me on with my jacket.'

'And?'

'And your favourite films are *Jason and the Argonauts* and *The Truman Show*.'

'Correction, the original *Jason and the Argonauts*.'

'The original *Jason and the Argonauts*.'

'And?' he says.

'And you thought the parents of the children throwing wedding cake should be put in stocks, so that we could lob stuff at them.'

'Full marks.' Tom gently lowers me back down to earth.

He pays for our pub lunch with his winnings, in spite of my protestations that the money is his. After our meal, he retrieves a pair of chinos he stashed in my car before our walk and goes into the toilets to change out of his jeans.

'I don't want your dad to think I'm a complete slob,' he says, as he heads for the Gents.

'See if you can do something about your hair, then,' I say. Our exertions in the playground have left it even messier than usual.

Tom emerges with his jeans bundled under his arm and his hair sopping wet. The trousers are smarter than denim and frayed hems, but I'm not sure his blue plaid shirt goes with them.

Dad lives twenty minutes' drive away, in the large, detached house I grew up in. It's too big for one person, but he doesn't want to leave the home he shared with Mum. Her presence still permeates it. Despite Dad's dislike of clutter, he has left her ornaments on the shelves and her trinkets on the bedroom dressing table. And there are photos of her everywhere, most taken by him.

There's no reply when I ring the doorbell. I buzz again, for longer. Then I knock, hard, hurting my knuckles.

'For heaven's sake, where's he got to?' I lean sideways, peering through the window into the living room. No sign of him. I half hope he has forgotten we're coming and gone out. If he isn't here, he won't find out we're engaged – not yet, at least. The fewer people who know, the better, until I'm ready to cope with the practical side of married life. The more people who hear about our engagement, the more pressure we'll be under to set a date. With a date comes a deadline I'll have to meet and I can't fix myself to order.

'I'll have to let us in.' I fish out my spare key and jiggle it in the lock. There's a knack to turning it, which I've lost. Eventually, it gives.

'Dad?' The house is silent.

Tom follows me into the living room. 'I hope everything's okay.'

'So do I.'

When I reach the patio door, I spot Dad at the far end of the garden. He's down on one knee on the neat lawn, apparently pointing his digital camera at a nondescript shrub.

I'm relieved, and disappointed, to see him.

I unlock the door and slide it open. 'Dad, we're here.'

He looks up, startled. 'Clare! Is that the time?' He beckons us over. 'Look at this.'

As I reach him, I gesture towards Tom. 'Dad, this is Tom. Tom, my dad, Brian.'

Dad is still balanced on one knee. 'Hello, son.' He points at the border in front of him. 'Isn't that amazing?'

Tom leans over. I mirror him. Dad's musty cologne envelops me.

'It's a snail,' I say.

'See the patterns on its shell? The texture of its body?' Dad fiddles with the camera. He turns the screen towards us, revealing a close-up of the snail. 'I'm trying out my new lens.' He flicks to another shot, and another, and another.

'Dad, how many photos have you taken?'

'I don't know. Twenty, thirty.'

'Of a snail?'

Since Dad retired as a financial planner, photography has become a consuming passion.

'Are you coming in now?' I say.

He fires off another couple of shots and stands up, wincing.

'Dad, are you all right?'

'Just my arthritis.'

The right knee of his corduroy trousers is wet and muddy. Moisture veils his fisherman's sweater. A buttoned-up shirt collar is visible underneath. Dad pulls out a cotton handkerchief and reaches down to rub at the dirty knee. As he straightens, he winces again.

'You need to look after yourself, Dad.' As I try to hug him, the camera digs into me. I kiss his cheek; his beard rasps my skin. The pleasant-unpleasant scratchiness is familiar and comforting. I pull away.

Dad tucks the handkerchief into his pocket and shakes hands with Tom. 'It's a pleasure to meet you, son.'

As we follow Dad back down the garden, I realise he's wearing his tartan slippers. We go in through the kitchen door. Dad flip-flops ahead of us across the tiles, leaving footprints. Mum would have gone berserk; not only is he tramping dirt in, but he's doing it in footwear reserved for indoors. Tom and I have already crossed the house in our shoes, but now I slip mine off and nudge him to do the same.

While Dad gets changed, I put the kettle on. By the time I carry the tray into the living room, he and Tom are standing together by the mantelpiece. Dad is wearing a clean pair of identical corduroy trousers and has removed his jumper, leaving his shirt fastened to the neck.

'Your dad's showing me photos of your mum. She was a lot like you. Very pretty,' says Tom. He lifts one of the frames from the shelf.

'I only wish I'd inherited her hair.' Mum's was thick, wavy, strawberry blonde: a combination that made it worth growing long. Mine is fine, straight and a muddy shade of fair. Fiona secured the hair trump card: Titian red that she wears in a sleek bob.

I sit down on the sofa, putting the tray on the coffee table in front of it. Tom replaces the frame and joins me. Dad hovers by the fireplace, looking at each photo again.

'Come on, Dad. Your tea'll get cold.'

He settles in the armchair at Tom's end of the sofa and reaches for his drink. As he takes a sip, he pulls a face. 'No sugar?'

'I thought you'd cut it out. Weren't you trying to lose weight?'

Dad leans back and pats the belly that strains his shirt. 'Didn't seem to be making much difference.'

'It wouldn't, if that's all you've done. Your cupboards are full of biscuits and cakes.' I worry about Dad's health, about losing him prematurely, too. And I'd rather talk about his diet than the real reason we're here.

'They're for visitors.'

'You must get a lot of visitors.'

'Not really.' Dad sips his tea, grimacing. Droplets bead his greying moustache.

Tom chips in, 'I see you play the piano, Mr Thorpe.'

'Call me Brian, son. I have a go. Gwen, Clare's mum, now she was a great pianist. And a great singer.'

'Dad's too modest. He's really good.'

'Maybe you could play at...' Tom stops.

I frown at him. Dad sips on.

'Dad, we've got something to tell you,' I say. This is it, no going back. My heart rate quickens.

'Yes?' says Dad.

Tom clatters his cup into its saucer and puts it on the table. 'Mr Thorpe. Brian...' He looks at me.

I nod.

'I've asked Clare to be my wife. She's said yes, so I was hoping you'd give your blessing. I know it's the wrong way around and you don't know me from Adam...'

I squeeze his hand.

'Sorry,' Tom says. 'Bit nervous. I just want you to know how much I love Clare and I'll always look after her and—'

'Of course you can marry Clare,' says Dad. 'Get her off my hands, eh?' He claps Tom on the shoulder. 'Congratulations. To both of you.' He's too far away to offer me any congratulatory gesture.

'Get me off your hands? Honestly, Dad!' I've barely been a blip on his radar for the last twenty years.

Dad looks thoughtful. He rubs his thumb up and down his chin, tracing the line of a scar. Up and down, up and down. His beard hides the mark, though I know it's there. A dog bit him as a child; he's still wary of them.

'Just remember,' he says, 'the most important thing in a marriage, in any relationship, is communication.' He intones the word like a preacher.

'True,' says Tom.

I crash cups and saucers from the table back onto the tray. 'Communication? Oh yes, we're brilliant at that in this family. Thanks for the advice, Dad.' I lift the tray and stand up.

Tom mumbles, 'I haven't finished.'

As I put the tray down again, his tea slops over the rim into the saucer. 'I'll get some biscuits,' I say. 'Let me know if I miss any more of Dad's words of wisdom.'

They don't speak again until I'm in the kitchen. From there, I can't make out what they're saying. Maybe they're talking about me. I'm suddenly embarrassed by my sarcasm, though it was probably lost on Dad. Abandoning my quest for biscuits, I head upstairs to the bathroom.

I sit on the edge of the bath, gripping the cool enamel.

Dad is the last one to give advice about communication. It's not just me and Fiona he doesn't open up to. He never did with Mum, either. She constantly rowed with him about it. They were one-sided rows; Dad never fought back. And then she argued with him about that, about not even fighting.

She would plead, 'Tell me. Tell me what you'd like?' Whether it was a paint colour, or where to go on holiday, or which friends to invite for dinner.

'You choose, dear. I'll be happy with whatever you want,' was Dad's perennial reply.

Mum's responses swung between frustration and contempt. She vented her feelings by slamming doors or tearing off in her old, red Mini.

I would wait by the window, until she came back, worried that one day she might not. I had friends whose parents had separated. At least mine were together, even if they were unhappy.

One afternoon, I heard her in the kitchen, shouting at Dad again. I listened from the hall. Something about the row sounded different.

'You have to face facts, Brian. Stop burying your head in the sand,' she said. 'In a few months' time I won't be here.'

'Things could change, Gwen.'

'They won't. You have to start making your own decisions.'

'I don't know how I'll manage without you.'

'You'll have to. You won't have any choice.'

I was scared this was it. Dad had finally driven Mum away. I ran into the kitchen, crying. 'Mum, don't go. I don't want you to go.'

Mum glanced at Dad, shook her head. She pulled me to her. 'What on earth are you talking about, Clare? I'm here. I'm not going anywhere.'

'Promise?' My face was buried in her chest.

Mum squeezed me tighter. 'Promise.' Her voice sounded funny. I didn't believe her. It didn't make sense, after what she'd just said to Dad. She gently pushed me away. 'Now go and tidy your room and get ready for dinner.'

I think that was when it all started.

Mum expected us to clear up after ourselves; she said if we

wanted to live in a pigsty, that was up to us. So my room was already neat, with the bed made, clothes put away, and books and toys stacked on the shelves. Mum must have thought it was a mess, though, if she'd asked me to tidy. If I did it better, it would make her happy. And if she were happy, maybe she would stay.

I decided to line up the school equipment on my desk. Ruler, hole punch, stapler, compass – from the longest item on the left to the shortest on the right. They looked nice like that, so I did the same with the things on my dressing table and the toys on my bed. From the tube of hand cream to the pot of cherry flavour lip balm. From the biggest teddy to the smallest doll.

I was searching for something else to do, when Mum stuck her head around the door. 'Dinner's ready, Clare.' She pulled back; she had barely glanced at my room.

'Mum, is my room all right?'

'Your room? Yes, it's fine.' She didn't look; I didn't care. She was happy, that was all that mattered. 'Come on,' she said. 'Your dinner'll get cold.'

My heart thumped with delight. Mum was happy. Everything was going to be all right. And it was – for a while. Over the next few days, Mum and Dad didn't argue. It was as if I'd cast a spell over the house. I couldn't let the magic fail, so I kept tidying my room the same way.

Then, one day, it didn't work; Mum shouted at Dad again. I thought it was because I'd done something wrong, left something out of place. The next day, I was extra careful to position things exactly as I had that first time.

As the weeks went by, though, it wasn't enough. Mum was tired, distracted, scratchy with us. The magic had worn off. The only way to get it back was to make my room even tidier. I extended my efforts into places no one could see: inside drawers and wardrobes. And so it spread. It seemed the only way to make things right with my world, to control it. If anything did go wrong, it would be my fault.

The night Mum died, I was sure I'd done everything right. She shouldn't have left us, but she did. I must have missed something.

What I'd missed was that for five months she'd been fighting cancer. That there was nothing anyone could do to stop what happened. To stop her being too tired to listen to me, let alone play with me. To stop Fiona being so angry, or Dad becoming more and more withdrawn. They all hid the truth so well I didn't realise she was ill until the very end. Then she went to bed and didn't get up again.

Now I know the truth: none of it was my fault. Knowing that doesn't make it any easier to undo the damage.

I get up from the edge of the bath and head downstairs. On the way, I open the door to my old room. The air smells stale. The decor is a hybrid of little girl things and a young woman's paraphernalia, untouched since I left home at twenty-two. Everything is exactly as it used to be. Blindfold, I could put my hands to any item. New patterns govern my life, yet the old ones lurk just beneath the surface. Like one oil painting hidden under another. The old patterns are tattooed on my mind. If I can't forget them, what hope do I have of rubbing out those that have replaced them?

I shut the door and head downstairs.

Dad is next to Tom on the sofa. They're going through an album of Dad's travel photos.

Tom looks up, his eyes bright with enthusiasm. 'Your dad's been to some amazing places. I'd love to travel, but it's tricky with work – and Charlie. I don't like leaving him in kennels at his age.'

'Other people manage.' I sit in the armchair Dad has vacated. Neither of them seems to have noticed how long I've been gone – or the lack of the biscuits I'd promised them.

'We'll have to sort something out for our honeymoon, anyway,' says Tom. 'What about Venice or Paris? We won't be away too long, then.'

'You should ask Marilyn,' says Dad. 'She's travelled a lot in Europe.'

'Who's Marilyn?' I say.

Dad flushes slightly. 'A friend of mine.'

I know all Dad's friends: not many and definitely no Marilyns.

'A friend? I didn't know you knew anyone called Marilyn?'

'Yes. Yes, I do.'

'And where did you meet her?'

'At the hospice. She works there.' Dad closes the album, fiddles with the plastic cover.

Tom looks concerned.

'Don't worry, Tom. Dad's not a patient. He works there as a volunteer on reception.'

'Wow, that must be difficult,' says Tom. 'Rewarding, though, I guess?'

'What does Marilyn do?' I say, before Dad can respond to Tom.

'She's a social worker.' Dad puts down the album and picks up another. 'Tom, I think you'll like these. It's Madeira. Beautiful gardens. I travelled there with some photography friends.'

'And how can we get in touch with her?' I say.

Dad frowns. 'What do you mean?'

'You said she knew about Europe, that we should ask her.'

'Yes, yes, indeed.'

'So?'

'So. Yes.' Dad's face brightens suddenly. 'Sunday lunch! Come for Sunday lunch. Two weeks' time. Marilyn's doing a roast. Fiona and Dave are bringing the children.'

Fiona knows about Marilyn, then.

Tom smiles. 'That'd be lovely. I can't wait to meet the rest of the family.'

'What about Charlie?' I haven't survived Tom's first visit yet; I'm not ready to contemplate the next one. 'Vicky may not want to help again.'

'I could come for the day,' says Tom. 'Charlie would love the garden and he's great with kids.'

Not great with Dad. I don't think he's listening, though. He turns to the next page of photos. 'Look at this strelitzia. Isn't it splendid?' He doesn't wait for Tom to answer. 'Botanical Gardens, Funchal, Madeira, twelfth of October, 2012,' he reads.

He always writes the exact location and date of every photo in his tiny, italic handwriting, even if they remain the same page after page.

Dad only mentions Marilyn again indirectly, as we leave. 'So, we'll see you for lunch?'

'Wouldn't miss it,' I say.

Dad has a new woman in his life; I won't believe it until I see it. Even if I'd rather not.

9

'So your dad's got a girlfriend, eh?' says Tom, as we're driving back. 'Good for him.'

Can we say girlfriend when Dad is nearly sixty? Lady friend? Too old-fashioned for me. Partner? Too modern for Dad. She's neither. She's just Marilyn.

I force a smile. 'I didn't think I'd see the day.'

'Has he been on his own since your mum died?'

'As far as I'm aware. It's not something he usually talks about.'

'Must be serious, then.'

That's what worries me. For years, I've wished Dad would move on. Now that he has, I'm uncomfortable with it.

Mum's death transformed her into a saint in Dad's eyes. He forgot the rows, the times they spent in silence at opposite ends of the house. He elevated their life together into a model marriage – a perfect relationship cut short in its prime.

I wanted him to be realistic, to stop idolising Mum. I didn't think, after all this time, he would replace her. The idea upsets me. My head tells me no one will ever really take her place. My heart isn't so sure.

'What about your mum and dad?' I say.

'What about them?'

'When am I going to meet them? I presume you haven't told them we're engaged?'

'No. I didn't want to say anything until I'd talked to your dad.' Tom shuffles in his seat. 'I'll tell them next time we speak, but it's a bit tricky to visit. Dad works weird shifts and Mum's out and about a lot—'

'They only live in Warwickshire, don't they?' It's almost all I know about them.

'Yes.' He uses his sleeve to rub a hole in the steam glazing the passenger window.

'So we could go up one Sunday when I'm at yours. We'll fit

around their commitments.' I can behave like a normal bride-to-be, even if I haven't yet figured out how I'll manage the role of wife.

Tom peers out of the window.

I put the blower on, to clear the fug. 'Tom?'

'Okay, I'll ask them.'

'You don't sound very enthusiastic.'

'We're not that close, that's all.'

'I know the feeling. My dad's never been very interested in me or Fiona.'

Tom shakes his head. 'It's more than that. I'm an actual letdown to my parents.'

'A letdown? How?'

He wipes the rest of the window clean. 'With Dad being a doctor and Mum a teacher, they expected me to do something similar. Not digging and weeding.'

'You're a landscape gardener with professional qualifications and your own business, for goodness' sake.'

'Two staff are hardly an empire. I do all right for money, but I should have made more of it. All the lads I've trained have gone on to bigger and better things. I don't know…' Tom shrugs. 'Once my marriage was over, there didn't seem any reason to push myself.'

'It's still an achievement. I'm sorry they're not proud of that, Tom. I am.'

'Thanks, beautiful.' He grins at me. 'Then, of course, there's being divorced and not wanting children. Always popular with parents.'

'They're going to love me!' Tom and I share an apparently rare genetic pre-disposition to remain childless. He and his ex-wife thought he'd grow out of it. The fact that he didn't drove them apart and stalled his future relationships. Which, in turn, it seems, has stalled his career.

'You can join Vicky and me, as the black sheep of the Henson family,' says Tom. 'Welcome to the flock.'

I understand now why he's so close to his youngest sister: Vicky's lack of either career or stable relationship must fall far short of her parents' expectations. Their remaining offspring provide some compensation: Susie the banker and Liz the lawyer have four children between them, whom Tom dotes on.

'Maybe I could help, if you wanted to build up the business?' I hesitate, unsure whether to meddle. 'With the admin, at least?

I can barely tell a daisy from a dahlia, but I'm a dab hand at filing and spreadsheets.'

'Really?' he says. 'You'd do that?'

'Only if you'd like me to.'

'I'd love you to…though you might regret the offer when you see the state of my paperwork.'

He may well be right, if it's anything like his cottage.

As we approach the flat, dread begins to gnaw at my stomach. The hours away from home dissipated my anxiety, but by the time we pull up outside, I'm dizzy with panic at the thought of Tom coming in again.

'I'd better take you to the station, once you've picked up your stuff,' I say. 'The next train's in half an hour.'

'I could catch the one after, to give us a bit more time together?'

'Don't you want to get back for Charlie?'

'Another hour won't matter. If you'd like me—'

'The Sunday service is erratic. Better not leave it too late.'

'You really are a worrier. There are plenty of trains,' says Tom. 'Mind you, I probably shouldn't hang about too long. Vicky'll be keen to get off.'

Once inside, he goes straight to the bedroom.

'I'll help with your things.' I collect his toiletries and stand over him as he stuffs them into his rucksack, along with his few clothes. 'All done?'

'I didn't have much.'

'Let's get going, then.'

'Anyone would think you were trying to get rid of me!' He stands up and follows me into the hall.

'I don't want you to miss your train.' I'm already at the front door.

'Hang on, I need to pop to the bathroom.' Tom puts down the rucksack. I grab it before it scrapes another wall.

He emerges a few minutes later. 'You tighten your taps way too much, Clare. You'll damage the washers.'

'Hark the plumbing expert!' I know he's right, but I have to be sure the water is off; the taps not running is insufficient proof. The truth is, sometimes I can hardly turn them on again.

'I'm just saying. You don't want them seizing up.' He lifts up his rucksack.

'Now who's stressing?' I say.

At the station, Tom hovers in the train doorway until the last minute. 'I'll come down again soon,' he says. 'It's not fair on you, driving all the time.'

'I don't mind. It keeps my car from rusting to a standstill.' I kiss him quickly. 'I'll see you at the cottage next weekend.'

Tom gives me a long look and kisses me back, hard.

'Let me know when you're home,' I say. 'Have a safe trip!'

'Well, as I'm not driving, that's hard to control, but I'll do my best.' He grins at me. 'Stop worrying!'

He slams the door shut and blows me a kiss, as the train moves off. I hold out as long as I can, waving from the platform. When I think he can't see me any more, I run to the car. I'm desperate to put things straight at the flat.

Once home, the size of the job hits me. Tom may not have moved much, but I have to check everything. All I can do is tackle one room at a time, scanning each surface and every piece of furniture for gaps and errors in the patterns. My few ornaments spaced equidistantly. Toiletries angled at the corners of the bath. The clothes airer standing parallel to the bathroom wall. Glasses lined up in descending order of size, from left to right. Papers pinned to my noticeboard at a forty-five degree angle. And on and on and on. The rules are endless, but the patterns are so familiar that divergences are easy to spot. Then I find myself moving things I know Tom hasn't touched and putting them back, just in case. My progress around the flat is painfully slow. Straightening, plumping, lining up, centring.

The rooms are dotted with presents from Tom − guilty reminders of why I have to stop this obsessive behaviour.

In the bedroom is a watercolour seascape that I paused to admire during a Sunday amble amongst the artists' stalls at Bayswater. Tom sneaked back later to buy it, on the pretext of getting us drinks.

Tacked to the kitchen notice board − at the perfect angle − is his Christmas gift: two tickets for *The Comedy of Errors* at Regents Park Open Air Theatre. A present at odds with his dislike of cultural pursuits, but something he knew I'd love.

And amongst my CDs is a compilation he put together: songs chosen to express his feelings, mixed with some of my favourites. I pull it out and study the photo on the front: a shot of us at London Zoo, laughing at the size of the gigantic ice cream cones we're holding. I trace the outline of Tom's face; I want to be with this loving, thoughtful man. For now, though, the compulsions preventing that are stronger than any other desire. I tap the CD back into position and move on to the next task.

Halfway through, the phone rings. I have both hands on the vase of tulips, making minuscule adjustments to ensure that it really is centred on the bookcase; the flowers themselves are a lost cause. I let the answerphone pick up, but release the vase; I can't carry on until the interruption is over.

It's Tom. 'Hi, just to let you know I survived the train journey. Hope you're having a relaxing evening. Talk to you later.'

Relaxing? Hardly, and I'm nowhere near finished. Because someone else has been here, it's harder to get things perfect. I put one item in position, tweak it until it's right, and then step back and see it isn't. Objects take on a life of their own, appear to move the instant I let go of them. Place, step back, check, tweak. Step back, check, tweak. Step back, check, tweak. I want to stop, walk away. I can't. I can't until it feels just right, however long that takes. Tweak, check. Check, tweak. Again and again and again.

To begin with, my mind is as busy as my fingers. Worries and memories spin in a shifting kaleidoscope I can't pin down or resolve. They divert me from the job at hand. Tom. Dad. The wedding. Marilyn. Mum. From one to another and back again. Gradually, though, tidying works its magic. My focus shifts from my thoughts to getting things right. I'm hypnotised by what I'm doing, hypnotised out of thinking.

An hour and a half later, I'm done. I've eradicated every sign of Tom's intrusion. I make a final check. A cursory glance around each room, to ensure nothing is out of place. It's all perfect again. Now, just for a moment, I need to savour that perfection. I sit in the middle of the living room floor and breathe deeply. Calm seeps through me.

The phone rings; the calm shatters. Unwilling to move, I let the answerphone kick in.

It's Fiona.

'Clare, are you there? I need to talk to you. Pick up, please. Clare? Would you please pick up if you're there?'

She treats me as if I'm one of her wayward teenage students: as Head of Maths at her school, she spends her days exercising discipline. She'd be easier to deal with if she left the bossiness at work.

I admit defeat, crawl over to the phone. 'Hello, Fi. I was in the bathroom. Sorry.' I slump against the sofa; it shifts under my weight.

'Oh, you are there! Good. Dad's just been on, very excited

about you and Tom. When were you planning to let me know?'

I stand up and nudge the back of the sofa with my hip until the feet drop into the dents sculpted in the carpet. 'We only saw him this afternoon! I haven't had time.' Sitting down on the floor, next to the phone table, I'm careful not to touch anything.

'For a two minute call?' Fiona sighs. 'I felt such a fool finding out that way.'

'Sorry, Fi. I didn't expect him to phone you.'

'It's very sudden. You've only been together a few months, haven't you?'

'I'm not pregnant, if that's what you think?'

'I wasn't suggesting that. I meant, how well do you know him?'

'I know I love him, that's all that matters.' I refuse to give any ground to Fiona. Any reason to doubt the wisdom of our engagement. 'Dad was happy to give us his blessing.'

'When has Dad ever not been happy to go along with what other people want?' Fiona says. 'So, when's the wedding? You'll need to let people know, so that they can plan.'

Plan what? All people have to do is keep a day free. 'We haven't fixed a date yet. Later in the year. Some time.'

'You need to get organised. Venues book up quickly. You can't expect other people to do it for you.'

'I'm not expecting anyone to do anything. We'll find somewhere, but there's no hurry.'

'Relationships are a partnership. Tom can't do everything.'

'Tom won't be doing everything. I'm not a child, you know, Fiona. I can look after myself.'

She snorts. 'We'll see.'

I could strangle her when she says that. *We'll see* means *No, you won't* or *You'll fail. We'll see*, she said, when I announced I wasn't going to university. *We'll see*, when I said I wanted to do business studies at college instead. *We'll see*, when I told her I was leaving home.

'I presume you're having a church wedding?' says Fiona.

I'm embarrassed to realise I don't know. 'Yes.'

'Well, let me know when you do finally work out a date. We don't want to be away.'

As if that's likely. Her husband, Dave, works as a salesman, which takes him all over the world. With the amount of time he spends travelling on business, they rarely holiday as a family.

I unpeel the 'Call Fi' note from the phone's base unit and screw it into a ball. 'By the way, you phoned last week. What was that about?'

'I'm hosting a birthday party for one of Sophie's friends. It's the last thing I need, but her mum's broken her ankle, so I could hardly say no.' She pauses. 'I thought you could give me a hand? Help with the food, organise games, that kind of thing. It's too late to book an entertainer.'

She must be desperate to ask me.

'When is it?'

'Next Saturday.'

'It's a bit short notice.' I'd rather not spend an afternoon with a room full of shrieking six-year-olds.

'I did call you last weekend, Clare.'

'What about Dave?'

'He's working.'

I give up. 'What time's the party?'

'Three to four-thirty.'

Fiona lives in Uxbridge, in a beautifully refurbished Victorian semi. I'll have to drive straight from there to Tom's. 'All right, I'll see you at three.'

'Make it one-thirty, please. We'll need to get things ready.'

'Right. One-thirty it is.' That's Saturday wiped out, then. I'm about to hang up, when I remember something else. 'Fi, do you know Marilyn? Dad's new friend.'

'Friend? She's a bit more than that!'

I feel like a little girl again. Out of the loop. Secrets between Dad and Fiona.

'Since when?' I say.

'Before Christmas. They met at some do at the hospice.'

'Is it serious?'

'Seems to be. She's good for him. Brings him out of himself. You know how hopeless he is. And Sophie and Harry love her.'

'You've met her?'

'A couple of times. It's nice for the children to have her around, with Dave's mum being so far away. Marilyn treats them like grandchildren.'

My throat tightens. Marilyn has taken Mum's role as grand-mother. 'Dad's invited us for lunch with all of you to meet her,' I say.

'So he said. It's just as well. I don't know when I'd have met Tom otherwise.'

I didn't know I had to have my boyfriends vetted by Fiona.

'You'll like him, Fi. He and Dad got on really well.'

'I'm sure. Look, I'd better go. The children are creating havoc. See you Saturday.'

She's gone without congratulating me on my engagement.

10

Tom's visit has unsettled me. Now that the flat is back to normal, I can't bring myself to change it. I have to regain my equilibrium before my next attempt at treatment. Although I retrieve the self-help book from under the bed, I leave it untouched on the coffee table all week. Untouched and lined up with the edge of the wood.

I'm up early on Saturday to get to the jeweller's. Tom and I had agreed that I should collect the ring, but not wear it until we were together.

The assistant is adamant though. 'We do need you to try it, madam, to check the size.'

Reluctantly I slip it on. It's a perfect fit. The feel of the metal against my skin is alien, though – akin to an itch. I slide the ring off and rub the base of my finger with my thumb, to ease the sensation.

He puts the ring into a silk-lined box, snaps the lid shut and drops the box into a small boutique bag. Outside, I fold down the top of the bag, wrap the cord handle around its stiff card and push it to the bottom of my handbag. The package disturbs the usual balance inside, but fear of losing the ring temporarily overrides the anxiety caused by the disruption.

Back home, I pack up the car and set off for Fiona's.

She answers the door with a red balloon in her hand and an air pump tucked under her arm. She's wearing a green polo shirt over a pair of grey, boot-cut tracksuit trousers, which is unusually relaxed for her, though still high-end: the top is Ralph Lauren.

'Thank God you're here. Can you take over with these?' She thrusts the balloon and pump at me and heads for the kitchen. 'I've still got food to prepare. Could you come and help when you're finished?'

'Hi, Fiona, nice to see you, too.' I pull a face at her back.

As I enter the living room, Sophie and Harry throw themselves at me.

'Auntie Clare, look.' Sophie grabs my hand and pulls me to the floor. Harry follows. Balloons, sweets and sheets of newspaper surround us. The sheets are from the Financial Times; Dave likes to play the stocks and shares.

'We're making parcels,' says Sophie. She plonks a ragged bundle onto a sheet, balances a sweet on top and folds the paper. She sticks it together with a twisted length of tape that four-year-old Harry has been holding for her.

'See.' She lifts up the parcel and the sweet falls out. Sophie frowns and sticks out her bottom lip. 'That keeps happening, Auntie Clare.'

I take it from her, put the sweet back inside and re-stick the paper.

Fiona strides into the room. 'What are you doing, Clare?'

'I'm giving Sophie a hand.' Which must be blindingly obvious. What she means is, *Why aren't you blowing up balloons?*

'For goodness' sake, Sophie. It's a simple enough job, you don't need Auntie Clare's help.'

'Fiona, give her a chance, she's only six.'

'She's old enough to do it by herself.'

Sophie pouts and tilts her chin defiantly at her mother. Harry looks as if he's about to cry.

I pick up the bag of balloons and the pump. 'Why don't you two do the balloons? Sophie, you hold them on the pump and Harry can put in the air. I'll knot them when you're finished.'

'I want to pump.' Sophie pouts again.

'Take it in turns. And no arguing over who does which colour balloon.' I latch one onto the pump to get them started.

Sophie pinches her fingers around the neck of the balloon and Harry starts pumping.

Fiona turns on her heel. 'You'll never get them done that way.'

No doubt she'll continue to eavesdrop on our progress, or lack of it, from the kitchen.

An hour later, I've wrapped all the parcels and hung up the balloons. I go into the kitchen to help Fiona. She's packing the party bags with expensive gifts: lacy tights, hair clips and Green & Black's chocolate.

'We're done,' I say.

'Really? The children need to change, then.' She sticks her head out of the kitchen door. 'Sophie, Harry, go upstairs and get ready, please. Your clothes are on your beds. Sophie, you can help Harry.'

Sophie marches past, clutching Harry's hand.

'Good girl,' I say.

As they clomp upstairs, Fiona looks me up and down. 'What are you wearing for the party?'

'This.' I gesture at my long-sleeved tee shirt and jeans.

'Oh.'

'What's wrong with it?'

'It's not really party wear.'

'I'm not really a guest. And it's a children's party, not Oscars' night.'

'Still.'

Still, there is clearly a dress code even for party skivvies. I ignore her and get on with the sandwiches: chicken liver pâté.

'Isn't this too rich for children?' I say.

'My two love it. It's better than that tasteless meat paste muck Mum used to give us.'

The rest of the food is equally upmarket. Platters of shop-bought canapés are all over the kitchen: pinwheels of smoked salmon and soft cheese; mini vol-au-vents; and olives, anchovies and gherkins on cocktail sticks. Not the sort of things I ate when I was six. I didn't try an olive or anchovy until I was in my twenties. Children must be more sophisticated nowadays.

'Can I leave you to it?' Fiona says. 'I have to get changed.' She disappears without waiting for an answer.

Her absence gives me a chance to snack while I prepare the food, having missed lunch to travel over here.

Sophie and Harry come back downstairs. Sophie is wearing a blue velvet dress, with white lace at the neck and cuffs. A matching hair band holds back her brunette pageboy cut. With her white tights and flat pumps, she looks like Alice in Wonderland's dark-haired twin.

Harry has on a white shirt, navy corduroy trousers and a clip-on bow tie perched at a jaunty angle.

In the hall, I squat next to them. 'Don't you look a treat?' I straighten Harry's tie and smooth down a strand of his hair. It's the same colour as Fiona's, the same floppy texture as mine.

'Auntie Clare,' Sophie whispers, 'I couldn't do up my dress.' She lifts her hand to the back of her neck, her fingers fluttering helplessly.

I gently turn her around and fasten the three tiny pearl buttons.

Fiona appears on the stairs. She's back in her usual black and white: crisply tailored black trousers and a white shirt. The only bright spots are her flaming hair and the silk scarf tied around her neck like a cravat. Her scarves, always with accents of green, are her trademark – today's is a geometric print, of black, white and emerald green diamonds.

'Are we all ready?' She eyes the children, studiously avoiding me. At the bottom of the stairs, she picks up a vase of white lilies from the marble-topped table by the front door. 'Blast, I meant to move these earlier.' One of the flowers bobs against her shoulder, scattering rust-coloured pollen over her shirt.

'Fi,' I say, 'you've got—'

'What now?' She stops on her way to the kitchen.

'Nothing.'

She shakes her head and carries on.

A few minutes later, the doorbell rings: it's the birthday girl. Her father delivers her with thanks, apologising that he has to get back to work. The other guests quickly follow: ten girls and a couple of mums who stay to help. They've also brought crisps and drinks. The snacks they empty into Fiona's bowls are lurid shades of yellow and orange, with a cheesy-feet smell. Fiona tucks their fizzy drinks behind the low-sugar squash she has bought.

The other mums, also in jeans and casual tops, help me organise the games: musical chairs, blind man's buff and pin the tail on the donkey. They pitch in enthusiastically, after some initial bemusement at the lack of magician, clown or bouncy castle. The children also seem to enjoy the novelty of more old-fashioned entertainment.

Later, as they sit down to eat, Fiona takes me to one side. 'You've got them far too excited. Could you do something quieter after tea?'

I settle for pass the parcel; it doesn't turn out quite as planned.

When the package lands in Sophie's lap, she tears into the paper, only to find there's no sweet. An escapee from one of her not-quite-stuck-together layers. I glance around the circle. Harry is sucking on something, although the parcel hasn't stopped at him yet.

Sophie fingers the shreds of paper. 'Where's my sweet? Where's my sweet?'

'Sophie, don't make such a fuss, please.' Fiona dips into a spare bag of sweets. 'Have one of these.'

'Nooo,' Sophie wails. 'I want a parcel sweet.' She crosses her arms, her bottom lip trembles.

'Don't be so silly, they're all the same.' Fiona leans over and drops a sweet in front of Sophie. She picks it up and throws it across the room.

'Sophie Mercer, behave yourself or you'll go upstairs!' Fiona flushes, while the other mums adopt middle-distance stares.

Sophie's eyes fill with tears, her chest heaves. Soon she's howling. Tears and snot dribble and mingle on her face. Harry, ever devoted to his sister, joins in.

'Sophie, Harry, stop, for goodness' sake!' Fiona lifts her hands in apparent despair.

Harry's sobbing reaches a new level. He starts coughing. His face turns red.

'Fi, he's choking. He's got a sweet in his mouth.' I run over to kneel beside him. As I reach him, he coughs up the sweet.

'Thank God for that,' I say. But he's still coughing. Then the coughing turns into retching.

Fiona shoves past me, pulling her scarf from her neck. She gets to Harry just as he vomits. She holds the scarf in front of him. A torrent of yellowy-orange sick pours onto it. Fiona cups her hands and a pool forms in the delicate silk. In seconds, it creeps towards the scarf's edge. I'm mesmerised by the sight of it.

'Don't just sit there, Clare. Do something,' she says.

The other mums have shepherded the girls to the far end of the room. I'm on my own. I run into the kitchen for tea towels. When I get back, Harry has stopped retching. A trickle of gunge oozes like lava from his mouth.

Fiona turns towards me. 'Hold a tea towel under my hands. Harry, stay still.'

He goes rigid, his eyes wide and teary, his mouth open. I reach in front of Fiona. She lowers the scarf onto the tea towel. The heavy warmth of the vomit penetrates the layers of silk and cotton.

'Stay there,' she tells Harry. She holds another tea towel above my hands, under his chin. 'You can put that straight in the dustbin outside.' She nods at my bundle.

'What about your scarf?' I say.

'I'm hardly going to wear it now, am I?'

Carefully I get up, pulling the corners of the tea towel together. The vomit slops about inside, the movement stirring up its sour smell. My throat constricts. I grit my teeth and breathe deeply. Fiona will kill me if I'm sick, too.

The party peters out after that. Fiona gives Harry a wash and the girls watch a film until their parents arrive. It's strangely quiet once they've gone.

I help Fiona clear up. Soft-cheese-smeared salmon strips curl and shrivel on paper plates. The contents of the cocktail sticks have been dismantled, but not all eaten. The vol-au-vents and sandwiches have vanished, though, as have all the cheesy snacks – into Harry and back out again, I suspect.

I take the empty bowls through to the kitchen, where she's washing up.

'Looks like the E-numbers won the day,' I say. 'No wonder Harry was sick.'

'It's not easy getting them to eat the right things.' Fiona scrubs the bowls hard. 'It's a constant battle. Children aren't just about having fun.'

'I know.' I hand her another bowl. 'I suppose we weren't much different. It's a wonder we didn't turn pink, with all the strawberry Angel Delight Mum gave us. Remember?'

'Exactly. She was hardly the perfect mother, either.' She crashes the snack bowls onto the drainer.

'Is there anything I can do to help in here?' I say.

'No, thanks. Just keep an eye on the children till I'm finished, will you?'

I retreat to the living room. Sophie and Harry are on the floor watching the rest of the film. They're too close to the television; I leave them to it. Fiona won't like it, but I prefer being good cop. I perch on the sofa behind them.

After a few minutes, Harry twists around. 'Auntie Clare, I'm thirsty.'

'All right, sweetheart, I'll get you a glass of water.'

I go into the kitchen. Fiona is at the sink, a tea towel pressed to her face, a party bag in her hand.

'Fi? What are you doing?'

'Nothing.' The cloth muffles her voice. 'Clearing up.' She turns away from me.

I go up to her, put my hand on her arm. 'Fiona, are you all right?' She twitches convulsively. I take my hand away. 'Fiona?'

She turns around. Her eyes are red. 'I forgot to give them the party bags!' She holds up the bag, her hand shaking slightly.

'Not to worry. Sophie can take them into school on Monday.'

'It's not the same. I messed it up. I messed it all up. I can't even throw a decent children's party.'

I've never seen her like this. She's always so together, so in control.

'Fiona, you didn't mess up, it was great. They loved it.' I pat her shoulder, noticing that the lily pollen has smeared into her shirt like a bloodstain. Unsure whether to hug her, I let my hand drop.

'They didn't. They hated the food and goodness' knows what got into my two. They behaved like spoiled brats.'

'They were tired and over-excited. All children get that way. Remember how we were? Our games always ended in tears.'

Fiona sniffs and straightens her shoulders.

'You're probably tired, too,' I say. 'None of this will seem such a big deal in the morning.'

'Maybe not.' She puts the party bag down.

'When's Dave back?'

'Tomorrow evening.' She bends to put the tea towel into the washing machine.

'You should ask him to help more,' I say.

'There's no point. He's hardly ever here.' Fiona slams the washing machine door shut. 'I have to deal with everything. I always have.'

Bustling past me, she marches into the living room. I trail behind her.

She shakes her head at the children. 'Sophie, Harry, how many times have I told you not to sit so close to the television?'

They shuffle backward on their bottoms.

Brisk and brusque, Fiona is back in charge. Yet I can't help wondering what just happened.

11

The front door of Tom's cottage opens directly onto the living room. As he ushers me in, he glances at me. 'What do you think?'

'About what?'

Charlie ambles over and nudges my leg with his nose.

'I've tidied up. Can't you tell?'

I look around. The cottage certainly isn't as dishevelled as usual. Nothing is dangling off shelves or out of drawers. It's cluttered, yet the clutter is more contained.

'Very nice.' I make for the stairs, to dump my bags in the bedroom.

'And I bought these.' He pats one of four new cushions on the sofa.

'Is this your way of telling me you're gay?'

'Cheeky!' Tom throws the cushion at me.

I catch it, letting my overnight bag drop to the floor.

'I got a table and chairs as well. Come and see.' He walks into the kitchen.

I put my handbag down, on top of the overnight bag, and follow him, hugging the cushion to me.

Squeezed in the corner of the kitchen is a tiny table with fold-down leaves. Two collapsible chairs lean against it. Tom pulls up the leaves and unfolds the chairs. 'Do you like them?' he says.

'They're a good size.' It would be churlish to mention that the beech veneer doesn't match the oak kitchen units. I don't want to discourage his new-found domesticity. The muddy wellies and DIY works-in-progress have even disappeared.

'I'll cook tonight and we can eat in here,' says Tom, 'like at your place. It was great having dinner at a table instead of takeaways off a tray! Why don't you shower while I make a start?' He pours me a glass of wine to take with me.

On my way through the living room, I toss the cushion back on the sofa. Upstairs I unpack my clothes and toiletries. On top of the chest of drawers are several half-used bottles of aftershave and cans of deodorant. Scattered amongst them are nail clippers, a key ring, a couple of CDs, a broken pencil and various scraps of paper. I clear a space in the muddle for myself. At Tom's, I put my things down without hesitation, without lining them up and endlessly tinkering. In someone else's home those urges vanish. I don't think about what I do, don't worry about it. The mess probably helps. There are no lines to follow, no patterns to complete. If I lived here, though, I would have to create patterns, link objects as if by ley lines.

As I come downstairs after my shower, Tom shouts something from the kitchen. I lean over the banisters. 'What did you say?'

'Don't come in!' The door crashes shut. Charlie pads over to paw at it, whining.

I carry on down into the living room. 'Come and sit with me, Charlie. He'll let us in soon.' I curl up on the sofa. Charlie twists his head to look at me and then turns back. He paws and whines until the kitchen door opens a few inches. Charlie sidles in.

'Hey, what about me!' I say. The door is already closed.

I sip my wine, browsing a coffee table book of landscape photography. Ten minutes later, Tom charges out, slamming the door behind him. 'Nearly there. Don't go in.' He thunders up the stairs and is back down in a few minutes.

'Can I come in now?' I say.

'In a sec. I need to sort out the music.' He squats in front of the CD cabinets. His head tilted sideways, he fingers through a shelf of cases. Reaching the end, he starts again.

'Where the hell is it?' Tom leans back and scans the shelves nearby. Lunging forward, he pulls out a disc. 'Here we are! Since when does *k* come after *n*?' He brandishes a *Keane* album at me. 'I've told Vicky to put things back where she finds them. Jeez, you wouldn't think it was that difficult.' He stands up, flushed, with sweat glistening on his nose. 'Madam, your table is ready.'

I take his outstretched hand and he leads me into the kitchen. It's hot, despite the back door being ajar. The cool April air makes no impression on the cooking fug. My underarms instantly become damp. I chose to put on a long-sleeved woollen dress, expecting the usual cottage chill.

Candles light the room. A vase of spring flowers decorates the table.

'This is lovely,' I say.

Tom lets go of my hand to pick up a tea towel. He swipes it over his face and drapes it back on its hook. 'Take a seat. I hope the food's okay.'

At each place setting is a starter of smoked salmon and buttered brown bread.

Tom slides the CD into a player on a ledge above the table and sits down.

'Before we eat, I wanted to give you this.' He reaches into the top pocket of his flannel shirt. He fishes about for a second and takes out his mobile phone. Digging deeper, he pulls out my engagement ring.

'You've been in my handbag!' I say.

'Yeah. I guessed it would be in there. I hope you don't mind?'

'Well, it's…I don't know. A bit of an invasion.' I feel sick. 'Handbags are private space.' And mine is a microcosm of my world, a portable sanctuary in times of stress, an obsessional comfort blanket.

'God, I'm really sorry, Clare. I did feel a bit funny about it, but I didn't want you to give this to me, to give back to you.' Tom holds the ring as if it might burn him. 'I promise, I didn't snoop and I put everything back as I found it. I hope I haven't spoiled the evening?'

'No, of course not.' He seems so upset, I can't keep on at him. 'Just don't make a habit of it!'

'I won't, believe me.' He beams and holds out his hand.

I put mine in his.

'Thank you for saying yes.'

Although I smile back, my mind is elsewhere. Distracted by the thought that he has touched my bag, by not knowing how he's left it. The uncertainty is unbearable.

Tom slides the ring onto my finger, but it sticks on the middle knuckle. He pushes.

'Ouch.' My eyes prick with tears.

'Sorry. Damn, I can't believe it doesn't fit.'

'It must do. It was all right when…I was sized last week. My hands are hot. Maybe I should wash them.'

I get up and hold my fingers under the cold tap until they hurt, wishing I could numb my mind the same way. The vision of my disordered bag gnaws at me – a mental weight pressing down on me from the bedroom above.

I dry my hands on the tea towel and Tom tries again. This time the ring slides all the way. The base of my finger tingles at the contact.

He raises his wineglass. 'To us.'

'To us.' Echoing the words unthinkingly, unable to focus on the here and now. 'Sorry, Tom. I need to pop to the bathroom. Back in a minute.'

I race upstairs and tiptoe into the bedroom. The floorboards creak. I halt, cringing, listening – until I realise that the music will drown out any small noises.

My handbag is on the floor, as I left it, except the zipper is half open. Next to it are the ring box and jeweller's bag. I open the handbag. Inside it's as if a whisk has stirred the contents. Nothing is where it should be. My heart races, I feel light-headed. What has Tom done? What on earth has he done?

I kneel next to the bag. The quickest way to sort it out is to empty it. I upend it onto the floor. My purse lands with a thud and flies open, spilling coins. I gather them up as fast as I can, fumbling and dropping some.

'Clare, are you okay up there?' Tom's voice comes from the bottom of the stairs.

I jump.

'Clare? I thought I heard something fall. Is everything all right?' His voice is nearer.

I freeze, purse in one hand, coins in the other. 'I'm fine, fine. Down in a minute.' I wait, motionless, holding my breath.

The stairs creak. Is he coming up or going down? If he's coming up, I don't have time to replace everything without getting caught.

The kitchen door shuts. I breathe out. My hands are shaking. I feel like a criminal.

Although I have to be quick, I can't stop myself checking each item is in the right position. Finally, I'm ready to zip up the bag. As I leave the room, I give it one last glance.

On the landing, I remember the outside pockets. It's unlikely Tom opened them, but not impossible. I return to the bedroom to empty and repack them, even though they appear untouched. At the door, I stop to stare at the bag once more. It's where it should be. Everything inside is where it should be. I clench my fists and force myself to turn away.

Creeping across the landing to the bathroom, I flush the toilet.

Back downstairs, I say, 'Sorry I took so long. I was looking at my ring.'

'Glad you like it.' Tom grins. 'Shall we go to the pub for last orders? I'd like to introduce you to everyone, and you can show it off to them.'

I'd rather not. Everyone includes Bex. Bex, the barmaid. Bex, the ex. Tom dated her a year or so ago for a few months. They split up amicably and she has a new boyfriend, yet she won't leave Tom alone. She's phoned for help a couple of times while I've been with him: a broken boiler once, a jammed lock another time. She treats him as her personal handyman and he hasn't yet rejected the role.

When we get to *The White Horse*, only one woman is serving behind the bar. She's sunbed-tanned and beautifully made-up. It must be Bex. As she slowly pulls a pint, she tosses a head of long, dark curls. My hair feels limper and duller than ever.

She spots Tom as we approach the bar. 'Hey you, to what do we owe the pleasure? Don't usually see you on a Saturday night.' She smiles at him.

A man perched on a stool nearby scowls.

'I brought Clare in to meet you all,' says Tom. 'Clare, this is Bex. And Keith, her boyfriend.' He gestures at the man on the stool.

Keith nods and picks up his pint. He's a tattooed bruiser.

Bex reaches over the bar to shake my hand. Hers is tipped by nails immaculately manicured with blood red varnish. 'Nice to meet you, Clare. You're a lucky woman.' She winks at Tom. 'He's quite a catch.'

'Bex, please!' Tom runs his hand through his hair.

Keith glares at him.

'Usual for you, Tom?' Bex says. 'And Clare?'

'A glass of Merlot, if you've got it? Thanks.'

Bex pushes Tom's pint towards him. 'Oh, yes, hearts broke all over the village when we heard our Tom was engaged.'

He flushes. 'I don't think so. Most of the women are old enough to be my mum.'

A woman in her forties at the other end of the bar leans forward. 'Oi, we'll have less of that, Tom Henson. Old enough to be your mum, my foot! Older sister, more like.'

'Sorry, Caz, I didn't mean you.' The flush spreads to Tom's neck.

'Aw, Caz, leave him alone, he's blushing,' says Bex.

Keith snorts.

Bex ignores him. 'Anyway, when are you going to fix my leaking tap? You promised to do it last week.'

'Sorry, Bex, I forgot. We've had a lot on at work. Tuesday evening?'

'It's a date.' Bex pours my wine.

Tom pays, picks up the glasses and heads for a table in the corner. I follow him.

'It'll be quieter over here,' he says.

'I thought you wanted me to meet people?'

'I did, but I'd rather not stay at the bar with Keith there. I don't think he likes me.'

'Was it the scowling or the snorting that gave it away?'

I take a seat facing out into the room. Tom puts down the drinks and sits down at right angles to me, with his back to the bar.

He smiles ruefully. 'I wouldn't want to get on the wrong side of him. Did you see his muscles?'

'He's just jealous.'

'Of what?'

'Of you. Of the attention Bex pays you. You do seem very close.'

'That's ridiculous! She's just a friend.'

If that's the case, I wonder why he accepts her proprietorial manner?

Behind him, Bex leans over the counter with her phone to take a photo of herself and a man sitting next to Caz. Bex's mane of curls hangs over the man's left shoulder.

'She's very glamorous,' I say, 'and she has lovely hair.' I watch Tom carefully for his reaction.

'High maintenance, though, with all that make-up and stuff.' He picks up his beer and gulps at it.

'That's normal these days. Every other shop is a tanning salon or nail bar.'

'You don't use them,' he says.

'No, but I'm not normal.'

'That's what I liked about you, at the wedding.' Tom reaches around the table leg to caress my thigh.

'What, that I'm not normal?'

'No, the fact that you looked more natural. That I could actually see what you looked like.'

'Go on, tell me more.' It's my turn for the game of why-did-you-go-out-with-me.

'You were by far the prettiest woman there.'

'And?'

'And the most classily dressed.'

'And?'

'And the funniest. With the cutest, freckliest nose.' Tom scoops up a blob of foam from his beer and deposits it on the tip of my nose.

'Thanks, that's nice.' I catch the froth with my forefinger and wipe it onto his sleeve.

'Oi, that's my best shirt!'

'It's the same as all the others.' Flannel, long-sleeved, chest pocket, checked.

'Okay, well, it's the newest.'

'And?' I say. Our game isn't quite over.

'And you agreed that the parents of the kids throwing wedding cake should be put in stocks for us to chuck stuff at them.'

I'm almost persuaded, but there is still the aberration of Tom's relationship with Bex to be explained. 'So, if you like all that's natural, how did you end up with Bex?'

He takes a swig of beer. 'She's a good laugh.'

Which can be interpreted any way you like.

'That was the only reason?' I say.

Tom looks sheepish. 'I suppose she kind of threw herself at me. It was just a bit of fun really. We knew it wouldn't last. Apart from anything else, she really wants kids.'

'And she was aware you don't?'

'Oh, yes. After what happened with my ex-wife, I didn't want to lead anyone else up the garden path...' His face crumples; he's never forgiven himself for the hurt he caused his ex. 'I wouldn't have had a serious relationship with any woman who wanted a family. Bex and I called it a day after a few months.'

He might have done; I'm not convinced she has. Perhaps she thinks she can talk him into fatherhood? It's hard to believe she only wants him for his DIY skills; she must have other friends who could ease the burden of her domestic crises.

'So, when did you become a plumber?' I say.

'I can fix a tap.'

'And Keith can't?'

'Apparently not.'

Tom's problem is, he can never say no. One day it will get him into trouble.

12

The engagement has taken on momentum. Dad knows about it. Fiona knows about it. In fact, Tom's entire village knows about it. I even have a ring now. Yet I've made no progress towards being able to share a home. I'm ashamed of that failure and panicky as to what it means for my future — our future. Tom and I won't have one, unless I can work things out, and I can't lose him, when it's in my power to prevent it. I have to step up my efforts before it's too late.

The next evening, I try again to make a mess. Not what the average person means by a mess, though: dirty clothes on the bedroom floor; piles of books and paperwork on every surface; and boxes of half-eaten pizza festering in the kitchen. For someone like me, a mess is more subtle: a mess is anything that is not-quite-just-so. Just enough not-quite-just-so to induce discomfort — even moving things a fraction of an inch. The trick is to resist putting them back. The longer I resist, the less uneasy I'll feel. Allegedly.

The theory doesn't translate so easily into practice.

I start by putting away my laundry: tee shirts and work shirts that I've already ironed, and underwear. The work shirts are draped over hangers and the tee shirts folded into squares, ready to lay in the drawer, with their edges lined up. I pick up the first, shake it out and loosely refold it. The seams are no longer aligned, the arms are crumpled. It looks horrible. No, feels horrible. Giving up control of one small piece of fabric has allowed my anxiety a way back in. Instantly, I'm edgy and unsettled.

Kneeling down, I open the drawer and drop, rather than place, the tee shirt on top of the pile inside. It lands an inch off to the right, leaving the one underneath visible. I stare at the rogue tee shirt; my fingers itch to move it, to relieve my unease. I clench my fists and wait to stop feeling uncomfortable. And wait. Ten minutes later, I'm still waiting for the anxiety to dissipate. I go into the living room and check the self-help book — it warns that it can take up to three hours to feel better. I can't spend three hours putting away every pair of socks and pants, every tee shirt, every shirt; it will take me all week. I steel myself to put everything away in one go and deal with the solitary – but huge – anxiety hit that will follow.

I open drawers, insert items any old how, and close them again. The same with the shirts. I hang them up without folding in the arms or making sure the hangers are evenly spaced. Five minutes later, I'm finished. The job usually takes at least half an hour.

In the living room, I sit down on the sofa and wait to feel better. Although I can't see the clothes, they are in my mind's eye. Each item in its new out-of-place place.

I have to force myself to stay seated, banging my heels against the floor to quell the agitation in my legs and feet that would otherwise propel me away to fix things. I squeeze a cushion to still my hands and arms. Obsessive urges tug at every part of me, like the strings of a sadistic puppet master. The biggest pull of all is in my head. It's the source of the twitching in every limb.

When I was ten, that same pull had a simple, if flawed, logic: tidy up to keep Mum happy, to stop Mum and Dad fighting, to make sure Mum didn't leave. It made some kind of sense, while being as illogical as superstitiously touching wood. There is no longer any sense, any logic. I am not trying to allay fears of a specific catastrophe, only the fear of the anxiety that disorder provokes – an unfocussed, inexplicable anxiety. The fear is no less, though, for its lack of a real source. The truth is, by gaining control of my environment, I've lost control of myself, and the tactics I adopted as a child are now more likely to drive away those I love than keep them by my side.

As I wait on the sofa, that indefinable anxiety continues to rampage around my mind. I wish I could unscrew my head and set it aside, until the feeling has gone. I need a distraction, like a smoker tormented by nicotine cravings, or a dieter by hunger. Want a cigarette? Find something else to occupy your hands. Want a doughnut? Have a glass of water to fool your stomach. Feeling anxious? Think about something else.

I pick up a magazine from the pile on the floor: a bridal one that I impulsively bought at the Tube station newsstand. I shut myself in the bathroom and run a bubble bath. Lying back in the hot water, I flick through the pages of beautiful dresses, flowers and cakes. With the worry about living with Tom, about being married, I'd overlooked the fun part: the wedding. I turn down the corners of pages picturing my favourite dresses, floral arrangements and outfits for bridesmaids and pageboys. By the time the water has chilled to lukewarm, my head is full of ideas and plans. I'm relaxed, happy, optimistic.

As I close the magazine, I realise the lower edge has become crinkled with moisture. Damp corrugations now irrevocably mar its glossy pages. I shiver as I drop it onto the floor.

Out of the bath, I quickly dry myself and put on my dressing gown. Padding through to the bedroom, I pull open my underwear drawer. The untidy piles inside greet me like a slap in the face. I'm transfixed, my hands clutching the edges of the drawer. In seconds, the anxiety has engulfed me as completely as it did an hour ago.

I have to put everything back as it should be; this time, I can't resist. With shaking fingers, I straighten the underwear, smoothing each item until it lies neatly on the one beneath. The same with the tee shirts, refolded first. Then the shirts, arms tucked in and hangers re-spaced. There is a frenzied edge to my movements, controlled as they are, wrought of my desperation to put things right.

Eventually, it is all back to normal.

Normal brings some sense of relief, but it's late and my efforts have exhausted me. I'm depressed by how hard this is. I thought I wasn't as bad as other people. Thought my obsessions didn't have the same grip, that I could give them up any time I wanted.

Yet I've failed again. Failed like a smoker having a secret puff or a dieter raiding the fridge. I collapse into bed, lonely and defeated. Pressing my face against the pillow, I begin to cry. I don't know how to do this.

13

I need someone who understands the problem and how to deal with it. Someone who has been there, done that and bought the immaculately folded tee shirt.

I know there are support groups for people like me, though I've never been to one. Now is the time to try. On the Internet, I discover the nearest meets about ten miles away and the next get-together is on Thursday evening. They run for two hours, starting at seven-thirty, so I'll be back in time for my usual bedtime phone call with Tom. He won't even know I've gone.

Until then, I give up any attempt to help myself. I can't face another failure. Once I've been to the group, it will be easier.

By the time Thursday comes around, I'm having second thoughts. I can't open up to a room full of strangers. They might not be as bad as me, they might think I'm odd. I won't know, though, unless I go – and I have to do this for me and Tom.

After half an hour's drive through the rain, I'm hunting deserted residential streets for the church hall where the group meets. A bell tower looms out of the darkness. Parking on the road outside the church, I crunch across gravel to the hall behind. I push at the entrance door. It creaks open. Inside, it is quiet. I wonder if I have the right place. The wind cuts through my thin fleece. I shiver and start to back out.

A door opens inside and a grey-haired woman hurries out. She stops when she sees me. 'Can I help you?'

'I'm…I'm here for the group.'

'The support group? They're in there.' She waves behind her. 'I'm Heather. I lead the meetings.'

I step inside and let the entrance door shut behind me. 'I'm Clare.'

'Welcome, Clare. Please make yourself comfortable,' says Heather. 'I'll be back in a minute.' She disappears down the dark corridor.

I walk towards the door. Standing in front of it, like Alice at the rabbit hole, I hesitate. It's not too late to leave.

A gust of wind blasts me from behind. I turn around. A tall, middle-aged man comes in. He strides up to me, rubbing his hands. 'Shocking weather, isn't it? Are you going in?' He pushes the door open and waits to let me through.

'Yes, thanks.' I duck under his arm.

Several people sit in a ragged circle in the middle of the hall. Curtains cover the windows on the wall opposite, where rows of chairs are stacked. To the left is a stage, with a piano on one side. Yellowing strip lights illuminate the room.

The man I came in with approaches the group, greeting some people by name. He collects two chairs and slides them into a gap in the circle.

I'm still by the door.

He catches my eye. 'Why don't you sit here?'

'Thanks.' I cross the room to join him. Draping my fleece and handbag over the back of the chair, I sit down.

'I'm Michael. Pleased to meet you.' My new friend smiles at me. He's good-looking, in an old-fashioned film-star way, with eyes the same clear, light blue as Tom's. A blazer and crisp white shirt offset his good looks.

'Clare.' I return his smile.

A woman on the other side of me leans forward. 'I'm Evelyn.' She's in her mid-fifties, thin and twitchy. A bunch of keys rattles between her fingers.

'Hi, Evelyn, I—'

'Clare,' says Michael, 'do you know how this kind of group runs?'

'No, I haven't been to one before.' I smile apologetically at Evelyn, as I turn my attention back to Michael.

While he explains, I glance around the room. There are twelve people, including me. Eight women, four men. To my relief, they all look normal.

A few do seem stressed. One young girl zips and unzips her handbag, muttering to herself. Beneath the hubbub of conversation, I hear an occasional number. She appears to be repeatedly counting from one to four.

A few seats away an elderly, balding man cleans his hands with a wet wipe. When he's finished, he folds the cloth, passes it to a woman sitting next to him and rests his hands in his lap, palms upwards, as if about to start meditating.

Their rituals are the visible signs of the distress that is the hallmark of our condition. The distress that differentiates it from the quirky habits that others claim make them obsessive-compulsive, but which have no foundation in anxiety.

Heather comes in, weighed down by supermarket bags. She hoists them up onto the stage, by the piano, and takes the chair opposite me, next to Wet Wipe Man.

'Good evening,' she says. 'Thanks to all of you for coming out in such horrible weather.' She looks around the circle. 'We're quite a big group tonight. Could I suggest family members and carers set up at the other end for networking first?'

Some people gather up bags and chairs. A woman next to the counting girl touches her arm. The girl looks up from her bag. She's holding it so tightly her knuckles are white, and she's on the verge of tears.

The woman peers into the girl's face. 'Will you be all right?'

A man on the other side of the woman tuts and stands up. 'See you over there.' He snatches up his chair and heads for the other group.

The woman follows him a moment later. They must be the girl's parents.

The girl zips and unzips her bag several times. I'd like to tidy my own, to relieve my stress, but this is too exposed an environment. The desire not to be observed keeps me in check. For the girl opposite, her compulsions seem to have overridden any such qualms.

We're left with five women and two men – Wet Wipe Man and Michael. Everyone tugs their chairs forward to close up the gaps.

'Let's begin with introductions,' says Heather. 'Tell everyone your name and a little bit about yourself.' She glances at me. 'For those of you who are new, I'm Heather. I used to be severely affected by obsessive-compulsive disorder – mainly contamination fears – and I've been running this group for six years.'

She turns to Wet Wipe Man. 'Albert?'

It's no surprise to learn that he is also worried about contamination. 'It's that filthy outside these days. I don't go out much, just here really. It's hard on the wife.' He gestures towards the woman beside him. 'Betty doesn't drive, so we've got people to do the shopping. I make 'em leave it on the step. I can't have 'em coming into the house, bringing muck in.' He shudders.

After Albert is a hoarder. She's compelled both to buy new things and keep rubbish. Her home is filled with a jumble of stuff she doesn't need, with barely space to move. The polar opposite to my flat. Strange that we have both ended up here.

Then Michael. To my surprise, we share the same problem.

'Must be something to do with my Navy background,' he says. 'I do like things to be shipshape. Pardon the pun.' There are a few polite titters at what is probably an old joke.

Heather turns to me. 'Clare, isn't it? Would you like to say a few words?'

'I'm like Michael.' I glance at him and he nods encouragingly. 'Except I've never been in the Navy!'

Laughter ripples around the group.

Heather moves onto Evelyn. She's obsessed with checking, especially her front door. While she talks, she fiddles with her keys.

Next is a woman who shares Albert's contamination issues.

Then, finally, Counting Girl. She introduces herself as Katie. She is quiet and well-spoken, with huge manga eyes. She is compelled to do everything four times. 'Checking stuff, cleaning my teeth, getting dressed.' Her voice wavers. 'It takes ages to finish anything.' She glances at the other group. Her father is slumped in his seat, arms folded. More quietly, she says, 'Mum's okay about it, but Dad gets really angry.'

'Thanks, Katie,' says Heather. 'Thanks, everyone. Let's find out how you've all got on in the last month.'

Albert has hard evidence of his progress. 'I've hardly bought any soap or cleaning stuff and I'm down from three packs of wipes a day to one.'

The woman who hoards reports that she has held a car boot sale to reduce her stash. A small round of applause greets her news.

Then it's Michael's turn. He isn't as forthcoming as the others.

'Things are much the same,' he says. 'I don't want to waste the group's time on me. Perhaps we should move on to Clare?'

I glance at Heather. Her eyes are still on him. 'Let us know if you'd like to speak later,' she says. 'Clare? Would you like to say anything tonight? No pressure. If you just want to listen, that's fine.'

I'm nervous, but if I don't speak, what's the point of being here?

'I think it started when I was ten,' I say. I tell them about Mum, about Tom and his proposal, and my renewed, and failed, attempts to deal with my obsessive-compulsive habits. Everything that has led to my being here tonight. Once I've started, it's easy. The murmur of understanding that runs around the group spurs me on. They know where I'm coming from, even if they don't all have the same kind of compulsions.

I finish, drained and relieved. Michael smiles warmly at me. I smile back, happy to be with these new friends.

'Have another go at the self-help,' says Heather, 'and ask your doctor to refer you for therapy.'

Albert snorts. 'Don't hold your breath, love.'

'What do you mean?' I ask.

Heather answers for him, 'Albert has a point. It can be difficult to get the right treatment within a reasonable timeframe.'

A couple of others in the group nod in agreement.

'You need to persevere,' says Heather. 'If you'd like an advocate to assist you, let me know. Some people find it hard to present their case to medical staff.'

'Thanks.' The revelation has only confirmed what I already knew: I don't have time to wait for professional help. Now, though, there are people who know what I'm trying to achieve on my own. People with, if not expectations, at least hopes of me. I'm answerable to them, as well as myself.

'Tell us how you get on next time,' says Heather.

By the time we get to Katie, we're an hour into the session and the other group has disbanded for refreshments. Katie's mother stands by the stage, setting out cups and drinks. Katie watches over her shoulder, as her father heads for the door. She doesn't speak until he has left the room.

'I'm a bit better,' she says. 'I was only fifteen minutes late for a meal out last week.' She looks over her shoulder again. 'The thing is, I'm worse when I'm stressed and Dad makes me stressed. He's always watching me.'

'Could your mum help, Katie?' says Heather. 'Ask him to take the pressure off a bit?'

'She's tried. He stops for a while and then he starts again,' Katie says. 'I just want him to leave me alone, let me do things my way.' Her head droops and her long, dark hair falls over her face.

'Remember, though, Katie,' says Heather gently, 'you're trying to change the way you behave. Your family can't pander to your rituals. It may seem easier for all of you if they do, but, in the long run, it will only make matters worse.'

Katie nods, her head still down.

I'm surprised any of them manage to live with husbands, wives, parents, children. And vice versa. How does someone else live in a hoarder's mess? How does Evelyn's husband cope, when she takes forty-five minutes to lock the front door? When do the partners of those with contamination issues ever get a turn in the bathroom?

I'm amazed to find that most of them, like me, get on with life, in spite of their problems: going to school and work, and maintaining relationships. I wonder how many more of us are out there, secretly struggling on.

'Let's wind up for a short break,' says Heather. 'We'll rejoin the others afterwards to get their feedback.'

Michael walks over to the stage with me. 'Can I get you anything?'

'Orange juice. Thanks.'

He pours two cups. 'Careful, I've overfilled them,' he says, handing me my drink. His own slops over the rim and onto his fingers. He puts the cup down and reaches into his trouser pocket with the other hand, pulling out a folded cotton handkerchief with initials embroidered on it: 'M R'. He shakes out the fabric, wipes his fingers, and then re-folds it – lining up the edges to make a neat square – and puts it back in his pocket.

'What's the R for?' I say.

'Ryder. Michael Ryder.'

'Well, Michael Ryder, apart from my dad, you're the only man I've ever met who uses a proper handkerchief.' I hold out my juice. 'Here's to getting better. And proper handkerchiefs.'

'Proper handkerchiefs.' Michael picks up his cup and lifts it to mine, at the same time delving into the pocket of his blazer to pull out a business card. 'If you need someone to talk to, call me any time, day or night.' He hands me the card.

'Thank you. It's great that you have the same problem. I mean, not great for you, but for me. Well, obviously, it's not great for anyone, but…God, sorry! I don't know what I mean.'

He touches my arm. 'No need to apologise, Clare. I trust I can be of assistance.'

'Thank you. Again.' Flustered, I glance at the card. 'Security consultant?'

'I started my own company when I left the Navy,' he says. 'With my experience, I can really pull in some money.'

'Why did you leave the Navy?' He seems too young for even early retirement.

'Smashed up my back in a car crash. Pretty much good for nothing after that. Nothing I wanted to do, anyway. I didn't want to be stuck behind a desk.'

I slip the card into the back pocket of my jeans. 'You must have seen a fair bit of the world?'

'Indeed.' Michael reels off a list of countries, which leads him on to an anecdote about an encounter with a venomous snake.

I watch him as he talks. He's in his mid to late forties, handsome, but with a prominent, bony nose. His dark brown hair, greying at the temples, is neatly combed back in spite of the blustery weather. Lines radiate from the corners of his eyes. He seems warm, friendly, amusing.

'You must miss the travel?' I say.

'I still have to, for work. More than I'd like. Living in hotels is a chore. I'm always happy to get back to base.'

Albert appears at our side. 'All right, Michael? You don't usually stay to chat. To what do we owe the pleasure?' He winks at me. 'Bit of a strong, silent type is our Michael.'

Michael gulps down the rest of his juice. 'Actually, I do have to dash. Early start tomorrow. It was good to meet you, Clare. Speak to you soon, I hope.'

He touches my arm again, before lifting his hand in farewell to the group. No one notices apart from Albert and Heather. Heather is staring, as if she has been watching us. She raises her hand too late; Michael has already gone. She looks at me for a moment and then Evelyn approaches and diverts her attention. I feel as if I've been caught red-handed. At what, I don't know.

14

Sunday is our date for lunch at Dad's – and to meet Marilyn. On the day, Tom changes into his new meet-the-in-laws' look of slicked-down hair, chinos and shirt.

As we have to travel in convoy from the cottage to London, I give him Dad's landline and mobile numbers. 'Just in case.'

'Just in case what?'

'In case the van breaks down, or you get stuck in traffic or—'

'Clare, we'll be travelling on the same roads. And if I do have any problems, I'll call *you*.'

'Well, there's no harm in having them. You might need them one day, in an emergency.'

He keys the numbers into his phone and we set off, with Charlie in tow, curled up on blankets in the back of Tom's van.

When we arrive, Sophie and Harry wave from the living room window. I wave back, as I get out of the car. A moment later, Dad is at the front door, the children behind him. Their squeals prompt Charlie to start barking. Dad looks edgy, though Charlie is on a lead twenty feet away.

'It's all right, Dad. Tom'll keep Charlie in the garden. Sophie, Harry, run through to the patio and you can say hello to him.'

The children skitter off.

I only hope Charlie doesn't tear up the immaculate lawn and borders. He's used to the countryside and the wilderness surrounding Tom's cottage. Dad's garden is his pride and joy – second only to his camera.

'Hi, Brian,' Tom shouts. He turns to whisper to me, 'Is your dad okay?'

'He's nervous of dogs. Can you take Charlie around the back?' I point towards the side gate.

'No problem, I'll make sure he stays out of the way. C'mon, boy.' The pair of them amble off. At least it's sunny, so we can leave Charlie outside.

I retrieve a bunch of irises from the passenger seat and walk up to the front door.

Dad backs away to let me in.

'Don't I get a kiss?' I say.

Dad shuts the door, pats my arm and kisses my cheek. 'Of course, dear.'

A fresh, herbal smell wafts over me. 'Have you changed cologne?'

'Mmm, what? Oh, yes. Marilyn's idea. Said it was more modern or some such. Can't say I notice the difference.'

'Dad, your old one was horrible and you must have been using it for thirty years.'

The kitchen door opens. Cooking smells pervade the hall, as a dumpy, but attractive woman comes towards us. 'Darling, why didn't you tell me Clare had arrived? Honestly, isn't he hopeless?' She smiles. 'I'm Marilyn.'

'Pleased to meet you. These are for you.' I give her the irises, taking in her long-sleeved tunic top, wide-legged trousers and sandals. The weather is too cold, and Marilyn's feet too gnarly, for open footwear. I decide to keep my shoes on, as well: Mum's 'not indoors' rule has obviously gone the same way as Dad's old cologne, at least for guests – he's still in his tartan slippers.

'I love irises, thank you,' she says. 'Where's Tom?'

'Out the back, with the children and his dog.'

'Congratulations on your engagement. May I see your ring?'

I stretch out my hand. Marilyn supports it with her own plump one. Flour streaks her wrist.

'Oh, Clare, it's beautiful. A lovely design. Isn't it, Brian?'

'What? Mmm, yes.' Dad peers at the ring. I doubt he could distinguish between one from a Christmas cracker and the real thing.

Marilyn withdraws her hand. 'I need to finish preparing lunch. You must tell me all about it later. I do feel I've missed out, not having a daughter.'

'Not much to tell, I'm afraid.' I twiddle with my ring.

'I'm sure that's not true.' Her eyes flick to my twisting fingers. 'Brian, will you give me a hand, please? The apple pie needs to go in the oven.' She heads back into the kitchen, her silver-grey hair swinging against her back. At nearly waist length, it's too long for a woman in her fifties.

'Marilyn's apple pie even beats your mum's,' says Dad, following her. I'm surprised he knows which is the oven; he lives on microwaved meals.

I hover in the hall, at a loss as to what to do.

Fiona appears at the top of the stairs. She's in her uniform of white shirt, black trousers and scarf – a smudgy pattern, in dusty, olive leaf green – though the cravat-tied, silk square is askew at her neck. She looks pale.

'Hi, Fi. How are you?'

'Overworked, overtired. As usual.' She comes down the stairs.

'The children will be out of your hair for a while. They're playing with Tom's dog.'

'Great. Now they'll want one of their own.'

'Why *don't* you get a dog? It'd be good security, when Dave's away.'

She brushes past me. 'And another thing to look after. No, thanks.'

God, is there anything she isn't negative about?

In the living room, Fiona pours a glass of red wine from the bottle open in the middle of the dining table. 'Want one?' she says.

'Bit early for me.' I sit down on the sofa. 'Is Dave here?'

'No, he's working.' Fiona watches the children through the patio door.

'On a Sunday?'

'Why should Sunday be any different? He works day and night, whether he's travelling or not.'

'Fi, that's crazy.' I can't help feeling sorry for her, so often left the lone parent.

'He says he has to, to pay for everything. As if *I* don't contribute. As if *he* doesn't want a big house and two cars.'

'You don't think...' I'm stepping into a minefield. 'You don't think there's anyone else, do you?'

'Of course not.' She swivels around and glares at me. 'What a ridiculous suggestion! Whatever makes you say that?'

'It just sounds like a familiar story. You know? Working late, never at home.'

'Dave's not devious enough for an affair,' she says. 'He can't even keep Christmas presents secret.'

'I'm sorry. I shouldn't have said anything. Shall we go into the garden?'

'No, thanks. I don't want dog hairs all over my trousers.'

I leave her to her wine and join the others outside.

Fiona watches us from indoors. Next door, Dad and Marilyn potter in the kitchen, like an old, married couple. A tableau of domestic bliss that's twenty years too late.

I introduce Tom to Fiona when we go back in for lunch.

'Pleased to meet you.' He beams at her.

'Likewise.' She smiles. Her eyes, sweeping quickly over him, contradict the sentiment; clearly, he is wanting in some way, in spite of his efforts with his appearance.

'Come on, Tom.' I take his arm and usher him to the table. At least my partner is here, even if he doesn't meet Fiona's unfathomable grooming standards.

As we settle down to eat, Dad bustles around with his camera.

'Don't often get all the family together,' he mutters. The fact that he won't be in the photos, and that Dave isn't here, seems to have escaped him. He urges us into pose after pose and ends up on the patio, shooting through the open door, temporarily forgetting about Charlie snuffling about at the top end of the garden.

'Come along, darling, your food's getting cold.' Marilyn calls Dad to heel. 'And you can hardly talk to people from out there.'

He dithers a moment longer, adjusting his lens cover, and comes in.

As I field questions from Marilyn about the wedding, I realise Fiona hasn't asked to see my ring. Instead, it's Sophie, sitting next to me, and with her little girl eye for sparkle, who spots it as I reach for the vegetables.

'Auntie Clare's got a luuurrrverly ring! Can I have a go? Pleeease!' She bounces in her seat, dropping her fork under the table.

Fiona intervenes. 'Sophie, sit still and get on with your lunch. Though I don't know how you're going to eat without a fork.'

Sophie pouts and picks up some chicken with her fingers.

'Sophie!' says Fiona.

Sophie leans down for her fork.

'Leave it!' Fiona gets up and goes into the kitchen.

While she's gone, I slide the ring off and take Sophie's hand. 'Try it on.' I put it on her middle finger. It rolls around, leaving the stone underneath.

'Ooh,' she says.

'Here.' I right the ring and squeeze her fingers together to hold it in place.

Sophie stretches out her hand. 'It's *beeeyoootiful*. I'm a princess.'

Fiona, bringing in a replacement fork, frowns. 'Clare, you shouldn't indulge her. She'll think being naughty gets her what she wants.'

Tom, on the other side of me, says, 'Maybe you should take the ring back, Clare. It might get lost.'

Sophie scowls at him. 'You're mean, Uncle Tom.' She looks just like Fiona.

'Sophie! Don't speak to Tom like that,' says Fiona. 'Any more of that behaviour and we'll be going home. Now, say sorry and give Auntie Clare her ring back.'

'Sorry,' Sophie mumbles into her lap.

'She might as well keep the ring on for now,' I say. 'It's hardly going to get lost while she's sitting six inches away from me.'

Fiona registers her disapproval with a shake of the head and Sophie eats the rest of her meal using only her fork, while the fingers of her other hand remain clamped against the band of white gold.

Towards the end of the main course, there is a lull in the conversation. The silence lengthens, sliding into uncomfortable.

I'm grateful to notice a diversion, in the shape of Marilyn's silver locket. 'That's a pretty necklace.'

'Thank you, it's antique.'

'Do you keep photos in it?'

'Yes.' She fumbles with the locket's catch, prises the front open and holds it up. 'My sons.'

One boy is about twelve, the other maybe ten. The older one is blond and serious, the younger dark-haired, with a cheeky grin.

'Very cute,' I say.

'They're ancient photos.' Marilyn snaps the locket shut. 'They're in their late twenties now.'

I pick a cold roast potato out of the bowl in front of me with my fingers. 'What do they do?' I bite into the potato like an apple.

'Richard, my older son, is a graphic designer. He lives in Australia, with his wife and twin girls.'

'Do you see much of them?'

'No. I've never met the girls. They're nearly two.'

'That's a shame. And your other son?' I finish the potato and reach for another, concentrating on that rather than Marilyn.

'I don't know,' she says.

'You don't know what?' The potato is halfway to my mouth.

'I don't know what my other son's doing. We lost touch several years ago.'

'Oh.' I put the potato down on my plate. 'I'm sorry to hear that.'

The table goes quiet. Seconds pass.

Sophie gazes at one adult, then another. She sticks her bottom lip out. 'When are we having pie?'

Everyone laughs.

'Now, my dear,' Marilyn says. 'We'll have it now.'

The pie is bland; something's missing. A few mouthfuls in, I realise what: cloves. Mum always put them in her apple pies. What her food lacked in aesthetics, it made up for in taste. She was a talented, but clumsy, cook: her arms always scarred by burns from the oven.

Dad wolfs down his helping and has seconds. 'Good, isn't it? Even better than your mum's.' Pastry crumbs decorate his beard.

'Very nice,' I say.

'Much better than Mum's,' says Fiona. 'I don't know why she insisted on using cloves. She knew Dad and I didn't like them.' Fiona always picked hers out, leaving them to float like drowned beetles in the accompanying cream.

'Well, I did,' I say. 'Sorry, Marilyn.'

'No need to apologise, my dear. Each to their own. I find them a little overpowering.'

Lunch over, I persuade Sophie to return my ring. 'You're going out to play, sweetie. We don't want it to get lost in the garden.'

She scowls and curls the fingers of her left hand into a fist. 'I won't lose it.'

'But if you do, you'll never be able to wear it again, will you? Never ever.'

The logic of that argument defeats even Sophie's petulance and she hands the ring back with only the most fleeting of pouts.

Tom and I volunteer to wash and dry the dishes. By the time I get to the pudding bowls, the debris has dried on. I plunge them into the water to soak. Tom carries on drying, while I retrieve the last bits of crockery from the dining room.

Dad and Marilyn are standing by the patio door watching the children play outside. Or, at least, Marilyn is. Dad is watching Marilyn. He reaches to lift a wisp of hair away from her face. She turns and smiles at him. I clear my throat. Dad lets his hand drop.

I pick up the pie dish and a spoon with broccoli stuck to it. 'Anything else for washing up?' Avoiding eye contact with Dad and

Marilyn, I scan the living room. Fiona is on the sofa, skimming a broadsheet.

Back in the kitchen, Tom is putting the crockery away. I retrieve a pudding bowl from the suds and scrub at it.

'Are you trying to get the pattern off that bowl?' he says.

'Sorry?'

'You've been rubbing at it for ages. I think we can safely say it's clean.'

I put the bowl on the draining rack. Tom picks it up and shakes off the foam. 'What was all that about with Marilyn?'

'All what?' Did he see her and Dad just now?

'Her son.' He switches to a horror-film-voiceover drawl. 'The mystery child no one talks about.'

'You know as much as I do.'

When we've finished, Tom goes outside to feed Charlie. I head upstairs to the bathroom.

The door is closed, but not locked. I open it. Fiona is at the basin, running water into a glass. She jumps.

'Sorry, I didn't know you were in here,' I say. She has reverted to old habits: as children, we never locked the bathroom door.

Fiona gulps half the water, puts the glass down and leans against the basin. She is even paler than earlier.

'Fi, are you all right?'

She nods – and then grimaces. I step towards her.

'I'm fine.' She waves me away. 'Must be something I ate.'

'Marilyn's apple pie?'

'Of course not.' She takes a deep breath and sits down on the edge of the bath. 'I'm all right. Just a bit dizzy.'

'Perhaps it's the wine?'

Her eyes widen. 'Hardly. I only had a glass.'

'You were drinking on an empty stomach.'

'It's just a bug.'

I hover by the door. 'You haven't seemed yourself lately. I'm worried about you.'

'You needn't be. I can look after myself. And everyone else. I've been doing it long enough.'

'Well, maybe you shouldn't. Maybe you should let other people lend a hand. At least with the children. Get a baby-sitter, for goodness' sake.'

'A baby-sitter won't fix things.'

'What things?' I take a couple of steps into the room. 'Tell me.'

'Talking won't help.' She grips the rim of the bath.

'No, please do tell me, Fiona. What is so terrible about your life, apart from a husband who works too hard?' I move closer.

'Things aren't always what they seem, Clare.'

'Don't I know it!'

'You never had to give anything up. Never had to wait for what you wanted.'

'So that makes my life perfect? Well, I'm delighted to hear I've got no problems.' I turn in mock exit.

'That's not what I said.'

I twist back around, lean down so that our faces are almost level. 'It's what you meant. What you've always thought. That I had it easy compared with you. I'm sick of your martyr act, Fiona. I didn't ask you to look after me, to put your life on hold.' The tiled walls amplify my already loud words. I straighten up.

'I had to, anyway.' She's unusually quiet.

I can't shout at her if she won't shout back; I lower my voice. 'Shouldn't you blame Dad for that? I couldn't do anything about it. And I can't change things now, can I?'

Fiona sighs. 'No, no one can. Nothing ever really changes. Just when you think it has, you're dragged back to square one.'

'What do you mean? You're talking in riddles.'

She stands up and turns towards the basin. 'I need to freshen up. I'll see you downstairs.'

'Fiona, what's going on?' She's only a foot away. I could touch her; I don't.

'Nothing. Nothing that words will change. Leave me alone now. Please.' She clutches the basin with both hands, bows her head.

'Fiona, tell me.'

She's stiff, silent.

I walk out, shutting the bathroom door behind me. A few seconds later, the key turns in the lock.

Fiona will think I'm spying, if I wait for her to finish. I'll have to use Dad's en suite. Tiptoeing into his room, I feel like a child again, sneaking in to dab on Mum's perfume or dress up in her clothes. Our parents' room was their sanctuary, accessed by invitation only. Mum always knew when I had secretly intruded. I never put things back as they were and her citrussy perfume lingered on my skin, even after I tried to wash it off.

As I creep through the room, I spot women's toiletries on the dressing table: face cream, perfume and deodorant. I unscrew the scent and sniff: the smell is sweet, sickly.

Something is missing from the table, though: Mum and Dad's wedding photo. The photo of Mum has gone from the bedside cabinet, too. It's identical to the one I keep in my bedroom: the portrait of Mum reflected in the same dressing table mirror that now reflects Marilyn's toiletries.

In the en suite, there are more female products: facial wash, lilac-scented talcum powder and a woman's razor. Marilyn is here to stay.

Back downstairs, I find her squashed on the sofa with Dad and Tom, engrossed in Dad's photo albums. Fiona is outside the front of the house, pacing up and down the drive as she talks on her mobile.

The children pounce on me, beg to have a jigsaw race. Sophie, dragging a huge toy bag behind her, grabs one of my arms, Harry the other. They pull me to the floor, beside the dining table.

Sophie fishes a puzzle out of the bag. 'Auntie Clare, you do this one.' The picture is of a fairground scene populated with Disney characters.

'This is for me.' She selects a smaller Cinderella jigsaw. 'And this is for Harry.' Harry's, the smallest, features Thomas the Tank Engine.

'Nanny Marilyn, count to three for us to go,' says Sophie.

Nanny Marilyn. Tears well up in my eyes at the thought of what Mum has missed. Distracted, I don't hear the end of the count.

'Come on, Auntie Clare!' urges Sophie.

Once started, I employ my usual tactic of picking out the corners and edges first. Next to me, Sophie randomly selects pieces.

'Sophie, sweetheart, it's easier if you do the corners, then the edges,' I say.

'Why?'

'Because it's better to have a frame to build on.'

'Why?'

'I'm not sure, it just is.'

'Okay.' Sophie continues with her arbitrary selection process. She slots another two pieces together. Her picture is taking shape. Mine has only four corners and two half edges.

Harry copies his sister, as usual. 'Edges are boring, I like the bobbly bits.'

Sophie storms ahead, connecting pieces left, right and centre. I adopt her approach, but quickly get flustered. The picture seems to merge with the carpet; I can't see what I'm doing. My heart thumps, as I battle to get the pieces in order.

'Finished!' Sophie flings her arms in the air.

Harry is just behind her. 'Finished,' he yells, throwing his arms up, too.

Tom laughs. 'Clare, they've absolutely hammered you.'

'They've probably done those pictures a hundred times,' I say.

Fiona walks into the living room. 'Come on, you two, we need to get going. Pack up your toys and go to the toilet, please.'

'Mummy, I want to play again,' Sophie says.

'What have I just said? Put the jigsaws away and go upstairs,' says Fiona.

Sophie pouts, but breaks up her puzzle, tips the pieces into the box and slides it back into the toy bag. Harry follows her lead.

I'm still busy with mine; I can't leave it unfinished.

Sophie tugs at my arm. 'Auntie Clare, you have to put your jigsaw away. Mummy says.'

'In a minute, sweetheart.'

As the children run out of the room, Fiona tuts. 'Clare, you're not setting a very good example.'

'Must be my upbringing,' I say. My head is down, eyes focussed on the jigsaw. I slot the last piece into place and study the picture for a few seconds: its completeness is satisfying. I break it up and shuffle the pieces back into the box.

I stand up and offer it to Fiona. 'Happy now?'

She silently takes it from me.

As we wave her and the children off from the hall, Tom whispers to me, 'What's going on with you two?'

I shrug. 'Just the usual sibling stuff.' I can't explain what I don't know.

Something is wrong, but I can't help Fiona if she won't open up or get past old wounds.

15

Tom heads home directly from Dad's, not wanting to let Charlie loose in the confines of my flat. I'm grateful not to add to my stress with an impromptu visit. Meeting Marilyn has already unsettled me, as has Fiona's odd behaviour.

As a result, unpacking my overnight bag takes as long as ever. In spite of my visit to the support group, it seems I still can't tackle my obsessive behaviour at times of high anxiety. It's a week since my last, failed attempt to mess things up. If I carry on like this, another week will slip by, then another. Before I know it, it will be too late. Tom and I will be married, my secret will be out, and my marriage over as soon as it has begun.

I need help before the next meeting, so look out the card Michael gave me. A call is too intrusive late on a Sunday evening and a text easier to ignore, if he now regrets his offer of help. *Gd to mt u at grp wd be gr8 to chat if u hv time Clare.*

He replies a few minutes later, *Would you like to meet up? I could do 8 on Wednesday, at Granvilles, Islington? Michael.*

He's the only person I know who shuns abbreviations and uses full punctuation in text messages. Perhaps he's as unused to texting as Tom is.

Tapping out a return message of acknowledgement and gratitude to Michael, I hesitate before adding, *Lkng frwrd to it.* Send. Clutching the phone, I wait for his response.

Me too. See you then. Michael.

It's rare for me to be out late during the week. I invent a colleague's leaving drinks for Tom's benefit.

'Funny day to go,' he says.

'She's owed holiday. Her last two days are leave.' I don't like telling even white lies, and this one is distinctly off-white.

'Holiday? Ah, those were the days. When I was young, free and worked for someone else,' says Tom.

'I might be late, so don't worry if I don't call. I'll text when I get in.'

Granvilles is a high-ceilinged, airy wine bar – all pale wood, soft lighting and modern art. On weekdays, young professionals from the local firms of solicitors, architects and accountants come here to kick back before heading home. As I step inside, the air conditioning blasts me. It's too cold for a chilly April evening and a sharp contrast to the stuffy Northern Line Tube train I've just left. I shiver in my flimsy raincoat.

Michael is sitting at a table against the wall. He must have come straight from work, as he's in an expensive-looking suit and tie. In front of him is a glass of white wine. I reach him before he sees me.

'Good evening. You're punctual.' He stands up.

'Ditto,' I say.

'Navy training.' He smiles. 'I'm not used to civvies being on time.' He pulls out a chair for me; he shares Tom's chivalrous approach.

I shrug off my coat. Michael reaches for it. 'I'll take that for you.'

'Thank you.'

He walks over to a nearby row of hooks to hang it up, while I sit down.

Back at the table, he taps the oversized wineglass. 'I'll get us a bottle of this.'

'Oh, all right.'

'Do you prefer red?'

'I drink both. Red when it's cold, white when it's hot.'

'It's nearly summer,' he says.

I shiver again in the chill. 'White'll be fine, thank you.' I open my handbag and reach for my purse.

'No need for that. My treat.'

'Thank you.' I close my handbag.

Michael walks over to the bar. He has a commanding presence, accentuated by his military posture and business dress. It sets him apart from the rest of the male clientele, who have abandoned their ties and jackets and are slumped around the room in varying degrees of alcoholic stupor.

Tom is equally handsome and imposing in a suit, but I've only seen him wear one at the wedding where we met and our engagement dinner. Even smart casual would be a nice change from the tee shirts, flannel shirts and jeans that he's welded to.

Michael is back within minutes with the wine, another enormous glass and an ice bucket. He pours me a drink, tops up his own and slides the already half-empty bottle into the container.

'How on earth did you get that?' I've never seen an ice bucket in a wine bar.

'I asked for it. Why should I spend thirty pounds on a bottle of wine and drink it lukewarm?'

We chink glasses.

After only a few minutes, the words are flowing easily between us. We chat about anything and everything except our shared problem – work, the weather, books, television shows – until we get onto me and Tom.

'So, it's been quite a whirlwind romance,' says Michael. 'What is it, six, seven months?'

'About that. We met at the end of September.'

'Not easy to sustain when you live so far apart.'

'Actually, having a long-distance relationship brought us closer,' I say. 'Because I was able to keep part of myself hidden, I could open up in other ways. It's the first time I've really let myself fall for someone.' I take a gulp of wine, suddenly embarrassed at revealing so much to a virtual stranger. 'Of course, now that I actually want to marry him, I've come unstuck!'

'So, tell me how I can help,' says Michael.

I put down my glass. Gripping the stem, I turn it, around and around. The bottom scrapes the table top.

He puts his hand over mine, stopping me. 'Clare?'

I look around. The wine bar has filled up. Almost all the tables are occupied and the bar is crowded. Friends and colleagues laugh and chat. The bar staff grin, as they serve drinks and flirt with the customers. A couple at a table nearby hold hands and gaze into each other's eyes. I envy them all their carefree air. None of them seem to have a worry in the world. I wonder if they look at me and think the same.

'It's getting busy,' I say.

'Clare? What can I do to help?' Michael persists.

I turn back to him, pulling my hand free of his. 'I don't know. I don't know what you can do. I don't know what anyone can do.' I rotate my engagement ring. The skin underneath it feels sore, irritated.

'Tell me what the problem is,' he says.

'You know what it is. I can't stop my compulsions. It's too hard. I need to know how you did it. Do it.'

'Why do you think you need to?'

I frown. 'Because Tom and I can't live together unless I do. I love him and I want to marry him, but I can't do that unless I change.'

'Why not?'

We're going around in circles.

'Michael, what are you getting at?'

'Let me ask you this. Were your compulsions a problem before Tom proposed?'

'Not really. Just time-consuming.'

'Do they impact on your life?'

'Not a great deal. I work around them. They've made it difficult to have much of a career, but, then again, I'm not particularly ambitious.'

'So, the real problem is Tom?'

'I suppose…'

'Then why don't you ask him to fit in with you?'

The wine has gone to my head. I can't follow Michael's train of thought. 'That's not right, is it? I thought other people shouldn't pander to our behaviour?'

'It's not pandering. It's compromise. What about if Tom wanted to watch the football and you didn't? You wouldn't stop him, would you?'

'No…'

'Or he wanted to eat lunch earlier than you, or go to bed later, or go out with his friends?'

'I see what you mean.' It suddenly makes sense. I have to fit in with Tom. With his dog, his sister, his ex-girlfriend, his work. Everything and everyone that makes demands on him and intrudes on our time together. I feel a rush of anger that I have taken all this on me. Of course Tom should do his bit. I wonder how I didn't see it before.

The advice I've read and heard still worries me, though.

'Why don't they say that, then? I mean, the books and Heather.' She's been through this herself and the others seem to trust her expertise.

'They're not living in the real world.' Michael shakes his head. 'For heaven's sake, I've heard of therapists making people touch toilet seats and wipe their hands over their face. No one in their right mind does that, do they?'

'I suppose not,' I say. 'So, have you ever lived with anyone?'

'I was married for nine years.'

'And your wife was all right about your habits?'

'Fine.' He waves his hand dismissively. 'She fitted in with them. She always said she had a Jekyll and Hyde life. Tidy when I was on shore leave, untidy when I wasn't.'

'Being tidy was the good side?'

Michael takes a sip of wine. 'Of course. She was better off than her friends, forever clearing up after their husbands.'

'Do you have children?'

'Heavens, no. I was never keen on the idea and she didn't want to be what amounted to a single parent.'

'Why did you split up?' I say.

'We grew apart. We hardly saw each other while I was in the Navy. When I left, we realised we didn't have anything in common any more.'

'It wasn't the compulsions?'

'Not at all. It was all perfectly amicable.' He lifts the wine out of the ice bucket and tilts the bottle towards my glass.

I cover it. 'I've had enough, thanks.'

Michael nudges my hand with the bottle neck. 'Go on, help me finish it. I'm a glass ahead of you.'

I give in. If I drink slowly, I'll be all right. I don't want to be woozy on the Tube journey home.

'You and your wife have stayed friends, then?' I say.

'I'm afraid not.' He rams the empty bottle back in the bucket. Ice and water slop over the side. 'She's remarried and her husband doesn't like her being in touch with me.' He takes out his cotton handkerchief to mop up the spilled water. As he wipes, a strand of his combed-back hair drops over his forehead like a dark scar.

'So I should definitely tell Tom?' I say.

'Absolutely.'

At least Michael and the book agree on that. He must be right about the rest of it. He has lived with this, with someone. He knows better than anyone how to cope.

'The sooner you tell him, the sooner he'll learn how you like things,' says Michael. 'Get him into your flat and show him the ropes. You need to be honest, otherwise what is there to a relationship?'

A pang of guilt shoots through me. Tom doesn't know I'm here. Michael is right about the need for honesty. Washing the guilt away with more wine, I'm surprised to see how little I have left. So much for drinking slowly. I lift my glass up and waggle it at Michael. 'You're a bad influence.' I giggle.

He smiles, as he folds his damp handkerchief and tucks it back into his pocket.

'I can't imagine how most of them in the group live with partners,' I say.

'Neither can I. Arthur is infuriating, constantly crinkling that wretched packet of wipes.'

'He's doing well, though, not using so many.'

'And as for that hoarder woman...'

'I know. It's a shame. She seems really nice.'

Michael snorts. 'Darned odd, though.'

Is that what he thinks of us? I need to know. 'So, you find the others...strange?'

'Well, I certainly can't relate to any of them.'

My heart sinks.

'Not the way I relate to you,' he continues.

'Really?'

'Of course. We're not like them, Clare.' He leans across the table. 'We're different.' His light blue eyes lock onto mine. They remind me so much of Tom's. 'We're completely different.'

I'm hot. The volume of bodies now filling the bar has defeated the air conditioning. I fan my face with my hand, turn my head slightly, to break Michael's gaze.

'You're the first person I've met who's like me,' he says. 'No one else really understands me. That's the problem. I think you do, don't you, Clare?'

'Yes. Yes, I think so.' I'm not sure, though. My thoughts flit like bats, hard to catch. It must be the wine: I've drunk more than usual, and too fast. I take a deep breath, sit up straight and try to concentrate.

Michael is still staring at me. 'There's no need to be afraid.'

'What do you mean? Of what?'

'Of anything. Whatever happens, everything will work out for the best.'

His face seems to waver. I clench my hands together in my lap, tensing the muscles in a bid to ward off the dizziness. My ring has swung to the underside of my finger and the stones dig into the palm of my other hand. I squeeze my hands together more tightly. Pain spikes in my right hand and the fog clears a little.

'I need to go to the bathroom,' I say. My chair tips back as I stand up, rocking into the person behind me. I murmur an apology and scoop up my bag. Michael rises with me, sitting down only after I've moved away.

The toilets are in the basement. I pick my way down the stairs, clutching the handrail. Down here, it's cool and quiet. At the basin, I splash water on my burning cheeks, hold my wrists under the cold flow. The dizzy feeling leaves me. As I dry my hands, I peer in the mirror. I'm pale, with shadows under my eyes. It's time to go home.

Michael stands when I get back to the table.

I don't sit down. 'Sorry, Michael, I'm worn out. I should make tracks.'

He glances at his watch. 'I'll get our coats.'

He brings them over and helps me into mine. 'Your collar's twisted,' he says. 'Let me.' His fingers brush the back of my neck, as he pulls and straightens the material.

On the way to Angel station, the fresh air and drizzle blow away the last of the alcoholic cobwebs clouding my thoughts. My mind is made up. 'I'm going to tell Tom,' I say.

'Good girl,' says Michael. 'He has to do his bit.'

'You're right.'

'I only want what's best for you, Clare. And if he really loves you, so will Tom.'

The train is crowded and noisy with late-night revellers. We squeeze in near the door, gripping the overhead rail. We sway backward and forward with the train's movements – towards and away from each other, again and again.

We travel together to Camden, where Michael has to change to the northwest branch of the line.

As the doors open, he bends towards me. 'Call me if you need anything.'

His lips brush my cheek, catching the corner of my mouth. He's stepped off the train, before I can say anything. A wave of people surges past me from inside the carriage, to be replaced by those waiting on the platform. The doors swoosh shut behind them. I gaze out of the window, as the train pulls away; the crowds have swallowed Michael.

I close my eyes and put my hand to my face. The skin tingles where he kissed me.

16

At home, I find an answerphone message from Tom. 'Hey, beautiful. I know you're out. I just wanted to say goodnight. Hope you had fun and gave your colleague a good send-off. Call me if it's not too late when you get in. I'll be up till midnight.'

It's eleven-fifty. The phone bleeps as I delete the message. A few minutes after twelve I text Tom, as promised, to let him know I'm back safely.

I'm headachy from lack of food and too much wine. Although a glass of water takes the edge off the hunger, I still can't sleep. My heart races from the alcohol and Michael's words bounce around my head.

Come morning, I'm exhausted. In the light of day, though, everything is clearer. I feel better for having decided to talk to Tom. Michael is right; I have to be honest.

Easy to say with more than two days to go until I see Tom. I have plenty of time to work out how to explain things – how and when and where. So I tell myself over breakfast.

And again that evening.

And the following morning.

Friday evening. Twenty-four hours to go. Still lots of time to think about it.

I don't.

Michael texts me, *Have you told Tom?*

I message him back, *No wnt to do in prsn wl do tmrw.*

He responds in seconds, *Good, the sooner the better.*

Saturday afternoon. I can think while I pack. I try, but can't even decide how to open the conversation.

Tom, we need to talk – sounds as if I'm dumping him.

Tom, there's something I have to tell you – he'll think I'm pregnant.

Tom, do you know what obsessive-compulsive disorder is? – he's not on *Who Wants To Be A Millionaire?* for goodness' sake. Though maybe he should call a friend or ask the audience; they might explain it better than I can.

On the drive up, with no distractions and time running out, I finally get my thoughts straight. I learn my lines like an actor, rehearse out loud what I will say and how. I'll be calm, play the whole thing down. *It's not a big problem, Tom, just something I ought to mention.* The opening line still eludes me. I hope that, when the moment comes, so will the words.

Tom takes that moment out of my hands.

We're on the sofa, Charlie at our feet, having a glass of wine before dinner. Tom puts his hand on my thigh. 'Anything wrong, beautiful?'

'No, I'm fine. What makes you say that? I've only been here ten minutes. What could be wrong?' I put my glass down. 'This is lovely wine. What is it?'

'Just the usual: Chilean Merlot. Your favourite, isn't it?'

'Yes, thanks.' I bend to ruffle Charlie's ears. He slobbers over my shoes. 'How's Charlie?'

'Charlie?'

I look over my shoulder at Tom. 'His hips.'

'Still creaky, with this damp weather.' Tom's forehead crumples as if he's trying to remember something. 'Never mind Charlie, it's you I'm worried about.'

'Me? Why?' I settle back against the cushions.

'You don't seem yourself.'

'In what way?' Oh God, he's guessed. No, that's crazy; how could he have?

'You're a bit quiet.'

'Give me a chance, I've only just sat down!'

'No, I mean, generally. You're not as bubbly,' he says. 'Your dad's worried as well.'

'Bit late for him to worry,' I bristle. 'And how do you know that?'

'We both heard you and Fiona arguing, that Sunday we went for lunch. He seemed concerned about it.'

'Fiona and I always fight. It's not unusual for siblings, is it?'

'I don't argue with my sisters.'

'Only because you let them trample all over you.'

'I hardly ever talk to Susie and Liz. How can they trample all over me?'

'Vicky, then. You let her take advantage of you.'

Tom scowls. 'This isn't about me, it's about you.'

Charlie whines. Tom leans down, tickles his tummy, sits up again. 'Is it the wedding?' he says. 'You haven't been very enthusiastic. I thought women normally loved that sort of thing?'

'I'm not normal.' I cross my eyes and stick my tongue out at him.

He squeezes my leg. 'Clare, I'm serious. Is it too soon? We can wait, if you want?'

'No, it's not that, it's… I've had a lot on my mind.' I take a gulp of wine and put my glass down on the table.

'Anything I can do to help?'

This is it, this is my opening. I'm still not ready. 'No, it's not you, it's me.' Brilliant.

Tom's hand tightens on my thigh. 'Oh, God, I was right—'

'No, no, I don't mean it like that! It really is me.' I twist in my seat to look him in the eye. 'Tom, I have to tell you something. It's hard to know where to start.' I've forgotten everything I practised, yet I can't turn back now. And if I can't tell him, I'll never be able to tell anyone.

'Clare? Please, tell me. I'd rather know, whatever it is.'

'I've got obsessive-compulsive disorder.' I wait for a lightning strike, a thunderclap, for the earth to stop spinning.

Tom frowns. 'What? The cleaning thing?'

'Yes. No. I mean, yes, some people clean. I don't. I…tidy things.' Put that way, it sounds inconsequential.

'Is that it?' He looks bemused. 'I thought something terrible had happened.'

'I'm a bit extreme.'

'Extreme tidying? Is that some weird sport?' Tom laughs.

'Tom, I mean it. I really do have a problem.' My eyes fill with tears. I need him to take me seriously.

'Sorry, beautiful. I didn't mean to take the piss. I just don't understand.' He strokes my cheek.

I blink hard, clear my eyes. 'I say tidying, but it's much more than that. I have to have everything in exactly the right place. It upsets me if it isn't, if someone moves something. I don't see how we can live together with me like that.'

'I still don't get why it's a problem. You're okay when you're here, aren't you? And this place is hardly tidy.' His eyes scan the living room.

Only now do I notice that it's more cluttered than a few weeks ago. Not yet as messy as before, but sliding towards it.

'It doesn't work like that,' I say. 'Your home doesn't bother me. It's my flat, my car and my desk that I need to have right. What'll happen when it's our home? You won't keep things how I like them.'

'I will. I only live like this because there's no reason not to. Charlie doesn't mind a mess, do you, boy?'

Charlie lifts his head.

'Honestly, Clare, I reckon this isn't the problem you think it is. I've seen stuff on TV about people who wash their hands hundreds of times a day or keep cleaning their house. You're not like them, are you?'

'No, I'm not.' Michael doesn't think so, at any rate.

'You're not exactly Howard Hughes.'

Howard Hughes, wealthy recluse and tragic poster boy for the disorder. The one most people think of, if they think of the condition at all. The one who reinforces its association with insanity.

'No!' I say. 'I'm nothing like Howard Hughes.'

'There you are, then,' says Tom. 'Why didn't you tell me before? I was starting to worry.'

'It's not that easy. At what point in a relationship is it a good idea to admit you're a bit bonkers? You don't want to scare someone off from the start and then… I don't know, things get serious and it's even harder.'

'You're not bonkers, Clare, don't say that. And why should it be hard to tell someone you love, and who loves you?'

'It's hard precisely because of that. There's more to lose if they reject you.'

'Why would they, if they love you?'

'Your wife did, didn't she? After she found out you never would want children.'

Tom runs his hand through his hair. 'I suppose that is why I put off telling her. I knew it would finish us.'

'See?' I don't want to be hurtful, yet I need him to understand why I've held back.

'But tidying – or whatever you call it – is hardly the same thing as not wanting children. Honestly, Clare, it's not a big deal.' He puts his arm around my shoulders and pulls me to him.

As I lay my head on his chest, I decide not to push the point. He doesn't appreciate the extent of the problem, because I haven't explained it properly. Perhaps it doesn't matter; if he doesn't see this as an issue, why should I? I should be happy it went so well; after all, he's offered to fit in with me. When I move into the cottage, we'll both keep things my way. My life might even be easier.

'How did you manage with other boyfriends?' says Tom. 'Didn't they move stuff?'

'I never lived with any of them.'

'They must have visited? I know you haven't had any long-term relationships, but still...'

'I didn't let them.'

'Didn't they think that was peculiar?'

'None of them ever said so. I just pretended to have flatmates I didn't get on with.' I'm glad Tom can't see my face; I'm embarrassed to admit my past deceptions.

'Is that why you offered to drive up here every weekend?' says Tom.

I suddenly feel hot. 'I didn't know what else to do. We couldn't keep meeting in town, we needed some privacy.'

'We certainly did!'

'Cheeky.' I poke Tom in the ribs and look up at him. 'So, didn't you think it was odd that I always came up to the cottage?'

'Not at first.' He shrugs. 'It was easier for me. I could come home from work, crack open a beer and then, there you were. No packing, or traffic jams, or worrying about who'd look after Charlie. Bit lazy, really.'

The very thing I'd banked on. 'Easier for me, too,' I say. 'I could relax here, because I knew you wouldn't find out about...the other stuff.' The geographical distance between us had closed an emotional gap that had hindered previous relationships. With the fear of exposure removed, I'd been able to open up more, yet still guard my secret. 'I'm a different person here, but I suppose that's wrong. You need to know the real me. I'm sorry.'

'No need to apologise,' says Tom. 'I'm just relieved it's nothing else. I was beginning to wonder...'

Untangling myself from his arms, I sit up, perching on the edge of the sofa to face him. 'Yes?'

'No, it's silly.'

'Go on.'

'Well, I had to invite myself to your flat and when I was there you seemed really anxious and grumpy and I got the distinct impression you didn't want me to come again and...' Tom takes a breath. 'And it didn't look as if anyone lived with you, but your neighbour didn't know about me and it just seemed like... I thought there might be someone else—'

'What! You know I'd never cheat on you. I love you, Tom.' I'm hurt, yet the hurt is tinged with an inexplicable guilt. 'You've put two and two together and got an almighty wrong five. How could I possibly have someone else, when I spend every weekend with you?'

'I don't know. I thought they were working or... I don't know. My imagination got the better of me. Past experience, I guess...'

'Oh! I didn't realise.' A failed marriage and an unfaithful lover. Poor Tom.

'No, no, not me. Just...past experience. I was afraid to ask, in case I was right. I'm so sorry. It seems ridiculous now, especially as you'd said yes to getting married!' He grasps one of my hands in both of his. 'You know I love you, too, Clare?'

'I know.' I wonder what scars he's carrying, but don't press him. He'll share them with me in his own time. 'I'm sorry. I'm to blame for not explaining things to you.'

I stretch forward to kiss him. My mouth tingles at the touch of his full lips. Then I remember Michael's kiss and the guilt takes a shape.

'I promise, there's no one else,' I say.

17

Tom is determined to prove he can fit in with me. By the time I leave on Sunday, he has persuaded me to have him sleep over at my flat the following weekend. It will be the May Day bank holiday, so we compromise on a one-night stay. Baby steps.

'I want to show you this can work,' he says. 'I'm not really a slob.'

'I know you're not. You weren't last time you visited, but I still found it hard having you there.'

'This time you can tell me how you do things. It'll be different.'

And it is – only not in a good sense.

The warning sign comes during one of our weeknight chats. Tom has looked up obsessive-compulsive disorder on the Internet and found advice for family and friends. 'It says not to fall in with the behaviour. Not to become a victim of it. Are you sure I should do things your way?'

'Yes, I am. Why did you go behind my back? Don't you trust me?'

'Of course I do. It's just that this is all new to me and I needed to find out more. You're the most important thing in my life, Clare. I'll help however I can. I wasn't checking up on you or trying to prove you wrong.'

'Yet you've given up already! You're not even prepared to try my approach.'

'I am. I was just asking. I don't want to make things worse.'

'You won't make things worse. You'll be helping me. At least give it a go, Tom.'

'I told you, I will!'

When Saturday comes around, I don't bother to mess up the flat. It's a relief not to worry about what Tom will think of it.

I collect him from the station late afternoon. This time he's worked most of the day, to make sure Barry and Steve toe the line. He's come straight here from one of their jobs and arrives sweaty and dishevelled.

'Sorry, I'll grab a shower when we get back to yours!' He kisses me, but spares me a grimy hug.

Back home, he slips off his trainers at the front door. He picks them up by the laces and dangles them in front of me. 'I'm learning,' he says.

Inside, he opens the hall cupboard and leans down to put the trainers on the shoe rack. His rucksack slides off his shoulder and towards the wall. I grab it, stopping it inches from doing any damage. 'Could you be careful of the paintwork? It marks easily.'

'Sure thing,' he says.

I put my own shoes on the rack and adjust Tom's. It's a dry day, so no mucky, wet laces this time.

'What are you doing?' he says.

'Straightening your trainers.'

'Oh, okay. Why?'

'Because they look nicer like that.' Articulating why I do what I do, it suddenly sounds silly.

'Can't say I notice the difference. Is that one of your tidying things?'

'Yes.'

'I thought you meant putting things away?'

'I told you, it's more than that. It's how you put them away as well.' I stand up and walk down the hall to the bedroom.

'Right,' he says.

I've cleared one of the small, top drawers in the dressing table for him. My thinking is if he puts everything in there, I won't care how he does it. I won't know, so long as I don't open the drawer.

I can't stop myself. How could I ever have hoped I'd be able to, when I'm compelled to order the inside of all my cupboards and drawers? In my world, out of sight is never out of mind.

As soon as he goes into the bathroom for his shower, I take my chance. The contents are a chaotic heap: a jumper and two tee shirts jumbled with underwear, toiletries and an iPod. It will only take a few minutes to sort out, though. I fold the clothes and put them in a pile, with the edges aligned and pushed up tight against the front left-hand corner of the drawer. Wrapping the wires and earphones around the iPod, I centre that on top of the clothes. Finally, I stand the toiletries up along the right-hand side of the drawer, in ascending order of size from front to back. I slide the drawer shut carefully, so as not to jolt anything out of place.

Seconds later, Tom walks back in, a towel around his waist and his hair dripping wet. I lean towards the dressing table mirror and poke at a non-existent spot on my chin.

He comes up behind me and kisses the back of my neck. Cold drops of water splash onto my skin. I shiver.

'Sorry, beautiful, can I get to my things?' I step sideways and he opens the drawer – his drawer. He stops, his hand still on the knob. He stares at what's inside.

'Did you do this?' he says.

'No, the drawer fairy did.'

He pulls out some underwear and a tee shirt, making the iPod fall off the clothes' pile. 'Why did you fold everything?'

'Your clothes were getting crumpled.'

'Clare, I don't mind crumpled underpants and socks.'

'What about the rest?'

'It's just casual stuff that I don't iron, anyway. And why are my toiletries all stood up like that?'

'I could smell aftershave. I think it's leaking.'

'Jeez, Clare, is there nothing you don't worry about? What about the deodorant stick and shaving foam?'

'Well, since I was doing the bottle...'

He raises his eyebrows. 'That's kind of extreme.'

'I told you. You said you could deal with it.'

'That was before I knew about this.' He waves his hand over the open drawer. 'Is all your stuff the same?'

'Yes, but all you have to do is put things back where you find them. That's not extreme, is it?'

'I suppose not.'

'No more extreme than storing your CDs alphabetically.'

'But the rest of my house isn't like that, not even my books. It's just that I've got so many CDs, I can't find anything if they're not in order.'

'You do get annoyed if they're not, though.'

'It would annoy anyone. I mean, it's easy enough to do.'

'Exactly.'

Tom sighs. 'Okay, I admit defeat.'

'So you'll put things back where you find them?'

'Yeah.'

'You're sure?'

'Positive.'

'That works for me,' I say.

And I really think it will. I haven't allowed for the fact that his idea of back-where-you-find-them and mine are poles apart.

After an evening of tidying up after him, I realise there's no difference between this visit and the last. He's incapable of returning anything to within an inch of where it was. Watching him, I have to fight the urge to slap his hands away from objects. Fight the urge to scream at him to stop moving things. Just stop, stop, stop. Please. I could cry with frustration.

As with his previous visit, by bedtime I'm drained, both mentally and physically. I sigh as I collapse into bed and drag the duvet over me.

'You okay?' asks Tom. He props himself up on his elbow to look down at me.

'Yes, just tired. Exhausted, actually.' I stretch up to peck him on the lips, before rolling over to turn off my bedside lamp. 'Goodnight. Sleep well.'

'Goodnight. You, too.' He hesitates and then swivels away from me to switch off the light on his side.

I sense his tension, his unspoken questions, as he lies beside me in the darkness, but I don't know what to say, how to explain. Eventually, I hear his breathing slow into sleep and I relax, too.

The last straw comes when I go into the bathroom after him on Sunday morning. The china toothbrush holder, usually centred to the basin taps, is now left of the cold one. As I move it back, I catch the bottom on the tap. The holder cracks down the middle. The two halves drop into the basin and shatter into smaller fragments around the brushes.

'For God's sake!' I pick up the larger chunks of debris and deposit them on the side of the bath. Tiny shards glint in the basin and the toothbrushes' bristles.

Tom puts his head around the door. 'Everything okay?'

'No. I wouldn't have broken this, if you'd just done what I asked. Why did you move it? You didn't need to, to use your toothbrush.' I toss the brushes into the bin near the door. 'What a waste! It was almost brand-new.' I'm close to tears.

He steps into the bathroom. 'Are you hurt?' He takes hold of my hands, gently turning them palm upwards. On my right thumb, two small cuts ooze red beads. He reaches over to turn on the tap. 'You need to rinse those, make sure there's nothing stuck in your skin.'

I put my hand under the water. The blood streaks across it like veins across marble. Bloodied water swirls down the plughole.

Tom rummages in the medicine cabinet for plasters. 'It's not the end of the world.'

'But why did you pick it up?' I still don't understand what he was doing. It's as if he's deliberately tormenting me.

'I like the design. I wanted to see where it was from.'

'Asda. It's an ordinary toothbrush holder from Asda.' I feel weary. 'Tom, why is it so hard to do things my way?'

He hands me the plasters and leans against the wall, folding his arms. 'I don't know. I have no idea why you make it so difficult.'

'What?' I struggle to peel open a plaster without blood smearing it.

'It's impossible. I've tried my best, but I'm walking on egg shells.'

'You're kidding? I haven't said anything about the mess, I've just run myself ragged clearing it up.'

'Clearing it up! There's nothing to clear up. There is no mess. Or not what any normal person would call a mess. And you didn't have to say anything. I could see you watching me.'

'You didn't realise I was watching last time. Christ, I wish I'd never said anything.' My hand shakes, as I wrap the plaster around my thumb.

He hasn't finished. 'I can't measure up to your standards. I can't put things back exactly the same. No normal person could.'

Again, those words: normal person. I'm not a normal person.

'Michael's ex did,' I say. 'It wasn't a problem for her. Why is it such a problem for you?'

'Michael? Who the hell's Michael?'

I take out another plaster and carefully press it against the second cut.

'Clare?'

'I thought I'd mentioned him?'

'No, you haven't. Who is he?'

'He goes to my support group. For obsessive-compulsives. He's got the same form of it as I have. He's been really helpful, given me loads of advice. He says it's a question of give and take.'

'He mustn't be as bad as you, then. You don't seem to have much give. And since when did you go to a support group?'

'I've only been once.'

'You seem to know this Michael pretty well.' Tom is still leaning against the wall.

117

'That's how these groups are. People open up.' I can't tell him about going out with Michael – not now. I walk out of the bathroom, brushing past Tom. 'He's a lot like you, actually...except he understands me.'

He follows me. 'Well, if he's so perfect, maybe you should marry *him*!'

I spin around to face him. 'Don't be ridiculous. All I'm saying is, he understands the way I am.'

'Then maybe he could explain it to me?'

'I'm sure he could. I'll give you his number!' I turn into the kitchen, to retrieve a newspaper from the recycling, to wrap up the broken holder.

Tom's mobile rings before he can respond. 'Vicky, hi. Everything okay?' She's on cottage and dog watch again.

His voice becomes muffled, as he walks into the bedroom. I strain to hear him through the kitchen wall. 'I'm not sure, Vicky. I know you need a job...don't get upset...Vicky, don't...okay, okay, I'll give you a hand with it when I get back.'

He comes into the kitchen, tucking his phone into his top pocket.

'Everything all right at home?' I ask.

'Yeah.'

'What did Vicky want?'

'Nothing. It doesn't matter.' He props himself against the counter.

'It does matter.'

'For God's sake, Clare, why? Why does it matter? We've more important things to talk about.'

'Because she's always after something. You've helped her again and again. Why won't you help me? The first time I ask, you give up.' I sit down at the table.

'I haven't given up. I want to help. I just don't think this is the best way.' Tom pushes away from the counter and paces up and down. 'I'll go crazy trying to keep up with you.'

'I'm crazy, am I?' He thinks it; I want him to admit it.

'That's not what I said. But I don't think you can carry on like this.'

'You think I should change?'

'Yeah.' He stops and looks at me. 'Don't you?'

'You're not so keen to change Vicky or Bex.'

118

'To my knowledge, neither of them has a mental illness.' Tom almost shouts the last two words. They're like a punch in the face.

'The way they behave, there's something wrong with them. You said it yourself. Vicky has hang-ups. That's just a nice euphemism. And what about you?' I say.

'Me? Why do you keep dragging this back to me?' His eyebrows arch in bewilderment.

'Because you let people walk all over you, get you to do what they want.'

'Like you, you mean?'

'No, that's different.'

'It's exactly the same, Clare.' He steps forward and bangs his fist on the kitchen table. His face is a foot away from mine. 'Jesus, can't you see that?' He takes a deep breath, straightens up. 'Look, I don't know much about this, but I think your friend Michael is wrong.'

'You don't know anything about it. You might be an instant plumbing expert, but believe me, you don't have a clue about psychiatry.'

'God help me, no I don't. You know, honestly, if you *had* been living with someone else, it would have been easier to deal with than this!'

'Well, I'm not the only one whose head's messed up. Get your own sorted out, before you give me advice.'

Tom stomps towards the kitchen door. 'I've had enough of this. This is your problem, not mine. Stop trying to turn it around.'

'Where are you going?'

'Home.' He slams the door behind him.

'Tom…' I don't know what to say to stop him.

18

I stay seated at the kitchen table, shaking. I don't want Tom to leave like this, yet I can't go to him.

I wait – and wait.

Eventually footsteps thud back down the hall. Is he coming into the kitchen? I stand up, wanting and not wanting to face him.

The hall cupboard door swishes open and closed over the carpet. A couple of minutes later, the front door bangs shut. He's gone.

I don't know how he'll get to the station. He won't know which bus to catch and it's a three-mile walk. I doubt he even knows the way.

I toy with the idea of going after him, but it's pointless. I won't know what to say and I suspect, like me, he'd rather be alone. He'll just have to ask for directions.

In fact, I need rescuing more than he does. My plans have failed, he thinks I'm crazy and our future together looks more uncertain than ever.

Temporary salvation comes, as usual, in the shape of tidying. I work my way around the flat, getting everything back to normal. Including, as I reclaim my territory, myself.

I may have reduced my anxiety to a manageable level, but I still don't know what to do about Tom.

I don't; Michael will. I call him, rather than text. His mobile goes to answerphone, the message short and businesslike. Just hearing his voice reassures me; he'll know what to do.

'Hi, it's Clare. I need to talk to you. Things have gone really badly with Tom. Please call me as soon as you get this. Thanks, Michael.' My voice cracks on his name.

I check my mobile a dozen times an hour for texts or missed calls, even though I'm in earshot of it all day. Nothing. Neither Tom nor Michael make contact. All night I worry about Tom. Worry he'll no longer want to be with me, now that he knows what I'm really like.

A text the next morning puts my mind at rest, *I'm sorry. I'm tryg to undrstnd. Cll tnght. Cht then. All my lv T.*

I smile. This is how other people, people outside my family, deal with problems: they talk. Tom and I don't need to have secrets. We can get through this.

He's working today, in spite of the bank holiday and the matching holiday rain. I don't want to embarrass him in front of Barry and Steve, so leave a message on his home phone. 'Hi, thanks for your text. I know this is hard for you, it's hard for me, too, and I know you're trying. Love you. Talk later.'

In the early evening, the phone rings. Assuming it's Tom, I don't screen the call. I should have.

'Hello, Clare?' The woman's voice sounds familiar.

'Speaking.'

'Clare, it's Marilyn.'

Marilyn? Marilyn! Why is she phoning me? There can only be one reason.

'What's happened? Is everything all right with Dad?' My panic is replaced within seconds by anger. Dad's ill and he's kept it from me and it's going to be too late. Again. I expect Fiona already knows.

'Your father? Brian's fine. It's you I'm calling for,' she says.

I sit down on the sofa, relieved and confused.

'I'm sorry, Marilyn, I've no idea what you're talking about.' I sink back amongst the cushions.

'Tom mentioned you have obsessive-compulsive disorder. I wondered if I could help?' Her voice has softened. She sounds like the agony aunt on the local radio station.

'He did what?' I sit bolt upright. My cheeks burn. I'm mortified. 'Does Dad know?'

'No, dear. And Brian isn't aware I'm calling. I won't tell him unless you want me to?'

'No, I absolutely do not want you to. I don't want anyone to know.' Including her, but it's too late for that. 'What exactly did Tom say?' I won't give away more than I have to. I lean forward to tug the coffee table straight.

'Only that he was worried about how you were tackling the issue.'

The issue? Now I'm an issue.

Marilyn continues, 'From what he told me, he may be right.'

I snort. Tom, the instant authority on everything.

'I'm not sure why you're getting involved? Isn't it for us to work out?'

'A hazard of being a social worker, I'm afraid. It can be hard to switch off.'

'Well, I'm not one of your clients.'

'I know. And I know that sometimes asking for help can be hard.'

The platitude curdles my stomach.

'I'm quite capable of asking for help, and I have – just not yours.'

'Of course, it's not my field, but I can put you in touch with a colleague, if you'd like?'

What I'd like, is for everyone who doesn't understand to leave me alone.

'I don't need anyone else. I told you, I already have someone helping me. He knows more about the subject than any therapist. He really understands me.'

The table is still not parallel to the sofa. I tweak it again and stand up to check the lines from above. They're perfect. I sit down.

'I can't claim the same understanding, dear, though I do have a great deal of counselling experience.'

'It didn't do you much good with your son.' The words are out before I can stop myself. 'Marilyn, I'm sorry. I shouldn't have said that.'

'No, you're right. I should be able to practise what I preach. It isn't always that simple.'

The sadness in her tone defuses my anger. 'What happened? Why are you estranged from him?'

'Nick's a drug addict. He's been in and out of rehab for years. He moved away after the last time he relapsed and we lost touch.'

'When was that?'

'About four years ago.'

'I'm sorry. That must be incredibly difficult for you.'

'Nothing I said or did made any difference. I can't dwell on it.'

She must, though. How can she not?

'He might get better one day,' I say.

'Possibly. The point is, I learned from trying to help him.' She sighs. 'I discovered how hard it is to admit to addiction. And to overcome it.'

'But I don't have an addiction.'

'It's not so very different, is it, dear?'

Going cold turkey is certainly no easier. 'And you don't think Tom should help?' I say.

'Not in the way you want him to.'

I'm starting to doubt the value of Michael's experience. It seemed to carry more weight than any advice I'd read or heard, but perhaps he and his wife were the exception. Even if Michael was right, and Tom should adapt to my ways, he can't – or won't. Our future together still depends solely on me.

'You won't say anything to Dad about all this?'

'Of course not, dear.'

Before she rings off, Marilyn insists on giving me her number, which I jot down on a sticky note that I press to the corner of the coffee table. Only then, do I wonder how she got mine – presumably by poking around at Dad's.

'Come over again soon,' she says. 'Your father would like that.' I doubt it. 'I will. We will.'

When the phone rings again later, I let the answerphone kick in.

It's Tom. 'Hey, beautiful, got your message. So, we survived our first row, eh? Next time, can you call me a cab? That station's a bloody long walk—'

I pick up the phone and perch on the edge of the sofa. 'Tom, hi.'

'Hey, Clare. How you doing?'

'I've been better.'

'Sorry to hear that. Bad day at work?'

'No.' I hesitate. 'Marilyn called earlier.'

'Oh? I didn't expect her to phone you. I meant to tell you I'd spoken to her.'

'And telling me first would have made it all right?' I unpeel the note with her number on it from the coffee table.

'What do you mean? Made what all right?'

'Tom, I don't appreciate everyone knowing about my problem, about us. What the hell were you thinking?'

'Ah, that. Yes, sorry. I didn't plan to tell her. I rang her for honeymoon ideas last week, and she was asking how you were and, I don't know, somehow it all just spilled out.'

'Well, I wish it hadn't.' Tucking the phone under my chin, I fold the note into a tiny plane. 'How did you get her number, anyway?'

'I rang your dad. You gave me his, remember? Just in case.' He sighs. 'Look, Clare, I'm out of my depth here and I suppose I just needed somebody to talk to. Marilyn's very discreet, she won't say anything—'

'So she said, but now she knows something my family don't and…it feels wrong.' I launch the plane into a nose dive into the waste paper basket next to the sofa.

'I'm sorry, Clare, I'm doing my best to support you. Isn't that what you wanted?'

I thought it was; it's not any more. The truth is, I regret telling Tom. I've complicated our relationship for nothing. Now he's made things worse, by dragging Marilyn into the situation. It was easier when my compulsions were a secret.

'Tom, I think we should have a break from one another,' I say.

'What? Where's that coming from? Are you calling off our engagement?'

'No! No, not at all. I just need time on my own to start getting better.'

'Why, Clare? You don't have to do this alone. I'll always be here for you. You just need to help me understand.'

'I don't know if I have the strength to help myself, let alone anyone else. I don't want to have to explain what I do, and why. All I want is to stop doing it.'

'You don't have to shut me out, though, Clare.'

'I don't see any other way, Tom. I'm sorry. Please let me do this. A few weeks apart is nothing compared with the rest of our lives together. And we won't have that, unless I begin to sort this out. I think you were right – it's me that has to change, not you.'

He sighs. 'Okay, but what about the wedding?'

'We'll have to postpone it. I can't cope with all the arrangements, on top of everything else.'

'There's not much to postpone. We haven't even set a date.' He sounds defeated.

'Then, we'll postpone setting a date.'

'What will you tell your family?'

'Nothing. They don't need to know. We'll be back on track soon and no one will be any the wiser.'

His silence tells me he's not convinced. He doesn't have a choice.

'I love you, Tom.'

'I love you, too.'

As I hang up, I'm drained, yet elated. I've wiped the slate clean and in a few weeks we'll be able to start again.

But a clean slate can be a dangerous thing.

19

The end of the week looms and I've made no progress with my cure. Instead, I've contrived reasons not to start: I was home too late, or was feeling too tired, or had ironing to do. Ironing? I hate ironing.

I've pushed Tom away, to get better, and already I'm failing him. I wish I could talk to Michael about it all; at least I wouldn't have to explain myself to him. He still hasn't returned the message I left on Sunday, though. Countless times since then, I've picked up my phone to call him, but resisted. He's already given up an evening to talk things through with me and we hardly know each other; I don't want to take advantage.

Guilt at so much wasted time finally spurs me on. In the absence of anyone else's help, I have to find my own way to do this. I resolve to dedicate the coming weekend to my mission; it should be easier with two days of no distractions.

At work on Friday afternoon, my mobile rings. Abandoning my filing, I scramble back to my desk and dig the phone out of my handbag. The screen displays the words 'unknown number'. I sigh. It's bound to be a sales call. 'Hello?'

'Hello,' a woman's voice says. 'Is that Miss Clare Thorpe?'

'Yes,' I say warily. 'Who is this?'

'My name's Wendy Harrison. I'm the secretary at your niece and nephew's school, St Michael's. I'm calling on behalf of Mrs Mercer...your sister. It's about the children.'

'Oh God! Are they all right?' I sink into my seat.

'They're fine. It's your sister. She's been taken ill. She needs you to pick up the children and look after them.'

'What's wrong with her? Why didn't she phone herself?'

'Miss Thorpe, your sister's had emergency surgery. The hospital called us.'

Hospital? Surgery? That doesn't sound good. My heart races. 'What's happened to her? Where is she?'

'I'm sorry, I don't know any more than that. I'm sure she'll be all right.'

'You don't know that.' My voice is wobbly.

'Miss Thorpe, please try not to worry. I expect the Head will be able to tell you more. What about the children?' She's calm, patient; she's obviously used to emergencies and neurotics.

'Yes, of course. I'll be there as soon as I can. Will Dave – Mr Mercer – collect them later?'

'I understand he's abroad on business. He can't get back till Monday morning.'

'Monday!' I can't take the children all weekend. I can't have them *in my flat* all weekend.

'Yes. Now, Miss Thorpe, do you know where our school is?'

She gives me the address: a mile or so from Fiona's house. The head teacher will stay with the children until I arrive. My panic makes it hard to take in what she's telling me.

It's an hour home on the Tube and a forty-five minute drive to Uxbridge, and it's already two-fifteen. Pleading a domestic emergency, I leave work straightaway. My boss doesn't quibble; she has two young children and regular childcare crises of her own.

On the way, I try to calm down and make plans. The children can sleep in my bed; I'll take the sofa. A mental inventory of my food supplies reveals little that will appeal to them. We'll have to shop on the way home. I'll need to buy clothes, as well; I don't have the key to their house to collect any. Dad may have, but diverting to his place and back to Fiona's will take hours. Easier to pick up cheap outfits at the supermarket. And toiletries. And toys. And? What else?

My head spins with the practicalities of the children's visit. The biggest worry is how I'll cope. I wasn't able to deal with one person, for one night. How will I manage with two people – two little, uncontrollable people – for three nights? It's inconceivable – and unavoidable.

In the head teacher's office, the children perch on chairs at her desk. They're both engrossed in colouring.

She stands up to shake my hand. 'I'm Mrs Fellows. The children have been looking forward to seeing you.' She reminds me of my own primary school head teacher: the kind of woman who makes you feel safe.

Harry slides off his chair. He's cute in his school uniform, yet also more grown-up. A mini version of his dad – though I doubt

Dave wears his tie twisted halfway around his neck.

He hands me his drawing. 'I did a dinosaur picture for you. Look.' Purple spikes straggle across the top of the paper.

'That's lovely,' I say. 'What kind of dinosaur is it?'

'A stegosaurus, silly!'

'And what are you drawing, Sophie?' I say.

Sophie, still seated, hasn't even looked at me. 'Mummy being poorly,' she says.

I lean over her shoulder. The figure has a bandage on its head, with tufts of orange hair poking out underneath.

'That's very nice, Sophie.'

Turning back to Mrs Fellows, I ask, 'Has my sister had an accident?'

'I'm afraid I don't know, Miss Thorpe. The hospital was only at liberty to say that she'd had surgery.'

Please let it not be anything life-threatening. I hate being in the dark, hate this lack of control.

She gathers papers off her desk. 'Miss Thorpe, I'm terribly sorry, I must dash. I have a meeting to get to.'

'Of course. I'm sorry to have kept you. Thank you for your help.'

She shows us to the school entrance, giving me directions to the hospital as we walk.

'Sophie, Harry, I'll see you on Monday. Have a lovely weekend with your Auntie Clare.'

They chorus, 'Bye, Mrs Fellows,' as she clangs the gate shut behind us.

Then she's gone. I want to shout after her, beg her to stay and take care of everything. I've never looked after Sophie and Harry for longer than an afternoon or an evening. Done no more than played for a few hours and provided a snack. Standing with them, beside the deserted playground, I've never felt more alone.

Harry tugs at my sleeve. 'Where's Mummy?' His bottom lip trembles. His blazer hangs off one shoulder and his satchel trails on the ground.

'She's poorly, sweetheart. I'm looking after you for a few days. Didn't Mrs Fellows tell you?'

'He's just being a baby,' says Sophie, prim and neat next to her dishevelled brother.

'I want Mummy,' he wails.

I bend down and hug him. 'We'll see her soon and, anyway, we're going to have lots of fun, aren't we?'

Harry's sniffles become sobs. His chest heaves. A repeat of the cheesy-snack-vomit episode appears imminent.

'Hey, guess what?' I say. 'I'm going to get lovely food and toys for you and Sophie. How about that, eh?'

He pauses mid-sob. 'T–t–toys?'

'You can choose whatever you want.'

He thinks. 'A Lego lorry?'

'Whatever you want.' I'm relieved the sobs have stopped.

Sophie glowers at me. 'Mummy says he can't have that till his birthday and that's ages away.'

Harry looks worried.

'Ages and ages and ages,' says Sophie.

Harry's chest rises and falls. He's gearing up for more sobbing. I can't let him be sick on his school doorstep.

'Well, I'm not Mummy and I say he can have what he wants. You can both have what you want.'

Sophie smiles triumphantly. God knows what she'll pick; I don't care. Whatever it takes to keep them happy and vomit-free.

Driving up the A40 back to north London, I'm stiff with fear. The rush-hour traffic is heavy and fast moving. Halfway back, we're caught in a downpour that defeats even the highest wiper speed. I can hardly see anything ahead of me. Terrified of crashing and killing us all, I hug the inside lane, well below the speed limit. It doesn't help that I don't have child seats. The children are strapped into the back as securely as possible, but I pray no police pass us. Irate drivers tailgate the car and then overtake, sounding their horns. One gives me the finger. I suppress my usual stream of invective. It won't do to send Sophie and Harry home with a new vocabulary.

Reaching the safety of Asda's car park, with the rain over, I relax a little. The children scramble out of the car.

When Sophie sees where we are, she wrinkles her nose. 'Mummy doesn't like this shop. She says it's cheap and nasty.'

'Does she? Well, it's all I can afford.'

I wheel the trolley inside, the children either side of me. The idea of sending them home dressed courtesy of *George* makes me smile. Fiona will whip off the clothes quicker than you can say 'Why pay more?'

The food shopping takes ages. By the time we've argued over

fish fingers or sausages, white bread or brown, yoghurt or fromage frais, it's five forty-five. Harry drags his feet, complaining he's hungry. I tear open a packet of teacakes and give him one.

'Do you want one, too, Sophie?' I offer her the bag.

'You haven't put any butter on.' She wrinkles her nose again.

'Well, I don't have a knife and I'm not spreading margarine with my finger.' I fold the open end of the bag over and put it back in the trolley.

'All right.' She holds out her hand.

I pick out underwear, tee shirts, jeans and a sweatshirt for Harry. I let Sophie choose her own clothes. She only wants items decorated with hearts, even the socks. We trail up and down the aisles, finding everything from embroidered hearts to a heart-shaped zip-pull. I put my foot down over the diamanté-studded knickers. They can't be comfortable. Plain, pastel cotton is a safer bet. She offers only a tentative nose wrinkle in complaint.

Agreeing to Harry's toy was a mistake. The lorry is enormous and costs £34. I can't back down now. Time to move the goalposts.

'Harry, this is an early birthday present, all right?' I say.

'Okay.' He shrugs. His birthday is in October, six months away. He knows as well as I do that I will have forgotten the lorry by then.

Sophie peers at the box. 'It says, "age five to twelve".' She puts her hands on her hips and scowls. 'Harry's only four.'

Maybe that's why Fiona was putting him off until his birthday? It's too late to worry about that.

I get off lightly with Sophie. She settles for a cheap princess dressing-up set: plastic sandals, tiara, wand and jewellery. The key attraction is that almost every piece features a heart.

'This isn't my birthday present, Auntie Clare.' She drops the box into the trolley. Her birthday is less than two months away; she doesn't intend to be short-changed.

Before we leave, the children select toothbrushes. Harry's is red and yellow, with a picture of Tigger. Sophie's has a Disney princess on a glittery purple handle.

One shopping trip, and a couple of hours in, and I'm worn out. I'm not the only one. By the time we get home, the children are exhausted. Sophie has shadows under her eyes and Harry's face is even paler than usual. His freckles stand out against his white skin.

I rustle up fish fingers, peas and oven chips, but they barely touch their food. Skipping baths, I get them ready for bed. I've forgotten to buy nightwear, so old tee shirts will have to do. The children are swimming in them, with Harry's down to his knees. They flap their arms and run around the bedroom like demented bats, giggling hysterically.

With all the noise, I nearly miss the phone. I dash into the living room to grab it.

'Hello?' I say, breathlessly. As I walk back into the bedroom, the caller is drowned out. 'Shh, Sophie, Harry, I can't hear!'

'Hello, Clare? It's Dave.'

'Dave, hi, where are you? Children, it's Daddy.'

The giggles stop. Sophie and Harry run over and press themselves against my legs.

'I'm in New York. I can't get a flight till Sunday night. Are you okay with the kids for the weekend?' He sounds strained and tired.

'Absolutely, no problem.' Fingers crossed behind my back.

'I'll come straight from the airport on Monday and take them to school, so that you can get off to work. I'll call when I land.'

'That's fine. Do you want to say goodnight to them, Dave? They're just off to bed.' I hand the phone to Sophie. 'Say night-night to Daddy and then let Harry talk to him.'

She clutches the phone in both hands. 'Daddy, we went to Asda and I've got a tee shirt with jewels on and boring pants 'cause Auntie Clare wouldn't let me have the ones I liked and we had chips for tea.'

I groan inwardly.

Harry is satisfied with whispering, 'Night-night, Daddy.'

I take the phone off him. 'Dave, can you hang on a sec? Into bed, please, you two. I'll be back in a minute to say goodnight.'

They snuggle under the duvet, giggling again.

In the living room, I push the door shut. 'Dave, what's happened to Fiona? The school said she'd had surgery.'

'I don't know. All the hospital would say was that it was some kind of internal bleeding and she'd be fine.'

'Internal bleeding! Jesus, that's serious. Is there…is there something wrong with her? Something she's not telling me?'

'If there is, she's not telling me either.'

'Maybe that's because she never sees you.'

The line hisses with his silence. Then he says, 'Clare, this isn't the time or the place.'

'You're right. I'd better go, make sure the children aren't getting up to mischief.'

'Of course.' He hesitates. 'Thanks, Clare. We do appreciate your help.'

'See you Monday, Dave.'

I hang up and go to say goodnight to the children, but they're already asleep. They look small and lost in the expanse of a double bed. I kiss them and turn off the light.

Now to see what havoc they've wrought on my flat.

20

As I step into the living room, I stop dead. 'Oh, my God!' It looks as if it's been burgled. My palms begin to sweat, as I scan the damage.

Someone, probably Sophie, has turned my coffee table into a shop. My few ornaments are set out alongside a selection of magazines, books and CDs. In front of them are scraps of paper marked with prices. Sophie's dressing-up set lies, unopened, in the middle. Coins from a pot of loose change are strewn between the table and the sofa, some stacked in piles according to denomination.

Beyond the table, a low wall of sofa and scatter cushions surrounds the television. Harry's work – his new lorry stands on top.

My PC, which sits on a desk at the other end of the room, is on, but the screensaver has kicked in; stars fizz across a black sky. I walk over to it and jiggle the mouse. The monitor glows back into life; to my relief it displays only a Disney website.

Everywhere I look, something is out of place. Sheets of printer paper, decorated with squiggles, litter the floor in front of the desk. Blue and black ballpoints, lids off, threaten to dribble ink onto the beige carpet. Soil is scattered around the yucca and palm that stand either side of the sofa.

I've only myself to blame. While I prepared the children's meal, I banished them from the kitchen, scared that one of them would have an accident. That fear overrode any anxiety over the mayhem that might ensue from leaving them to their own devices. Danger trumped disorder, but I wish now that I'd chosen to live dangerously.

My stomach churns. I feel dizzy and panicky at the thought of how long it will take to clear up. After Tom's first visit, I spent hours tidying and he hardly touched anything.

I turn my back on the room and escape to the kitchen: an oasis of bare, shining surfaces. Leaning against the cool wall tiles, I close my eyes and breathe slowly and deeply, girding myself to tackle the mess.

I don't want to deal with it, but I have to sleep in there, and the floor has turned into an obstacle course. If I get up in the night, I'm bound to trip over something. I sigh and push myself away from the wall; I have to sort it out.

And I have to abandon my plans to start my cure – the mess the children have made is far too much to constitute a first step in my recovery.

I find myself taking even greater care than usual, as I replace every ornament, CD and book, every magazine, cushion and pen. Each is tweaked, checked, tweaked, checked, tweaked, checked. Again and again and again. Restoring my flat to normal provides a sense of control that I don't have over Fiona's illness or looking after the children.

Finally, I walk slowly around the room, making sure each item is where it should be, that the patterns are complete again. The usual scan from the doorway isn't enough. There has been too much disruption to be sure, from a distance, that I haven't missed something. Three circuits satisfy me.

It has taken two hours to do one room and I'm exhausted by the mental effort.

Before I move on, I check the answerphone message that I noticed flashing during the first lap – listening to it then would have interrupted my scan and meant starting it again. The phone must have rung while I was vacuuming up the soil. I dreaded waking the children, yet couldn't leave the dirt to get ground in.

I press *Play*.

'Clare, it's me. Dad. Dave called. About Fiona. Er, call me back if you can.'

Then whispering behind him, before he adds, 'Marilyn says hello—' His voice becomes distant, as if he has turned away, 'What was that, dear?' Then louder again, 'Marilyn says if you need help with the children, give her...us a call. Bye.'

It's nine-thirty – not too late to phone him back. I don't have much to tell him, though, and I don't want Marilyn's help. Seeing her again would only give her another opportunity to interfere between me and Tom. I scribble 'Call Dad' on a sticky note and attach it to the phone's base. Then peel it off and put it back, straight this time.

I leave the living room, taking the toys with me; there's no place for them in there. As I close the door behind me, I look up and down the hall. The children's backpacks are on the floor, next to their shoes. I bend to pick them up and spot the mark on the wall made by Tom's rucksack.

I wonder what he's doing tonight. The absence of our daily chats has made it seem far longer than four days since we last spoke. I wish I could call him and share my worries about looking after the children, but I asked for time and space to get better; I can't go running to him whenever it suits me, even if this latest challenge is nothing to do with my recovery.

I run my fingers over the graze in the paintwork. Under the kitchen sink, I have a tin of the same apricot white emulsion. A dab of that will blur the scar, yet nothing will conceal it completely. It will always be noticeable, if only to me.

I have to find a home for the children's things. As with anything alien to the flat, I'll have to alter my patterns to accommodate them. New objects always cause a visual jolt, until they have bedded in. An easy solution to the children's stuff is to store it in the hall cupboard. I squeeze the shoes onto the rack and line up the bags and toys behind them.

The bathroom is an equally quick fix. The children were in and out too fast to disturb much.

Only the bedroom left. With the children asleep, it will be a challenge.

The door creaks as I open it. I stop, hold my breath. Not a murmur from the bed. I leave the door ajar, with the hall light on, hoping that will be enough to see by, but half the bedroom is still in darkness. I tiptoe to the bedside table on Harry's side to pick up my torch. I feel over the surface, inch by inch, as if reading Braille. In spite of visualising exactly where the torch is, I can't find it. My fingers bump up against a box of tissues, which falls to the floor. I wince at the clonk. There is no reaction from the children. I put the tissues back and finally find the torch. Flicking it on, I cup one hand around the lamp end, to narrow the beam.

Slowly, I shine the torch across the bedside tables and the chest of drawers. Apart from the children's clothes, on an armchair in the corner, everything looks the same as always. This shouldn't take long.

I spin the torch's light over the floor to the dressing table.

Oh, my God.

Every single item has been moved and between the jumbled containers are blobs of cream and small puddles of perfume. Sophie must have come in to play while I was cooking. A table of toiletries

– and my few cosmetics – must have been a magnet to a six-year-old girl. I can't believe I didn't notice until now. Getting the children to bed and talking to Dave took all my attention.

The only way to fix the dressing table is to clear it, wipe up the mess and put everything back. Holding the torch between my teeth, I retrieve the box of tissues and make a start. Taking things off is one thing, putting them back another. Not only do I have to be quiet, it's impossible to judge distances in the wavering torchlight. I can't tell if things are evenly spaced.

Suddenly I stop. What the hell am I doing? This is ridiculous. I'm creeping about in the dark, trying to put things straight that no one can see. I shake my head. The torch swings left and right and then slides out from between my teeth. It hits the dressing table and bounces to the floor. I freeze at the noise.

'Mummy?' Sophie's voice.

I pick up the torch and go over to her. 'It's not Mummy, sweetheart. It's Auntie Clare.'

'I heard a big bang. I'm scared.'

'It was only me. I dropped something. Go back to sleep.'

'Mmm.' She's already dozing off.

After that, I have to stop. She might not be so easily pacified if she wakes a second time.

I creep out of the room, the job not even half done. I have to accept that things won't get back to normal until the children have gone; right now, that seems a very long way off.

21

Exhausted by the day's stresses, I go to bed early. Bed being a fusty sleeping bag on the sofa, with underwear replacing my nightdress – I forgot to look one out and daren't venture back into the bedroom.

I don't sleep well. The sleeping bag is too confined, the sofa feels like a mortuary slab under my bony shoulders and hips, and my bra digs in, whichever way I lie. I'm tempted to take it off, but Harry might walk in. Fear of traumatising him keeps me trussed up. I toss and turn, trying to get comfortable.

Sleep would be difficult whatever the bed or nightwear. My mind buzzes with problems I can't resolve. Every thought leads to another worry. Fiona. Sophie and Harry. Tom. Dad and Marilyn. Worse than any of these concerns is my discomfort at the flat being a mess. If I could only tidy up, I could cope with anything. The chemical oblivion of drugs or alcohol is not for me; I just need the mental oblivion of my rituals to distract me from my other worries. Like consolidating debts, I hide all my problems in one that is much bigger.

My last time check, on the DVD player display, is three forty-five. After that, I drift off.

A persistent tapping on my head wakes me. I blearily open my eyes. Sophie is standing by the sofa.

Instantly awake, I struggle to sit up. 'Sophie, is everything all right?' I squint at the time: six-thirty.

'I'm bored. Why aren't you up?'

I never stir before nine-thirty at the weekends. 'Is Harry awake?'

'No.'

'Go back to bed and I'll get up soon.'

'When?'

'Soon.'

She wrinkles her nose. 'That's not what Mummy does.'

'I'm not Mummy. I'll be up in an hour. All right?'

Another wrinkle of the nose and she stamps off. Minutes later, she taps my head again.

I keep my eyes closed. 'Sophie, I told you I'd get up later.'

'It is later. We've been waiting ages.'

I open my eyes. Harry is now next to Sophie. 'Where's my lorry?' he says.

'In the hall cupboard. Don't move anything else!'

He scampers out of the room.

I look at the time. Seven-thirty. I don't feel as if I've been asleep for another hour.

'All right, I'm getting up.' I wearily unzip the sleeping bag and swing my feet to the floor. I run my fingers through my hair; bits stick up all over. With the children up, I won't have chance for a shower. I'll have to glue it down with spray.

Harry comes back into the living room. 'You're in your pants!' He giggles.

I pull the sleeping bag around me and wave them away. 'Bathroom, both of you. Now, please. I'll be through in a minute to help you.'

They run off into the hall, shrieking and pushing each other. I wonder how they have the energy at this hour.

In the bedroom, the duvet is half off the bed and the pillows are on the floor. The things I put back on the dressing table have been moved again. I sigh. I'm so tired this morning that I'm numb to the sight: my physical exhaustion has momentarily neutralised my body's usual stress response.

Wailing from the bathroom diverts me. I pull on my dressing gown and go to investigate.

Sophie and Harry are standing in front of the toilet, staring into the bowl.

'What are you two doing?' I lean over them and see Harry's toothbrush head down in the water. 'How on earth did that happen?'

'Sophie made me,' he says, tearfully. 'We were playing sword-fighting and she hit my hand, and that's cheating because you're s'posed to hit swords, and it hurt and—'

'You're a big baby,' she says. 'When Mummy and Auntie Clare were little, they had boiling oil and burning arrows and they really hurt. And sometimes they'd chop your head off and put it on a spike—'

'Sophie, enough of all that nonsense, please!'

Harry resumes his wailing, hiccuping out his retort between howls. 'I'm...not...a...baby...I'm...four!'

'Stop that, Harry!' I roll up my dressing gown sleeve. 'I need to get this out, before it gets stuck in the U-bend.'

'What's one of those?' says Sophie.

'It's the bit at the bottom.'

'Which bit?' She peers down the toilet.

'Sophie, I don't have time for a plumbing lesson. Pass me a rubber glove, please.' I point to the pair draped over the toilet brush.

'Eurgghh,' she says, pinching the cuff of one between her thumb and forefinger and passing it to me, at arm's length.

I snap it on and fish out the toothbrush. 'Harry, please stop crying. I'll get you another one.' Throwing the brush in the bin, I peel off the glove and reach across the toilet to put it back with its partner.

''Xactly the same?' He sniffs.

'Exactly the same.'

'Red and yellow, with Tigger?'

'Red and yellow, with Tigger.' Fingers crossed they haven't run out of that design. 'But only if there's no more sword fighting. Promise?'

Harry nods earnestly. 'Promise.'

'Good. In the meantime, I'll have to look out a spare toothbrush for you.' An adult one will be far too big, but needs must. 'By the way, Sophie, Mummy and I were not born in the Middle Ages. That was hundreds of years ago.'

She frowns. 'So, what's middle-aged, then?'

I suppress a smile. 'I'm not middle-aged either, Sophie, but I'll explain later. I'm not answering any more questions till you're both washed and I've had a cup of tea.'

Once they're settled at the kitchen table with bowls of cereal, and I'm armed with tea, I go into the living room to phone Dad.

As he picks up, I hear a click – a lamp being switched on. He must still be in bed.

'Hello?' he says. Shuffling noises and whispering. In bed with Marilyn.

I try to wipe the picture out of my mind. 'Hi Dad, it's Clare.'

'Clare? What time is it? Is something wrong?'

'It's just after eight. Sorry, I didn't realise it was so early. I'm returning your call. About Fiona?'

'Fiona. Indeed. Dave said surgery...' His voice fades.

'For internal bleeding.'

'Yes. Very worrying.'

'The hospital say she'll be fine.'

He's quiet for a moment. 'Clare, is Fiona ill?'

'I don't think you bleed internally if you're well, Dad.'

'I mean—'

'Is it something terrible? Is she dying? Not as far as I know. I don't always know everything.'

Dad clears his throat.

'Look, I'm sure it's nothing serious,' I say. 'We'll find out when she comes home.'

'We're visiting her this afternoon,' he says.

'Are you?' For Christ's sake, why is he quizzing me, then? I peel off a sticky note and press it to the edge of the phone stand, underneath, and parallel, to the one that says 'Call Dad'. I take another and line it up with the blank one.

'We'll let her know you were asking after her.'

'Dad, please! Asking after her? She's my sister, not some passing acquaintance.' I lift off one of the unused notes and put it back on the pad. 'Give her my love and tell her I hope she's better soon.'

'Your love. Yes, indeed.'

'And let me know what you find out.' I remove the second clean note and return it to the stack, running my forefinger up and down the jutting edge of the replaced sheets.

'Yes. Bye, now.'

He hangs up before I reply. 'Love you,' I tell the dialling tone, screwing up the reminder to call him and flicking it into the bin.

I go back into the bedroom to check on the children. Harry is on the bed. He's turned the duvet and pillows into a mountain and is pushing his lorry up the side. Sophie is perched on the stool in front of the dressing table. As I come up behind her, I'm horrified to see what she's done. No mess this time: the bottles, pots and cans are, instead, in neat rows. Undeniably lined up, even if not according to my patterns. She's busy coiling a necklace into my jewellery box.

'Sophie, what are you doing?'

'Hi, Auntie Clare.' She tucks the end of the necklace into the box and closes the lid, not looking around.

'Sweetheart, why's everything lined up?' I'm not sure I want to know.

''Cause it looks nice.'

The worst possible answer.

'It looks nice like this, too.' I reach over her head and lift a pot of cream out of its designated line.

'No!' She grabs my wrist. 'You mustn't.'

'Why not?' Please let her not be like me.

''Cause it's a shop and the shop man gets cross with the ladies if it's not right.'

So, she's playing at being a shelf-stacker. At least her lines have a reason – more of a reason than mine. I put the pot back.

'All right, well we can play shops later. How about going out for the day?'

'Yeah!' Harry leaps off the bed and runs up to me, winding his arms around my legs. 'Is Mummy coming?'

'Mummy's not very well, remember?'

His face crumples.

'We'll still have fun, though.' I unravel his arms and squat in front of him. 'It'll be an Auntie Clare Adventure.'

Harry brightens. 'Like when we went to the zoo and had burgers and Mummy was cross because she said we shouldn't eat that rubbish?'

'Something like that, yes.'

Sophie chirps up, 'And like the fair when we were sick because of the candy floss and Mummy said the teddies we'd won were tat and we had to give them to the jumble?'

'Er, yes. Only I don't want anyone being sick today, thank you.' Not when I have to clear it up.

Whatever we do, at least it will get them out of the flat. The more we're out, the easier the weekend will be.

I help the children to dress and leave everything else as it is: the bedroom a play area, the living room a camp site. While they're up, tidying is as futile as baling out a leaky boat. As fast as I put things right, they'll mess them up. Their force is every bit as relentless as the ocean.

Once they're in bed, I'll get as much of the flat back to normal as I can. The thought of waiting until then bothers me less than I expected. Perhaps it's because I haven't lost control; I've chosen to give it over to the children. For now.

22

I dither outside the door of my flat, locking, unlocking and re-locking it, assuming the children won't notice that I keep turning the key.

Harry is otherwise occupied, watching a spider scuttle along the skirting board.

Sharp-eyed Sophie is not. 'What are you doing?'

'Locking the door.'

'You're taking ages.'

'I'm checking it.'

'Why?'

'Because you have to be careful.'

'Why?'

'Because sometimes people...' I don't want to frighten them. 'Never mind. Let's get going.' I twiddle the keys one more time, marking the action mentally with the word *tarantula* – evidence I locked it, if I begin to doubt myself later.

Downstairs I sort through the post, keeping a watchful eye on the children, as they hop about on the front step outside.

'Anything for me?' Janet, my neighbour below, appears in the entrance hall. She's tugging a small suitcase behind her. 'I was on my way to see you. I'm off to Paris for a long weekend. Back Wednesday. Could you pop my post in and keep an eye on things?'

'No problem. Do you still have my spare keys, by the way?' She's scatterbrained enough to have lost them.

She frowns. 'The ones with the orange bow? I'm pretty sure they're on the rack in the kitchen.'

Pretty sure? God, she is hopeless.

'Have a look when you take the post in,' she says. 'Better dash, my taxi's waiting.'

'Got your passport and tickets?'

'I hope so.' She ducks her head to ferret inside her handbag. The roots of her bottle-blonde hair are showing. 'Here you go!' She brandishes the documents.

'Don't lose them,' I say, as Janet charges outside. Chances are she'll leave them in the cab.

I take the children to an urban farm for the morning, which is marred by only the odd tantrum or sulk. After lunch, things go downhill.

It's dry and mild, so I decide we should go to the local park. The last time I came here was with Tom. Despite the stress of his visit to my flat, we had fun: vying to outdo each other on the swings; Tom teasing me on the seesaw; and my reminiscing about what first attracted me to him. I wish he were with us now – he's a big kid at heart and adores his own nieces and nephews. The children would love to see him and Charlie again; maybe one day we'll all come here together.

The play area is crowded with other youngsters and their parents, but I manage to find a free swing for Sophie.

She won't let me push her. 'I can do it on my own!'

I leave her to it, once I'm sure she won't fall off, and lift Harry onto a small rocking elephant: one of a circle of animals, each propelled by a large spring at its base.

'Don't rock too hard,' I tell him. Some children are lurching backward and forward so vigorously, they'll catapult into the air if they let go. 'I'll come and get you off in a few minutes.'

My plans to relax with a magazine on a nearby bench are thwarted by my fear of something happening to Sophie or Harry. I glance up to check on them every few seconds.

Five minutes in, Sophie stomps up to me.

'I'm bored,' she says, adding a half-hearted pout.

I haven't even finished one article. 'Play for a bit longer, sweetheart. I'll call you when it's time to go. Try something else, if you're fed up with the swings.'

'I don't like anything else.' She scowls, but wanders back to the swing and plonks herself down on it. She hangs there, scuffing her toes in the bark chippings. Every time I look up, she glares at me. I abandon the article for quicker reads: letters, fillers and the agony column.

A few minutes later, Harry tugs at my arm. 'I've hurt my knee. I want Mummy.'

'Which knee?'

'This one.' He points at his left leg.

I push up his jeans. 'I can't see anything. What did you do?'

He looks down. 'It might be the other one.'

I lift the right leg of his jeans. 'I still can't see anything. What's the matter with it?'

'It feels funny. I want to go home.' His bottom lip quivers.

It's only three. I'd hoped to stay out for at least another hour.

A shriek from the swings makes me jump. Sophie is standing over a much bigger girl, spread-eagled on the ground. I run over to them, pulling Harry behind me. He tries to limp; my speed turns the movement into a hop.

'Sophie, what's going on?' I let go of Harry and reach down to help the girl up. She swats my hand away and scrambles to her feet.

'She said I had to give her a go.' Sophie lifts her chin and folds her arms. 'She said to push her higher. It's not my fault!' Her fearful eyes are at odds with her defiant stance.

'You pushed too hard!' The girl grabs a fistful of Sophie's glossy brown hair. 'You did it on purpose, 'cause you wanted my swing.'

'It was *my* swing,' Sophie yelps, flailing her arms, as she tries to wriggle free.

Harry whimpers.

'For God's sake, stop it!' I prise the girl's fingers open and release Sophie. 'I'm sure it was an accident. There's no need for all this. Where are your mum and dad?' I scan the park, catching disapproving looks from some of the other adults. No one comes forward to claim the girl, who appears to be only nine or ten-years-old; she's too young to be here alone.

'I'm going to get you, just you wait.' The girl spits at Sophie and runs off.

'Eurgghh, Auntie Clare, get it off, get it off!'

Spit glistens on her cheek. I wipe it away with a tissue. 'You're all clean again.'

She flaps her hands. 'It's still there, Auntie Clare. I can feel it. Here.' She turns her left cheek towards me.

'Sweetheart, it's as dry as a bone.'

The whimpering next to me gets louder.

'Harry, will you stop that noise,' I say.

'It doesn't feel right.' Sophie scrunches up her face.

'Only because I've been rubbing it.' I stroke her cheek. 'I think we should go home. We've had enough excitement for one day.'

Harry chips in, 'And my knee hurts.'

'For goodness' sake, your knee's fine.' I take each of them by the hand and we set off. Harry's whimpering mutates into hiccupy sniffles. Sophie keeps touching her cheek. They hold onto me more tightly than usual.

Tea, baths and bedtime follow without fuss; they're both worn out. Harry doesn't even complain about my failure to replace his Tigger toothbrush. With all the upset of the day, I overlooked that errand.

He's asleep within seconds of getting into bed. Sophie lies still next to him, while I whisper a story to her. Afterwards she gazes at me, wide-eyed and pale. 'Auntie Clare, will that horrid girl get me?'

'No, of course not, sweetheart. She doesn't even know where you live. You're quite safe.' I pull the duvet up under her chin. 'Settle down and go to sleep.'

She pulls her arms out from under the covers and feels her cheek with trembling fingers, her eyes still big and frightened.

'Hold on.' I fetch the pot of face cream from the dressing table.

Perched on the edge of the bed, I scoop some out. 'This'll make your face smell lovely.' I smooth the cream into her skin. She half closes her eyes. I dot a blob onto her nose. 'Your turn.'

Sophie rubs at the cream, as if at an itch. She smiles. 'It smells like flowers.' She visibly relaxes and lets me tuck her in.

Outside the bedroom, I gird myself. It should be my turn to relax; I can't. I have today's mess to clear up. The children's room is a no-go area, as I can't risk disturbing them, but there is still the rest of the flat. The memory of how long it took last night drains me before I start. Repeatedly ordering the same things doesn't usually defeat me. Then again, the volume of work is normally less, and not so hard or so pointless. In a few hours, Sophie and Harry will undo everything I'm about to put right. Yet I can't resist the force driving me. I push myself away from the door and trudge into the living room. The sooner I start, the sooner I'll finish.

It isn't soon enough. I'm too tired to concentrate. If I can't concentrate, I can't be sure I'm doing things correctly. I have to check, again and again. Is that pile of magazines straight? Is the remote control where it should be? Are the cushions at the prescribed angle? I'm just not certain.

Eventually I'm done. And done in.

Slumped in front of the television, I channel-hop while I eat a microwaved spaghetti carbonara, feeling suddenly lonely. This is the first Saturday evening I've spent apart from Tom in months. He's probably enjoying a carefree night out at *The White Horse* with his friends: his usual weekend pastime before we met. He probably had dinner there, too, to avoid cooking. I hope Bex isn't behind the bar.

While I eat, I check the room. Everything appears different from the sofa: all the angles look wrong. Half a dozen times I get up to tweak an item, only to sit down and see it's still not right. The pasta cools and the sauce congeals, while I tweak and check, check and tweak. Up and down I go. Up and down, like a robot with no control over its movements. I can't bear the lack of control and yet I can't fight it.

At eleven, I crash out on the sofa. As frazzled as the children, I fall asleep within minutes, too tired tonight to notice any discomfort, or for my worries to keep me awake.

So tired, I forget until morning that Dad didn't call about Fiona.

Sophie's head tapping wakes me again, though she's let me have a lie-in this time: it's six forty-five. I don't even attempt negotiations about staying in bed.

How can anyone stand this routine, day in, day out, and on so little sleep? A perpetual hamster wheel of cajoling them to wash and eat and get dressed, of playing games and breaking up fights, of taxiing them to school and friends and ballet and Beavers. Doing it all again the next day, and the next, and the next, for weeks and months and years. The thought alone makes me tired.

The children are weary, too, and still pale. Peaky, as Mum used to say when I was under the weather. Abandoning plans for another day out, I settle for the idle aunt's option: the television. To supplement that, I fish out every so-called children's film I own.

Idle Aunt's brainwave secures a thumb's up.

'Yeah!' says Harry. He scrabbles amongst the DVDs. 'I want *'spicable Me.'*

'Mummy doesn't let us watch television in the morning,' says Sophie.

'I'm not—' I say.

'I s'pose it's okay, though.' Sophie catches my eye. 'Have you got *Happy Feet?'*

They lie on the floor, two feet from the screen, to view Harry's choice first.

Sipping tea, half following the story, I wonder if it's too early to call Dad. I don't want to catch him and Marilyn in bed again. Thinking that puts the image in my head, which is just as bad.

I might as well risk it. I take the phone into the kitchen and shut the door.

It takes several rings for Dad to pick up. He sounds out of breath. My imagination goes into overdrive.

'Hi Dad, it's Clare.'

'Oh, Clare, hello. Is something wrong?'

'Er, apart from Fiona being ill, no. How did you get on at the hospital?' I tweak the line-up of cleaning products and sponges next to the sink.

'Fine. Yes, fine.'

'Did you find out what's happened?'

'Not really.'

'Not really? Either you did or you didn't!' I could scream at his vagueness. Instead, I straighten the already straight tea, coffee and sugar jars on the counter. 'Do you know what kind of ward she's on, at least?'

'Ward? Mmm… It seemed to be general.'

Helpful. I roll my eyes. 'A general surgical ward?'

'Yes, yes, that's it! A surgical ward.'

The Spanish Inquisition would have had it tough with Dad.

'Did Fiona not tell you?'

'No. Mmm…you know Fiona. She just gets on with it. She looked well, though. That's the main thing, eh?'

'Honestly, Dad, you are hopeless.' I shake my head in despair. He can't even bring himself to communicate properly when one of his own daughters is in trouble. 'I'll go and visit her when Dave gets back.' And make someone tell me something.

'Very good, dear.'

'Enjoy the rest of your day, Dad. Love you.'

'Yes, indeed. Bye, dear.' The line goes dead.

In the living room, I curl up on the sofa and we all watch one film after another. By the end of the third, the bright images have hypnotised me. I can't imagine moving, can't imagine anything beyond staring at the screen.

We stop only for food and toilet breaks. During those breaks, I realise that the children's mess is spreading like a rampant weed. Given their inactivity, I don't understand how; it's as if they're telekinetic. I watch as the mess strangles my home, clinging to the knowledge that I can partially reclaim it once they're asleep, and in twenty-four hours they'll be gone. I'll no longer have to accept short-term, small-scale fixes; life will return to normal – my pre-cure normal, at least. Until then, my world of order shrinks to the sofa, my island sanctuary. Every time I get up, I plump and rearrange the cushions. It's all I can do for now.

Dave calls in the early evening, to let me know what time he'll arrive tomorrow. The children exchange a few words with him.

Sophie offers the highlights of the weekend. 'A nasty girl spat at me and we watched television all day today and Auntie Clare said a rude word.'

When? I don't remember swearing.

Harry doesn't help. He jigs with excitement as he tells his dad, 'My toothbrush fell down the toilet and I hurt my knee and Auntie Clare wouldn't give me a plaster.'

What about the farm and the playground? Being a parent, even a stand-in one, is a thankless task.

I reassure Dave, 'His knee's all right and they were too tired to go out today and—'

'Clare, don't worry. I don't know what we'd have done without you. See you tomorrow.'

At bedtime, Sophie hugs me tightly and says, 'Auntie Clare, is Mummy going to die?'

'Of course not.' I'm horrified she thinks that. 'She'll be home soon.'

Sophie lies down next to Harry. 'Only, Olivia's mummy went to hospital and she died and then Olivia and her daddy went away.'

Harry looks anxious. 'Are we going away with Daddy?'

'No. No one's going to die and no one's going away.' As soon as the words are out, I wish I could suck them back in. I can't promise either of those things. Not indefinitely. 'Daddy'll take you home tomorrow and you'll see Mummy very soon.'

'I don't want to go home,' says Sophie. 'I like it better here.'

I'm pleased, even a little smug. I know I shouldn't ask why. 'Why?'

She purses her lips. 'Because Mummy and Daddy get cross and shout.'

'And Mummy cries,' says Harry, 'all the time.' He nods sagely.

'No, she doesn't, silly. Only when Daddy's not there,' says Sophie.

'All mummies and daddies fight,' I say. 'It's nothing to worry about.' I hope they believe me; I don't believe it myself. Fighting is one thing, Fiona crying is another. I'd assumed her tears at the birthday party were a one-off.

'But can we still come again?' says Sophie.

'We'll see what Mummy says.'

She pouts. 'She'll say no, like she always does.'

'You never know,' I say.

Sophie snuggles down, still pouting. I tuck Harry in. He's hugging his lorry to his chest. I have no idea how he'll sleep like that, though his eyelids are already drooping.

So are mine. I retreat to the sofa again. Surfing between mindless television programmes, I give myself five minutes' break before I sort out the flat. Just five minutes, then I'll get on.

I wake with a start. Glancing at the DVD player, I realise it's half past one. I've been asleep for three and a half hours. Groggily, I sit up and flick off the television. I have to tidy the flat.

Taking in the mess around me, though, I'm overwhelmed. It's too much to deal with. Just. Too. Much.

'Sod it!' The words ring out in the dead-of-night silence. 'No, really, I'm not doing it.' As if I'm disobeying someone, or something.

I stand up, fetch the sleeping bag from behind the sofa and unzip it. I get undressed quickly and climb in.

'Sod it,' I say, as I turn out the lamp. 'Sod it all.'

23

At six, I wake to the memory of my revolt. Eyes still closed, I let that memory sink in. Remember what I did – or rather, did not do. I wait for a reaction, for the racing pulse or churning stomach. Nothing. I open my eyes and gaze at the mess around me. I feel a slight jolt inside, like the stutter of a car on a cold morning, and then my body settles into an unfamiliar smooth running. I breathe in, slowly sit up, as if sudden movement might trigger a reaction. Still nothing. I'm a little scared; it's as if I've lost part of myself overnight. The calm should be welcome, but the mental vacuum is strangely unnerving and my body feels underoccupied without any of the usual stimulating effects of anxiety.

I tiptoe through the debris of DVD boxes, unwashed mugs and discarded sweet wrappers to the bookcase. An empty vase sits on top, exactly in the middle. Identical decorative candles stand six inches either side – never lit, to maintain their perfection. I nudge the vase a couple of inches off-centre. Stepping back, I consider the new arrangement. My heart rate goes up. Thank God.

I keep looking at the vase, waiting for the anxiety to dissipate. For once, it doesn't take long. Perhaps because I've moved something in an already chaotic environment. The vase is less out of place for not being the only thing out of place. Whenever I've tried to create a mess before, it stood out like the first scratch on a new car. The progress may be small, possibly fragile, but it is progress. The first embers of optimism glow in my mind.

I'm as much of a mess as the flat, having skipped washing during last night's rebellion. My mouth is stale, my skin greasy, my hair a Worzel Gummidge mop. As I'm up ahead of my usual head-tapping alarm, I manage to shower and clean my teeth before the children surface.

Sophie complains about wearing her school clothes from Friday. She has no choice; I overlooked washing them. A quick press with the steam iron freshens them up enough to pass for clean.

By seven, we're all dressed and breakfasted.

I dump her and Harry in front of the television to work on their square eyeballs while I tidy up. This time it's the kind of tidy-up normal people do for visitors: shuffling papers and magazines into loose piles, throwing stuff in cupboards, clearing up dirty crockery. My flat has been transformed into a home that's actually homely.

Half an hour later, the intercom sounds.

'Daddy!' The children race to open the flat door, while I buzz Dave into the entrance downstairs. They hop about in the doorway, jostling each other.

'Settle down, you two,' I say, as I join them.

Dave comes into view, trudging up the stairs. He smiles at Sophie and Harry, who run onto the landing, squealing. Dave reaches the top step and kneels down to hug them. Stubble stands out darkly against his skin, as do the shadows under his eyes. He looks shattered.

They swap kisses and then Dave stands up. 'Let's get inside before we wake the entire building.'

He steps forward and leans in to kiss me. 'Hi, Clare.' He's wearing a suit that gives off a musty odour of sweat and work and travel; Dad used to bring the same smell home. Flecks of grey glint in Dave's hair and the wrinkle above his nose is carved deeper. He has aged in the four months since I last saw him.

I touch his arm. 'It's good to see you.' Unexpectedly, it really is. I regret that we have lost touch, that my view of him has, of late, become second-hand, filtered through Fiona's bitterness and frustration. Seeing him again, I remember what a fundamentally decent man he is.

Dave's shoulders sag, as he moves inside. The children run on ahead, back into the living room. He bends down and unlaces his shoes. 'God, it's good to get out of these.' He flexes and stretches his toes, as he straightens up.

'You look tired. Feel free to freshen up.' I wave in the direction of the bathroom. 'Help yourself to anything you need. Can I get you a drink?'

He smiles wearily. 'Thanks. Coffee, please. It might help with the jet lag. I'm too old for all this gallivanting.' He heads down the hall, shrugging off his jacket.

He's ready just as the coffee is. The minty smell of mouthwash wafts into the kitchen with him. The front of his hair is wet, with bits sticking up like Harry's. I take his jacket from him and hang it over the back of one of the chairs.

'Thanks.' He sits down at the table.

'It's more comfortable in the living room,' I say. 'I'll bring your coffee in.'

He shakes his head. 'I'm not up to whatever that is.' A children's show blares across the hall.

I smile. 'I know what you mean.' I hand Dave his drink and take a seat opposite him.

'Having kids around is a shock to the system, isn't it?' he says.

'You can say that again.' He'll never know how much of a shock.

'They seem happy, though. You've done all right, kiddo.'

Kiddo. He's always treated me like the little sister he never had. I'd have preferred an older brother; things might have worked out differently. At least I wouldn't have had to contend with a reluctant substitute mum.

'How's Fiona?' I say. 'Have you heard any more?'

'No. The hospital says she's on the mend, but she wants to talk to me about it herself. I'll call in this afternoon. I'm sure everything's fine.'

'Dad wasn't able to tell me anything, either. Phone me when you have any news.' I'm far from sure things are well. 'And how are you?'

'Same old, same old. You know?'

'Fiona said you were working hard.'

'Did she now?'

Thin ice looms. I step onto it. 'It's a shame you see so little of her and the children.'

'I don't think she would agree. She prefers it when I'm not at home.'

'That's not true, Dave. She's under a lot of pressure.'

'Well, if she is, she's brought it on herself. She insists on doing everything. God knows what she's trying to prove. It doesn't make her an easy person to be with.' Dave rubs his face. 'Sorry. I shouldn't have said that.'

'I know what you mean, believe me.'

'Still, I don't want to drag you into our problems.' Dave looks at his watch. 'Crikey, the kids'll be late.' He gulps his coffee, standing up as he tilts the mug to catch the last drops. 'Sophie, Harry, let's get ready to go, please.'

I fetch the bags of new clothes and toys and the children's school backpacks.

Sophie takes hers and looks inside. 'Where's my lunch, Auntie Clare?'

'Lunch?' Stricken, I look at Dave. 'Sorry, I didn't think. I could quickly do some sandwiches? I've got pâté.'

'I don't like pâté.' Sophie wrinkles her nose.

I know that's a fib; Fiona said the children love it.

'Don't worry,' says Dave. 'They can have school lunch for a change.'

'Eurgghh, I don't want school lunch.' Sophie's nose twitches like a rabbit's.

'Sophie, stop making a fuss. I don't have time to argue,' says Dave.

She stamps her foot. 'School lunch is horrid!' She stamps again.

'Sophie, stop that! What on earth has got into you?' Her father's tone puts an immediate end to both her arguing and stamping.

At the front door, I smile to see Dave checking that the loose ends of his shoelaces are the same length before tying them. Sometimes he pulls them backward and forward through the holes, again and again, until they're right. I can relate to the habit, but it's just another source of irritation for Fiona. He even does it when he's in a hurry, like now.

Sophie is too busy sulking to say goodbye. Harry, cuddling his lorry, gives me a damp kiss.

'Thanks, again, Clare,' says Dave.

He shepherds the children down the stairs. The outside door slams shut and they're gone.

24

I can't wait to tell Tom how much I've achieved. The children's visit was one long exposure exercise, with no choice but to accept the mess. If I can do it for them, I can do it for him.

I call him when I get in from work. We haven't spoken for a week – not since the night I suggested we have time apart. So much has happened that it feels longer.

His response isn't what I expected. 'This is a surprise. I thought we were on a break?' His words are muffled, as if his mouth is too close to the phone.

'That doesn't mean we can't talk.'

'I didn't know the rules.'

'Are you all right? You don't sound yourself.'

'I'm okay. Hang on a sec.' His voice becomes distant. 'The wineglasses are in the second cupboard along, top shelf. Sorry, I moved them.' Then, louder, 'Hi, I'm back.'

'Tom, if this is a bad time…' Whoever is with him appears to be familiar with, and comfortable in, his cottage. Vicky?

'No, it's fine. What's up?'

'I wanted to let you know I'm making really good progress,' I say.

'With your tidying and stuff?'

'Yes.' What else would I be making progress with?

'Already?' He sounds surprised – or is it disappointed?

'Yes, already. Fiona's not well, so I had the children to stay and I actually coped. With the mess, I mean. Not at first, but then something clicked.' It's as hard to explain as it was when I first opened up to him.

'That's great, Clare. Don't get too carried away, though, will you? It's only been a week. You shouldn't try to run before you can walk.'

No ordinary week, though. The intensity of the last few days has been the equivalent of weeks of my previously half-hearted self-help.

'I'm not getting carried away, but it's a start, isn't it?' I wonder why I'm bothering. It's as if he doesn't want me to get better.

'Of course, it's fantastic, and I'm really pleased for you. I just don't want you to be disappointed if there are setbacks. From what I've read, they're to be expected.'

Instant expert Tom again.

'I know that. I know there's a long way to go, but I thought you'd be happy about how well it's going?'

'I am, beautiful, I—' In the background, I hear a female voice, the words indistinguishable, and high heels clacking on the cottage's stone floor. 'Yeah, it's Clare,' says Tom. 'Er, Bex says hi.'

'What's she doing there?' Bad enough that she sees him at the pub; this is a real invasion of my space – what I soon expect to be my space, anyway. Jealousy curdles my stomach; she's so glamorous, so together, compared with me.

'She brought me a bottle of wine… As a thank you… For mending her leaky tap.' I don't need to see Tom to know he's blushing.

'I'd better leave you to it, then. Whatever *it* is,' I say.

'Jeez, Clare.' He lowers his voice. 'It's not like that.'

'Like what? Look, I'd better go. I've got things to do. Bye.'

'Please, don't. Clare? Please. I love—'

I hang up.

As my breath comes faster, my mouth goes dry. I can hardly think straight. Bex seems to rule Tom's life. I don't trust her, and now I'm no longer sure about him. No sooner are we apart, than she's back on the scene. She might fling herself at him again; she might have already done so. And then what?

Retrieving my mobile from my handbag, I log onto Facebook and key in Tom's name. He hardly ever posts, but I bet she does – the last time I saw her, she was taking a selfie with a customer – and they're bound to be friends. They are. I click on her name to get to her page. If she's discreet, it won't tell me much, but it's my only possible source of information.

I see the photo straightaway: she and Tom cheek to cheek, with a couple of men I don't recognise gurning above them. The shot was posted on Saturday, with the simple tag *at The White Horse*. I scan her timeline, but there are no other photos of her and Tom in her recent past, and only one or two featuring her boyfriend, Keith.

Clicking onto her photo gallery, I scroll through to when she and Tom must have been a couple: there is shot after shot of them.

They look good together – happy and relaxed in every picture. Seeing them like that adds to my torment. My heart pounds. Have the feelings they shared only a year or so ago really gone?

They seem to be much more than friends, even now, and Bex's current *Relationship status* is, I notice, blank. Yet I still can't quite believe it of Tom. I just don't know any more and not knowing is hard to bear. I log out of Facebook and put the phone back in my bag.

The uncertainty has rendered the mess around me suddenly intolerable, propelling me to put it right. As my hands tidy and straighten, I grow increasingly disappointed with myself. Disappointed that I've let the situation upset me so much. Disappointed that, in moments, I've allowed it to undo everything I've accomplished. I wonder whether I'll be able to regain that ground and, if I do, how quickly I might lose it again. I try to shake off the disappointment, to restore my budding optimism – and disprove Tom's warning.

When I've finally finished, I realise that I haven't yet heard from Dave. It's nine; he must have been to the hospital by now. I phone him to find out.

'Clare?' He sounds drowsy.

'Sorry, did I wake you?'

'S'okay, I must have nodded off.' Scuffling and a stifled yawn. I picture him sitting up, rubbing his tired eyes.

'Any news on Fiona?' I peel a sticky note off the pad. My hand hovers over the base of the phone. Then I put the note back. I have to try to stop.

'Not much I can tell you, I'm afraid. I meant to call earlier. The kids…you know?'

'What do you mean, "not much"?' He's as bad as Dad. One side of the dislodged sticky note hangs over the rest of the pad. I pick at its edge, lifting it slightly, and press it down again – like picking at a scab.

'Fiona asked me not to tell you. I'm sorry, Clare.'

I close my eyes, visualise my ten-year-old self standing in the living room doorway. Mum, Dad and Fiona in a huddle on the sofa, whispering. Dad holding Mum's hand. Fiona crying. The whispering stops when they see me. They drift apart slowly and silently, like moving underwater, and carry on as if nothing has happened. No one speaks about it and I don't ask. It's easy to believe I imagined it. Until it happens again. And again. Each time, I retreat from the silences into tidying. Then Mum dies and I understand. I didn't imagine those moments of isolation. They were part of a nightmare I was living without knowing it.

I won't go through that again, won't be cut off from the people I love, because they want to shield me from pain. That kind of loneliness is more painful than any grief I might be spared.

'Dave, you have to tell me. I have a right to know.' My voice wobbles, my eyes fill with tears. The child is just beneath the surface.

'I'm sorry, kiddo. I promised.'

The tears roll down my cheeks. He wants to tell me; he understands how important it is to me. Fiona doesn't, or she wouldn't have gagged him.

'Clare, please don't get upset,' says Dave.

I grind the tears away with the heel of my hand. 'I'm fine. So long as Fiona is?'

'She is, it's just…'

Please, Dave, please.

'It's not what you think,' he says. 'You have to believe me. She isn't seriously ill.'

'I believe you,' I say.

I don't, though. I won't until I see Fiona for myself. The only way to discover the truth is to tackle her face to face.

25

Fiona's bed is at the end of the ward, next to the wall. She's sitting bolt upright, the covers smooth over her legs, flicking irritably through a glossy magazine. She stands out from the patients around her, with their slumped bodies and rumpled bedclothes. Although she appears focussed on the magazine, she doesn't stop on any page long enough to read it; as if she were in a doctor's waiting room, expecting to be called at any moment, not really belonging.

As I approach her oasis of order, I realise she isn't immune to her circumstances. She's wearing an old-fashioned, long-sleeved nightgown, with a pattern of roses swirling across it. Possibly donated by Marilyn – it certainly won't be from her own wardrobe. And her hair is lank; the russet bob has lost its shine and sharp edges. Her customary well-groomed look is decidedly frayed, in spite of her finishing school posture.

She looks up. 'Clare! I didn't expect to see you.'

I lean over to kiss her. Up close, dark circles are visible under her eyes. 'Why not? It's normal to visit people in hospital.'

'I'll be out in a couple of days. It's hardly worth it.'

'Still. I wanted to.' I hold out a box of her favourite chocolate truffles. 'I brought you these.'

'Thanks.' She puts down the magazine, takes the box and then immediately hands it back to me, nodding towards the bedside locker. 'Could you put them in there for me? I can't reach.'

'Of course.'

The locker is between the bed and the wall. I walk around and open it. An identical box of chocolates is on one shelf. From Dave, probably. I put my box on top and push both to the back corner, to line them up.

'What are you doing?' says Fiona.

'Nothing.' I close the door.

Back on the other side of the bed, I pull up a hard-backed chair. It's low, forcing me to crane my neck to maintain eye contact with her.

'Thanks for having the children. I know they can be a handful,' she says. 'I hear Sophie was creating about not having a packed lunch?'

'They were fine,' I say. She would have to focus on that oversight. I'm sure Dave's report included more positive elements. 'Anyway, how are you feeling?'

'All right.' She rubs her temple. 'Or I would be, if it weren't so ridiculously hot. Between that and the noise, it's intolerable.'

'Are you sure you're all right?'

'It's just a headache.'

'Do you want a painkiller?' I unzip my handbag.

Fiona raises an eyebrow. 'I'm surrounded by medical staff, Clare. If I need a painkiller, I'll ask for one.'

'Of course, sorry.' My chair seems to shrink; I feel even smaller. I re-zip the bag and sit quietly for a moment. I haven't considered what to say to her. How to broach the subject of what's wrong. Being in a hospital, though, it's the most natural thing to talk about.

'I was wondering what's, er...what's the food like?'

'The food? Dreadful.' Fiona's face twists, as if in pain. 'It would make you ill, if you weren't already.'

I can't ignore the opening. 'About that, Fi...'

Her head turns sharply towards me. She knows that I know the subject is taboo.

I fiddle with my handbag zipper. 'What was...is wrong with you? Exactly.' I force myself to look at her.

'Clare, you know I don't want to talk about that.' Her expression and tone are those of a teacher admonishing a pupil – I'm sure she's had plenty of practice with her students. Any second now, she'll tell me she's not angry, just disappointed. I feel as if I'm getting smaller and smaller, as if the floor is coming up towards me – like Alice after the miniaturising potion.

'You must understand why I'm concerned, though?' I say.

'No, I don't. Dave told you there was nothing to worry about, didn't he?'

'He said it wasn't serious, but internal bleeding's hardly a minor problem.'

Paper rustles on the bed behind me. I glance over my shoulder. The occupant, a woman in her fifties, is reading a soaps' magazine. Her body is stiff with listening. It's easy to forget we're in public. Sitting by Fiona's bed creates the same illusion of privacy as

158

a restaurant table. An illusion that tricks you into sharing secrets with strangers.

'I just need to know, Fi. Why did you have to have surgery?'

'No, you don't need to know,' she says. 'All that matters is I'm all right now.'

'Fi, don't shut me out. Don't. Not this time.'

'Please don't make a scene, Clare. You're not a child.'

'Then don't treat me like one! Tell me. I'm not leaving till you do.' I lean back in my seat and cross my arms. The chair digs painfully into my back. I don't care; I won't move, however long it takes. They'll have to carry me out at the end of visiting hours.

Fiona picks up her magazine, stares at the cover. I stare at her.

Our corner becomes a vacuum of silence in the ward's bustle. As the minutes pass, the silence gets deeper, thicker, pushing back the noise around us.

'Fi, tell me!'

She slaps the magazine down on the bed. 'For goodness' sake! I was pregnant, it was ectopic, it's over. It's over, Clare.'

'Oh, Fiona, I'm so sorry. Why didn't you tell me?'

'Because I didn't want all this fuss.'

'You've lost a baby. What do you expect?'

'It wasn't a baby, though, was it? It was just something growing in the wrong place. Like a tumour.'

A sharp intake of breath comes from the bed behind me.

'Fiona! That's a horrible thing to say.'

'It's true, Clare. It was never going to be a baby.'

'But you thought it was, until this. How did you know something was wrong?'

Her eyes flit around the ward. 'Clare, do we have to talk about this?'

'I just want to know what happened.'

'What happened was I thought I had a bad stomach. Then my tube ruptured and I collapsed. That's it.'

'Jesus, you could have died!' Like Mum.

'Yes, but I didn't, so there's no point in dwelling on it.'

A flurry of activity nearby distracts me. I twist around. A middle-aged man and a teenage girl have arrived at the soap fan's bedside. Presumably her husband and daughter. The woman looks pleadingly at Fiona, then me. Her silent entreaties are futile; she has to give her attention to her own family, to their hugs and kisses and chat. She'll miss the end of this particular story.

I turn back to Fiona. 'Your hormones must be all over the place. You'll need time to get over it, whatever you say.'

'Believe me, Clare. There's nothing to get over.'

'It might hit you when you're not expecting it.' I reach for her hand. She pulls it away.

'Clare, please listen to me. I'm not in shock and I'm not upset. I didn't want a baby; it was just another accident.' She shakes her head. 'God knows how, I hardly ever see Dave.'

'What do you mean, another accident?'

Fiona lets her head drop back on the pillows, closes her eyes. 'Clare, please.'

'Do you mean Sophie? Or Harry?'

She ignores me.

'Or both?'

She opens her eyes, wearily says, 'Sophie, if you must know. Sophie was an accident.'

'A happy one, though?'

'Hardly. Dave had to talk me out of an abortion.'

I gasp.

'Don't, Clare, please. Don't look at me like that.' The words are beseeching, rather than imperative.

'Like what?'

'Like I'm a terrible mother. I'm not. I love Sophie. I love both my children. That doesn't mean I wouldn't have done things differently.'

I could weep for Sophie. How can Fiona really love her, if she'd rather have aborted her? 'I don't understand,' I say.

She sighs. 'You should. You know I had to put my life on hold to look after you. University, teacher training, career. Just as I was getting somewhere, I found out I was pregnant. It was like some bad cosmic joke.'

'It's not my fault your life turned out that way. If anyone's responsible, it's Dad. Why do you never take it out on him?'

'He was depressed. He couldn't cope. He could hardly look after himself.'

'Well, neither could I, Fiona. I was a child. You can't blame me for that.'

It has gone quiet behind me. The family next to us has tuned in to our miserable soap.

'At least Dad knew Mum was dying,' I say. 'At least you both had a chance to prepare. What about me? How was I supposed to deal with it?'

'I know, we should have told you. Mum made us promise not to. What could I do?' Her eyes fill with tears. 'What could I do, Clare?'

'What? I thought you'd all agreed I was too young to be told?' As a teenager, I'd repeatedly challenged Fiona about Mum's illness being secret. 'Why didn't you tell me the truth?'

A tear rolls down her cheek. 'I didn't want you to be angry with Mum. It was bad enough that you'd lost her.'

So she let me be angry with her instead – the only one left to blame, with Mum gone and Dad too remote to reach.

I'm stricken by the revelation, and by having distressed Fiona so much. 'I'm so sorry, I didn't know—'

'Is everything all right over here?' A nurse appears at my left shoulder.

'Fine, thank you,' I say.

The nurse glances at Fiona. 'Mrs Mercer needs to rest now. Perhaps you should pop back tomorrow?' She's throwing me out, albeit charmingly.

'I'll do that. Thank you.' I stand up, lean over to kiss Fiona's damp cheek. Her skin is hot.

'I'll see you soon.' As I turn to leave, I stumble over my chair.

The man sitting by the next bed half rises and grabs my arm. 'Steady, love, I've got you.'

His wife tuts. 'For Gawd's sake, Derek, stop mauling the girl.'

Her husband goes red, lets go of my arm and sits down. Their daughter stares at me for a moment and then looks away. If I'm leaving, the drama is over.

I stumble out of the ward, my vision blurred by unshed tears. I feel every patient, every visitor, every nurse, watching me walk out. Everyone, I'm sure, except Fiona.

The tears trickle down my face as I weave through the corridors. I duck my head to hide them. No one pays any attention. Teary-eyed visitors are hardly unusual.

At the main hospital entrance, I look for somewhere to sit down, to compose myself. There aren't many spare seats; I squeeze between a fat man with a bloodied bandage around his arm and a woman with a toddler on her lap.

My heart thumps. My fingers clench and unclench around the

strap of my handbag. I need to calm down. Opening the bag, I make the checks that usually serve to soothe me.

I don't feel any better when I've finished. The hubbub around me has shattered my concentration; I can't be sure I've checked properly. I start again. As I pull the zip open, my elbow jabs the fat man's stomach.

'Mind what you're doing!' He rubs his belly.

'Sorry.' I zip up the bag. I have to complete the checks without interruption; they won't work otherwise. I begin again. I press my elbows into my sides and tug at the zip. Then, check, check, check the contents. Next, the outside pockets. I unzip the first one, but feel someone watching me. I look up. The toddler, flushed and feverish, stares at me with wide, blue eyes.

Sweat trickles down my back. I have to get out of here. I push myself to my feet, offering no apology as I jog the man next to me again. He grunts in protest.

Outside I gulp in the cool evening air as gratefully as if I've been held under water. I sway as I breathe slowly, deeply.

In the sanctuary of my car, I go through my handbag again. It takes three attempts to run the checks uninterrupted. A car alarm bursts into life halfway through the first. On the second, a boy roller-blades past. The third time, I hold my breath against any distractions, which is almost a distraction in itself. Finally, though, it's done. I have recovered enough to drive home.

Back at the flat, I cave in completely to my urges. Safe from prying eyes and interruptions, I can check and tweak and straighten for as long as I want. For as long as it takes to stop thinking about Fiona and Mum.

I feel guilty for blaming Fiona all these years, but it was her choice: she could have told me the truth when I was old enough to hear it. Let a dead woman be the rightful target of my rage, rather than allowing it to damage a living relationship.

And what about Mum? In the twenty years since her death, my unconditional love hasn't wavered. My feelings are too fossilised to change now: it's too late for me to be angry with her.

The phone rings. I freeze with my hand on a vase. Perhaps if I stop dead, it won't feel like an interruption; I can carry on when the caller has hung up. Obsessive-compulsive musical statues.

The answerphone greeting plays out, followed by a booming voice. 'Clare? Michael, here. Just returning your message—'

With all that has happened in the last few days, I'd forgotten that I hadn't heard back from him. I loosen my grip on the vase, inadvertently nudging it to the right. Making a mental note to reposition it later, I lunge to grab the phone before he hangs up.

'Michael! Hi, it's great to hear from you. How are you?'

'Good. Very good, in fact. I've been overseas, tying up a tricky deal. All signed and sealed now. Should be a nice bit of business. Quite a money-spinner.'

'Congratulations.' I sit down, suddenly weary.

'The client operates all over Europe, so lots of potential work.'

'Sounds promising.' I straighten the sticky notepad on the table. 'You got my message?'

'Yes. Couldn't call till I was home. Wall-to-wall meetings. You know how it is?'

'Of course.' He's here for me now, that's the main thing.

'So, what's wrong?' says Michael.

'What isn't?' I gabble it all out to him. The argument with Tom. Our temporary separation. Fiona's emergency admission to hospital. Looking after the children. My fleeting progress in dealing with my compulsions.

'Why don't we meet up and sort all of this out?' He's firm, businesslike. 'Nothing is ever as bad as it seems.'

'I'd like that,' I say. 'I'd like that very much.'

We arrange to meet at Granvilles again, on Saturday. Four days to wait, yet already I feel better. Michael may have been slow to call back, but his timing has turned out to be perfect. He says we'll sort things out and I believe him.

26

In the morning, I remember that the next support group meeting is on Thursday: only two days away. Michael must have forgotten, too; he didn't mention it yesterday. We won't have privacy to talk, but it will be good to see him, and his friendship makes this second visit less nerve-wracking. I text him a reminder, but he must have become tied up with work again, as he doesn't respond.

It's mild on the evening of the meeting, with a hint of summer in the air, and I feel optimistic as I shoulder open the heavy door into the hall.

A small group of people is already assembled; Michael isn't amongst them. I grab a chair from the stacks against the wall and join the circle. Albert is a couple of seats away, clutching a packet of wet wipes. He winks at me and hands the packet to his wife, Betty, who is sitting between us.

'Down to ten a day and I've had me ten,' he says. 'Don't want to blow it, eh?'

'Good for you,' I say.

Albert smiles proudly. Betty, who was part of the carers' group last time, gazes lovingly at him. I envy them their relationship.

Katie, the counting girl, is also here, with her mother, though her grouchy father is absent. Katie is pale and drawn, and looks as if she's been crying. She clutches her handbag to her chest. Her lips move; I can't hear what she's saying. Her mother's arm is around her rigid shoulders.

I mouth 'Hi'. Only Katie's mother responds, with a fleeting smile.

Over at the stage, Heather unpacks drinks and plastic cups. A thin, young man talks earnestly to her. He has a nervous tic: his head jerks, as though he's recoiling from a succession of slaps. With every movement, his dark, tousled hair quivers.

The door to the hall creaks open; someone holds it ajar for a moment. My heart races. I can't tell if it's Michael. A metallic clanking makes everyone look around. A woman carrying a mop and bucket hobbles in.

Heather steps forward. 'Annie, sorry, we're in here this evening. Can you come back later?'

The cleaner edges backward out of the room, looking cross.

I slump in my seat, disappointed.

The door opens again. I straighten up. This time it's an overweight woman wearing a bright silk scarf like a turban. She sits down next to me, smiling at everyone. Wisps of hair curl around her neck. She seems to have very little, presumably the result of chemotherapy. I'm ashamed to be coping so badly; at least I don't have cancer to contend with.

As the woman scans the group, I catch her eye and smile.

She holds out her hand. 'Hi, I'm Ruth.' My knuckles click under the pressure of her grip. She's strong for someone enduring such toxic, energy-sapping treatment.

'Clare. Hi.' I pull my hand away as quickly as I can without being rude.

Heather takes a seat, between Katie and Albert. Albert greets her. Katie continues murmuring under her breath. Her big eyes are vacant.

The man with the tic is last to sit down, Ruth on one side of him, Katie's mother on the other. He sprawls in his chair, his long legs stretched in front of him. His bony knees poke through rips in his jeans.

It's seven-thirty. Time to start. I will the door to open, for Michael to appear. He must be caught at work.

With only seven of us this time, including the two family members, we all stay together. Again, introductions follow Heather's welcome. There are no newcomers this evening: Ruth and the man with the tic are regulars, who were unable to attend last time.

As Ruth talks, the reason for her scarf becomes clear: she's a hair puller. A different kind of obsessive urge that I now remember reading about in my self-help book: trichotillomania.

She's cheerful about her hair loss. 'The doctors say most of it won't grow back, so I'm going to buy loads of wigs and have some fun.'

'Like Cher?' says Albert.

Betty offers to look out an old beehive wig. She turns to Albert. 'It's in the loft, isn't it, dear?'

'You needn't think I'm going up there, with all that dust and the

Lord knows what else.' He shudders. 'Sorry, love,' he says to Ruth.

Everyone laughs.

The main issue for the man with the tic, Neil, is his intrusive thoughts about hurting his parents.

'I live with 'em, 'cause I can't get a job,' he says. 'I'm stuck in my room all day. Dunno what might happen otherwise. Mum brings food up and leaves it outside, and I've got a telly and stuff, you know? S'boring, though.' His head jerks. The dark halo of his just-out-of-bed hair vibrates. 'Makes a change bein' 'ere.'

Then it's back to Albert for a full progress report: in his case, short, sweet and successful. 'We've saved a fortune on wipes and soap and cleaning whatnots.' He beams. 'And now that I'm not stuck in the bathroom all day, I've got more time for the wife.' He turns towards her. 'Not sure she thinks that's a good thing, though.'

Betty tuts. 'Don't talk so daft, Albert.'

It's my turn before I've decided whether to summarise my last month as good or bad. I quickly opt to focus on the good: my own improvements have been temporary, but, with Michael's help, I can build on them. I only wish he were here now.

'I had to have my niece and nephew to stay for the whole weekend and it went really well,' I say. A minor embellishment of the facts. 'It made me see things differently.' Which is true.

'Well done,' says Heather. 'Have you been doing the self-help exercises?'

'As much as possible.'

'And have you told your boyfriend?'

I fiddle with the strap of my handbag. 'Yes.'

'How did that go?' Heather's voice is gentle.

'Not so good. We're working on it.' I smile. 'On the whole, things are all right.'

'Why didn't it go well?' says Heather.

Damn, I thought we'd finished.

'He said my compulsions weren't a problem. He didn't really understand what they involve.' I look to the door. Michael, where are you?

'It can be difficult for other people at first,' says Heather. 'Give him time.'

'I will.'

'Good. Is there anything else you're concerned about?'

'No, I don't think so.' I say. 'Well, I did wonder about one thing… Is it true that Tom shouldn't compromise?'

'What do you mean by compromise?' Heather leans forward.

'You know.' I twirl the handbag strap around my fingers. 'Doing things my way to help me.'

Heather frowns.

'Not exactly my way, of course,' I say. 'I just mean, more tidy. And putting things back where they were.'

'Remember what we discussed last time, Clare?' says Heather. 'Other people shouldn't pander to your behaviour.'

The room is stuffy, the air oppressive. The underarms of my tee shirt are getting damp. 'But that's not what…'

'Yes?' she says.

I look around the group. They're all watching me, waiting. Even Katie has come out of her stupor to stare at me with bleary eyes.

'It's just that…I know someone with compulsions, whose ex-wife was happy to fit in with them,' I say.

'Ex-wife?'

'It's not what you think. That's not why they split up.'

'Nevertheless, I doubt his ex was as happy as your friend has led you to believe.'

'I'm sure Mi…' I clear my throat. 'I'm sure my friend's telling the truth. Why wouldn't he?' I wish Michael were here to back me up.

'I don't know, Clare, and he's not here for us to ask.'

I look sharply at Heather. Does she know who I mean?

'Just keep working at your exercises,' she says. 'And no compromises!'

'Okay. Thanks.' Her view is clear and confirms my resolve to go it alone in tackling my problems.

She turns her attention to Ruth. 'Are you managing to resist the hair pulling?'

Ruth flushes. 'What's the use? It's too late.' She fingers a tendril of hair at the base of her neck. I tense, hoping she doesn't pull any out.

'It's never too late,' says Heather. 'The doctors may be wrong about it not growing back.'

Ruth's eyes fill with tears. 'But it's so hard.' Her earlier flippancy and cheerfulness were obviously a façade.

'I know what you mean,' I say. Ruth can no more snap out of hair pulling than I can snap out of my need for order and perfection. Than either of us could snap out of any illness, mental or physical. The condition may cause distress, but addressing it is equally anxiety inducing.

Ruth smiles weakly.

'Everyone finds it hard,' says Heather. 'We're here to support each other.'

Neil and Katie have made no progress either.

While Neil talks, his head jerks violently. The jerks become stronger and more frequent as he goes on.

'Mum and Dad don't get what's goin' on,' he says. 'It was okay to hang out in my room when I was a lad. I'm twenty-three now, for fuck's sake.' His head jerks three times in quick succession. 'Sorry about the language, ladies.' His eyes flit around the circle.

'And you haven't talked to anyone else about this?' says Heather.

'Who'm I gonna talk to? I ain't got no friends no more. This tic's so bad. Who'd want to be seen with me?'

'Is that what they say?'

'Nah, but I can tell. I must be a right joke to 'em. Fucking Nervous Tic Neil.'

'Are any of them still in touch with you?' says Heather.

'Yeah, I ain't going out with 'em, though. I don't want 'em taking the piss.'

'I'm sorry to hear that, Neil. If they want to see you, they must like you. Most of us don't bother with people we don't like.'

'S'easier bein' on my own. They'd run a mile if they knew about all them things I think about Mum and Dad.' He grunts. 'It'd be all right if I had me own gaff. Fuck, I can't even go in the kitchen, 'cause of the knives.'

I've never had those kind of thoughts, but I'd feel the same as Neil, if I feared hurting someone I loved.

'Least here, I can't do no one no 'arm, you know?' he says. 'I can't go nowhere else to get away. People laugh at me, jerking around like a fucking freak.' He jerks again, twice. 'Sorry, sorry.'

I can't imagine his world; it's no better than being in prison.

'Spend more time with your parents,' says Heather. 'You have to expose yourself to your fear, to prove it's unfounded.'

'Yeah? Well, don't blame me when it all goes wrong.' Neil shakes with a series of tiny twitches. 'For fuck's sake.' He leans forward, rests his elbows on his knees and puts his head in his hands. He clutches his tangled hair. 'Sorry, guys. Sorry.'

'Don't worry, Neil,' Heather says. 'Let's move on to Katie.'

Katie doesn't want to talk. She hangs her head, her hair falling over her face, while her mother speaks. 'Katie's dad walked out at the weekend. He's gone to his brother's. He'll be back; he just needs time away from it all. Katie mustn't blame herself.' She strokes her daughter's hair off her face, her own twisted with concern.

Katie's eyes fill with tears. Her throat rises and falls as she swallows.

'She won't listen,' says her mother. 'I made her come tonight, so you can tell her.'

'Katie, your mother's right,' says Heather. 'You're doing your best, and so's your father. It's tough on all of you.'

Katie shakes her head, her chin trembling.

'Let's all have a chat in the last half-hour about what our family and friends can do to help us, and how we can help them,' says Heather.

The atmosphere is subdued, as we break up for drinks. An hour of such intense emotion and mental struggle is draining, even for those with good news to share.

After pouring myself a juice, I join Albert and his wife.

'Any idea where Michael got to this evening?' I say.

'Michael? Not a clue, love,' says Albert. 'Thought you'd know better than us. You seemed quite taken with him.' He nudges me with his elbow.

'Hardly, I'm engaged, remember.' I waggle my left hand at him – and realise I didn't put my ring back on after showering. I let my hand drop.

'Maybe he took a shine to you.' Albert winks. 'He doesn't usually hang about afterwards.'

'I don't think so.' I'm flattered all the same.

'Albert, don't embarrass the girl!' His wife slaps at his arm.

'I'm just saying—' he insists.

'Well, don't!' She slaps his arm again.

'He's a funny cove, any road,' says Albert. 'Doesn't have much to say for himself. He's…what's that word, Betty?'

'Antisocial?' She arches an eyebrow.

'No, no. He's…' Albert's forehead furrows. 'Enigmatic! That's it, enigmatic.'

'Enigmatic, my foot! Downright strange, I say.' Betty turns to me. 'Sorry, dear, I shouldn't talk about your friend like that.'

'No, that's all right. Each to their own,' I say.

Their comments are incomprehensible, though. Michael has only ever been kind to me.

27

I get home to an odd answerphone message from Dad. 'Marilyn's asked me to invite you over. Tomorrow night. For dinner.'

A woman's voice whispers in the background: Marilyn herself, no doubt.

'There's someone she'd like you to meet,' he says. Then, after more whispering, 'Sorry. At seven. For dinner. Hope you can come?'

Dinner at Dad's is the last thing I need, let alone with a mystery guest, but as I reach for the phone to make my excuses, I hesitate. The tone of his final words was odd. I replay the message and hear the note of desperation straining his voice. Curiosity gets the better of me. Something is up and, for once, I'm going to find out what. I leave a return message, accepting the invitation.

When he opens the door the following evening, I do a double take. I saw him less than a month ago, yet it might as well have been a year. His beard has gone, as has his uniform of baggy, corduroy trousers and button-through shirt – length of sleeve determined by season. He's wearing jeans and a yellow polo shirt that reveals weight loss around his midriff. I glance over his shoulder, as if my real dad might be hiding behind this alien being.

'What's with the new clothes?' I peck his cheek, recoiling involuntarily at the smoothness of his skin. It's like kissing a stranger.

'Don't you like them, dear?' Dad fingers the open neck of his top.

'They're fine, just...different.' At least Marilyn hasn't got *him* into a tunic. 'And what's happened to your beard?'

'I shaved it.'

'I didn't think it had upped and run away. I meant, why have you shaved it?'

He touches his finger to the snail trail scar running from his lower lip to the bottom of his chin. The skin around it is pink, like new skin after a burn. I've never seen his scar; in fact, I've never seen his chin.

'Marilyn says it makes me look younger.'

I tilt my head and study him for a moment. Try to see him objectively, rather than as deforested Dad.

'She's right,' I say. His beard was greyer than his hair; it made him look old. Without that, and his frumpy clothes, he's no longer an unkempt man of the hills. 'It was a shock, that's all. You don't look like you any more.'

Dad shuffles his feet. He's wearing his threadbare tartan slippers. Thank God. No sandals – or, worse, mules or espadrilles.

Marilyn appears in the hall. 'I thought I heard voices.' She stretches up to kiss me. Her cheek is soft and powdery. Something has changed about her, too; her skin glows, her eyes sparkle.

'What do you think about your dad's new look?' she says. 'He took some persuading, but as I told him, he's fifty-eight, not eighty-eight. No need to dress like an old man.'

Yes, fifty-eight, not twenty-eight. I wonder whether he can really carry off jeans? They're a supermarket brand, though, with an elasticated waist – designed for middle-aged men.

'He's lost so much weight, too.' She pats the not insubstantial remains of his belly. 'It's taken years off him. He'd pass for forty-eight, don't you think?'

Dad blushes.

'I suppose...' I have no desire for him to look as if he fathered me in his teens.

'I'll get Nick,' says Marilyn. 'He's been looking forward to meeting you.' She walks through the kitchen to the back door, her long, silver-grey hair swinging to the rhythm of her hips.

'Who's Nick?' I ask Dad.

'Her son.'

'Which one?'

Dad ambles into the living room. 'The younger one. The junkie.' He says *junkie* as if it's a foreign word he's unsure how to pronounce.

'I thought they'd lost touch?' I follow him to the patio window.

Marilyn is at the end of the garden, her arm linked through that of a tall man in chinos and a pink polo shirt. Perhaps she dresses him, too.

'They had. He turned up a few days ago.' Dad rubs his scar. 'He said he'd given up drugs for good and was making a new start.'

Nick is smoking. He lifts his chin and blows a perfect smoke ring. Marilyn looks up at him, laughing.

171

'Marilyn must be delighted,' I say.

'Yes, indeed.' Dad is still rubbing his scar. The skin around it pales under the pressure and then flushes pink again. Pale. Pink. Pale. Pink.

I itch to pull his hand away from his face.

He abruptly stops rubbing. 'He wants to start some daft business.'

'What kind of business?'

'Floatation tanks, I think he called them.' He enunciates *floatation* in the same way as he did *junkie*.

'They're supposed to be great for stress.'

Dad harrumphs. 'Lot of nonsense.'

He doesn't believe in stress or treatments for it. Stiff upper lip and get on with it, is his attitude. And look where that's got him over the last twenty years.

'Where's he found the money for that?'

'He wants Marilyn to lend it to him. I've advised her against it.'

'Why?' I say. 'I bet it's quite lucrative. It could be a good investment.'

'Not if she has to re-mortgage. Not at her age. I don't want her throwing good money after bad.'

Dad has obviously dusted off his financial planner's hat. He used to dispense advice to me and Fiona, urging us, from our early twenties, to plan for the future with savings, pensions and property investments. I let him help me buy my flat, with some of Mum's life insurance, and ignored the rest of his tips.

'Where's Nick living?' I say.

'With Marilyn – for the moment.'

'A loan and bed and board? He knows which side his bread's buttered.'

Dad casts a nervous look in the direction of the garden. Nick blows another smoke ring. Marilyn tugs on his arm.

'They can't hear me, Dad. They're too engrossed in each other to pay us any attention, anyway.' In fact, I wonder why Marilyn's so keen for me to meet her son; I'd have expected their time together to be sacrosanct, until they'd re-established their relationship.

A pained look crosses Dad's face. He's like a child usurped by a new sibling.

'Don't worry, Dad. They're bound to be like that at first.'

'Indeed.' He stares out of the window.

Marilyn waves to him and begins to lead Nick down the lawn

towards the house. Just before the patio, he stops. He drops his cigarette and grinds it into the grass with his heel.

Dad winces.

The back door slams. A moment later, Marilyn guides Nick into the living room. She said her sons were in their late twenties; he could pass for younger. I expected evidence of his drug abuse: a gaunt face, hollow eyes, a collapsed septum. Instead, he looks fit and healthy – and his nose is intact.

Marilyn releases his arm and gestures towards me. 'Nick, darling, this is Clare, Brian's younger daughter.'

Nick grips my hand a fraction longer than necessary. 'Hi, Clare. Good to meet you. I've heard a lot about you.'

'Sounds ominous.'

'Sorry, terrible cliché.' He grins. 'I'm hopeless at introductions.'

I don't believe that. He's the stereotypical handsome bad boy – from his curly, black hair to the twinkle in his eye and the dimple in his chin. He must charm every woman he meets. Nearly every woman: I've never been one for bad boys.

'If that's true,' I say, 'you won't get very far with your new business!'

Nick's grin drops a notch. 'Your dad told you my plans, then?'

'Yes. You must like a challenge? Being self-employed isn't easy.'

'I've been through worse,' he says.

Marilyn looks up at him proudly. 'I think you two will find you have a lot in common. Why don't you have a chat, while Brian and I get on with the cooking?'

The light dawns. Marilyn likened my obsessive-compulsive disorder to an addiction; she wants me to meet Nick to put me on the right path to recovery. I wonder how much she's told him? I don't have a client's right to confidentiality, after all.

I glance at Dad. He looks puzzled. Great, now he must be wondering which of Nick's problems I share: drugs or lack of money.

'Dinner will only be ten minutes,' says Marilyn. 'I've made your favourite, Nicky – apple pie.'

'You always did spoil me, Mum!'

Marilyn goes back into the kitchen and Nick saunters into the living room as if he owns the place. Dad trots behind Marilyn, while I follow Nick.

'Wine?' He gestures towards a bottle of red open on the dining table.

'A small one, thanks. I'm driving.'

Nick pours our drinks and brings mine over to me. 'I understand your sister's been in hospital? How is she?'

'She's fine, thanks. Much better.' I remember her standing at that table, watching the children play in the garden, when we were all here for Sunday lunch just a few weeks ago. She must have known then that she was pregnant. Perhaps that's why she was unwell after lunch: the first sign something wasn't right.

'Nothing serious, I hope?' His dark eyes watch me over the rim of his glass.

'No. She was due to be discharged today.' I move away from him, to sit on the sofa under the window. A lavish bouquet of lilies and roses dwarfs the coffee table in front of me. Dad's becoming a regular romantic.

'Your dad will be relieved.'

'Of course.' I roll the stem of my glass between my fingers.

'By the way, congratulations on your engagement.' Nick sits down in the armchair Dad normally occupies, bumping the coffee table as he squeezes in. The flowers vibrate, the lilies shedding pollen onto the wood beneath them.

'Careful! You'll knock Dad's flowers over.'

'Sorry. Actually, I got them, for Mum. Least I could do. Do you like them?'

'Very nice.' He probably used money he'd borrowed from her to buy them.

He seems to know all about our family; it's time to find out about his. 'Are you…attached?' I say.

'Yeah. I've been with Lucy for three years. She's a great girl. Stuck by me through all the crap. Don't think I'd have got clean without her.'

'That's nice.' I roll my engagement ring around my finger.

'I reckon we'll get married, too.' Nick stares at my left hand.

I stop fiddling and clench my fist.

'Your Tom sounds like a good bloke,' he says. 'We should all go out for a drink some time.'

'That might be difficult,' I say. 'It's a long way to travel and his dog…' And I don't want you to meet him. 'Excuse me, I need to wash my hands before dinner.' I stand up and make my escape, dawdling upstairs until Marilyn calls us.

She and Dad sit at opposite ends of the table. The extension

174

leaves are pulled out, making it longer than usual. With Nick and I on either side, it's like eating in a stately home.

The meal is torturous. Marilyn simpers and smiles, while Nick basks in her maternal spotlight. They talk about everything from his childhood to floatation tanks. Everything apart from his drug habit and their estrangement. I'm sure even the original prodigal son didn't enjoy such a homecoming. Dad and I are virtually silent. The upside is, Marilyn is so focussed on Nick, she doesn't ask about Fiona.

Dad, isolated at the other end of the table, opens a second bottle of wine, which he ploughs through almost single-handedly. Slumped in blank-eyed bliss, he seems oblivious to the interminable stories and memories.

Not being able to drink to excess, I'm unable to benefit from the same alcoholic immunity. Finally, I butt into a story about Nick winning a drawing competition when he was seven. 'How about some of your delicious apple pie, Marilyn?'

She frowns, as if unsure who I am, and then recovers herself. 'Of course. Where are my manners?'

She gets up and walks around the table. As she passes Nick, she pauses to kiss the top of his head. 'I can only do that when you're sitting down.' She laughs.

Dad straightens up in his seat. She sashays past him into the kitchen, hips and hair swaying, and his shoulders sag again.

Marilyn carries in the pie and a jug of cream on a silver tray. From her ceremonial air, you'd think they were the Crown Jewels.

Dad takes a couple of mouthfuls of his pudding and a glug of wine. He pulls a face. 'Wine tastes funny now.' He pushes his bowl away, the pie half-eaten.

I manage a small piece, marvelling again at how insipid it is.

Nick wolfs down two slices. 'Better than ever, Mum!'

'I'll clear up,' I say, as soon as he puts down his spoon.

He starts stacking crockery.

'I'll do that.' I reach for the bowls he's collected. 'You carry on talking to your mum.' If they can find an anecdote they haven't revived yet.

In the kitchen, I put on an apron and run hot water into the washing-up bowl.

Dad drifts in with a stray spoon. 'Something I meant to ask.' His words are slurred. 'Fiona?' He looks hopefully at me.

'Fiona?' I stall.

175

'Yes. Fiona. Wh…wha's wrong?'

'Nothing's wrong, Dad. She's fine now. Why don't you go and sit down?'

He frowns. 'Nothing's wrong?'

'Nothing.'

'Splendid, splendid.' He wanders off.

Thank God for alcohol.

Thank God I'll be home soon.

I'm celebrating too early.

Nick comes in. 'Just going to make some coffee.' He flicks the kettle on and leans against the counter next to me.

I crash dishes and cutlery about in the bowl, to put him off talking.

'I'll give you a hand,' he says. 'Where are the tea towels?'

'I can do it.'

'I know you can, but I'd like to help. We're both guests.' He opens one drawer, then another.

For heaven's sake. 'They're in the next one along,' I say. Where Mum always kept them.

Nick opens it, pulls out a towel and picks up a plate. 'Do you think you could rinse them first?' he says. A thumbnail-sized blob of foam decorates the surface.

'How?' I gesture at the single sink. 'If it's too much trouble, don't worry. I'll do it myself.'

'You don't like me, do you?' he says.

'I don't know you.'

'Maybe you think you do?' Nick wipes a bowl. 'You know I used to be a drug addict. You must have had preconceptions? Someone you can't trust? Someone who steals to pay for their habit?'

'Of course not.'

A plate slips out of my hands back into the water. It hits another hidden beneath the suds. I dredge it out and inspect it for damage. A chip interrupts the clean line of the rim, but I'm unsure whether the blemish is new. I scrub the chipped plate clean and stand it in the rack.

'Track marks? A busted nose?' says Nick.

'I don't know what you take…took. How would I know what to look for?'

'That's the point, you don't. Whatever our poison, we druggies come in all shapes and sizes. You'd be surprised.'

I scoop foam into the next bowl as I remove it from the water. Nick holds it over the rack, until the bubbles slide off.

'Maybe not,' I say. 'Most people aren't quite what they seem.'

'Yeah, we've all got some shit going on.'

I don't want to talk about my shit, not to him. Marilyn's wrong; Nick and I have nothing in common.

Standing the last of the crockery to drain, I empty the water down the sink and reach behind me to untie the apron strings. The double knot of the bow has tightened and my nails are too short to get a purchase on it. My arms twisted behind my back, I pick blindly at the fabric.

'Damn it,' I say. 'What the bloody hell is wrong with this thing?' Hot and bothered from my struggles, I could cry with frustration.

'Let me.' Nick puts down the tea towel and moves behind me. He gently lifts my hands away from the knot.

I feel a tug, the apron pulls tighter around my waist, and suddenly I'm free. The strings fall to my sides.

'There.' He clasps my shoulders. His breath is on my neck. 'You're all right now.'

'Thank you.' I shrug off his hands as I lift the apron over my head.

'If you ever need help—'

'Why would I? Anyway, I thought it was you that needed help?' I hang the apron on a hook on the back of the kitchen door.

'Only money, and money's easy to sort. It's the other stuff that's tricky. I've been through the mill more than once and learned a fair bit along the way. What works, what doesn't.' He drapes the tea towel over the draining rack. 'Look, the offer's there, if you want to take it up.'

'Thank you.' I know I won't. I don't need his help or Marilyn's. I have Michael.

Abandoning Nick to his coffee making, I go into the living room to say goodnight. Marilyn is on the sofa, glasses perched on the tip of her nose, doing a crossword. Dad is asleep in his armchair, his head drooping at an awkward angle. He's holding a glass of wine at a dangerous tilt, the drink on the verge of spilling. I prise the glass from his hand and put it on the table next to him. He grunts, but doesn't wake.

I kiss him on the forehead and whisper, 'Night, Dad. Love you.'

Marilyn looks up and mouths, 'Are you off?'

177

I nod and she gets up to see me out.

In the hall, she says, 'I do hope you and Nick had a good chat?'

'Er... Yes.' My hand is on the front door latch. 'Thanks for dinner.'

'Wait. Where is Nick?' Marilyn twists towards the kitchen. 'Nicky, come and say goodbye to Clare.'

'It's all right, there's no need to disturb him.'

I open the door and step outside. Nick comes up behind his mother.

She smiles. 'Ah, there you are, darling.'

'Not staying for coffee, Clare?' he says.

'No, I have to get going.' I back down the drive. It's starting to rain. I wheel around, lift my handbag over my head and make a dash for the car.

'See you soon,' shouts Nick.

I hope not.

28

A knock at the door wakes me on Saturday morning. I answer it in my dressing gown, to find Janet from downstairs with a parcel for me.

'The delivery man left it with me yesterday. You were out when I came up last night.'

'Thanks, Janet.' I take the bulky, padded bag from her. 'How was Paris?'

'Great. Apart from losing my credit card on day one!' She rolls her eyes. 'Thanks for taking my post in.'

'No problem,' I say. At least it gave me an excuse to verify that my spare keys were still hanging up in her kitchen; the ribbon bow made them easy to spot from the door.

Back inside, I study the front of the parcel. Sleep-bleary, I can't identify the childlike handwriting, although it is familiar. Walking into the kitchen, I open one end of the bag and slide out a bubble-wrapped bundle. A piece of paper taped to it says, 'Saw this and thought of you. Tx.' Tom, of course. I feel a surge of warmth at the thought of him, followed by an almost physical ache; I miss the touch of his soft lips and his strong arms.

The bubble wrap is in several layers. I carefully unroll it and tip the object inside onto my hand. It's a toothbrush holder identical to the one I broke when Tom last stayed here. I smile. He's unlikely to have just stumbled across it. He doesn't even shop at Asda and the nearest one must be miles from the village. The present is odd, yet thoughtful.

Then I wonder, is it to ease a guilty conscience over spending time with Bex? Or worse. Almost immediately, I shake my head at my own foolishness: an unfaithful lover would hardly choose a toothbrush holder as an apology.

I dump the padded bag next to the bin and take the holder into the bathroom, to swap it for the tumbler I've been using instead. As I slot in my toothbrush and adjust it to the right angle, it occurs to me that a second brush would balance the holder.

I want to phone Tom to thank him, but he'll be at work, making the most of the May sunshine and longer days, and I'll be on my way out by the time he gets in. I text him a quick message, instead; I can always call tomorrow.

Later I'm pricked by guilt, as I complete my evening's outfit of plain skirt and sparkly top with a pair of emerald earrings that he gave me for my birthday. Saturday nights are usually our time. It seems strange to be spending this one with another man, yet Michael is my best hope for getting through this, and I'm doing this for Tom – for me and Tom.

Delays on the Tube mean I arrive at Granvilles half an hour late. I can't see Michael in the throng and wait by the entrance for a moment, unsure what to do. The din of the weekend mob reverberates off the high ceiling. He won't hear his phone above the noise; I'll have to look for him.

Zigzagging across the room, I murmur 'Sorry, excuse me' on a loop, as elbows clash and drinks spill. In spite of the air conditioning, the room is hot. Sweat is running down my back by the time I reach the bar. Scanning the counter, I catch sight of a blazer-clad Michael on a stool at the other end. He's looking at his watch. Deep lines ridge his forehead. I wave. He doesn't see me. Squeezing between the bodies separating us, I edge towards him. Fingers crossed he doesn't move.

'Michael!' I touch his arm.

He turns, frowning. 'Are you all right? I was wondering what had happened to you.'

'Sorry. The trains were running late and then I couldn't find you,' I shout.

Michael slides off his stool. 'We'd better head off. I've booked us a table at my favourite little Italian.'

He carves a path through the crowds, but I keep up with him for only seconds, before a young woman cuts in front of me. 'Soz,' she says, as her cleavage swivels beneath my nose.

When I catch Michael up at the entrance, he's frowning again.

'Sorry, someone walked between us,' I say.

'We need to get a move on.' He pushes open the door.

'I didn't know we were eating. I had pasta before I came out.'

'Perhaps you can just have a drink, then?' He strides off and I have to scamper not to be left behind.

At the restaurant, the waiter welcomes Michael by name and steers us to a corner table, near the door.

The room is cool and quiet – a haven after the heat and clamour of Granvilles, but hardly the *little Italian* I'd pictured. There is no clue, from the chic, minimalist decor, as to what country's food might be on offer. I'd expected a warm, cosy cliché of dusty wine bottles, decorative bottles of herbs in oil, and pictures of Italian landmarks. Instead, there are rows of arty, black and white photographs on white walls, hung over tables set with immaculate white cloths, heavy looking silver cutlery and sleek glassware.

The waiter pulls out a chair for me and then Michael.

'That's better.' He relaxes into his seat, to my left, and smiles at me.

The waiter hovers beside me. 'Can I take your coat, madam?'

'No, thank you.' Once I've cooled down, I may need protection from the chill of the air conditioning. I drape my jacket and handbag over the back of my seat and begin to relax too.

Michael keeps his blazer on. He looks as debonair as usual, a white shirt contrasting with the navy jacket and his crown of dark, neatly combed hair.

The waiter disappears and returns with a bottle of white wine and an ice bucket. 'Your usual, sir?'

Michael nods. 'Thank you.'

I'm hot enough not to mind that it's not quite white-wine-drinking weather. We clink glasses. The wine is bone dry. A flash of taste and it's gone – as easy to drink as water.

Michael chooses Parma ham with figs, followed by black squid ink spaghetti. 'You should eat something,' he says.

I'm not hungry, but order a simple tomato and basil topped bruschetta.

We engage in small talk until we've finished the first course, when he asks, 'So, how are things with Tom?'

'No change. I haven't spoken to him since I phoned you.'

'His attitude is disappointing. It's not as if what you requested of him was unreasonable.'

The waiter clears the plates. I take a gulp of wine from my huge glass: each could hold about a third of the bottle.

'I don't know about that any more. Everyone else says I'm the one who should change. I'm beginning to think they're right.'

Michael shakes his head. 'I don't believe—'

The waiter returns with the spaghetti and diverts him with the offer of freshly grated pecorino cheese. I sip my wine, waiting to regain his attention.

Eventually we're alone again.

'What were you saying?' I ask.

'I was going to say that I think you're wrong. I don't believe Tom wants you to change.'

'What do you mean?'

Michael's eyes are fixed on me. 'You said he was surprised that you'd called?'

'Yes. He didn't expect us to speak when we were on a break.'

'You'd assume he'd be pleased at your progress, though?' He twirls spaghetti from his plate, maintaining his gaze.

'Yes, and he wasn't.'

'So, you try to change for him and he's still not happy?'

He's right. Tom was negative about my efforts. What did he say? *You shouldn't try to run before you can walk.* I can't win, whatever I do.

The waiter glides over. 'Is everything satisfactory, sir, madam?'

'Excellent, thank you,' says Michael.

I smile and nod.

'More wine?' The waiter plucks the bottle out of the ice bucket.

'Thank you,' says Michael, before I can object.

The waiter tops up our glasses, although they're still almost half full.

Michael looks at me. 'If Tom doesn't want you to change, why should you? Who are you doing it for?'

'I don't know,' I say miserably.

'Clare, I've got to be honest, I don't think Tom is able to deal with who you really are.'

'But he said he wanted to help me—'

'Of course he did. He knew that was what you wanted to hear.' He puts down his knife and squeezes my left hand in his right. 'Has he initiated contact since you split up? Tried to discuss things?'

I shake my head. The parcel with its brief note hardly constitutes proper communication. In nearly two weeks, the only significant contact has been one way: from me to him. One way and unwelcome.

My eyes well up. I bow my head.

Michael lets go of my hand and fishes out one of his initialled handkerchiefs. 'Here.'

I take it, wipe my eyes and ball the damp cotton into my fist.

'Don't be upset, Clare,' he says.

'I thought…' I swallow hard, as the tears return. 'I thought

'I could make it work.' I dab at my eyes again, determined not to cry here, and slide the handkerchief into my jacket pocket.

'I know. Still, it's better you find out how Tom feels. Better now than when you're married.'

Is it? It doesn't seem that way. I was convinced Tom was the one. Convinced, if I changed, that we could live happily ever after. Now I can't imagine happily ever after with anyone, as the same problem will always surface. Tom is a kind, sensitive man; if he can't deal with this, no one can.

'If I change, he'd feel differently, though,' I say. 'I still don't understand why he wouldn't want me to do that?'

Michael sighs. 'There's another thing. You said his ex was with him when you called. Hadn't they recently split up when you met Tom?'

'About six months before.' I take another swig of my drink, my heart racing.

'I think Tom has another agenda.'

'Oh, God, no!' I've been so naïve. I should have listened to my gut instinct; Michael voicing the same suspicion has now reinforced it.

How was it Tom described Bex? *A good laugh…a bit of fun.* She's a much easier option than me, whatever their other differences.

'I'm sorry, Clare. Sometimes the truth is hard.' Michael lays down his cutlery and grasps my hand again, in both of his. His grip is strong, reassuring. 'Everything will work out for the best. I know it will.'

The alcohol swirls my thoughts. I hope he's right; I can't be certain of anything any more. I'm hurt that Tom has given up on me so quickly, that his love was so easily shaken, that he has turned out not to be the man I thought he was. I feel foolish for believing our relationship was solid and real and meaningful. The only thing solid about it now is the ring on my finger.

'You need a man who accepts the real you,' he says. 'I do, Clare. You have to believe me when I say that.'

I look into his pale blue eyes. 'I do,' I say.

The waiter approaches, to serve the last of the wine. He upends the empty bottle in the bucket and takes it away, before returning a moment later to remove the plates.

His eyes sweep over our linked hands as he works. 'I hope you're enjoying your evening, sir, madam? Would you like dessert?' He reels off the menu. His voice seems far away; I don't take in what he's saying. The lines of his black jacket blur against his white shirt. I blink, try to focus.

Michael says something that I don't catch. The waiter nods and moves away.

A few minutes later, he brings over two flaming sambucas.

'In one,' says Michael, 'on the count of three. One, two, three.'

I blow out the flame and down the drink. I cough, as it scorches a trail down my throat. The afterglow comforts me. Michael orders another round.

While we're waiting for the liqueurs, a flower seller sidles into the restaurant and up to our table, a basket of single roses on her arm. Michael gets out his wallet and slips her a note in exchange for a red rose in a thin tube of clear Cellophane.

As she pockets the money, the waiter bustles over and ushers her out, apologising to us for the intrusion.

Michael presents the rose to me with a small bow of the head.

'It's very kind, but you shouldn't—' I say.

'I should. You deserve to be spoiled.'

'Thank you.' I raise the bloom to my nose, but it gives off no scent. I peel back the top of the wrapper to expose the petals and smell it again – still nothing. 'It's lovely,' I say.

When we leave the restaurant later, I slide the stem into my handbag. Michael takes my arm and I lean into him, letting him steer me to the Tube station. I'm woozy in spite of the fresh air. I feel as if I'm floating, watching us from above.

The train is full of couples, holding hands, or hugging, or kissing. They make being in love look so easy. The sight depresses me.

'You're quiet,' says Michael.

'I'm tired.' I slouch deeper into my seat.

At Euston, passengers pour out of the carriage. A woman in stilettos teeters past. She overbalances and steps sideways, the heel of her shoe stabbing into my foot. I yelp in pain; she carries on, oblivious. I lean over to rub my foot, tears filling my eyes. The train jerks into motion.

'Are you all right?' says Michael.

'No. No, I'm not.' The tears begin to fall and then I can't stop crying. I sob into my knees, my shoulders heaving.

'Hey, hey, steady on.' He rubs my back. 'You're all right.'

I'm crying too hard to speak. He pulls at my shoulder, trying to make me sit up. I resist, embarrassed to be sobbing in public.

'Clare, come on.' Michael pulls at me again.

I let myself be dragged upright and bury my face in his chest.

He strokes my hair, whispering, 'You're all right. You're all right. It's going to be fine.'

The train lurches to a standstill, but the doors stay shut; we must be in a tunnel. Without the racket of the train's movements, the carriage is quiet, and my sobs are loud in the stillness. I try to get a grip on myself.

I lift my head to look at Michael. 'I'm sorry.'

'For what?'

'For this.' I dig in my pocket for his handkerchief. 'I must look a mess.'

'You look beautiful. As always.'

My heart pumps faster.

The train jolts forward.

'You can't go home in this state,' says Michael. 'Have a coffee at my place and I'll get you a cab later.'

'I'm all right, honestly.'

'No, you're not. Come with me. You shouldn't be on your own when you're so upset.'

The tears bubble up again. 'All right,' I say.

As we stand up to change at Camden a few minutes later, I remember the last time we were here. Remember my face tingling from Michael's kiss.

He leaps off the train ahead of me. I hang back in the carriage. He turns and reaches towards me. 'Hurry up, Clare, the doors are closing.'

I take his hand and step down onto the platform.

29

We arrive in Hampstead ten minutes later. I'm not familiar with the area; I only know the Heath – and that the property prices are out of my league. Michael's one-man business must be doing well.

His flat is at the top of a Victorian conversion. I stumble up the stairs behind him, fuzzy and light-headed.

He ushers me in. 'Can I take your jacket?'

'I'll keep it on for now, thanks.' The hall is cool, with its white walls and black and white tiled floor. The only furniture is a coat stand to the left of the door.

Michael drapes his blazer over a hanger on the stand and does up the buttons and smooths the lapels, before turning back to me. 'Coffee?'

'That'd be lovely.' It'll help to clear my head.

He leads the way into a kitchen so immaculate that it appears unused. It's like a photo in a brochure: all pale oak and brushed steel, with mirror-bright chrome appliances, a stone floor and granite worktops.

'This is lovely,' I say. He wouldn't think much of my MDF cupboards and adhesive floor tiles.

He stands a cafetiere, cups, saucers, teaspoons and a milk jug on a tray. While the water boils, he measures out the coffee, tearing off a sheet of kitchen roll to wipe up the stray grains that scatter across the work surface.

The wine has made me thirsty. 'Could I have some water as well, please?'

'Of course. I've got filtered in the fridge.'

I move towards the huge, space-age appliance in the corner.

Michael raises his hand in a policeman's stop gesture. 'I'll get it.'

He takes a glass from a shelf and opens the fridge. The water jug is in the doorsill. He fills the glass and replaces the jug, carefully adjusting the angle of the handle; apparently he prefers it to be parallel to the sill edge.

As he shuts the fridge door, he seems to become aware I'm watching him. 'Everything all right?' he asks.

'Fine, thanks.'

He passes me my water.

'Thank you.' I gulp it down in one and stand the glass next to the sink.

Michael picks it up, washes and dries it, and replaces it on the shelf, before turning back to the cafetiere to depress the plunger. 'Nearly there.'

'I'll just pop to the bathroom.'

He gestures down the hall. 'First door on the left.'

The bathroom is that of a four-star hotel – shiny tiles, glittering enamel, white towels lined up over heated rails, and loo roll folded to a point. The toilet is so pristine, I hardly like to use it.

At the mirror, I take in my ruffled hair and bloodshot, shadowed eyes. As soon as I've had my coffee, I'll go home.

I tidy my hair and splash cold water on my face. Lifting a towel off the heated rails would disturb the order, so I bend to dry myself on one. Once it's damp and crumpled, the display is spoiled, anyway. It's a familiar problem: if you aim for perfection, deviations are glaring.

In the living room, Michael fiddles with the stereo. Music fills the room. 'Do you like Mozart?' he says.

'What I've heard of his music, yes.' My knowledge of classical composers is limited to an old collection of compilation CDs, picked up free in the Sunday papers.

'Help yourself to coffee. I'll be back in a minute.' He walks out of the room.

The tray is on a low table in front of a brown leather sofa. I sit down, placing my handbag at my feet. My skirt rides up, exposing the back of my bare legs to the cool leather. I keep my jacket on. The flat feels chilly in spite of the mild evening.

I fill the cups and warm my hands on one, as I look around. Spotlights illuminate the high-ceilinged room, which contains little furniture; the effect is to make it seem cold, though it's decorated in creams and browns. A rug covers the wooden floor between the table and the wall, which is dominated by a plasma screen television. A couple of deep bookcases hold paperbacks and DVDs. On top of one is the only greenery: a row of six tall, single-fingered cacti, spaced evenly along the length of a low trough. On the other is a large aquarium, occupied by half a dozen long-finned, black and white striped fish. The ideal pet for those with obsessive-compulsive disorder: contained, and with no accompanying slobber, hairs or muddy paws. I watch them swimming idly back and forth, as the coffee's warmth permeates my body.

Michael comes back in. 'Coffee all right?'

'Great, thanks. What kind of fish are they? They're very restful.' I'm still a little out of it and their movement contributes to my trance-like state.

'Angelfish. Did you know they contain the same poison as puffers?'

'No, I didn't. I'd better avoid eating one, then!'

He gestures towards the wall behind me. 'What do you think of my latest art purchase?'

I twist around, to see a plain cream canvas, highlighted by a single light.

'Come and look,' he says.

I join him in front of the painting.

'It appears to be blank, but see here...and here...and here.' He points out tiny specks of colour, barely visible even close up.

'Mmm, interesting idea.' I prefer more accessible work, but like the fact that he's engaged by art.

Michael rests his hand on my shoulder and leans in closer, as he directs me to more dots. His fingers brush the right-hand side of my neck. I jump.

'You're missing an earring,' he says.

'What?' I reach up to my ear. The lobe is bare.

'An emerald stud, isn't it?'

'Yes.' I frantically scan the floor.

Michael crouches down.

'It might have come off while I was washing.' I head for the door, panic building at the idea of losing Tom's present.

'I'll keep searching in here.'

In the bathroom, my eyes skim over the sparkling surfaces that will make the twinkle of an earring hard to distinguish.

My hunt comes to a standstill when I notice the towels. The one I used is no longer crumpled. I finger it. It's not just flat, it's also dry. Mine couldn't have dried that quickly. In the corner stands a wooden linen basket. I lift the lid. On top of the pile inside lies a folded white towel. I press my hand to it and find it's damp. Something is still not right: it's too damp. Mine must have dried, after all – and ironed itself? Then I see that the marble surfaces I splattered with water are dry as well. Wiped down with the towel in the basket – my towel.

The whole room looks exactly as it did when I came in earlier. Even the end of the loo roll has, I now notice, been restored to a perfect triangle. I close the basket lid and push down on it, to ensure it's shut. To ensure I leave no evidence of my activities.

I walk back into the living room.

'No sign of your earring, I'm afraid,' says Michael. 'I'll keep an eye out for it. It must be here somewhere.' He sits down and picks up his coffee.

'Thanks,' I say, but I'm not hopeful. The tiny stone could have caught on something and been pulled loose at any point in the evening. Maybe when I was leaning against him as we left the restaurant, or as I rested my head against his chest on the train.

For a moment, I'm teary at the loss. Then I realise there's no longer any reason to be sentimental over Tom's gifts. As I join Michael on the sofa, I take out the other earring and put it into a small, zippered pocket in my purse. It seems pointless to keep it. Even if the missing one does turn up, I won't want to wear them again; the associated memories will be too painful. Yet I know that I will never throw away the remaining stud.

Michael pulls a face. 'My coffee's gone cold. I'll heat it up in the microwave. How about yours?'

I shake my head. 'It's fine. I've nearly finished, anyway. Thanks.'

He gets up and disappears into the kitchen.

It's obvious, from my limited exposure to his home, that it's the same as mine: everything in its place and everything back in its place. He said he wasn't like the others in the group; he's right. What's different is that his ordering doesn't bother him or those around him. His lack of concern makes it unlikely he even has obsessive-compulsive disorder – and a mystery why he joined the group; he doesn't want, or need, any help.

The nature of our habits is the same, though, even if his haven't arisen out of anxiety. He's the only person I know who could possibly understand what I do.

He returns with his steaming cup of coffee. 'Penny for them?' He sits down next to me, putting his drink on the table.

'I was thinking how nice it is to be with someone who really gets me.'

'Ditto.'

189

'You don't know how much it means to me, Michael.' I look into his blue eyes.

'I do, Clare. I do.'

I lean towards him and kiss him quickly on the lips. Immediately I rock back away. 'I'm sorry, I shouldn't have done that.'

'Why not?'

'Because—'

'There is no because, Clare.' He cups his hand under my chin and presses his mouth to mine. His lips are thin, firm; they feel odd at first. For a second I think of Tom's soft, full mouth. My head spins.

Michael pulls back, gazes into my eyes. 'This is right, Clare. We're right. You must know that?'

'I do,' I say.

He takes his hand away from my face and slides it up my naked thigh. As his mouth meets mine again, his tongue parts my lips and I begin to kiss him back.

30

When I wake at eleven, the other side of the bed is empty. I roll onto my back and stare at the ceiling. Memories of the night before gradually pierce the fog of sleep and hangover.

Michael carefully removing my clothes and laying them on a chair.

Michael methodically working his way through a gamut of foreplay techniques.

Michael quietly coming, while I chased orgasm to the brink, only to have it driven back by fatigue and alcohol.

My heart thuds, my head pounds. I feel sick. I wish I hadn't had so much wine. Wish I'd refused the sambucas. Wish I'd gone home.

Wishing won't change anything. I would have ended up in this position sooner or later. I was drawn to Michael the first time we met. Now that we've slept together, I'm able to admit that. There's so much about him that is attractive. There's so much, in fact, that he shares with Tom: his good looks, his chivalry, his romantic gestures, the drive to run his own business – even his desire to remain childless. My realisation last night of his singular understanding of my obsessive behaviour finally tipped the balance.

In the cold, sober light of day, though, the evidence against Tom is no longer convincing. It's all circumstantial. I don't know what he feels about me, or our relationship. I don't know that he's gone back to Bex. I don't know anything, because I haven't asked him. I haven't given him the chance to explain.

I squeeze my eyes shut. Everything seemed so complicated before; it's so much worse now. Flinging my arm across my face, I groan. Less than two weeks into my temporary separation from Tom, and what have I done? What the hell have I done?

I wonder whether I should leave; after all, staying will only compound the situation. Leaving won't undo it, though. I've taken an irreversible step, which means I've already lost Tom, whether I stay or go. Whatever *he* has or hasn't done, *I* have ruined everything.

My eyes well up at the thought, yet I can't dwell on it. I can't think about whether I've misjudged Tom and what I might have lost as a result. All I can do now is focus on what an alternative future might bring.

And I have to stay, to see whether that future might include Michael.

Clattering from the kitchen reassures me that he's in no hurry for me to leave, but if I'm getting breakfast in bed, I need to perk myself up a bit.

I scramble from under the covers. Dragging on the silk robe hanging on the back of the door, I go into the bathroom. It's as perfect as before. If Michael has been in here, he's left no trace.

I wash my face and clean my teeth with my finger. Much as I'd like to take a shower, I daren't; I'd have no clue how to restore order afterwards. There's no sign of a flannel to give myself a vertical sponge bath, and my hair is unsalvageable without washing it or applying vast quantities of hairspray. I make do with leaning over the basin and slopping water from my cupped hand onto my head. The water spills, flooding the surrounding surfaces. I wipe them down with my towel, but then I'm stuck. If I put the towel in the linen basket, the gap on the rail will be obvious, as I've no idea where the spares are. If I hang it up, it will look untidy and the ones underneath will get wet. I opt for what appears to be the lesser of two evils and drape the towel over the rail.

A knock on the door startles me.

'Clare? I'm going out to get the Sunday papers.'

'Hold on.' I tug the towel straight and open the door.

Michael is crouched in the hall, doing up his shoelaces.

'Hey.' I wrap my arms around my body, holding the robe tight against my skin.

'Good morning.' He straightens up. He's wearing a long-sleeved, white shirt, tucked into sharply creased navy trousers; he looks as if he's on his way to church.

He kisses me, his mouth hard on mine. He smells of soap and, from close-up, I realise his slicked-back helmet of hair is damp. He must have had a shower, although the bath is completely dry.

'I assume you don't need to shoot off?' he says.

'No, I don't have any plans for today.' Except unravelling the mess I've made of my life.

'I'll only be five minutes.'

The door closes behind him and I shiver in the sudden draught. As I spot my jacket, on a hanger on the coat stand with the buttons done up, I remember him easing it off my shoulders last night and shiver again.

I decide to lie down until he gets back. When I return to the bedroom, though, the bed has already been made, with a cream bedspread now covering the duvet and pillows. It's smooth and spotless and splays out in neat folds where it falls over the corners of the bed. I can't disrupt the hotel-cum-hospital look, so get dressed instead.

My skirt is crumpled, but relatively clean. My top is sweaty. Michael must have something I can wear. Behind the doors of the built-in wardrobe is a rail of mainly suits and shirts. The suits are grey, the shirts white or light blue, and the hangers are all the same distance apart; we have that habit in common.

I ease open a drawer at the end of the wardrobe. Balled-up socks lie in rows, like apples in a supermarket. The next drawer is full of close-fitting jersey boxers, in shades of blue and grey; folded into neat squares, they form a disconnected patchwork. I give up. Even if I find something suitable, removing it will destroy Michael's order. The smelly top will have to do. As I pull it on, my engagement ring snags on a loose thread. I stare at the ring for a moment. Overnight it has become a glittering guilt trip, a reminder of what I've done to Tom – to us. I slide it off and secrete it in the zippered pocket in my purse, next to the solitary earring.

In the kitchen, I nose around for breakfast materials; toast might ease my queasiness. Nothing. Whatever Michael was up to in here, it wasn't breakfast. I expect he'll get something at the shops.

I lie on the sofa to wait for him. He has left classical music playing and the violins drill a hole in my sore head. I get up to peruse his music collection: his tastes are middle of the road and outdated. Deciding against changing the CD, I retreat to the sofa and position myself so that I can watch his fish, hoping their lazy movements will relax me.

The front door opens and closes. Breakfast, at last. Michael comes in and hands me a two-inch deep pile of papers.

'I'll put the coffee on,' he says.

'I'd prefer tea, if you don't mind.'

'Of course. I'll get a pot going.'

'A mug's fine.'

He raises an eyebrow. 'If you're a builder. I like to do things properly. Warm the pot, fresh boiling water. You can't beat a well-made cup of Earl Grey.'

I wrinkle my nose at the thought of the insipid, perfumed blend.

He doesn't notice. 'Better than all those so-called breakfast teas,' he says, as he goes into the kitchen.

My head and eyes hurt too much to read, so I dump the papers on the floor. My stomach rumbles. I wonder what's taking Michael so long? Maybe he's heating up croissants. Or making scrambled eggs with smoked salmon. Or porridge with cream. Nothing as mundane as cornflakes for someone like him.

Nothing, in fact, turns out to be the answer.

'Here we are.' He brings in a tray loaded only with a cafetiere, teapot, cups, saucers, teaspoons and a milk jug.

'Aren't we having breakfast?' I say.

'I don't usually. Anyway, it's nearly lunchtime. I thought we could go out. The gastro pub around the corner does a good steak.'

The gnawing hunger pains intensify. 'Sure. That sounds great.' It sounds awful; a hunk of cow is not my idea of breakfast.

The Earl Grey eases my thirst, but gurgles around inside in a way that only emphasises my emptiness. Michael takes his time, savouring every sip of coffee, but eventually finishes.

'Let's clear up and be on our way,' he says.

'Why don't we leave it till we get back?'

'I'd rather not.'

'I'll do it, then.' I start loading the tray.

'No, no, you're a guest.'

'Still, I can't loaf around like the Queen of Sheba all day.' I pick up the tray and march into the kitchen.

Michael nips past me to the double sink and runs the hot water. 'I'll wash and rinse, you dry and put away.' He frowns. 'No, you wash and...'

I wait.

'No,' he says, 'I'll wash.'

Presumably it's easier to rearrange a cupboard than to wash everything again if I don't do it properly.

After I've dried each item, I slot it back in its place. My eye for detail compensates for the patterns being different to mine. I remember where things belong from watching Michael make coffee last night. In the kitchen – unlike the bathroom – I can follow the rules with virtually no effort.

I put the milk jug back on the shelf, angling it with the spout to the wall.

'The handle a little more to us,' says Michael.

I loop my forefinger around it and pull.

'That's it, stop. Stop. Good girl.'

He corrects me as necessary until everything is to his satisfaction. 'You're a quick study. I knew you would be.'

I feel like a performing poodle. Unfortunately, no foodie treat rewards my tricks.

He lets the suds drain away and picks up a luminously white cloth to wipe down the sink and surrounding surfaces.

I lean against the kitchen counter and watch. 'How would two people with set ways of arranging things manage if they lived together?'

'What do you mean?' He rubs at a mark I can't see.

'I mean, which would become the default?'

'Whichever made more sense.' He taps the tea and coffee containers. 'Labels to the front, you know what's in them. Simple.'

'How would you decide the right angle for a milk jug?'

'Whatever looked best.'

'That's subjective.'

'Nevertheless, easy to learn. You did.'

So, subjective means his way. Last night, he said I didn't have to change, that he accepted me as I was.

'Maybe you could divide things up, half one person's rules, half the other?' I say.

I need an answer. Our relationship may be less than twenty-four hours old, but I have to know where I stand before it's much older. I'm not prepared to give up all my rules in favour of someone else's. If I *am* going to give them up, it might as well be for a man without rules. For a man like Tom.

Michael's understanding of my behaviour is no help, if he simply expects me to mimic him. There's no reason we couldn't give and take, as any couple does in day-to-day decisions.

'Michael? What do you think? Half and half?'

He throws the cloth into the washing machine and pushes the door shut. 'You can't be that precise. It's not a science. You have to play it by ear.'

By his, I assume. I shiver. Only an hour or so ago, I contemplated a future with him. Now I wonder what sacrifices such a future would entail and whether I'd be prepared to make them.

I visit the bathroom before we leave. I shouldn't be surprised that Michael has restored its perfection, but I am. Surprised and disappointed. No wonder he took so long to make our drinks. In the time he spent on the bathroom, he could have rustled up a week's worth of breakfasts.

31

At the pub, Michael leads me to the last free table outside. As he pulls out a chair for me, he clanks it against the back of one at a neighbouring table. The occupant, a sunburnt young woman, scowls at him and edges her seat forward an inch.

He bumps her chair again. 'Excuse me!'

The woman ignores him.

'Michael, it's all right. I can manage. Can we just sit down, please?' I slide into the seat.

'Let's have the umbrella down.' He fiddles with the catch on the parasol.

'I'd prefer it up. I burn easily.' And the sun won't help my headache.

'It's a shame on such a beautiful day.' Michael frowns. 'I'll see if I can tilt it so that I'm in the sun.' He spends several minutes adjusting the umbrella, only for a nearby customer to complain that she's now in the shade. He tinkers for another five minutes before everyone is happy and he can sit down.

'They do a good Merlot here,' he says, scanning the menu. 'It'll go nicely with the steak. I'll get us a bottle of that.'

'Not for me, thanks. I overdid it a bit last night.' Pain stabs my temple.

'Just a glass. Hair of the dog, eh?'

'Michael, I don't want to drink. I really don't. Could you just let me decide for myself?'

'All right. It was only a suggestion. There's no need for such a fuss.'

Fuss? I wasn't the one obsessed with rearranging the pub's furniture.

I order the roast of the day and a sparkling water, with ice and lemon, and fight the flies for the bread that arrives with our drinks. It stands in lieu of breakfast, making the chicken that follows easier to swallow.

Michael's steak dribbles blood, as he cuts into it. The sight nearly makes me retch. I take a gulp of water and another mouthful of bread.

'Would you like to try some?' He spears a piece of bleeding meat onto his fork and holds it out to me.

I shake my head, nausea sealing my mouth shut.

The blood congeals on his plate, forming a reddish-brown stain. It seeps under the vegetables and contaminates them, too. I push my own plate away, my meal barely touched.

As I watch him eat, I realise he's still wearing his blazer. He must be baking. I long to tear it off him and tell him to relax. Long to ruffle his mannequin-perfect hair and tell him to have some fun, for God's sake.

My headache moves up a gear, as the afternoon heat builds. Flashes of light dance across my vision and I feel dizzy and queasy. Fortunately, Michael is intent on his food; we barely speak. It's a relief when he declines pudding, in favour of coffee back home.

Inside the flat, the air is thick and stuffy. While he makes the coffee, I struggle to open the sash windows. The effort makes me sweat and my grimy clothes suddenly feel filthy. I feel filthy. The windows must be locked, but there's no sign of the key. Defeated, I sink onto the sofa, my head thumping.

Michael brings the tray in and puts it on the coffee table. The contents, and their layout, replicate last night's tray. Perhaps it's a coincidence. Knowing him, I doubt it.

He turns on the stereo: violins again. The bows scrape across the inside of my skull.

'Any chance of something more mellow?' I say.

He looks surprised. 'This is great Sunday afternoon listening. You'll love it when it gets going.'

We've finished our coffee before the piece ends. Clearing up allows me to escape further musical torture.

Michael follows me into the kitchen. 'A woman after my own heart. Tidying up as you go.'

We repeat this morning's ritual: he washes and rinses, while I dry and put away. The clatter of crockery is unbearable, every sound another nail in my brain.

The pain distracts me and I place the cafetiere on the wrong shelf.

'No, no, not there,' he snaps. 'That's the teapot shelf. Next one down.'

I move it.

'The spout more towards me,' he says.

I nudge it a quarter of an inch.

'No, more.' His irritation envelops us like a bad aura.

I nudge it again.

'For pity's sake! I'll do it.' He reaches past me and adjusts it almost imperceptibly.

'Jesus, Michael, calm down. Other people can't do everything exactly your way.' All of a sudden, I know how Tom felt in my flat. No wonder he couldn't emulate me, if I can't emulate Michael. Then, I was the predator, tracking Tom's every move, now I'm the prey – and my stress is rising, just as his did.

'I thought you were different?' says Michael. 'I thought you knew what you were doing?'

'Well, forgive me for not mastering your house rules in less than a day.' I slap the tea towel down on the counter. 'This is no way to live. Constant niggling and watching and—'

'That's enough, Clare. You're in no position to tell me how to live.' His tone is as glacial as his blue eyes. 'I'm disappointed in you. You sound just like Angela.'

'Who the hell is Angela?'

Michael slots the last of the cutlery into the draining rack.

'Who's Angela, Michael?'

He empties the washing-up bowl.

'Michael, answer me.'

'My ex-wife. She's my ex-wife.'

The ex who was so happy to accommodate him? The ex he divorced only because they grew apart?

'You lied to me. You said she fitted in with you.' I groan. 'That's why I expected Tom to accommodate me. I trusted you!'

I should have placed my faith in Heather from the start, but I was so desperate for an easy answer, and Michael seemed to have that answer.

He tweaks the cafetiere again.

I grab his arm. 'Stop it! Just stop it!'

His hand bumps the milk jug out of position. 'Now look what you've done,' he says.

'No! Look what you've done.' I wave my arm wildly, taking in myself, Michael, the night before.

I run out of the kitchen into the bathroom, bang the door shut and lock it. Pressing my palms onto the marble surround of the basin, I lean over. I close my eyes and breathe deeply. Bile rises in my throat. I swallow hard.

I've screwed up. Completely screwed up. Betrayed Tom for nothing. For a man whose tyranny is harder to live with than my own. I've crash-landed into the worst of all worlds and I have only myself to blame.

I splatter my face with cold water. Droplets spray over the surround. I stare at them for a moment. Everywhere I've gone in Michael's flat, he has wiped me out. Every sign of me has been eradicated. It's time for me to make my presence felt. Scooping more water into my hand, I fling it over the edge of the basin. Then more. And more. Left, right, behind it, until the whole area is awash.

There must be something else I can do?

The shower? No, he'll hear that. Unless – I flush the toilet to hide the noise. Directing the showerhead up and down the tiles, I soak them from top to bottom. He'll need his entire towel collection to dry the walls.

I wipe my hands on one, crumpling it, and drape it wonkily on the rail. Wetting my hands again, I dampen the others, mashing them between my fingers and tugging them out of place.

Finally, the toilet roll. I unravel the crisp point and pull the paper down to the floor.

There's nothing left to do here now. I unlock the door and go into the living room.

Michael looks up from his newspaper. 'Have you calmed down?'

'Yes, thank you.' Strangely, my fury has dissipated.

'Good.' He pats the sofa next to him.

I ignore the gesture.

'I understand your reaction,' he says. 'When two people are so alike, it causes conflict.'

'We're not alike. I want to change, you don't.'

'Why do you want to change? You don't have to for me.'

'What about your rules?'

'They're not a change. They're a refinement of what you do.'

'Are you serious? Your rules are completely different. I might as well not have any.' I pick up my handbag from the floor and hook the strap over my shoulder. Last night's rose is still inside, hanging limply out of the peeled-back Cellophane. A petal falls to the floor. 'I should go. This has been a terrible mistake. I'm sorry.'

'No, don't, please.' Michael lurches to his feet. 'Please. I've waited so long to find someone like you, Clare. We can't throw this away.' The paper slips out of his grasp onto the floor. The pages separate and slide apart. He steps towards me and then turns back and squats to pick up the sheets. He pushes them together, lines up the edges and re-folds the pages.

'Look at you,' I say. 'Even now, tidying is more important than anything else. Than anyone else. I know you don't see it, but you're worse than any of us at the support group, because you think your way is the right way. You think everybody should be like you.'

As he straightens up, I turn and walk away from him.

Then, at the door, it comes to me. I stop, spin around. 'Oh my God. Is that why you go? To find a woman you can mould?'

Michael holds the paper against his chest like a shield. 'Of course not. What a ridiculous notion.'

'Why *do* you go, then? You say almost nothing about yourself, you don't like the others, and you always leave at the break. Except the day you met me.'

Now I understand his reluctance to engage with the group: he just uses it as a dating agency, hovering like a vulture for quarry. I might have been his first victim, I doubt I'll be the last.

'You shouldn't do that,' I say. 'People will get hurt.'

People have got hurt.

Tears fill my eyes, as I run out through the hall. I yank my jacket from the coat stand, sending the hanger crashing to the floor. Slamming the front door behind me, I clatter downstairs into the fresh air.

On the street, I pull the wilting rose out of my bag and toss it into a bin at the edge of the pavement. As I slide my jacket on, I feel the bulge of Michael's handkerchief in my pocket. I pull it out; it's crumpled and stiff with last night's tears, his initials distorted by the creases and stains. I drop the balled-up cotton into the bin.

I only wish I could discard the memories of what I have done so easily.

32

A shower and clean clothes only fix the external mess. My mind is a witch's brew of sadness, anger and regrets.

I slump on the sofa, trying to unscramble it all and work out what to do next.

Whether Tom has given up on me or not, I can't justify my infidelity, and the consequence is the same: I have to tell him our relationship is over. I cheated on him and that's a deal-breaker. It would be for me, if the situation were reversed. Splitting up is the right thing to do. Even if we did have a future, I couldn't face a lifetime of lying – of replacing my old deception with a new, and worse, one.

I can't tell Tom the real reason, though. He'd be hurt, his trust destroyed. What he doesn't know won't harm him. I have to contrive another excuse to break up with him – something that keeps the blame at my door. I'll say I can't change my obsessive behaviour. Won't change. Ironic, when the one thing I learned from Michael was that I have to. Inanimate objects can never again become more important than the people around me. I've already ruined the best relationship of my life, because I wanted everything my way. Literally. What a childish reason. I'm no better than a spoiled toddler.

I'll tell Tom face to face; he deserves that much. And maybe my suspicions about Bex are right, after all. He may welcome the news and we can both cut our losses and move on. Although I'd hate to have my own trust broken, it would alleviate my guilt.

I phone to arrange to see him as soon as possible; I have to get this over with.

'Hi, Tom, it's Clare—'

'Clare! God, I'm so glad you called.'

Hearing his voice breaks my heart all over again. I shiver. He wouldn't be so happy, if he knew why I'd rung.

Before I can say anything else, he carries on, 'Look, I know you were upset the other day. I mean, about Bex. Honestly, it was nothing—'

'Tom, can we get together? I really need to...' Tears choke my voice.

'Clare, are you okay? Clare?'

I take a deep breath. 'I'm fine. Just tired. Could I come up tomorrow?'

'Why don't I drive down? You must be worn out, with everything that's been going on.'

I am, but I'd rather be able to leave once I've said my piece. 'What about work?'

'I'll finish early, leave the lads to it.' He clears his throat. 'I've missed you.'

I close my eyes and sigh.

'Clare? We can go out if you're uncomfortable with me being in your flat?'

'No, no, there's no need for that, thanks.' He won't be there long. 'I should be back about six-thirty. Make it seven?'

'Okay, beautiful. I can't wait to see you.'

I put the phone down, dazed. In twenty-four hours, our relationship will be over. Two weeks to the day since I wiped the slate clean to fix myself, I'll have broken us.

Tom arrives dead on seven. I buzz him in and wait at the front door, still uncertain as to exactly how I'm going to finish this. My heart races, my palms sweat. I rub them up and down my jeans, feeling the hard nub of my engagement ring in the right-hand front pocket. I plan to give it back to Tom. If I still had both emerald earrings, I would return those, too; I don't deserve to keep such an expensive gift.

His tufty, blond hair bobs into view, as he clomps up the stairs. He grins when he sees me. My stomach flips. He's so handsome, even in his work-stained tee shirt and frayed jeans. In his hand, he clutches a bunch of floppy-petalled garden roses wrapped in tissue paper.

'Hey,' I say. I can hardly breathe, faced with the reality of what I'm about to lose.

'Hello, beautiful.' He gives me the flowers.

'They're lovely, thank you.' I dip my head to inhale their rich scent.

'Shop bought, I'm afraid. Mine aren't out yet.'

'They're still lovely.'

He leans in to kiss me lightly on the lips and I register the softness of his mouth, fringed with a day's stubble.

As I lead him into the kitchen, I'm unsure what to say. This feels like a first date, not the last.

Tom sits at the kitchen table, while I make tea. I expect he'll be on his way before he's finished it.

'You got my letter, then?' He breaks the silence.

'What letter?' I stir his drink, waiting for the sugar cubes to dissolve. Tiny pieces rattle like grit against the spoon.

'The one I sent with the toothbrush holder. I thought that was why you called?'

I go cold. 'No. I didn't get any letter. Let me have another look.'

The large, padded envelope that contained the holder is still propped against the bin. Retrieving it, I push the sides to widen the opening. Something white glimmers deep inside. I pull out a small, creased envelope. The bubble-wrapped bulk of the holder must have pushed it to the bottom.

I put down the padded envelope and hold up the small one. 'Is this it?'

'Yeah.' He shifts in his seat.

I slide my finger under the flap.

'No!' Tom reaches out his hand, half stands up.

I stop, the flap partially unstuck.

'No, please.' He blushes. 'Please, give me the letter.'

'Don't you want me to read it?'

'Not now.'

'Why not?' I lift the flap another half inch.

'Clare! Don't!' Tom's eyes are pleading, desperate.

'All right, keep your shirt on! I don't know what the big deal is.' I hand him the letter.

He almost snatches it from me and sinks back in his seat.

'Will you at least tell me what's in it?'

Tom lays the letter on the table and smooths the flap down. He's still blushing. 'It's kind of embarrassing.'

'What is?'

'The stuff I wrote.'

I'm lost. 'You said we could tell each other anything. Remember? Dark secrets and all. What have you done? Chopped down a plant you thought was a weed? Covered a garden in pesticide instead of fertiliser?' I regret my frivolity immediately.

'It's us. It's about us.'

'Oh.' Of course.

Tom stares at the letter, pressing on the flap of the envelope over and over, as if to re-stick it. 'I put it down on paper, because when we talk, we misunderstand each other and fight, and I thought I could say what I wanted without it coming out all wrong.'

Picking up our mugs, I go over to the table and sit down. 'Tell me, anyway,' I say, though I don't want him to. Something bad is coming. He's going to explain how he really feels about me, about my compulsions.

And yet – he said he was glad to hear from me, that he'd missed me and couldn't wait to see me. I don't know what to think any more.

'Okay, you've been warned. If this comes out completely garbled, it's your fault!' Tom folds the envelope, slides it into his back pocket and fixes me with those blue eyes. 'I'm sorry for walking out. I was scared because I didn't understand what you were doing and I didn't know how to deal with it and I suppose that made me angry and that's not very helpful and I'm sorry.' He looks down, runs his hand through his hair.

My ears buzz, I feel dizzy. I'm watching us from above, waiting for the axe to fall. 'And?'

Tom lifts his head. 'And I want us to try again and take one step at a time and work things out.' The axe falls. 'I thought you felt the same, because you phoned. Now I know you didn't read the letter and...' He wipes his forehead with the back of his hand. He looks as if he's about to pass out. 'I love you, Clare.'

The bad has happened. I thought he didn't care enough to make an effort with the real me. I was so keen to restore the status quo with his present of the holder that I overlooked the bigger gift. If only I'd checked the package properly. If only I'd found the letter before I went out with Michael. I'd have known then that Tom hadn't given up on me, that he did love me, that our relationship was everything I believed it to be. Was, but isn't any more. And I'm the one who has jeopardised our future, not Tom or Bex.

Now I'm on quicksand, uncertain which way to turn.

'Are you okay?' he says.

I bite my lip, nod.

'You're crying. That's not okay. Have I upset you? I told you it would come out wrong. I'm sorry.'

'No, stop. Stop saying sorry. You have nothing to be sorry for.' Tears roll down my face.

'So, are those happy tears?'

'Yes,' I lie, wiping my face with a tissue.

Tom shakes his head. 'God, I'll never understand women.' He strokes my hair. 'Come on, beautiful. I hate to see you cry, even if you are happy.'

The tears come faster. The tissue is soaked. 'It's me that should apologise. I should have listened to you all along.' I pull my head away from his hand. 'I shouldn't have expected you to compromise. I'm so sorry, Tom, I've spoiled everything.'

'What are you talking about? We had a row; we've made up. That's what happens in relationships.'

'Not just that. What's happened since. What I've done. I need to tell you. That's what I wanted to talk to you about.'

I understand now why people kiss and tell. Not to is a horrible burden.

'Clare, you don't have to tell me anything. Nothing you've done could be as bad as you think. It's not as if you've murdered someone, is it?'

I shake my head, sobbing. 'No, of course not—'

'Well, there you are.' He pats my shoulder helplessly. 'Clare, please stop.'

I try. Closing my eyes, I inhale deeply. My breath bubbles in my heaving chest. A future with Tom is there for the taking. If I forget my infidelity and don't tell anyone else. I breathe in and out slowly. That's all I have to do. Forget. Don't tell.

I open my eyes, look into his. They really are exactly the same light blue as Michael's. I won't tell, but I will never forget.

'Better?' says Tom.

'Sort of.'

'Go on, then. If it would make you feel more than sort of better, tell me.'

'What?' My resolve weakens. I pick up my mug, gulp the cold dregs.

'I mean, how bad can it be? Did you use a ruler to line up your tins? Or get up in the middle of the night to straighten your socks? You can tell me, whatever it is.' He grins at me, amused by his own suggestions; he thinks it's all about my compulsions.

I put down my mug, as drained as it is. 'You're right. It's things like that. Silly things that don't matter.' And with those words, I reclaim our future.

'I knew it. I knew you were getting in a state about nothing.'
Tom stands up, comes around to my side of the table and hugs me
from behind. He presses his cheek against mine, his stubble grazing
my skin.

His touch transforms my guilt into an almost physical pain. I am
The Little Mermaid, knives piercing me when I'm with the man I love.
I wish I were as blameless. And I wish I could be sure I wouldn't still
lose *my* prince.

33

'I'm sorry I have to dash. I've got an early start in the morning,' says Tom, after a second cup of tea. 'Are you sure you're okay? I don't want to go if you're still upset.'

'I'm fine. We can talk more tomorrow.'

I'm actually grateful when he leaves; I need time alone to reflect on the truth of my situation. Tom doesn't understand my behaviour, but that hasn't, after all, driven him away. Michael does understand, but his unwillingness to change negates the benefit of that understanding. His own, warped goals are all that matter to him. Only now can I see the extent of his disregard for others: from his domineering attitude in restaurants to his insistence on absolute adherence to his 'house' rules – from irritating to almost frightening. His chivalry and romantic gestures are a smokescreen, while everything Tom says and does is from the heart.

Even the offer of help from Marilyn's son, Nick, was probably better intentioned, and more honest, than Michael's. I'm sorry that I mistrusted Nick; his recovery makes him more of an inspiration than Michael will ever be.

My feelings for Michael may have evaporated virtually overnight, but it will take longer to get over the fallout. I'm devastated to have cheated on Tom and to be deceiving him further by hiding it. Yet I'm relieved, and happy, that our relationship has survived. Somehow, I have to reconcile those conflicting emotions. At least I have practice in covering things up.

I resist the urge to pour my confusion into a tidying frenzy. If I don't change, then my experience with Michael will have been a waste; something good has to come of it, something that will help me make the best of my second chance with Tom.

His roses are prime fodder for my new resolve. I dump them in a vase without fussing over the arrangement and trim only a couple of particularly long stems, ignoring those blooms that bob a mere half inch above the others. The vase is usually centred on top of the bookcase. Instead, I position it left of middle, so that the church candles either side are no longer equidistant from it.

I need to do more; I light both candles. It is a grand, no going back gesture; once they melt, they will no longer be perfect. The wicks blaze, liquefying the wax around them into uneven puddles and casting imperfect shadows of the vase and its roses against the wall behind them.

I step back and look at my new shrine to normal. As with my previous flirtations with disorder, the asymmetry jolts me like a static shock. I wait for the anxiety to subside and, while I wait, I realise that my guilt will follow a similar trajectory. Over time, its first, sharp pain will also dull, until it is transformed into something more bearable.

I wait for five, ten, fifteen minutes, until this messy corner loses its impact; I can look at it without a racing heart or sweating palms. Only a slight discomfort remains.

I leave the candles to burn into misshapen wax sculptures – Picasso remnants of their former perfection. Their destruction is enough for a first step. I have a whole flat upon which to wreak, if not havoc, at least disarray.

Every day, I nudge more things out of place and sit out the anxiety. When things get hard, I cheat: I retreat to an untouched area to soak up the perfection. Sanctuaries will be harder to find as time goes on; maybe, eventually, I won't need them.

And there is no such sanctuary from my guilt. I'm glad; I deserve this invisible punishment, for betraying a man who loves me and wants only the best for me.

Tom agrees not to visit again until I'm ready. In the meantime, he offers long-distance support. Every night I report my victories, and sometimes defeats, and he encourages me, without interfering. I have to do this on my own, but this time I'm not alone.

At the weekend, I travel up to the cottage. I haven't been there for a month, not since I first told him about my problem.

As he opens the door, Charlie pushes past him. He nudges my leg with his nose, his tail wagging.

I squat down. 'Hi, Charlie, good to see you, too.' This old dog's unconditional love is so touching. I give him a hug and he sits down, whooshing his tail backward and forward over the paving stones.

'Hey, boy, aren't you going to let me have a go?' says Tom.

'I missed you,' I whisper in Charlie's floppy ear.

'He's drooling down the back of your shirt, Clare.'

I let go of Charlie and stand up. He grins up at me, his tail still wagging furiously.

Tom wraps his arms around me and kisses me. 'You smell of dog.'

'Thanks, I love you, too!' I push him away. My guilty conscience makes it easier to hold Charlie, than be held by Tom.

Later, on the patio in the back garden, Charlie dozes next to me, as Tom and I sip white wine. Summer has arrived and insects buzz over the daisies and dandelions carpeting the lawn beyond.

Tom is shame-faced. 'It's a poor show for a gardener, isn't it? I find it hard to get down to, after a day of it.'

'Like a plumber who doesn't fix his dripping taps?'

'Something like that.'

'You could say it's deliberate. A wilderness area to encourage the butterflies.' I hold my glass out. 'To wildernesses and butterflies.'

He clinks his glass against mine. 'Wildernesses and butterflies.'

To an outsider – and, I hope, Tom – this must seem like any other evening we have spent together. For me, it's a performance. I'm acting the part of loyal girlfriend, feigning a normal relationship until it feels normal again. Committed to a path of deception, I have no other choice.

'You're not wearing your ring.' Tom squints at my hand.

'I must have forgotten to put it back on after my shower this morning. I'm always frightened it'll come off and get lost down the drain.'

In reality, I haven't been able to bring myself to wear it. After we met on Monday, I returned the ring to its box and haven't looked at it since. I'm determined that we will get married, but for now it is a reminder only of bad things: of my infidelity and guilt.

Yet it could provide a way to make a break with my immediate past.

'Tom, this might sound odd, but would you give it to me again? I mean, propose.'

'Oh-kay. Why?'

'It'd be like a fresh start.' As silly a notion as New Year's resolutions. Fresh starts don't need the right day or object, only the right attitude. Still, a symbolic gesture can't do any harm.

'Sure, why not,' he says.

'I won't wear it till then. If you don't mind?'

'Fine by me. More wine?'

He gets up to fetch the bottle from inside. As he passes me, he stops. 'Hold still.' He touches the back of my neck, making me jump.

'What is it? What are you doing?' I hunch my shoulders. 'You're tickling. I don't like it.'

'Stop jigging about!'

A moment later, Tom holds his hand in front of my face. A ladybird with six spots scurries along his forefinger. 'You had a guest,' he says. He shakes his hand and the ladybird flies away.

The hairs on the back of my neck are on end. I remember Michael touching me, when he noticed my earring was missing, and shiver. The memory is disturbing and a reminder of something else I have hidden from Tom. The remaining stud is still secreted in the pocket of my purse, but I haven't admitted to losing its twin.

Later we have dinner at the local Indian restaurant. While we're waiting for our starters, Bex walks in, followed by the muscle-bound Keith.

'Hey, you.' She winks at Tom.

Keith scowls.

'Hi, Clare,' says Bex. 'Haven't seen you in a while.'

I smile. 'Hi Bex, Keith.'

Keith nods. The warmer weather has driven him into a vest top; his over-inflated pecs distort the logo decorating the front. His hair is cropped close to his bullish head.

'Not working tonight, Bex?' says Tom.

'Got the night off for Keith's birthday.' She links arms with him; hers are like matchsticks compared with his tattooed monstrosities.

'Happy Birthday!' Tom and I chorus at Keith. He grunts something unintelligible in response.

Bex tosses her curly-haired head at Tom. 'I have a bone to pick with you, Tom Henson. You haven't returned my calls all week. My garden's a jungle since my lawnmower packed in.' She flutters manicured nails that I'd lay odds have never been near a garden.

'I've been busy. I doubt I'll make it in the next few weeks. I haven't even had time to cut my own lawn,' he says. 'I know someone who could repair your mower, if that'd help?'

A waiter squeezes behind Bex and Keith, hoisting a tray of steaming dishes over the diners at the next table.

'C'mon, Bex. Let's get sat down. I'm gagging for a drink.' Keith pulls his arm free and edges away.

Bex tosses her head again. 'Better keep birthday boy happy!'

As they walk off, Tom picks up a poppadom, breaks it into bits and passes a chunk to me. 'It's a pity your tidying doesn't extend to other people's places – like my garden. Why is that? I mean, why is it just your stuff that matters?' He scoops lime pickle from a steel dish in the middle of the table.

It's the first time he's asked me to explain myself.

'I'm not sure. It's all about control. You know, bad things happen, but at least I have power over something. Lining up my books or folding my tee shirts into squares or whatever.' I crumble my poppadom onto my side plate. 'Maybe I'm only compelled to tidy my things because they're more important to me. I don't really know...'

'I'm sorry, I'm making you uncomfortable,' he says. 'I don't want to do that. I'd just like to understand, if I can.'

'I know. It's hard. I don't understand it myself.' I mash the poppadom under my fingers.

Tom nods at the crumbs on my plate and passes me a fresh piece. 'Have another go!'

'Thanks. What's the pickle like?' I'd rather talk about Indian condiments than my mental health.

'Well, I've got third-degree burns on my throat, but otherwise it's lovely!'

I laugh and instantly relax. I still don't feel my old self with Tom, but maybe I'm on my way.

The real test comes when we get home – when we go to bed.

He is as attentive as ever, but I'm self-conscious under his gaze. I almost flinch as he runs his fingers over skin that I fear somehow retains an imprint of my deception. I tense, waiting for him to feel the change, to find me out.

He's oblivious; it's all in my mind. And that's the problem; too much is going on in my head for me to relax. The guilt acts as a strange kind of paralytic. I sense the physical contact, yet it brings me no pleasure.

I close my eyes, try to concentrate.

'Hey, beautiful, are you okay?' says Tom. 'You're frowning.'

Oh, Christ.

I open my eyes, murmur, 'Mmm, fine.'

He knows I love to watch him watching me. His Michael-blue eyes stare into mine and I freeze inside.

He reaches down between us and parts my legs. The initial soft pressure of his fingers builds into something harder, faster. He knows my body, knows what works — what should work.

It won't this time; I'm not going to come. If I don't, Tom will be concerned, apologetic. I can't face that; I don't deserve either concern or apologies.

I begin to moan, try to act what usually comes naturally. He's fooled; his fingers quicken to my rhythm. I step up my response. When I think we've both had enough, I judder and groan to my fake climax.

'Abstinence makes the heart grow fonder, eh?' says Tom.

My eyes fill with tears. He brushes one away as it rolls down my cheek. 'You are funny. I've never known anyone cry so much when they're happy. You never used to.'

'Maybe I wasn't this happy, then,' I say, and smile to prove how very happy I am.

He smiles, too, and moves gently inside me. When he comes a few minutes later, I cry again.

34

My breakfast tray is decorated with an egg cup full of daisies, which prompts me to suggest a focus for our morning.

'It's a beautiful day for gardening,' I say. 'From what you said last night, it sounds as if you could do with some help?'

'If you're sure you want the job?' says Tom. 'The pay's pretty lousy and there's no private healthcare or pension scheme.'

'I'll settle for unlimited tea and biscuits.'

'Deal! You weed and I'll hack and mow.'

We don matching uniforms of tee shirts and shorts – and sunscreen for me – and are soon sweaty with the effort. Towards lunchtime, I plead impending sunstroke to escape and prepare a snack of ham sandwiches and sliced apple. We picnic amongst the sweet-smelling grass cuttings. Charlie joins me in the shade, panting as he snuffles for crumbs. Tom sits a few feet away, in the sunshine, his capacity for soaking up ultraviolet rays apparently infinite.

I'm guiltily grateful for the distance that capacity affords me.

I am so happy to have another chance with Tom, so happy to be back with him. Yet, at the same time, my infidelity renders his presence almost unbearable. Every time he touches me, every time I laugh at something he says, every time I relax in his company, I remember – and the memory pulls me up short. The day is a world apart from last Sunday with Michael; I could almost believe that weekend never happened. The recurring stabs of guilt are proof that it did.

Tom grants me an unexpected reprieve: although it's a bank holiday weekend, he has to work tomorrow.

'I'm really sorry, I forgot to tell you,' he says, as we clear away the garden tools. 'Not that I'm kicking you out. You can stay here tonight and tomorrow if you want to. I won't be back late. We can have dinner before you go home.'

I'm torn as to how to react. Part of me screams, *Have a day off, for Christ's sake. Weeds won't conquer the world in twenty-four hours.*

The other part whispers, *Thank God I won't have to fake it again.* Not tonight, at least. With time, I hope, the guilt will loosen its paralysing hold on my body.

I elect to say, 'I'd better not stay. You'll be up way too early for me.'

'Have a lie-in after I've gone.'

'I won't get back to sleep. Once I'm awake, that's it. Don't worry, I've plenty to do at home.' Plenty being, trying to make a mess and live with it.

As I leave, Tom reminds me, 'Bring your ring next weekend, for me to propose again. If you still want me to do that?'

'Yes. Yes, I do.'

'Okay. But you do know everything's going to be all right now?' He looks deep into my eyes, as if he might persuade me by sheer force of will.

'I do.' I'm already determined to make sure it will be, whatever it takes. I have to.

And so I plan for Monday to be my first whole day surrounded by self-imposed disorder. My first real leap towards my future.

In the morning, I rearrange a few things in each room of the flat, depriving myself of any refuge from the disarray. Then I try to divert myself with magazines, washing and ironing, but am repeatedly distracted by the muddle around me. The experience strains my nerves so much that by mid-afternoon I am driven to put things right in the living room, to establish one safe retreat. As soon as I have, I think of Michael, of how I don't want to end up like him, and what I have to lose if I do. And so I unpick the order in the living room and endure the rest of the day with a knot in my stomach.

The result is that, for once, I'm relieved to return to the office after the break. So far, I've not attempted to generate mess at work. I'll move onto that when I've mastered the flat – one step at a time. In the meantime, the precise layout of my office equipment and the orderly piles of papers are balm to my soul.

I get in later to find a note from Janet amongst the post downstairs, *Been burgled. Scared to sleep here. Gone to Mum's for a few days. Could you collect post? On mobile if you need me. Thanks. Janet.*

God, no! Poor Janet.

Her flat is off the main hallway. There's no sign of the door having been forced. I go outside and circle the building. Her bathroom window is boarded up. It faces the garages at the back and isn't overlooked. The softest option in the block, given that the other ground-floor flat has metal grilles at the windows.

As I walk back around to the entrance, I glance up at my own flat. Thank God I live on the first floor. I shiver at the idea of someone invading my home.

Back inside, I finish checking the post. I wonder whether to put a notice on the communal board to warn the other residents. Nothing like this has happened here before. It's unsettling. Tidying will be hard to resist tonight; bad news always exacerbates my compulsions. Still, it's Janet's bad news, not mine. If I react to every incident that ripples my life, I'll never get better. I resolve not to let it affect me.

I head upstairs to my flat. As I turn the key in the mortise lock, it stops halfway through its usual rotation. I rattle it. It must be jammed. Turning it back, I try again. Nothing. No clunk of the bolt sliding across. Then I realise, it's already unlocked. My heart thuds. Jesus, I must have forgotten to lock it. I don't remember ever doing that.

I try to recall this morning's tag word. The landing was hot and stuffy, I was cradling a bunch of flowers for a colleague's birthday – and? Think, think. And I was worried about them wilting. Water! The tag word was *water*. I *did* lock the door.

So why is it not locked now? I shake my head. The tag word must have come to me before I actually did it. Idiot. That will teach me. I shudder at my near miss. With a burglar downstairs, it was the worst day to leave my door unsecured.

I put the key in the latch and click it open. A flyweight burglar could shoulder past such a flimsy device. The mortise I overlooked is the true guardian of my home. I shudder again. So close.

Pushing the door shut behind me, I slip off my shoes – and freeze. Something is on the floor in the middle of the hall. It looks like a fallen butterfly. My eyes take a moment to interpret what it is: my spare keys. The ones Janet holds. The ones I decorated with an orange ribbon bow, so that she couldn't lose them.

I drop my post and handbag onto the floor. My fists clench, my own front door keys dig into my palm. Flipping them around in my hand, I entwine my fingers through the connecting rings to create an impromptu knuckle-duster. A do-it-yourself self-defence tip from a glossy magazine. Faced with the reality of a possible intruder, the keys are a poor weapon.

I listen. The flat is silent. It's safe to move around, but I don't want to. I want to stay here and pretend this isn't happening.

A sickening certainty that I'm about to discover something horrible grips me. My life will be turned upside down and I can do nothing to stop it. Nothing at all, because it has already happened — I just can't see it yet.

I drop the keys and walk towards the living room. My body is out of my control. It moves without conscious thought, making me as helpless as the soon-to-be victim in a horror film. Approaching some unknown, yet certain terror.

I watch my hand press flat against the door and push. The door opens in slow motion. Bit by bit, until the entire room is visible. And the horror isn't a monster with blades for fingers. The horror is the room itself.

Everything is upturned, broken, tossed around as if by a tornado. The patterns are all gone, replaced by a crazed kaleidoscope of destruction.

My eyes dart here and there, registering the missing pieces.

The DVD player and most of my DVDs and CDs.

The phone.

The pot of loose change.

Some new stereo speakers.

Left behind are random survivors of my film and music collections. The old-fashioned and bulky stereo system. The PC, too old to be of any value. The monitor is shattered, though, and glass litters my desk.

The vase that held Tom's roses is in pieces in front of the bookcase. Water darkens the carpet beneath the shards. The flowers lie limp amongst the fragments, loose petals shrivelling around them.

The scatter and sofa cushions are all over the room, the smaller ones ripped open, their feathers like a dusting of snow on the carpet.

The piles of books and magazines have toppled. Plants lie horizontal. Ornaments are smashed.

The mosaic of debris has almost obliterated the carpet.

I stagger out of the room and crash the door shut behind me. Leaning against it, I close my eyes. My heart races. Nothing in my therapy has prepared me for anything like this — for this kind of devastation.

Opening my eyes, I move towards the kitchen. I'll stay in there. Just for a few minutes. Until I feel better. A cup of tea, get my head straight.

I push open the door, stop. Ketchup bleeds down the walls,

chocolate spread is smeared across them like faeces. At my feet spreads an evil-smelling swamp of pickle and mayonnaise and pesto and curry sauce. Glass from jars and bottles glitters amongst the rancid goo.

Backing away, I run to the bathroom. I reach the toilet just in time to heave over the bowl. To keep heaving until I'm empty. My eyes stream, as I retch drily.

I wipe my mouth with a handful of toilet paper and slump against the side of the bath, feeling cold and shaky. Too drained to imagine ever getting up.

I pull a towel from the rail and wrap it around me. Huddled under it, still shaking, I gaze around the room. All is ordered, unbroken, perfect. A haven against the maelstrom outside.

Reaching up, I lock the door. I'm safe now. The chaos can't get me in here.

35

I come to with a start. My neck is cricked and I'm cold and stiff, confused about where I am and why. Then I remember. Nausea revives with that memory, but there is nothing left inside me to feed it.

I unwrap the towel from my shoulders and stand up. My legs are wobbly. I don't know whether I passed out or fell asleep. I clutch the edge of the basin and stare at my pale face in the mirror above it. Stare for so long that I can't see who I am any more. Lose all meaning, like a word repeated too many times.

Unlocking the door, I cross the hall to the bedroom. I feel nothing as I register the mess of spilled creams and perfumes. The drawers pulled open, their contents tumbling out. The upended jewellery box. The cracked glass of the frame holding Mum's photo.

I feel nothing, think only, *I have to get out of here.*

I lift a small case down from the top of the wardrobe and lay the photo in it, before packing a few clothes. I have to ferret in the bottom of drawers and the back of cupboards for items not fingered by the burglar: mostly unfashionable or worn-out things, kept for the next charity shop clear-out.

In the bathroom, I fill a toiletry bag with the basics for a trip. I don't yet know where I'm going, only that I am going. At the door, I turn back. I pick up the toothbrush holder and add it to the bag. The zip won't close. I take the holder anyway.

Back in the hall, I stare down at the case. My life is in there now: a photo, some old clothes, a few toiletries and a cheap toothbrush holder. The random belongings of a bag lady.

I retrieve my handbag, post and two sets of keys from the floor. Only now do I notice the change to the label on the spare set: Janet has added the word *upstairs* against my name. The word that must have led the burglar here. How could she have been so stupid? Anger surges through me, yet I'm angrier with myself than with her. How could *I* have been so stupid as to trust her?

Sighing, I flip the case up onto its wheels and take a last look around. I've closed the doors to all the rooms. The flat is peaceful, the hall tidy, yet I can see what lies beyond it. The images are branded on my mind. Freeze frames of the collapse of my world.

As I leave, the front door slams behind me. I turn to lock it. Force of habit. There doesn't seem much point.

On the bottom of Janet's note, I scribble, *I've been burgled, too. Also gone away for a while. See you soon. C*, and slide it under her door.

I drive to a small hotel on the other side of town: one of a chain favoured by business travellers. Bland and anonymous. At reception, I feel sleazy. Like a prostitute or fugitive signing in at a remote motel. I am a fugitive of sorts.

I take my key and follow the receptionist's directions. Walking down the long corridor, in the carpeted silence, I could be the last person on Earth.

The door to my room is heavy. Leaning into it, I reach my sanctuary. The bedroom is clean, tidy, minimalist. Perfect. A vase of red silk roses is the only bright spot in an oasis of cream and beige.

Dropping my case, I wander around. Run my hand over the clean, polished wood. Take in the neat tray of refreshments, the precise fan of information leaflets. Watch the spotlights twinkle off the bathroom surfaces.

I don't want to spoil the look. Hiding my handbag and case in the wardrobe, I take off my shoes and lie on the bed, still in my work clothes.

I stare at the ceiling. My eyes wander over the blemishes pock-marking it, searching for constellations, geometric shapes, patterns of any kind. I make a hexagon and a square and find most of The Plough.

As I calm down, I let my mind drift to what has just happened.

I thought I'd done everything possible to protect myself, but no amount of checking, or locks, would have prevented the break-in. Although I berated myself earlier, I couldn't have foreseen how Janet would undermine my security. I can't anticipate every eventuality or avert every catastrophe, whether it's the result of a neighbour's foolishness, an accident or a natural disaster. I see that; I don't want to accept it. Don't want to accept that, sometimes, nothing makes a difference – neither superstitions and rituals nor practical measures. What will be, will be.

The light fades. I'm hungry and thirsty, yet don't have the energy to drag myself off the bed to make a drink or find food.

The room is airless. Traffic hums on the main road. Suddenly drowsy, I doze off to the sound.

A passing siren wakes me, both to darkness and the niggling feeling that I've forgotten to do something.

Tom! We speak every evening. Clicking on the bedside lamp, I check my watch: ten-fifteen. He'll be wondering what's going on. I get up, splash water on my face and rescue my handbag from the wardrobe. My mobile shows both a missed call and a text from Tom.

He answers on the second ring. 'Clare, hi, are you okay? Your answerphone isn't kicking in and I couldn't get through on your mobile.'

'Er...yes, the answerphone's playing up at the moment, and I didn't hear your call. Sorry.' I can't bring myself to talk about the burglary.

'No worries. What's new? Have you had a good day?'

'The usual. You know.'

'You sound down.'

'Just tired. I've got a lot on at work. How about you?'

'The same. Everybody wants their gardens ready for summer.' He chats on about his customers, while I make appropriate noises.

He suddenly breaks off. 'Are you sure nothing's wrong? You don't seem yourself.'

'Honestly, I'm fine.'

'Maybe you just need an early night? I'll stop rabbiting on and let you get to bed. So long as you're okay?'

'I'm all right, Tom. Really.'

'Okay. Night, then. Love you.'

'Love you, too.'

In the morning, I call in sick to the office, pleading a virus. My boss commiserates, saying there's a bug going around; her husband and a friend have been ill. I feel bad about deceiving her, but it works in my favour that I don't usually let her down; she never questions my rare sick days. In fact, I do feel awful: I slept badly and I'm faint with hunger.

Dressed in a faded tee shirt and cut-off jeans, I make some tea. Water from the bathroom mixed with long-life milk makes an unpleasant brew, but it eases my thirst, and the shortbread biscuits take the edge off my hunger.

The hotel is a stopover only place, with entertainment restricted to the tea tray and the television. I head into the town centre for a proper breakfast and to kill some time. Until when or what, I don't know. I gravitate from people-watching in cafés, to browsing bookshops, to reading the daily papers in the library. It's lucky that I don't work locally, and that none of my close colleagues live nearby, or I'd be trapped in my hotel room, watching chat shows and ordering takeaways.

By early evening, though, I'm running out of options. I go back to the café where I started the day. The menu lists everything from milkshakes and burgers, to fry-ups and roast dinners. Although it's early, I'm hungry again. If I eat now, I'll avoid the need for a meal at a more expensive restaurant later. The food is stodgy, but comforting.

The cheering effect is only temporary. Returning to the hotel, where no one knows or cares about me, I'm enveloped in misery. I trudge down the corridor, a prisoner forced back into my cell.

My loneliness is exacerbated by the fact that the cleaners have restored my room to its original perfection, obliterating what little impact I'd made on it: the refreshment tray has been restocked and returned its rightful place; the information leaflets I shuffled through restored to a perfect fan; and the used towels replaced and toiletries replenished. As if no one had been in the room. The perfection that soothed me yesterday now seems cold and impersonal. I've been wiped out, as I was by Michael in his flat. As I was by the burglar in my own.

I have to make my presence felt.

So far, I have only unpacked my toiletry bag. The contents, including the toothbrush holder, have been pushed to one side in the bathroom. I wonder what housekeeping made of the holder? I doubt many guests bring their own. I put it back in the middle of the shelf above the basin, where I left it this morning.

In the bedroom, I wipe out its anonymity by draping clothes over the chairs, moving the refreshment tray to the bedside table, pushing the leaflets into a pile and sitting on the bed to ruffle the covers. My last personal touch is to place Mum's photo in front of the dressing table mirror.

The lived-in look makes me feel more comfortable.

Not for long, though. An evening of mindless channel-hopping leaves me fidgety and restless. I have no idea what I'm doing here. No idea where another day of killing time will get me. I can't stay in this hotel forever, nor can I face going home. I need help to escape my limbo; I have to tell Tom what has happened.

I dive in as soon as he picks up the phone, 'Tom, I've been burgled.'

'What? When?'

'Yesterday, while I was at work.'

'Yesterday! No wonder you sounded out of sorts last night. Why didn't you tell me?'

'I couldn't bring myself to talk about it. I didn't even tell work this morning; I said I was ill.'

'You shouldn't be on your own. I'll come down to stay the night. Give me an hour.'

'I'm not at home. I'm in a hotel. I couldn't stay in the flat; it's been vandalised. I couldn't face it.'

'Oh, Clare, I'm so sorry. I can't imagine how horrible that must have been.'

Only as I begin to cry, do I realise I haven't until now. Through my sobs, I hear Tom asking where I am, saying he'll come for me. Eventually he stops talking and waits for me to stop crying.

'Clare, you have to let me help you. Is the flat secure? How did they get in?'

'They burgled Janet's flat and found my spare keys. She's so dozy that she'd written "upstairs" next to my name, so they could only be mine or my neighbours and—'

'Okay, okay, slow down. You'll need to get the locks changed, then.'

'I never thought of that.' Thank goodness for his practicality.

'I know a good locksmith. I'll give him a call, see if he can come down with me first thing.'

'Thanks, Tom.'

'Have you told the police?'

'No, I didn't think of that either. I was just so desperate to get away from there.' My voice is shaky. 'God, I'm useless.'

'You're not useless. You're upset. Don't worry, Clare, everything will be all right.'

'I hope so,' I say.

But with my home as damaged as my relationship, I don't see how anything will ever be right again.

36

I meet Tom in the hotel reception. Before I say anything, he hugs me tightly. This time his embrace feels reassuring, rather than awkward.

'How are you doing?' He pulls away and looks at me.

'I'm fine.' I choke back tears.

He raises an eyebrow.

'Honestly.' I do feel better for seeing him, for knowing he'll take care of everything.

'You should come and stay at the cottage.'

I shake my head. 'I need time on my own, Tom.'

'But this place must be costing you a fortune?'

'Not really.' And the bill will go on my credit card, to worry about another day; money is the last thing on my mind.

'Still, you'd be better off at my place, even with the higher train fares into work.'

'I'd rather—'

A small, wiry man comes up behind Tom and holds out his hand to me. 'Hi, I'm Andy, the locksmith. Sorry 'bout your flat.'

I shake his hand. 'Thanks.'

'Tom, mate, we need to get going,' says Andy.

'Sorry to keep you hanging about,' says Tom. 'Clare, we need to crack on. Andy has another job later this morning.'

They both turn and head outside. I hesitate.

Tom stops and looks back. 'Clare?'

I don't want to go, but nor can I stay here. It's not fair to leave them to sort out my problems – while I do what? Dawdle in cafés? Battle with housekeeping over the layout of my room?

'Coming,' I say.

We travel to the flat in Andy's van. Tom has left his with his trainees, Barry and Steve, making Andy chauffeur as well as locksmith. It turns out he's one of Bex's friends. I resent the connection, while realising how churlish that is; he's only here to help.

He parks the van at the back of the building. As we get out,

I look up at the windows. My kitchen and bedroom overlook the rear. Time and distance had blurred the images of the chaos inside. Now they come back into focus, as vivid and shocking as the real thing. The food mural disfiguring the kitchen walls, the wreckage on the living room floor, the violation of my bedroom. My courage fails me.

'I can't do it,' I say. 'I'm sorry, I can't go inside.'

'Don't worry,' says Tom. 'I'll check things out for you. It'll only be a quick recce. We shouldn't touch anything before the police get here.'

'Actually, I've been thinking about that... I'd rather they weren't involved.'

'But you won't be able to claim on the insurance if you don't report it,' he says.

Maybe not. All I know is I don't want more strangers tramping around my home. More unfamiliar hands touching my belongings, or boots grinding in the debris. The police will only make things worse, and a claim might be a waste of time; I doubt my insurance covers a burglar letting themselves in.

'I just can't bear the idea of them being in my flat as well.' I dig out my keys and hand them to Tom. 'Oh, I've just thought, I touched the spare keys, but there might have been fingerprints on them!'

'I doubt it; the burglar probably wore gloves. And if not, there'll be fingerprints all over the flat, anyway.' He kisses me lightly on the lips. 'Leave it all to me. I told you. Everything will be all right. Maybe the police don't even need to come around.'

'Shouldn't think they'll give a toss,' says Andy. 'It's just another burglary, isn't it? They never catch these bastards.'

Once he and Tom have gone around to the front of the building, I begin to pace up and down, like a prisoner on exercise time, scuffing the gravel with my toes and swinging my handbag to the beat of my steps.

Waiting gives me time to think, which I don't want to do. I need a distraction. I cross the grass surrounding the building and peer into Janet's bedroom window. Through the nets, I can see no mess, only an ordinary person's clutter. I check out the kitchen. The same. The key rack catches my eye, on the wall opposite the window. Several hooks are empty.

I walk along next to the sidewall, past the boarded-up bathroom window, and approach the living room at the front. Making blinkers of my hands around my face, I look inside. The room has an abandoned air, but is undamaged. Janet can't have cleaned up already; I doubt she's even back yet. Fury grips me. The burglar only vandalised my home. Why? I thump my hand against the glass. Why me? It's so unfair, when all this is down to her.

'Clare, what on earth are you doing?'

I swivel around. The front door swings shut behind Tom.

'I...' I step away from the window and squint into the sun at him. 'I thought Janet might be home.'

'You could ring her doorbell.' He gestures at the panel next to the entrance. 'You'll give her a heart attack, banging like that!'

'I don't think she's there.' I walk towards him. 'How are things upstairs? You know...?' I mean, is it as bad as I remember?

'Sorry, beautiful, he really went to town, didn't he?'

It is as bad. My eyes fill with tears and my head droops.

'I know how nicely you kept everything,' says Tom. 'It must be so hard for you.'

Maybe my tidiness triggered the burglar's destructive urges. Maybe I'm to blame, after all.

Maybe I deserve it for what I've done to Tom.

He puts his finger under my chin and tilts it up. 'Don't worry. I'll get contract cleaners in. It'll be cleared up in no time.'

I chew my lip.

'Are you okay with that?' He peers down at me. 'I don't think we can avoid having people in, unless you want to do it yourself? Cleaners will probably make a better job of it, have the right stuff for stains...'

I can't stand the idea of tackling it myself, but nor can I bear the thought of someone else doing it.

'I know. It's just...' It's just that I want the impossible. I want a genie to appear, to wish things back to the way they were. A fairy godmother to wave a wand and create beauty out of ugliness. 'That would be great. Thank you.'

'Good. The kitchen'll need re-painting, as well. I'll sort someone out to do that.'

Fantastic, cleaners and decorators. I might as well hold an open house. Having the police around suddenly seems the least of my worries.

'I need to get back upstairs,' says Tom. 'I just came down to borrow your phone. If I take some photos you can check what's broken or missing, when you're up to it.'

'Thanks.' I can't envisage ever being ready to look at those photos, but fish my phone out of my bag.

He takes a few test shots, following my instructions, and then asks, 'Where do you keep your insurance paperwork? I can look that out for you while I'm up there.'

'The black concertina file on the bookcase in the living room. Bottom shelf, left-hand side.'

After he has gone, I trudge back to the van. Inside I rest my folded arms on the dashboard and let my head sink onto them. I stare into the darkness of the footwell. The sun beats through the windscreen, my scalp burns. I stay like that until Tom opens the passenger door.

He climbs in, nudging me to the middle of the seat and handing me my phone. 'We're all done. And I've got your insurance stuff.' He brandishes a small bundle of papers. 'Good thing you're organised. If you like, I could give them a call? See what we have to do about reporting the burglary.'

'Thanks, Tom.' I like the way he has taken charge. Nothing fazes him.

Andy gets into the driver's seat.

'And thank you, Andy,' I say.

'No problem, love. Here are your new keys. Tom's got the spares, so he can let people in.'

The keys dangle from my fingers; they're new, shiny, perfect. The opposite of what is behind the door they now secure.

As Andy manoeuvres the van out of the car park, Tom fidgets next to me. 'Clare, have you got your engagement ring?'

I flex the fingers of my left hand, though I already know the answer. 'No, I haven't been wearing it. I was waiting till...' I glance at Andy. 'It was in my jewellery box, on the dressing table. In the little silk-lined box it came in.'

Tom runs his hand through his hair. 'I'm really sorry, Clare. They must have taken it. The box is there, but it's empty.'

'Oh no! If only I'd been wearing it—'

'It's not your fault, Clare. We agreed you wouldn't.'

'It *is* my fault. If we hadn't had a break and all those problems. My problems—'

Andy clears his throat.

'We'll replace it.' Tom squeezes my leg.

'It won't be the same. A replacement will never be the same.'
My eyes fill with tears. Tom presenting the ring again was supposed
to be symbolic of our new start. Losing it is a bad omen.

'I'm sorry, Clare. I wish I could undo what's happened.'

He looks so sad. Then I realise, this is not just about how I feel.

I brush away my tears and stretch over to kiss his cheek. 'I know
you do,' I say, 'and I know that I couldn't get through this without
you.'

He smiles and turns to press his lips against mine.

Andy clears his throat, more loudly this time. 'Oi, get a room,
you two!'

'Sorry, mate.' Tom blushes.

At the hotel, he sees me inside.

'God, I nearly forgot,' I say, 'I haven't paid Andy.' Sliding my
handbag off my shoulder, I move back towards the main doors.

Tom stops me. 'I'll do it.'

'You've done enough already.'

'It's fine. Settle up with me another day. You've got enough
expense with this place.' He sighs. 'I hate to think of you here on
your own, Clare. I wish you'd come and stay with me. I won't be
around during the day, you'll have the place to yourself.'

'I'm booked in till the weekend. They might charge me if
I cancel.'

'I doubt it. Even if they do, it's not as if you'll have to pay to
stay with me. You'll be spending the same amount, whichever bed
you sleep in.'

'I know, and I'm grateful for your help, Tom, honestly. I could
just do with some time to myself. Please.'

The truth is, although I now desperately need him, being
with Tom, day in, day out, will be too hard. My sense of guilt in
his presence too much to handle on top of everything else that has
happened.

'Okay, beautiful,' he says. 'Whatever you want, but don't forget,
the offer's there.'

Back in my room, I almost regret my decision, nearly run
outside to chase down Andy's van – housekeeping has been in and
everything belonging to the room is back in its place.

This must be what it's like to live with someone who has my
compulsions – or Michael's habits. The same rigidity governs this
room and visitors can only temporarily bend the rules of its layout.

No matter how many nights I stay, no matter how many times I flout those rules, eventually the room will revert to its status quo, as if I never existed.

I have to fight back, even if the fight is futile. I wearily begin to undo everything. Find new locations for the tea tray, the leaflets, the remote control – even the bible in the drawer. Only, I know, for them all to be put back tomorrow, and the day after, and the day after that.

In the bathroom, the toothbrush holder has retained its position in the middle of the shelf above the basin, where I left it this morning. That was my rule then, my decision. Now it has become part of the room's pattern. I take it down and place it next to the basin. Tomorrow I'll put it somewhere else. I don't want patterns any more – mine or anybody else's.

37

Eating breakfast in the café again the next morning, I long for my own kitchen, to be able to make a sandwich or a decent cup of tea whenever I want. I wonder when my flat will be habitable and how I'll cope with going back when it is. For now, my life is on hold, including my still fragile future with Tom. Eventually, though, the pause button will be released and I'll have to pick up where I left off.

As I watch the world go by from my table at the window, a group of teenage girls stops outside, talking loudly on mobiles and to each other. Two turn to examine their reflections in the glass above my head. One licks the end of a finger and smooths down her eyebrows. The other puts on lipstick, pressing her lips together until they vanish, and pouts at the window. They behave as if the glass were mirrored, as if I were invisible.

I concentrate on my food, waiting for them to move away, so that I can relax again. Then I realise, they're not in school uniform; it's half-term. Sophie and Harry will also be off and Fiona is meant to be convalescing. I could offer to baby-sit this afternoon; it will give the day a purpose.

It will also allow me to make amends for upsetting her.

Our encounters often end with animosity crackling between us, with neither of us expecting an apology or further discussion of what we argued about. Usually, though, we part on equal terms – each equally upset, each equally to blame. At the hospital, it was different: while we both ended up in tears, the upset was all of my making and Fiona was left more vulnerable. I have to say something – do something – to restore the balance.

I keep our phone conversation simple, trying to assess her frame of mind. With all that has happened in the last two weeks, I haven't had time to dwell on our fight, but Fiona might have done.

'I thought I'd take the children out,' I say. 'Give you a break.'

'I'm used to it, I can manage.' Her tone is abrupt, but no more unfriendly than usual.

'I know. Still, after the surgery…and everything.'

'All right. What time will you be here?'

'Eleven-thirty?'

'Fine. Though everywhere will be heaving by the time you get there. I can't imagine why you decided to take leave in the school holidays, when you don't have to.'

'Er, I'm just using up days I'd carried over.' I don't intend to tell her about the burglary or my escape to the hotel and dependency on Tom. She has little enough faith in my ability to fend for myself. 'I have to use them by the end of May or—'

'Will you have lunch here first?'

'No – thanks. We'll get something while we're out.'

I arrive at Fiona's with a colourful supermarket bouquet.

'Thanks, but you didn't need to,' she says. 'You're doing me the favour, aren't you?' She takes the flowers from me.

'I suppose so,' I say, 'but I thought they were pretty.' Maybe it's a good sign that she doesn't expect a peace offering; she obviously doesn't feel particularly hard done by.

As we move inside, I notice the customary white lilies on the table by the door. My orange gerbera and pink roses are garish in comparison.

The appearance of the children saves me from having to provide the real explanation for my gift. They fling themselves at me, shrieking and laughing. Talking over one another, they vie for my attention. I raise my eyebrows in mock bewilderment at Fiona.

She shakes her head. 'They've been like that ever since I told them you were coming. Sophie, Harry, go back outside and play, while I make Auntie Clare a cup of tea.'

The children scamper off and I follow Fiona into the kitchen. She walks awkwardly, almost with a limp. Laying the flowers in the sink, she flicks the kettle on.

'They haven't stopped talking about their stay with you,' she says. 'I must say, you managed better than I expected.'

The backhanded compliment encourages me to risk an apology. 'Fi, I'm sorry if I upset you at the hospital. I really didn't mean to.'

She clanks two mugs down and drops teabags into them. 'Clare, I don't think we need to go over all that again, do we?'

'No, I just wanted to say—'

'White, no sugar, isn't it?'

'Yes.'

Fiona pours the water. I sit down at the large table.

'So, how are you doing after the op?'

'Fine.' She winces, as she bends to get the milk out of the fridge.

'When do you go back to work?'

'Not for another month. The summer term's a terrible time to be off. God knows how much paperwork will have piled up.' She pours the milk into the mugs.

'It can't be helped. Your health's more important. How are you in yourself?'

She looks better than when I last saw her. Her hair has been restored to a sleek helmet and she's wearing her usual monochrome trousers and shirt, topped off with a green and white scarf tied too tightly around her neck to make out the pattern. Externally, at least, everything is back to normal.

'In myself?' She slides the milk back into the fridge.

'You know?' I jerk my head, translating the words I daren't say into a gesture.

Fiona interprets it correctly. 'I told you, I didn't want a...' She glances outside, through the open French doors connecting the kitchen and patio.

I follow her look. The children are at the bottom of the garden, playing on their swing set.

'I didn't want a baby.' She joins me at the table, with our teas. 'It was just a damned nuisance that I had to have a full-scale operation. I could have dealt with an ordinary pregnancy and been back at work the next day.'

Dealt with? She is so matter-of-fact.

'Anyway, enough of all that.' She cups her tea in her hands. 'Have you fixed a wedding date yet?'

The wedding? Christ. 'No, not yet. We've been too busy. There's no hurry.'

'If you keep saying that, it'll never happen.'

Sophie skips in. 'Is it time to go? Is it, is it?' She tugs at my arm.

'Sophie, stop bothering Auntie Clare. You'll spill her tea.'

Sophie pouts at her mother and turns a smile on me. 'Auntie Clare, can I put your ring on? Pleeease!' She holds out her hand.

'Sophie Mercer! I told you to leave Auntie Clare alone. What is the matter with you?'

I put my hands under the table, wrapping the right one over the bare fingers of the left. 'Sorry, Sophie, I'm not wearing my ring at the moment. Maybe another day.'

'If I had a ring, I'd never take it off. Never, ever. Not even in the bath.' Sophie frowns. 'Auntie Clare, if you don't wear Uncle Tom's ring, can another boy kiss you?'

Ring or no ring, it doesn't matter. Hardly an answer to give a child. 'Of course not! Whatever makes you say that?'

'We-ell—'

'Sophie, will you do as you're told and stop pestering Auntie Clare!' says Fiona.

Sophie ignores her mother. 'We-ell, on television, Auntie Clare, this lady—'

'I'm not going to tell you again, Sophie. You won't be going out, if you carry on like this.'

Sophie glowers at Fiona, heaves a pained sigh and runs out into the garden.

'I don't know where she gets her ideas from,' says Fiona.

I just hope that Sophie has used up all her attitude, so that we can survive the afternoon without mishap.

38

'Bekonscot Model Village? That sounds old-fashioned,' Fiona grumbles at me in the kitchen, after we get back from an almost tantrum free trip.

'They loved it.' I'm sitting at the table, watching her make Sophie and Harry's dinner, while they get washed and changed upstairs. 'Where did you expect me to take them? It was hardly worth spending a fortune at somewhere like Legoland just for an afternoon.' Transferring their car seats had cost us an extra half-hour before we'd even set off.

Fiona isn't used to doing budget days out, though. Not for her low-cost venues, free museums or picnics in the park. No, it's theme parks and zoos and boat trips and accompanying bags of pricey merchandise.

She leans down and opens the oven door to check on the children's food. 'I don't know, it just doesn't sound much fun.'

'Well, it was; they had a great time.' I slouch in my chair in sulky teenager mode. 'Anyway, I can't afford to spoil them the way you do.' Especially now, with a flat to be cleaned and refurbished. I doubt the insurance will cover everything, even if the company does pay out.

Fiona pulls out a baking tray, on which several small jacket potatoes wobble next to a couple of chicken breasts. 'Really, so what were you thinking, buying Harry that lorry?' She reaches up to the counter for a fork and stabs at the potatoes.

'That was different. He was upset you weren't there. I thought they both deserved presents in the circumstances.'

'He's got enough cars and lorries as it is. I'm forever tripping over them. I told him he couldn't have that one till his birthday.'

'Sorry, I didn't know.' I cross fingers that Sophie doesn't mention telling me.

'So long as they don't expect to have expensive things all the time.' Fiona slides the tray of food back into the oven, slams the door shut and drops the fork into the sink.

'Bit late for that.' I'm not the one who takes them on fancy holidays and dresses them from Next.

'It's never too late for anything – or so I'm told. Sophie! Harry! Dinner will be ready in fifteen minutes. Can you make sure your rooms are tidy before then, please.' She takes a bottle of white wine out of the fridge and tops up a glass on the counter. 'Do you want a drink?'

'A small one. Then I need to make tracks.'

She takes another glass from the cupboard over the table, splashes in some wine and passes it to me.

'Thanks. So, did you have a relaxing few hours?'

'Hardly. I was up to my neck in paperwork.'

And wine, by the look of it.

Fiona swivels back to the hob and deposits the wine bottle on the counter next to her. She drops pasta shells into a pan of boiling water and picks up her glass, sipping at it while she cooks. The ends of her silk scarf have escaped the confines of her shirt and dangle limply in the steam.

Keys rattle in the front door.

'Hellooo? Anybody home?'

Sophie and Harry thunder down the stairs with a chorus of squeals. 'Daddee!'

Fiona frowns. 'They're supposed to be tidying their rooms.'

Dave comes into the kitchen, Sophie at his side and Harry hanging off him like a chimp. While Dave supports Harry with one arm, the other is twisted behind his back, concealing something.

'Hey, kiddo, didn't expect to see you.' He grins at me and moves towards Fiona. 'Hello, love. Had a good day?'

'Busy, as usual. Clare took the children out this afternoon, so I've had a bit of quiet, at least.'

'Nice one, Clare,' says Dave.

'It's a pleasure.' I smile at him.

Dave whispers to Sophie and Harry, 'Shall I give them to Mummy now?'

They both nod, beaming.

Dave produces a bunch of yellow roses like a magician. 'Ta da! From me and the kids.'

Fiona looks up. 'Thanks. I'll find a vase later. Can you put them somewhere out of the way while I'm cooking?' She turns back to stir the pasta, wooden spoon in one hand, glass of wine in the other.

Dave lowers Harry to the floor. 'You're getting too heavy for your old dad.' He goes over to the sink, runs water into the drainer section and props the roses in it.

Sophie and Harry stay in the kitchen doorway, nudging one another and giggling.

'Wine, Dave?' I say.

'Please.'

I reach up to the cupboard above me for a glass and pass it to Fiona. She huffs, as she puts down her own to fill Dave's.

He peers into the pan. 'What are we having with the pasta?'

'I'm having pesto,' she says. 'I didn't expect you back.'

'I told you I'd be home for dinner.'

She snorts. 'You've said that before and it's ended up in the proverbial dog.'

'Are we getting a dog?' says Harry, eyes bright with excitement.

'Don't start,' says Fiona. 'I've already made it quite clear, we are not having a dog.'

Sophie pokes Harry. 'See! I told you.'

He pushes her back.

'Hey, hey, enough of that, you two!' says Dave. 'Go and play next door and not another squeak out of you.'

When they've gone, Dave sits down next to me. He slips off his jacket and drapes it over the back of the chair. A musty work smell emanates from it.

'Fiona, I told you things were going to change,' he says. 'If I say I'll be home early, then I will.'

Fiona concentrates on the pasta.

'I'd better go,' I say.

'Aren't you staying for dinner?' says Dave. 'It's the least we can do to thank you for having the kids.'

Fiona opens a cupboard and takes down a jar of pesto. 'I told you, I'm only making for one. Clare said she had to go.'

Dave stands up. 'Come on, I'll shove another pan on for us, eh, kiddo? Can't send you home hungry.'

The prospect of eating in a domestic minefield doesn't appeal – nor does another roast dinner alone in the café.

'Thanks,' I say.

Dave persuades Fiona to let the children eat in front of the television, so that we can enjoy our meal in peace. By the time he and I start, she's halfway through hers and well into her next glass of wine.

The first few minutes of silent eating pass amicably enough. I've never been a fan of so-called comfortable silences, though; couples eating in restaurants without exchanging a word strike me as odd.

I make myself busy grinding black pepper onto my pasta, helping myself to more salad, sipping my wine. Those activities only occupy me for so long. Finally, I crack under the tension and say the first thing that comes into my head. 'What's with the half day, Dave? Trying to get your work-life balance back?'

'Something like that.' He looks quickly at Fiona.

She tops up her wine, emptying the bottle.

I plough on, 'No point in earning money, if you don't have time to enjoy it, eh?'

'Absolutely,' he says. 'Water, anyone?' He gets up and goes to the fridge.

'I'm always saying that,' says Fiona, ''cept no one listens to me. Do they, Dave?' Her words run together. She has, I suddenly realise, quietly got drunk.

He returns to the table with a bottle of mineral water, pours a glass and puts it in front of her. 'Have some water, Fiona. Please.'

I've never seen her like this; it makes me nervous. In this state, she's an unknown quantity. The alcohol could make her maudlin or aggressive, tearful or amusing.

She ignores the water and takes another swig of wine. From the look on her face, amusing isn't likely.

Dave takes the bait. 'Fiona! You'll make yourself ill, drinking so fast. You're not used to it.'

'How do you know? How do you know anything 'bout me?' Fiona tugs at her neckscarf, lifting her chin as she pulls the knot loose. The bamboo-patterned silk falls away from her skin onto the floor.

Dave sighs. 'I don't think I do.'

'Well, that's not my fault.' Her voice is louder.

Dave stands up, shuts the kitchen door. 'Fiona, stop it,' he says in a stage whisper. 'You're embarrassing Clare – and me.'

'Am I, Clare? Am I embarrassing?'

I open my mouth to say I'm-not-sure-what.

She carries on. ''Cause I'd think this was nice. Talking 'bout stuff, 'stead of all those secrets. 'Cause I know you don't like secrets, do you, Clare?'

Dave catches my eye and shakes his head almost imperceptibly.

Fiona leans back in her seat. 'The thing is, Dave doesn't like me all that much. Not at all, really.'

Dave sits down. 'Clare, ignore her, she's drunk.'

'Says I'm difficult to live with. Same thing, isn't it, Clare?'

'I don't know.' I put down my cutlery. My appetite has gone. I've often wished Fiona and Dad were more open, but not like this.

'Is that right, Clare? Am I difficult? Am I? You can tell me. I won't mind.'

I hesitate.

'See!' She waves her arm, wine sloshing over the top of her glass. 'See! S'true. Told you. S'why Dave works all the time. I'd like to work all the time, but I can't 'cause...' Her face is puzzled.

Dave puts his head in his hands.

'Oh yeah, 'cause we've got children,' says Fiona.

I glance at the kitchen door, fearful those children might walk in.

'And I have to look after them. 'Cause I do everything. I fix everything, for everyone. Here's to Fiona the fixer.' She makes a lone toast, gulping back half a glass of wine.

'I should go,' I say.

No one pays any attention.

Dave leans towards Fiona. 'And fixing includes planning to get rid of a baby you weren't going to tell me about?'

'Way things worked out, didn't matter,' she says.

'But the fact you didn't trust me does. I'd have understood, if you'd explained. You never gave me a chance.'

I'm a child again, listening to my parents arguing, helpless to stop them.

'I really should be off.' I stand up to make my intention clear.

Dave jumps, as if he has just noticed me. 'You're right. I'm sorry you had to hear this. This is between Fiona and me.'

'No, no, s'not,' says Fiona. 'I fix things for Clare, as well.'

I clutch the edge of the table. 'Like what?'

'Bringing you up...and stuff. You know?'

'Oh, I know. You certainly fixed things. You and Mum and Dad. You fixed things good and proper. If it weren't for all of you, maybe I wouldn't be so screwed up. Maybe I wouldn't be in this mess!'

Dave groans.

'Screwed up?' she says. 'Don't think so. Not you. You're as normal as, as…anyone.'

'Normal? Me? You know nothing, Fiona. Nothing.'

Fiona and Dave's faces become a blur, as tears fill my eyes. Grabbing my bag from the back of my chair, I storm out of the kitchen.

'Hold on,' calls Dave. 'Don't go. You're upset. You shouldn't drive.' He follows me into the hall.

The children's voices chirrup from the next room.

'Nothing to worry about, kids.' He hesitates at the living room door. 'Everything's all right.'

'No, it's not,' I throw back at him. 'It's not.'

I don't think it ever will be.

39

Tom soothes me when we talk later. 'Don't let it get to you. Doesn't Fiona always niggle you like that?'

'Yes, but I thought things might be changing. That maybe we could be more open with one another,' I say.

I was wrong. Her frankness is dependent on her being at a low ebb: ill or drunk. And at those points, it becomes an unguided missile, blowing open secrets with no discretion, no purpose, no chance of resolution.

'I don't need all this right now,' I say. 'I just can't deal with it.'

'Look, it's nearly the weekend. You can chill out up here, forget all about it. I'll make a nice meal, spoil you.'

'That'd be lovely,' I lie. Tom's efforts to look after me and put things right only make me feel worse about my infidelity, and I'm still unsure how I'll cope with a prolonged period in his company.

'By the way, I've booked some people to clean your flat early next week,' he says. 'The decorators are going in a couple of days later. I'd do the painting myself, if we weren't so busy—'

'Tom, I don't expect you to redecorate on top of everything else!'

'I know, but I'd like to have saved you the expense,' he says. 'It'll be great to have it all sorted and get you home again, won't it?'

'Yes, absolutely.' I cross my fingers. I'm fed up with the hotel, but not fed up enough to face what's left of my home. The cleaners and decorators aren't miracle workers, after all; I know the flat will never be the same again.

I'm sick of killing time, though. In the morning, I call work and tell them I'll be back on Monday.

Before I head out for breakfast, and more aimless mooching, I write a note to housekeeping, asking them not to clean my room. Once again, I've left my mark on it and I don't want it erased. Poking a hole in the paper, I hang it on the door handle.

When I return, late in the afternoon, the note has gone. It has also been ignored; the room is back to normal – its normal. Fury surges through me. Can they not read? For a moment, I hesitate in the doorway, wondering whether to complain to reception. And say what? *Your staff are doing a perfect job.* It won't wash. I need another strategy.

I go out again, this time to the local supermarket, where I pick up supplies for a do-it-yourself breakfast tomorrow: orange juice, pain au chocolat and fruit. My room may be under siege, but now I'm armed for a face-off with housekeeping.

On my way to the till, I stop. I'm bored with stodgy dinners at the café, so re-visit the aisles to add a makeshift meal to my basket – a tuna salad, crusty roll and a small bottle of wine – and pick up cutlery from the discount store next door.

Back in my room, I transform the dressing table into a dining area, with tissues for napkins and a bathroom tumbler acting as a wineglass. Food, drink and television distract me until the middle of the evening and then anxiety resumes its grip. The weekend is nearly here and I'm not ready to see Tom – not ready to play loyal girlfriend for two days.

Before calling, I gird myself for another lie. 'Tom, I'm afraid I'll have to cancel coming up this weekend. I've been feeling rotten all day.'

'Sorry to hear that, beautiful. I was looking forward to seeing you. And I've bought a ton of food!'

I'm on the verge of backtracking, of telling him *I might be better tomorrow and as you've gone to so much trouble—*

'You don't sound too bad,' he says.

The hint of an accusation puts me on the defensive. 'Well, I feel it. It's one of those fluey things. I'm aching all over.'

'If you come here, I could look after you.'

'I'm not really up to driving. You know, I reckon I jinxed myself, by telling work I was ill.' Once I start lying, it gets easier.

'You're probably run down with the stress of everything. Look after yourself, eh?'

'I will. At least I won't give it to you.' Altruism is my final trump card.

The second I hang up, I regret using a small deception to avoid a larger one. A fake illness is as bad as a fake orgasm. Pretending on the phone is, at least, easier than in person and it's only a short-term measure, to tide me over until my guilt becomes more manageable.

I sleep in on Saturday and, when housekeeping knock, I'm still eating my pastries. The door opens, before I can swallow my mouthful and reply. A woman backs in, tugging a cleaning trolley behind her.

I dash across the room to stop her. 'Excuse me.'

She jumps and turns around. 'Ooh, you didn't 'alf give me a fright. I didn't think you was 'ere. You ain't usually.'

I stare at her for a moment. I'd imagined my nemesis to be the cleaning equivalent of an old-fashioned hospital matron: smart, brisk, efficient and definitely middle-aged. Not a scruffy girl who doesn't look old enough to have left school.

'D'you want me to do you later?' She peers over my shoulder. Maybe she thinks I'm hiding another guest.

'Actually, no.' I read her name badge. 'Thanks, Shavaun.' Shavaun?

My planned speech eludes me in the face of this slouching vision of unloveliness, who is now chewing her thumbnail. Her manicure is flaking and the diamanté tips are missing from several nails, while multiple holes punctuate her ears: four on one side, five on the other. Her overall is creased, her black shoes scuffed, and the whole look is topped off by badly dyed, blonde hair. Everything about her is untidy and uneven.

'Madam?' The word sounds odd, falling primly from her chapped lips – a rogue entry in her vocabulary.

'I don't need my room to be cleaned today, thank you.' I move into her personal space, to encourage her to leave. 'Or tomorrow. Or at all. Thank you, Shavaun.'

She doesn't budge. 'I gotta do all the rooms.' She lifts her head and stands a little straighter. 'That's me job. I don't want to get meself into no trouble.'

'You won't.' I smile brightly. 'I won't tell, if you don't!'

'You says that. I dunno...' She scowls. 'What if you change yer mind? They'll dock me pay.'

'I won't, honestly. I promise, you won't get into trouble.'

Her eyes dart about the room. 'What about tea bags? I bet you need tea bags?'

Damn, she's right. 'That's a good idea. Oh, and more milk and biscuits, please. Thanks.'

She picks the packets out of her trolley and bundles them at me. 'Soap? Loo roll?'

I can't remember and daren't go into the bathroom to check. She might take the opportunity to manoeuvre into the room. 'Please,' I say.

She arches a knowing eyebrow, before raiding her cart again. I take the soap and toilet paper from her, my arms almost full.

'Towels?' she says.

I can't hold any more. 'No, thanks. Better do my bit for the environment.'

'Eh?'

'You know? Saving electricity and water, and dumping fewer chemicals into the system.'

She shrugs. 'Whatever.'

'All right, then. Thanks very much.' I move forward another few inches.

She backs away, eyes fixed on me and pushing the trolley behind her.

As soon as she's in the hall, I catch the edge of the door with my foot and nudge it shut. 'Thanks again,' I say, as she disappears from view.

I dump my supplies on the bed and look around the room. Its untouched disorder screams rebellion.

Later I go out to stock up on library books for my weekend of self-enforced solitary confinement. Shavaun lurks in the corridor, leaning on her trolley and chatting to a colleague. I smile to reassure them I'm harmless. They fall silent until I'm past and then begin whispering to each other – no doubt speculating on the secrets concealed in my room.

She doesn't capitalise on my absence to sneak in; she must be more afraid of me than her supervisor. Nor does she go in when I return to work.

My colleagues sympathise with me over my illness, a few commenting on how tired I look. Guilt wobbles my smile of acknowledgement, yet what has happened is worse than any virus. Their sympathy is justified, albeit misdirected.

The backlog from my four days off litters my desk and sorting it out provides a welcome focus for my time. The days pass quickly, as I settle back into a routine.

On Thursday, Dad calls my mobile, bringing me up with a jolt.

'Clare? There you are!' he says.

'What's happened, Dad? What's the matter?' God, I'm turning

into him, assuming the worst of every phone call.

'Nothing.'

'Why are you calling me at work, then?' He never calls me here; it must be an emergency.

'Mmm, yes. Your phone at home. Seems to be a problem?'

Ah. 'Sorry, yes—'

'I'd like to talk to you about something. Can you come over tomorrow? At eight?'

I've never heard him speak so quickly or be so decisive, and he rarely manages so many words in one go.

'Of course. Are you sure there's nothing wrong?'

'Nothing at all, no. Nothing at all.'

The repetition of the denial makes me doubt it. I know he won't tell me anything until I see him, though; all I can do is wait.

40

Marilyn answers the door, wearing a kaftan patterned with swirls of bright blue and green. Stray, silver-grey tendrils of hair coil down her neck from a loose bun.

'Hello, dear.' She stretches up to kiss me, her skin cool against my hot cheek. Faced with her calm elegance, I feel frayed and fractious.

'Would you like some lemonade?' she says. 'I've made the old-fashioned kind. Your father loves it.'

'Thanks. Where is he?' I trail behind her into the kitchen.

'In the garden, dear. Taking photographs – again.' She looks over her shoulder conspiratorially.

I ignore the invitation to bond over Dad's obsession.

Marilyn fills two glasses from a jug clinking with ice cubes. 'Take one out to your father, will you, dear? He never thinks to come in for a break.'

Clutching the glasses, I push the back door open with my elbow. Dad is lying in front of a rhododendron at the top of the garden; he's so still, he could be dead. I walk towards him.

'Dad?' He doesn't move. 'Dad?'

'Damn,' he says. 'Little blighters.'

'Dad!' I'm only a few feet away.

He starts. 'Clare!' He puts down his camera and pushes himself up, first onto his knees, and then upright. His weight, combined with creaky joints, makes it a challenge to move from horizontal to vertical.

'I'm too old for this,' he says. Sweat glistens on his forehead and grass sprinkles the front of his polo shirt and jeans.

Kissing him, I feel his stubble, longer and softer than a day's growth. I hand him a glass of lemonade and bend to pick up his camera. The manicured lawn retains the imprint of his body. 'You had something to tell me?'

'Yes.' Dad gulps down half the drink.

'Do you want to go inside?' I turn back to the house, where Marilyn is flitting about the dining room, the sleeves of her kaftan billowing like giant butterfly wings.

'No.' He's as forthcoming as ever.

'Shall we sit down, then?' I gesture towards the bench in the corner.

Dad sinks onto the seat, looking uncomfortable – a naughty schoolboy outside the head teacher's office.

I sit next to him, sipping my drink, his camera on my lap.

Tilting his head back, he gazes at the sky. My eyes follow his to the glinting dart of a plane piercing the blue. I track it until it disappears behind a bank of crimped cloud.

Dad's forehead furrows. He looks down at his feet. I stare at the top of his head, willing him to make eye contact, to speak. I'm used to his silences; this one feels different, laden with the promise of something significant. Something bad. Anxiety gnaws at me.

I finish my drink and place the glass on the ground. 'Dad? What's going on?'

He shifts uneasily.

I clutch the camera in front of me like armour. Dad looks at the house. Marilyn has switched on the lamps. A soft glow spills across the patio. The tinkle of classical music wafts through the open windows.

He finishes his lemonade and carefully stands the glass under the bench. Straightening up, he says, 'I've asked Marilyn to move in with me.'

For a moment, I doubt I've heard right; then I start to laugh. I can't help it – the idea of Dad inviting a woman to live with him! Doubling up, I laugh until tears come to my eyes.

'Clare, please, you're getting my camera wet! Salt water is bad for it.' He pulls it from my grasp, as I sit up and try to compose myself.

Flapping my hand in front of my face, I choke out, 'God, I'm sorry, Dad, I didn't mean to, I...' And I'm off again, tears rolling down my cheeks in a mixture of amusement and relief.

Amusement, relief and then, suddenly, sadness. Sadness that Dad is moving on from Mum. Sadness that it has taken him so long to do so.

I don't know what to feel any more. Sad, amused, relieved. The emotions pour down my face in a salty cocktail.

Dad sits in silence until I calm down.

'I really am sorry,' I say. 'I don't know what came over me.'

He watches the sky darkening against the rooftops, his chin high and huffy.

'Dad, please. Talk to me.'

He sniffs, doesn't reply.

I lean towards him. 'I think it's great news.'

He narrows his eyes. 'You do?'

'Of course. I was surprised, that's all.'

Surprised not least because Marilyn is so different to Mum. Mum was vivacious, stroppy and stubborn. Marilyn is restrained, calm and reasonable. Maybe she is more suited to Dad for that very reason: two of a kind, not Mum's chalk to Dad's cheese. And Mum was thirty-six when she died. Perhaps, by her fifties, she would have mellowed into someone like Marilyn. I doubt she'd ever have worn kaftans, though.

'I presume she said yes?' I ask.

'Indeed. I'd hardly have told you otherwise.'

'When's she moving in?'

Dad shuffles his bottom on the seat. 'She already has. Bits and pieces, anyway.'

'Why didn't you tell me before?' I expect I'm last to know, as usual.

'I did try to call you at home, to ask you over—'

'About that...' No, it's not right to mention the burglary. This is his moment; I don't want to spoil it. 'Carry on using my mobile for now, will you? Till my landline's repaired.'

Marilyn appears in the kitchen doorway, silhouetted against the light. 'Are you two coming in soon? I'm making camomile tea.'

'On our way, dear.' Dad pulls a face and mutters, 'Cat's pee.'

'Dad!'

'Well, it is.'

'You should nip that in the bud, or you'll have a lifetime of it.'

'A lifetime. Yes, indeed.' He smiles and stands up.

I stack the glasses, leaving a hand spare to hook through his arm. As we head inside, I venture to tilt my face against his and feel his whiskers brush my skin.

When we reach the door, I unhook my arm and move away from him. "What's with the designer stubble? Too lazy to shave?'

'No, I thought I might grow my beard back,' he whispers, wiping his shoes on the mat. Marilyn is nowhere to be seen.

'Whatever for?'

'Didn't you like it, either?' He looks hurt.

'Of course, but the new you is growing on me, and you do look younger. Besides, I'm pretty sure Marilyn will notice if you have a beard. It's not exactly something you can hide.'

Dad strokes his chin, tracing the line of his scar through the silvery sheen. 'Mmm.'

Marilyn walks into the kitchen, catching him mid-stroke. 'Yes, it's about time you had a shave, darling. That stubble doesn't do my poor old skin any good at all.'

I elbow Dad in the ribs, as Marilyn turns away to pour the hot water.

She hands him a mug of tea. 'Let it brew for five minutes, to bring out the flavour. Tea, Clare?'

'Thanks.' The lemonade has quenched my thirst, but I can't let Dad suffer alone.

I take the drink and follow him into the living room. Dad sits on the sofa, depositing his tea on the side table. I make myself comfortable in the armchair he used to prefer.

He's not doing too badly, if shaving and drinking herbal tea are the only compromises he has to make. I have to concede that Marilyn is a good influence on him.

She comes in and curls up next to Dad, tucking her feet under her kaftan. 'Brian, did you tell Clare our news?'

I jump in, 'He did. Congratulations. I presume you'll sell your house?'

'No sense in keeping it. I plan to give some of the proceeds to Nick, for his business and his own place. He might as well have his inheritance, while I'm here to see him enjoy it.'

'Good idea,' I say.

Dad stares into his tea.

'Oh, it was Brian's suggestion that I sell up and move in. He says it's much more sensible than re-mortgaging to help Nick. Good job one of us is clued up about financial matters.' She strokes Dad's cheek. 'Your father's very wise.'

He looks up, a picture of wide-eyed innocence. 'Mmm?'

'He's that all right,' I say. Wise enough to know how to protect Marilyn, without distancing her from her younger son. A risky strategy, if things don't work out between her and Dad, but proof of feelings he would never admit to.

He levers himself up off the sofa. 'I'm going to get a jumper.' He retrieves his tea from the table and steps towards the door.

'Why don't you leave your drink, darling?' says Marilyn. 'You don't want to spill it.'

Dad hesitates. 'Of course, dear.' He frowns slightly, as he turns to replace the mug.

I suppress a smile. Spilling it – down the sink – was probably exactly what he did want.

Alone with Marilyn, I'm suddenly shy and cast around the room for something to talk about. My stomach flips, as I catch sight of gaps amongst the photos on the mantelpiece. I'm familiar enough with them to know which are missing. 'Where are Mum's photos?'

'I'm sorry, dear. Your father thought he should put them away – for me. I told him it wasn't necessary, but he was most insistent. I do hope you don't mind?'

'No, of course not. I'm hardly ever here and I have my own at home. I was just wondering.'

Marilyn leans towards me. 'By the way, I have a new photo of Nicky.' She holds up her locket and flicks open the catch. Adult Nick has replaced cheeky, young Nick, while her other son, Richard, remains frozen in boyhood.

'Very nice.' The response seems inadequate. 'He's a handsome man.'

'He is.' She shuts the locket. 'That reminds me. How's Tom? Have you two fixed a wedding date?'

'Er, no, we're having problems finding a suitable weekend.' I curl my hands around my mug and take a sip of tea. Dad's right; it's vile.

Marilyn stares at my left hand. I fold my right hand over it, hiding my bare fingers.

'No other problems, though?' she says.

'None at all.'

Not any more. After our split, we're almost back to where we started, the only difference being that the secret between us has changed. Whether the new secret is more or less of a threat to our future than the old one, I don't yet know. Either way, that future is in limbo, and will be so long as I stay at the hotel. Dad is moving on; it's time for me to do the same.

'By the way,' I say, 'could you let me have Nick's number some time?'

I'd like to apologise for my rudeness when we met. In the face of an addiction I didn't understand, I took a stance of mistrust and prejudice. Nick meant only well, I'm sure, yet I rejected him out of hand.

Marilyn smiles. 'Yes, of course. I'd be delighted if you two became friends.'

'Er... Actually, I just want to book a floatation tank session, once his business is up and running. Give him a bit of support, you know?'

Dad walks back in. 'Floatation tanks! Stuff and nonsense!' He sits down next to Marilyn.

'Brian, darling, you're so old-fashioned. I'm sure you'd enjoy the experience if you gave it a try.'

A vision of Dad floating like a bemused whale in swimming trunks pops into my mind. I shake my head to dispel the image.

'I should get going.' I put down my unfinished tea. 'It's late and I'm sure you two would like some time alone.'

'Not at all, my dear,' says Marilyn. 'Remember, this is your home. It always will be.'

It isn't really – not any more. I have to make my own home, one that I'm able to share with someone else.

Dad sees me to the door, bringing his tea with him, so that he can tip it into the flowerpot by the front step.

'Are you trying to kill that plant?' I say. 'Why don't you just tell Marilyn you've gone off camomile, or it disagrees with you, or you prefer peppermint?'

His face brightens. 'Clever girl!' He pats my arm.

'Not really, Dad.' He's wise about some things, very dim about others.

From my car, I watch him go into the living room. Marilyn is on the sofa; her silver head turns as he approaches. The room looks warm, inviting – the centre of a real home. The last time I saw it like that was the winter before Mum died. At dusk, she always left the curtains open until Fiona and I got in from school, the lighted window our beacon. I feel the same pull now as then. Nostalgia and longing ache inside me, as though I'm leaving home for the first time and the last.

Dad stretches over the sofa to close the curtains. I mouth *No* and press my hand against the car window. The pleading gesture becomes a wave goodbye that he doesn't see. The curtains slide together. For a moment, a sliver of light divides them and then that, too, melts into the darkness.

41

As soon as I get back to the hotel, I phone Tom. 'I was wondering, could I take you up on your offer to stay at the cottage?'

'Of course, beautiful, no need to ask. Do you want to come up tonight?'

'It's probably a bit late to set off now, thanks. Is tomorrow all right for you?'

'Perfect. Make it lunch time and I'll pop back from work to let you in. The decorators won't be done at your flat till Friday. You might as well stay here for the week and go home next Saturday.'

That makes sense; it will give me a whole weekend to settle back in, though I'm worried I'll immediately revert to the habits I'd begun to break before the burglary. It doesn't count that I've messed up my hotel room; it's a fake home and not so different from when I stay with Tom. Back in my own environment, I may relapse, like an alcoholic in a pub or a reformed smoker amongst cigarette-wielding friends. With so much now damaged or stolen, I know I won't be able to recreate my old patterns, but I may be tempted to devise new ones. If I give in to that temptation, my future with Tom will go on hold once again.

The following morning, I check out of the hotel and take a leisurely drive up to the cottage to meet Tom. He greets me with his usual bear hug and presents me with my own set of keys.

'You'll need some, anyway,' he says. 'I thought you might as well have them now.' He has looped the keys onto a ring decorated with a miniature wooden doormat. The mat is engraved with the words *Home Sweet Home*.

'Thanks.' My thumb rubs over the grooves of the letters.

'You can come and go as you please, do what you want.'

'I get the idea, Tom. I have used keys before!'

'Sorry! It's just so good to have you here.' He squeezes me again.

Tom goes back to work, leaving me to unpack. I quickly put my clothes away in the drawer he has cleared for me and hang a couple of items in the wardrobe. That's all the space I need for now, but at some point we'll condense two homes into one and have to negotiate over what to keep, and where. I wonder how any couple manages it, even without compulsions to contend with.

I also claim a corner of the chest of drawers, for Mum's photo. I prop it up and run my finger along the length of the crack in the glass, making a mental note to buy a new frame.

Once I'm finished in the bedroom, I pick out one of my library books and go downstairs, to the back garden. Charlie pads out of the kitchen to join me. As I make myself comfortable on a deckchair in the shade, he lies down on the grass beside me.

The book fails to grip me and after only a few pages my attention strays to my surroundings. Either the sun has generated a fresh sprinkling of daisies and dandelions on the lawn, or Tom's mower missed some last week. I toy with the idea of cutting the grass, but operating unfamiliar machinery is too big a challenge. Weeding, on the other hand, I can manage. I wander around, plucking intruders from the flowerbeds. Every time I pass a section I think I've cleared, I spot another weed. The job is made more frustrating by the knowledge that, in time, more will spring up – again and again and again.

At least Charlie enjoys himself; he becomes increasingly excited as we circle the lawn, perhaps mistaking our stroll for the prelude to a walk.

The doorbell interrupts us. Charlie's ears prick up and he turns around and trots back to the cottage. I hesitate over whether to do likewise. I'm not up to arguing with utilities' salesmen or Jehovah's Witnesses.

He barks a couple of times.

'All right, I'm coming.' I arrive at the front door to find him snuffling and pawing at the bottom of it. Nudging him aside, I ease it open.

Bex is on the front step, in shorts and a skimpy vest top, with a bulging bin liner at her feet.

'Oh, hi,' I say. What's her problem this time? Another leaking tap or broken gadget, or maybe whatever is hidden in the bin liner?

'Hi, Clare. Sorry to hear about the burglary. How are you doing?' She bends to pet Charlie, who is turning rings around her tanned legs. Her long, curly hair falls over her face. Insecurity and jealousy curdle inside me.

'All right, thanks. Tom's not here, he's at work.' I keep hold of the door, ready to shut it. 'I don't know when he'll be back.'

'Actually, it was you I wanted.' Bex stands up, tossing her head irritably. 'God, it's too blinking hot for all this hair.' She gathers up her curly mane and ties it into a loose knot at the back of her neck. 'I wish I had yours. I can't have mine short; it sticks out so much I look like a lollipop.'

'Thanks.' I run my fingers over my own cap of straight, boring and yet equally uncontrollable hair. 'Why did you want me?'

She bends over again and lifts the bin liner. 'I thought you might want these to get you started. They should all be done by next weekend.'

'What should?'

Bex rolls her eyes. 'Didn't Tom tell you?' She picks at the knot in the top of the bag with her manicured talons. Opening it, she gestures inside. 'I got him to bring over your clothes for us to wash and iron.'

'What?' I look into the bag and recognise a couple of tee shirts on top of the neat pile. 'Why?' Lost for words, I shake my head.

'Tom was going to ask the cleaners to put your clothes away. I told him he was an idiot and you wouldn't want to wear them as they were. Not after that scumbag had rootled through them.'

I can't help giggling. 'Poor Tom.'

'Well, honestly, Clare, men have no idea.'

'He has sorted out everything else for me. I've been a hopeless damsel in distress.' Bex is right about my clothes, though: the burglar fingering them was a violation.

'Still. Clueless, the lot of them.' Bex reties the top of the bag.

'So who's done all this?'

'Me and a couple of girlfriends. We had a right laugh. They brought their irons and boards and I cracked open a couple of bottles of Chardonnay. We're going to do it again with our own stuff. Ironing's way more fun, when you're drinking and nattering.'

'Thank you so much.' I hug her.

Hampered by the bin liner dangling from her hand, she squeezes me back awkwardly. 'No problem. I reckon I owe Tom a favour or two.'

'Have you got time for a drink?' I step back and gesture her inside.

'Always time for a drink. I'm not due at work for a couple of hours.'

I meant tea or coffee, but Bex unearths a half-full bottle of Pimms from the back of a cupboard: a relic from her days as Tom's girlfriend.

By the time he gets back, we've emptied the bottle, along with another of lemonade – and decimated his supply of ice cubes. Tom does a double take at the sight of us sitting together in the garden.

'Hi, Clare, Bex.' He loiters in the kitchen doorway, Charlie sniffing around him.

'Hey you, don't be shy. Come and say hello,' says Bex.

The affectionate tone no longer bothers me; I know from the confidences she has shared this afternoon that she's no threat.

Tom runs his hand through his hair and ambles over. He leans down to kiss me, delivering the smell of sweat, soil and the fading aroma of this morning's aftershave.

He straightens up and ruffles Bex's hair. 'Hi, Bex, good to see you.' He pats her head.

Bex and I snort.

'What?' says Tom. 'What's the matter?'

'Nothing,' I say. 'Why don't you get a beer and join us? Bex has something to tell you.'

When he comes back outside, she shares her news. 'Keith and I are getting married!'

'Really?' he says. 'I mean…congratulations!'

'Oh, and Bex and I thought a double wedding would be lovely,' I say.

Tom's face falls. 'Well, if that's what you want… I suppose… Do you?'

'Of course not, you twerp,' says Bex. 'Blimey, it's taken that much work to get the daft lug to propose to me. Imagine what he'd say about a double wedding!'

I laugh. 'I'm sure he'd love to compete with your ex for Best Dressed Groom of the Day.'

'Yeah, poor sod.'

Tom scowls into his beer. 'I liked it better when you two didn't know each other and weren't ganging up on me and Keith.'

Bex winks at me. 'That's what girlfriends and exes do. Do you want to know what else we talked about?'

'No, I do not! I think I'll finish my beer in the shower; it's safer.'

Over dinner later, I confess my old fears to Tom. 'I thought Bex was after you. It turns out she was only flirting to wind up Keith and provoke him to propose.'

'Dangerous game.'

'Not really. You wouldn't have done anything.'

'Of course not.' He looks up from his stir-fry, puts down his fork and reaches under the table to squeeze my thigh. 'You do know that?'

'I do.' I only wish I'd realised before it was too late. Before Michael.

'It's still a dangerous game.' Tom gives my leg another squeeze, gets up and goes over to the cooker. 'If you pick the wrong person to play with, things can get out of hand and that's it, game over.' He returns with the rice pan. 'Seconds?'

'No, thanks.' I shake my head. 'Game over?'

'As soon as you cheat on someone, the trust's gone.' Tom scoops rice onto his plate.

I breathe in sharply and something goes down the wrong way, making me cough.

'You okay?' he says.

I nod and take a gulp of wine.

He clatters the pan back onto the hob, sits down and picks up his fork. 'There's no getting back from that… There wasn't for my parents, anyway.' He stabs at his food.

'Your parents?' Presumably the *past experience* he mentioned, after admitting his fear that I was seeing someone else – long before my actual fall from grace. 'Which one? I mean…'

'My mum.'

'And you knew about it at the time?'

'Yes. Once Dad found out, Mum made no secret of it.'

'That must have been difficult. How old were you?'

'Twelve. Susie was nine, so she had some idea what was going on, but Liz and Vicky were too young to understand until later.' Tom pushes his food around his plate. 'I sometimes wonder about Vicky…'

'What?'

'She was only one when Dad found out about the affair and she doesn't look like either of them. I think that's why he's always treated her differently; he's just not sure.'

'Poor Vicky.' No wonder Tom's so protective of her.

'He and Mum drifted apart after that, which was tough on all of us. They lead pretty much separate lives now.'

'But they're not divorced?'

'No. Neither of them wants to give up the lifestyle. Mum enjoys the status and financial benefit of being married to a consultant, and Dad likes having someone to look after him and host dinner parties.'

'I can't imagine being in a marriage of convenience.' It's ironic that Tom's parents are so damning of his mistakes – actual and perceived – given their own dysfunctional situation.

'Dad's a fool to himself, for letting it carry on,' he says.

At least I know now that I was right not to tell him about Michael. Somehow, I feel better for that certainty.

'Bex wouldn't let it get that far with anyone, though, would she?' I say.

He smiles. 'No, you're right. She's a decent woman and I'm pleased you're getting on. It's nice for you to have a friend up here.'

'On the subject of relationships, Dad and Marilyn are moving in together.'

Tom grins. 'The old dog.'

'Tom! That's my dad you're talking about.'

'Sorry. Good on him, though.'

'About time. He's taken long enough to find another woman.'

'Not like me, eh? Got them swarming all over me. You, Bex...'

I flick rice at him. 'Two can play at that game. I could get used to Keith's muscles and he's very mean and moody. Women like that, you know?'

'I'm sure he's extremely appealing...in the right light.'

He clears the plates and takes them to the sink. 'Good news, by the way...' He turns on the hot tap to fill the washing-up bowl and the running water scrambles the rest of his words: something about a ring.

'What was that?' I say.

He turns towards me, his face flushed from the steam. 'The cleaners found your ring. It must have fallen out of the box when the burglar was trashing the place.'

'That's fantastic! I can hardly believe it.' Now I won't have to settle for a replacement. We'll pick up where we left off and things will go back to how they were.

'I'll collect it from them later in the week,' says Tom.

It's a good sign – the first in a long while. Right now, I'll take all the good signs I can get.

42

The support group meets on Thursday evening, when I'm still at Tom's.

Over breakfast that morning, I remind him about it. 'I won't be back till about half ten.'

'Do you have to go? You know what you need to do, don't you? How will the group help?'

He's half-right: I do know the theory, but I need the group's supportive pressure to ensure I put it into practice.

'They keep me on track, Tom.'

'I could do that, too, you know?'

'Maybe. It's different with them. They really...'

'Yes?' He stops with a spoonful of chocolate cereal and milk halfway to his mouth.

'They really understand. I'm sorry, I know you try, but...'

He shovels in the gloopy mess from his spoon.

'More juice?' I say.

He shakes his head. I pour some for myself.

'Will that Michael be there?' he asks.

Ah, that's why he's so concerned. He's not the only one. I dread my next encounter with Michael, but won't let it stop me getting the help I need. He has already done enough to threaten my recovery – and my future.

'I don't know. He usually is.' I affect nonchalance, as I butter another piece of toast.

'You won't let him lead you astray?' Tom runs his hand through his hair.

'What do you mean?' My heart skips a beat.

'With his advice. You said he had it all wrong?'

'Yes, he has. And no, I won't let him mislead me again.' That, at least, is true. Michael enjoys his habits, which means he doesn't even have obsessive-compulsive disorder, making him ill-equipped to advise anyone who does.

The sun blazes all day and the air is thick with accumulated heat by the time I set off.

Walking up the drive to the church hall, I spot a young woman in a pretty floral dress waiting outside the front door. She takes a few paces forward, stops and turns back.

I smile as I approach. 'Are you here for the support group?'

She bites her lip and gazes at the ground. 'Yes.' Her voice is so quiet, I can hardly hear her.

'Would you like me to show you where it is?'

She looks up. 'Are you...? I mean...' She's breathing heavily, as if from physical exertion.

She means, *Are you one of us?*

'Yes, I'm going, too. I'm Clare, by the way.' I push open the front door, holding it to let her through after me.

'Sarah. I'm Sarah.' She almost tumbles inside.

I lead the way through the inner door, into the hall. Scanning those seated in the centre of the room, I recognise Wet Wipe Albert and his wife, Betty, Evelyn, the door checker, and the young man frightened of harming his parents. His name escapes me until his head jerks with a nervous tic. Neil. Nervous Tic Neil. There are a couple of people I don't know, and Katie and her parents are missing. I hope she's all right.

No sign, either, of Michael.

Sarah follows me. I point out Heather, who is at the edge of the stage unpacking the refreshments. Sarah thanks me shyly and goes over to speak to her. I grab a couple of chairs and join the group, placing the spare seat to my right, between mine and Betty's.

Albert, on the other side of his wife, nods at me, unsmiling. He's clutching a wet wipe and a packet bulges in the top pocket of his shirt. Betty has an anxious look on her pale face.

Opposite us, Evelyn whispers to the woman beside her, whom I now recall was the hoarder from the first meeting.

A couple of seats away from Evelyn, Neil leans forward in his chair, his elbows on his knees and his chin propped on his fists. As he stares at the floor, his head's repeated jerks shake the dual pillars of his arms. He cups his hands around his cheeks. His head continues to twitch. Pushing his hands up to his scalp, he winds his fingers into his dark, messy hair.

A tension in the air deters me from speaking to anyone. Instead, I open my handbag and pretend to check my mobile is off.

The room is hot and stuffy. The evening sun shines through the windows behind me, making a patchwork of sunlit squares on the floor. I get up to open a couple of the lower panes, to let some air in.

As I sit down again, I notice Sarah hovering between the stage and the circle of chairs. I wave her over, gesturing at the empty seat next to me. She crosses the room and sits down, gripping her hands together tightly in her lap. Her body is tense and bent slightly forward, ready to take flight.

The door creaks open. Michael? No, an overweight woman I don't recognise. She strides into the room, her head held high. Her long, Titian-coloured hair – the same shade as Fiona's – swings about her shoulders. I realise it's Ruth, the hair puller from last time, who has replaced her turban with a wig. The artificial hair seems to have given her confidence.

'Hi, everyone.' She smiles, apparently unaware of the silence, and plonks herself next to Albert. She shakes her hair. The gesture is self-conscious, as though she's not yet used to her new locks.

Ten minutes to go. Will Michael turn up or not? The silence and the waiting are too much. I turn to Sarah, dredging for something innocuous to say. 'Everyone's very nice here,' I offer.

Feet shuffle. A chair leg scrapes on the wooden floor. Sarah smiles half-heartedly.

I plough on, 'You can talk as much or as little as you like and Heather's very good, she knows her stuff. It's really helpful.'

Sarah's eyes flick left and right, seeking escape, my approach as unwelcome as that of a street fundraiser.

The door squeaks open, drawing attention away from my rambling. Michael strides in. My heart thuds, as my anxiety spikes.

He takes a chair from the stack underneath the windows and surveys the group. His eyes alight on Sarah. He walks over to stand behind her and Betty.

'Excuse me,' he says, 'could I squeeze in here?'

Betty looks puzzled; there are gaps elsewhere in the circle. 'I suppose so. Don't you want to sit next to Clare?'

Michael clanks the leg of his chair against Betty's, ignoring her question.

She frowns. 'Budge up a bit, Albert.' She flaps her hand against her husband's left leg. He flinches as if burned.

'For heaven's sake, Albert. You've got trousers on. You won't catch anything,' she says.

'Betty!' Albert looks stricken.

A low wave of sound runs through the group: a medley of coughs and sniffs and throat clearing. Albert's reaction to his wife's touch confirms my suspicion that he has taken a downturn.

They both move to the right and Sarah to the left, nearer to me. Michael slides his chair between hers and Betty's and sits down. He keeps his blazer on, in spite of the heat.

I can hardly ignore him. I lean forward, around Sarah. 'Hi, Michael.'

He nods curtly. 'Clare.'

I sit back. Betty catches my eye and raises an eyebrow. Now I understand her comment about finding Michael strange. Her instincts were right: behind his greying handsomeness is a controlling and decidedly unattractive man.

He stretches out his hand to Sarah. 'Hi, I'm Michael. Pleased to meet you.'

Her face lights up, as she turns towards him. 'I'm Sarah.' Their handshake lasts longer than normal courtesy dictates.

'This is a good group. You should find it useful,' says Michael. 'If there's anything I can do to help, let me know.'

'Really? Thank you. Thank you so much.' Sarah visibly relaxes into her seat.

I smile wryly. I can hardly blame her; Michael's charm had the same effect on me. Hopefully, she'll turn out not to have ordering compulsions. He's taking a risk in offering help before he finds out, but maybe he's simply making a point: he's no longer interested in me. The feeling is mutual.

The meeting starts. We're a large group tonight, but Betty is the only family member or carer, so we all remain together. Heather is to my left and I'll be last to speak.

Most people report little change. Neil is still living at home and trying to avoid his parents. Evelyn is still checking her doors and windows. Ruth is still pulling out her hair — now from under her wigs.

Albert has had the worst month. He found a tiny fly in a pre-prepared salad. The discovery kick-started old issues about dirt and germs and triggered new fears over food contamination. He's up from ten wet wipes a day to more than forty, and his eating habits are haywire.

Betty is almost in tears. 'He checks every bit of food a dozen times before he'll eat it. Lunch took two hours today. It's worse than having a baby.'

Albert hangs his head, wringing a wipe in his hands.

'Sorry, love, it *is*,' says Betty. She makes to touch his arm, but stops her hand an inch above his sleeve.

As usual, Michael declines to speak. He listens closely, though, as Sarah takes her turn. She said little during the introductions. As she elaborates, it becomes apparent she has more in common with Neil than Michael: she suffers intrusive thoughts about hurting her best friend.

'The problem is, we share a house,' she says. 'It's getting ridiculous. I go out when she's in, have weekends away. I'm finding it harder and harder.'

Neil is attentive while she talks. The frequency of his tic even seems to diminish.

She carries on. 'I suggested we have locks for our bedrooms. I told her it was in case we were burgled. Really, it's so that I can't hurt her in the night. Why would I even think like that? I love her to bits.'

'Have you talked to your friend about this?' says Heather.

Sarah is horrified. 'No way! I'm scared I'll lose her, if I tell her the truth.'

Heather points her in the direction of her doctor, a self-help book and Neil, and the discussions continue, without any contribution from Michael. He sits military-straight in his seat, with his arms crossed and his body as rigid as his hair. He has a contemptuous look on his face. The moment Sarah failed his test, she exited his radar. To Michael she has become, like me, just another annoyance he has to tolerate in his search for a woman who will accept his behaviour. He may see the members of the group as irritating or odd – or both – yet he is the real odd one out, in refusing to accept he has any kind of problem.

When Heather gets to me, I hesitate over how much to divulge.

'Tom and I have worked things out. You were right about not asking him to compromise.'

Heather nods. 'Good.'

'I can't expect anyone else to do as I do. I realise that now. No one should live like that.' I sense Michael bristling two seats away. 'I'm working on messing things up. Or, at least, I was...'

'But?' says Heather.

'I was burgled,' I say, 'so I'm not at home at the moment.'

'How awful.' Ruth fingers her new hair. 'Did they take much?'

'I don't know.' I bow my head. 'I packed a few things and left. I've been at a hotel and now Tom's. I couldn't handle being at the flat. Everything was such a mess.'

'That's nothing to be ashamed of,' says Heather. 'We'd all find a burglary upsetting.'

'I know. Still, it's been more than two weeks. I'm worried about how I'll feel when I go home. Whether I'll even be able to face going inside—'

'How did they get in?' Evelyn, the door checker, is perched on the edge of her seat. She grips the wood either side of her legs as if she might fall off.

I look at Heather. She nods.

'My downstairs neighbour was burgled. She had my spare keys and the burglar found them.'

'No!' Evelyn sounds horrified. 'How did they know the keys were yours?'

'I'd just put my first name on them, but she'd added "upstairs", which meant they could only be for one of two flats.'

'Oh, my God!' Evelyn's face is white. 'Two of my neighbours have my keys. I must get them back.'

'What would you do then, if you lost yours?' asks Heather. 'It's sensible for someone else to hold spares.'

'But they might do the same as Clare's neighbour.' Evelyn's eyes fill with tears. 'Even if I ask them not to, a burglar might figure it out somehow.'

She's so distressed, all because of me. I have to do something. 'I doubt—'

Heather stops me with a slight shake of the head.

Evelyn gestures helplessly. 'I have to be sure. I can't cope with this...with this not knowing. Tell me it won't happen to me. Please.'

'I can't,' says Heather. 'No one can. I know it's hard, but it's the only way. Obsessions feed on reassurance.'

'I'm sorry I mentioned it,' I say.

'No,' says Heather, 'you should never feel you have to hold back, and this has brought out an interesting point about living with uncertainty.'

I'm not convinced. Evelyn is fingering her house keys like rosary beads. I've had the same negative effect on her as the fly in Albert's salad had on him.

'When do you plan to go home, Clare?' asks Heather.

'At the weekend.' I shiver. Less than forty-eight hours. In less than forty-eight hours, I'll be back – or fleeing once more.

'Good luck. Let us know how you get on. Okay, I'd like to propose that we finish the group work there for today, as feedback has taken a bit longer than usual. Could I suggest that you spend the last half-hour networking over drinks and I'll be available for any questions?'

As we break up, Sarah follows Michael, who veers towards the door.

'Excuse me, Michael?' Sarah addresses his back.

He turns and looks at her as though they've never met. 'Yes?'

'I was wondering. You said you could help and I—'

'I have to go. I'm already late.' He walks off.

'Oh. All right. Thanks. Maybe next time?' Sarah watches him leave the room.

I step up beside her. 'Did you find the meeting useful?'

'Yes, although...' She stares at the door. 'I had some questions and Michael did offer to help, only he's had to leave. He's very nice, isn't he?'

'What about Neil? He's had similar experiences to you.'

Neil is sipping an orange juice on his own, next to the stage. He catches Sarah's eye and smiles. She flushes and looks down. 'I don't know. He's a bit strange.'

'No more strange than you or I. Or Michael. I'll come with you, if you're not sure?'

'All right.' Sarah shoots a quick glance at Neil. 'If you stay with me.'

'I will.' And I lead the way to a lonely man who would never hurt Sarah in the way Michael would have done.

43

Fiona calls my mobile while I'm packing on Friday evening.

'At last!' she says. 'Where on earth have you been? I've left three messages for you at home.'

I'm surprised she got through at all; Tom must have replaced the phone in my flat.

'I'm at Tom's.' I sink down onto the bed.

'You should have told me. What if there'd been an emergency?'

'You could have got me on my mobile.' As she just has.

'Still. I was worried about you.'

'Why?' I tuck the phone under my chin and pick up a tee shirt.

'You seemed upset, last week, at ours. Dave thought I should call.'

So, it's Dave who's worried.

'Oh, that,' I say.

'You said you were…in a mess. Is there anything I can do?'

She does sound genuinely concerned. I line up the seams of the top, tuck in the arms and fold it into a square.

'Clare? Would you like to talk about it?'

She's probably hoping I'll say no, that just asking will have fulfilled her duty.

'Yes, I'd like that, but it's a long story, and it's not a good time right now.'

'All right.' Fiona hesitates. 'Perhaps we could go out for a coffee? Or something.'

This is unfamiliar territory for both of us. I meet her halfway. 'Coffee would be great. I'll call you next week to fix a date.' I start on another tee shirt. 'Fiona, I'm sorry, I have to go. Tom's cooking dinner and—'

'There's something else. I wondered if you could baby-sit a week tomorrow? Dave and I have to go out for a few hours in the afternoon.'

'Sure. Doing anything exciting?'

'Not really.' Her voice takes on a familiar guarded quality.

'What are you up to, then?' I pause, the tee shirt held aloft in front of me.

'I'd rather not say.'

I let the top crumple into my lap and take hold of the phone, pressing it closer to my ear. 'Fi, tell me, please.'

She sighs.

'Fi?'

'All right. We're going to counselling. Relationship counselling. Nothing exciting.'

Not exciting, perhaps, but promising.

'I'm glad to hear you're working things out,' I say. 'I really am.'

'It's Dave's idea. I'd rather we dealt with it on our own.'

'Sometimes the experts know better.'

'Maybe. So, could you baby-sit from about two?'

'Of course. I'd be delighted to.'

As soon as I've hung up, Tom's mobile vibrates into life. I lunge over the bed to retrieve it from his bedside table. *Vicky home* flashes up on screen.

'Tom! Phone,' I shout.

'Let it go to voicemail.'

'It's Vicky.' No reply. 'Tom, did you hear me? It's Vicky.'

'I'm getting dinner. She'll have to wait.'

Fine by me. I stretch to put the phone back on the table. It shivers to a standstill and jangles that a message has been left.

I struggle to eat my meal, anxiety about tomorrow constricting my throat. I wish there were some way to avoid going back. A week ago, it was easy to agree to, with all those days still ahead of me. Now only hours separate me from the inevitable.

After dinner, I retreat to the bedroom. Charlie follows, struggling on his stiff joints up the stairs. He whines occasionally, apparently sensing my mood.

Tom comes in later to find us both curled up on the bed.

'Vicky left a message,' I say.

'I'll check it in a minute. I don't suppose it's urgent.'

'Probably not.' Odds are another row with Sam that will blow over by morning.

'I want to get these bags downstairs first,' he says. 'Make a bit of space in here.'

Bex returned the rest of my clothes last night: eight bin liners full. Tom grabs two of them.

'By the way,' I say, 'I'm not leaving. Ever.'

'Really? How's that going to work, then?' He shifts both bags to one hand and hoists up another.

'I'll sell my flat, with all my stuff in it. I can manage with my toothbrush and my clothes.'

Tom raises an eyebrow. 'You don't need anything else? Like your books and your photo albums and your—'

'All right, some other things. But you've got to admit, it's an idea.' Right now, selling up and walking away from my flat is preferable to facing it.

'It is an idea. A very bad one.' He pretends to think. 'In fact, only a crazy person would come up with an idea like that.'

'I told you I was crazy. You wouldn't listen.' I sit up, grab a pillow and throw it at him.

He drops the bin liners and ducks. 'Yeah, definitely crazy.'

I launch a second pillow.

Charlie stands up on the bed and barks. I scramble up next to him and throw my nightie at Tom. As I scan the bed for another missile, he grabs me around the waist, swings me off the mattress, and spins around until I beg for mercy.

'I'm dizzy. I'm going to be sick. Stop!' I shriek.

He comes to a halt and lowers my feet to the floor, but keeps hold of me. 'Do you give up? You agree to go home?'

'We-ell,' I say.

He lifts my feet off the ground.

'I give up! I'll go home!'

'And you'll be happy about it?'

'And I'll be happy about it.'

I don't believe it, though, and I know, even as he lets me go, that Tom doesn't either.

44

Outside the flats the next morning, Tom asks, 'Do you want to go in on your own or would you like some moral support?'

'On my own, I think, if you don't mind?' I have no idea what my reaction will be. If it's bad, I'd prefer not to have a witness – especially one who has put in so much work on my behalf.

'Course not. Give me a shout when you're ready.' He runs his hand through his hair. 'Just to warn you, though...things aren't as they were. I don't want you to be disappointed.'

'I know.' I smile weakly. 'See you in a few minutes.'

In the communal hallway, the stairs rise ahead of me: a daunting climb with an uncertain outcome. I trudge up them like a prisoner going to the gallows.

At the top, I stop and stare at my front door, remembering the last time I stood here and the horrors awaiting me behind its innocent exterior. The eerie silence of the building adds to my apprehension.

I stall for a few more seconds and then unlock the door. The keys turn smoothly in the new locks. Taking a couple of deep breaths, I step inside.

The hall is as tidy as when I last saw it. I close the door and hesitate, before slipping off my shoes and moving forward. Veering to the right, I reach for the kitchen door handle, but visions of the food graffiti come flooding back and stop me in my tracks. I cross the hall to the living room instead, where at least the walls were spared the burglar's destructive touch.

As I slowly open the door and take in what I see, a strange feeling engulfs me. I grip the doorframe to steady myself and try to process my emotions.

The furniture has been rearranged in the now clean room, with the sofa, bookcases and computer table – the cornerstones of the patterns that previously governed the space – all in new locations. And different positions have been allocated to their contents, including my remaining books and ornaments and replacement items, like cushions, a phone and a vase of higgledy-piggledy roses.

The combination of familiar objects in unfamiliar positions creates an unexpected effect. The objects give the feel of home, while the changes make it seem like someone else's. I should be upset; I'm not. What I am, is relieved. In other people's homes I have no desire to create, or maintain, patterns.

I sit down on the sofa, sinking into the truly scattered cushions. The old anxiety about things being out of place is absent. This state of grace may not last; I may become trapped by these new patterns. For now, though, I'm grateful to feel as I do: more relaxed than I have ever been in my own home.

I still have the rest of the flat to explore, though.

In the kitchen, daffodil yellow paint has obliterated the food stains. The colour is a bold move away from my usual hints-of-white. It works, bringing out the warmth of the wooden units, restocked with the basics destroyed in the burglary.

Next door, in the bedroom, the mess of spilled creams and perfumes and broken glass has gone. The dressing table carries only my empty jewellery box and a few aerosols. The cupboards and drawers are bare, too, ready for my laundered clothes. It is the blank canvas of a hotel room between guests.

A sob rises in my throat. The worst is over. My home has, after all, been restored to some kind of normal. Like Pandora's Box, the evil has gone from it. I collapse onto the bed, crying.

A few minutes later, the door buzzer sounds. I take a moment to compose myself before answering.

'Clare?' says Tom. 'How are you getting on?'

'Fine.' I sniff.

'Can I come up?'

'I'll be down in a minute.'

'Are you sure you're okay? You sound funny.'

'It's the intercom. It makes everyone sound funny.'

In the bathroom, I check the extent of the damage caused by my tears: predictably, my nose and eyes are red and swollen. I splash cold water over my face, dab it dry and return downstairs. We still have to get all my clothes inside.

Tom is pacing up and down beside his van. He turns as I scrunch across the gravel and comes up to me. He peers at my battered face.

'I'm sorry, beautiful, I did what I could—'

'It's great, Tom. Thank you.'

'Are you sure? You don't mind that I moved things? I wanted to hide some ink stains that wouldn't come out of the carpet, but I can put it all back, if it's freaking you out? You can probably get new flooring on the insurance, only I couldn't do that, till the claim's sorted and—'

'Tom, stop, please. It's perfect.' I wrap my arms around him and rest my face against his shoulder.

'Really?'

'Really.'

'I was worried you'd hate it being so different.' He kisses the top of my head. 'You know, I still don't...you know...get it.'

'Get what?' I look up at him.

'What you do.' He flushes. 'The way you arrange things and all that. I mean, I've tried, but I just can't get my head around it.'

'Don't worry, I don't think many people can.'

'Still, it makes me feel a bit useless. Give me a failing plant or a broken chair and I'm in my element. I can grow things and fix stuff, but this...' He shrugs. 'I don't know what to do.'

'Do you think I'd have got this far without you fixing stuff? It doesn't matter if you don't get it, Tom. I'm the only one who can actually put myself right, but I know I can't do it without you.'

'Even if I'm just there in the background hammering like a Neanderthal?'

'Now, don't get carried away, you're not that smart.'

'Cheeky!' He tickles me under the ribs. I start giggling, which only encourages him to carry on.

A few seconds later, I'm doubled over and weak from laughing. 'Stop...stop...can't...take...any...more,' I plead. He relents and I straighten up, panting. 'Sorry...Tom...too...breathless...to...carry...bags.'

He grins and lopes off, adopting a slouched posture and scratching his head, as he grunts, 'Me carry. You rest.'

After a moment's respite, I join him. Between us, we quickly transfer the luggage into my flat.

As Tom offloads the last of the bin bags, he says, 'There you go. Once you've put this lot away, you'll be back to normal.'

I add a carrier bag of underwear to the pile. 'I've been thinking about that,' I say. 'I'm frightened that if *I* unpack, I'll put my clothes back exactly where they were.'

'Oh-kay.'

'If you did it, everything would be in a different place. Like the rest of the flat. It would really help.'

He raises an eyebrow. 'You mean, you fancy a cup of tea and a sit down?'

'No!' I say. 'I'm serious, honestly, Tom. I wouldn't ask, you've done so much already, only I'm scared I'll...' My voice wobbles. 'I'm scared I'll go straight back to how I was.'

'So, you want me to rifle through your underwear?'

'Not exactly, but if that's what it takes, feel free.'

'Right you are, I'll make a start.' Tom rubs his hands together with a lecherous grin. 'Let's get my paws on those lacy bras!'

While he works, I make us both tea and take in my new surroundings.

He's finished in half an hour – a fraction of the time I would have taken. I realise why when he leads me into the bedroom to show off his handiwork. On the wardrobe rail, he has mixed up skirts, trousers and shirts. The same muddle prevails on the shelves, which are a jumble of tops, shorts and scarves. And in the chest of drawers, half my pants and bras are tangled in one drawer, half in another. Elsewhere, belts fight with gloves, hats with tights, and socks with nighties. Tom lives in jeans and tee shirts; his own system must be a whole lot simpler. Faced with a woman's paraphernalia, he's lost.

'What do you think?' He's as proud as a child presenting its first unrecognisable painting.

'It's great.' I suppress a snigger at the sight of a suspender belt lying next to a woolly hat. I'll have to sort it all out later or I'll never be able to find anything. There is some method to my compulsive madness.

'One more thing.' Tom retrieves a plastic bag from the bed and pulls out a flat, bubble-wrapped parcel, which he hands to me.

'What's this?' I say.

'Open it!'

I unwrap the packaging to find an elegant, brushed-silver frame inside.

'I checked, it's the right size for your mum's photo,' he says. 'Do you like it?'

Tears fill my eyes. 'It's beautiful, Tom. I love it.'

'I can tell,' he says, 'because you're crying again!' He reaches back into the plastic bag and pulls out Mum's photo, still in its broken frame. 'Shall I do it?'

I nod. 'Careful you don't cut yourself.'

He eases the photo out and I wrap the old mount in the discarded bubble wrap, while he fiddles with the fastenings on the back of the new one. Picture installed, he stands the frame up on the left of the dressing table. 'It was about here, wasn't it?'

'No...but that's perfect. Thank you.' The light sheen of the frame beautifully complements the black and white image of Mum, reflected in the mirror of her own dressing table, brushing her hair.

'Good,' says Tom. 'By the way, I haven't put your ring back. I thought I'd hang onto it till I could give it to you properly. Make an event of it, like we planned.' He pats his top pocket, where the box bulges above his mobile phone. 'Is that okay?'

'Of course. If we're done here, shall we go and get some lunch? I'll treat you to a fry-up, if you like?'

'I think I deserve one, after a morning playing with your underwear!'

In town, we head for the café I haunted while at the hotel, which is now populated with both shoppers and Friday-night partygoers seeking a hangover cure in fried food. As we hover in the doorway, the owner points out the only space left: a table for two in the middle of the room, inches from one occupied by four young men. From their pallor and the fizzy drinks in front of them, they're amongst the hangover brigade.

Tom hesitates. 'It's a bit squashed.'

'We won't be here long.' I shimmy between the tables to the spare one and pull out a chair.

One of the young men sitting opposite, on the next table, smiles at me. 'Got enough room there, love?'

'Yes, thanks.' I sit down, dragging the table towards me to make space for Tom.

'All right, mate?' The same man nods at Tom.

'Er, yeah. You?' Tom looks bemused. He sits down. The sun is pouring through the full-length windows at the front. He squints into the light. 'Jeez, it's hot in here.'

The gentle breeze from the open door has little impact. I fan the laminated menu in his direction.

'The breakfasts are up there.' I indicate the blackboards running across the room at ceiling height behind him. He turns to read the faded, scratchy writing.

The café owner approaches to take our orders.

271

'We 'ave not seen you for a little time,' he says to me. He has a strong Eastern European accent, though everyone calls him Derek.

He delivers our drinks a few minutes later with a wink and a smile.

We can hardly talk, with the noise from the kitchen, the clatter of cutlery on crockery, the chatter and laughter, so I content myself with people-watching.

Derek brings our meals and Tom tucks into his as if he's famished. When he finally puts down his knife and fork, he heaves a satisfied sigh that reflects my own unaccustomed contentment.

'Would you do it now?' I say.

'Do what?' He frowns.

'Give me my ring.'

'Really, now?'

'Yes. Please.'

'Here?' He scans the noisy, crowded room, with its cheap tables and chairs, sticky sauce bottles and mottled mirrors lining the walls.

'Yes.'

'Why?

'It feels right. When I go home, I'll be starting over. We'll be starting over.'

'I wanted to make it special.' Tom looks disappointed.

'You did, the first time, but this will be special, too. Please.'

'If you're sure.' He fishes in his pocket and pulls out the box, flushing a little as he glances at the men next to us. Cupping the box in his palm, he opens it and picks out the ring. He puts down the box and takes my hand.

'Clare. I'd like you to…' He clears his throat. 'Sorry. Clare Thorpe, will you marry me?'

'Yes.' I grin at Tom. 'I'd love to.'

Before he can say anything else, the men alongside us start cheering and clapping.

'Good on you, mate.' The man who greeted us earlier thumps Tom on the back.

'Er, thanks,' says Tom.

Somehow, everyone in the café catches on and shouts their congratulations. Derek rushes out to join in, offering every table free drinks to celebrate.

Gradually the uproar dies down. The other customers resume both their meals and their own business.

'Well, that was surreal,' says Tom, 'and I haven't even given you your ring yet.'

My skin is sticky and hot, yet the ring slides on easily. I hold my hand up to the light. The diamonds' setting is even more beautiful than I remember.

'We should make a toast,' I say.

'With what?'

I lift my tea mug. Tom follows my lead, shaking his head in bewilderment.

As we clink china, I say, 'To us, take two.'

'Take two,' he says.

I only discover the truth about the ring three months later.

45

'You're not crying,' says Tom. 'I guess I wasn't very good, then?'

'Ha, ha, very funny! You know you were. I just don't cry every time.' I pull the duvet over my bare shoulders and snuggle up against his chest.

'It's no wonder men don't understand women. You cry when you're happy, you cry when you're sad...then again, you don't cry when you're happy—'

'Shh!' I lightly slap his chest. 'You're taking the shine off a very nice post-you-know-what glow.'

'Well, at least I'm not asleep.'

'It might be better if you were!'

I smile to myself. The days of crying after sex are over. Tom can make of that what he will, but in time he'll forget I ever did – and not crying will be the norm again.

When he starts to snore, I prod him into action. 'Rise and shine! It's a beautiful day. Let's not waste it.' An Indian summer has taken hold of September and sun blazes through my bedroom window.

'Okay,' he yawns. 'Can I use the bathroom first? I need a shower.'

'Sure.'

He blearily hauls himself upright and rubs his chin. 'Think I'll have a shave as well.' He climbs out of bed and collects his washbag from the dressing table. 'Won't be long.'

As he shuffles out of the room, I throw back the covers and get up, too. At the dressing table, I pick out the things I need to take into the bathroom. My toiletries are now kept tidy, but not military precise. When Tom is here, though – which is more often now – chaos reigns: his belongings always get mixed up with mine. I scan the items littering the table's surface, my fingers twitching with the desire to put things straight.

My old behaviours haven't deserted me yet. Every day is a battle, some with a successful outcome, some not. On bad days, I create patterns; on good days, I dismantle them again. Tom's visits, and their aftermath, still provoke bad days. I allow myself an outlet for the tension by doing small things: tidying a shelf; straightening my shoes; or lining up my drinks' glasses. Creating mini sanctuaries to reassure myself that control and order are possible any time I choose. Knowing the mess is reversible enables me to tolerate it.

Today, while Tom is in the bathroom, it's the turn of my purse. I fetch it from my handbag in the hall and begin to excavate the contents. Sorting the items in my bag has always provided a form of stress relief in public situations or emergencies. Tidying those in my purse or make-up bag – the next level of sorting – is reserved for private.

Delving into every flap and pocket, I pull out receipts, shopping lists and money-off vouchers, discarding those that are out of date and replacing what's left. Then I turn the coins to face the same way, adjust store cards so that the edges are parallel, and clip any loose stamps together, with the perforations matching.

The lone emerald earring still occupies the small zippered pocket: a reminder of my crime against Tom. One day, I'll admit to losing its mate – but I'll never confess how.

I put the purse back in my handbag, go into the kitchen to switch the kettle on, and return to the bedroom.

While I wait to use the bathroom, I sit at the dressing table, contemplating the mess. Amongst the toiletries are items discharged from Tom's pockets: house keys, car keys, a packet of mints, some loose change, and a bulging wallet, from which a ragged bundle of receipts protrudes.

Before I can stop myself, I pick up the wallet and fold over the ends of the receipts, so that I can tuck them inside. Doubling the thickness of the paper makes the wallet so full that, as I extract my fingers, they stick to the wad and pull the slips halfway out. As I try to push them back in, the papers crumple and tear beneath my fingertips.

'Damn it!' I should have opened the wallet first, to give me room to manoeuvre. Now I'll have to do that, *and* remove the receipts, in order to smooth them out. Poking around in Tom's things makes me uncomfortable, but I don't have any other choice.

As I lay them on top of one another, like playing cards, I carefully line up the top left-hand corners. Halfway through, I spot the receipt for my engagement ring, headed by the distinctive curly lettering of the jeweller's name.

I smile and carry on, but a couple of slips later, there it is again: the same shop, the same amount and, when I look closely, the same item reference. I compare the two, looking closer still, and spot the only difference: one is dated early April, a week after we got engaged, and the other early June, shortly after I was burgled.

I lift my left hand and stare at the band glinting on my fourth finger. The cleaners didn't find the original after the burglary, as Tom claimed; he secretly replaced it, to make me feel better. I finger the ring, as if I might suddenly detect a difference between this one and its predecessor.

The gurgle of water running away in the bathroom alerts me to Tom's imminent return. I don't want him to know that I know. Bundling up the receipts, I stuff them back in his wallet and fling it onto the dressing table. In spite of my haste – or perhaps because of it – I have almost replicated their original state of disarray. I doubt he'll notice my meddling.

The bedroom door creaks open and he wanders in, a towel around his waist. 'All yours.'

'Thanks.' I walk over to him and fling my arms around his damp body. 'I do love you, Tom Henson.'

He leans back and looks at me. 'What's brought that on? I wasn't gone that long, was I?'

I laugh. 'No, I just wanted you to know.'

He grins. 'I love you, too.'

If possible, I love him even more for his deception, for trying to spare me the pain of the truth. I wish I could tell him that, but I can't. I have my secrets; it's only fair to let Tom have his.

Contact Helen at www.helenbarbour.blogspot.com or follow her
on Twitter @HelenTheWriter